THE BLOCKBUSTER NOVEL THAT REVEALS THE NIGHTMARE BEHIND THE AMERICAN DREAM

Presidential candidate James Hawk and his brother Billy had declared all-out war on union corruption, zeroing in on the shadowy Louis Cordaro and his links to the Mafia. Through their Senate committee, they began to turn the screws tighter and tighter until Cordaro started worrying.

And when Cordaro started worrying, he sent shock waves through the entire fabric of American life, summoning secret allies and making deals with the most ruthless and powerful men in the nation.

Temporarily blocked by Cordaro's political connections, the Hawks turned to businessman Tor Slagle, whose billion-dollar empire was about to crumble under the weight of union pressure. With the help of beautiful Mikki Parker, Slagle accumulated enough evidence to put Cordaro away—but would he live long enough to give his testimony?

BALANCE
OF
POWER

Jack Peterson

LEISURE BOOKS   **NEW YORK CITY**

To me—I wrote it.

To the others from whom I stole time that could have been spent sharing our lives; I am forever grateful for their understanding.

To those who in real life dedicated their lives to the causes that inspired this book; I find words impossible to describe their contributions. I only hope their message, even in fiction, isn't lost.

A LEISURE BOOK

Published by

Dorchester Publishing Co., Inc.
6 East 39th Street
New York, NY 10016

Printed in the United States of America

Chapter 1

LITTLE EDDIE PARKER was only four years old on the day
that it happened. His stubbornness had in the past frequently led him to ignore his mother's pleading cries to
come in from the chilling late afternoon winter winds of
Chicago's north side, but this time he obeyed. He instinctively knew something was different. Something was
wrong.

"Eddie! Eddie!" his mother shouted, frantically flailing
her thin arms wildly from the upstairs bedroom windows.
"Get inside," she screamed.

Quickly, he stepped off his three-wheeler, pushed it
aside, and ran with his head down and chin buried in his
scarf to the foot of the steps where he looked up and saw
his mother already waiting. Using his tiny arms for mobil-
ity, he scrambled up the ten short steps where she scooped
him into her arms. She pushed herself back through the
doorway and ran as fast as she could, carrying her son to
the kitchen where the others were waiting.

Miss Pearl, the family cook, was standing between
Eddie's two older sisters, her comforting arms draped
around their shoulders. Her oily black skin contrasted with
the white and frightened faces of his teenaged sisters.
Eddie was too young to know real fear, but his mother's
voice had been different from anything he had ever heard,
and his sisters' silence began to make him feel uneasy.

"The cellar," his mother whispered loudly, pushing her
children through the stairwell inside the pantry door.

Eddie and his sister Sabrina scurried to the bottom of the stairs. His sister Teresa, at fourteen a year Sabrina's junior, had to be helped down the stairs because her leg was in a full-length cast. If it hadn't been for Teresa's temporary immobility, they would have left the house altogether. It was no time to be publicly strolling down the neighborhood sidewalks. They had to hide.

"Wait!" Miss Pearl shouted from behind. "What about the front door?" she asked, standing halfway down the stairs.

"My God! I left it open!" Mrs. Parker whispered hoarsely, her drawn face losing even more color.

"I'll get it, mum," Miss Pearl answered calmly. Hurriedly, she waddled back up the stairs as fast as her stump-like legs would carry her. A moment later the click of one dead bolt on the front door thumped loudly and the children could hear their mother exhale a heavy sigh of relief. Within seconds, Miss Pearl lumbered back down the stairs, slamming and locking the pantry door behind her.

It was at that precise moment that Eddie's mother saw the knife Miss Pearl brought from the kitchen. It was the one she had always used to carve meat for the family.

"What's that for?" Mrs. Parker demanded incredulously.

Miss Pearl's voice was defiant. "Ain't no white bastards gonna hurt this family," she hissed. "They'll have to get me first!"

Eddie's mother felt sick inside. She stared at Miss Pearl, a curious mixture of anger and sorrow filling her eyes. The taste of vomit lined her throat and she swallowed hard several times to hold it down. It was hard for her to comprehend, but she knew that the union problem at her husband's plant had finally come down to the violence he had constantly warned her about.

She believed in her husband. She knew his strength of character and moral convictions were the bonds that tightly sealed the cracks and leaks that developed in any marriage, including her own, but it was incomprehensible to her that God would permit a man who tried to live and work honestly to be subjected to the harassment of terror that had filled their lives over the past few months.

She could only remember bits and pieces of her husband's phone call a few minutes earlier—"To the cellar . . . Wait for me there . . . No time for you to get out . . . Home as fast as I can!"

There was something about the lights. Yes, the lights. Had she turned them off? Yes! No! Too late! Can't take the chance! God! It will be at least an hour before he gets home! All we can do is wait!

Kicking away at a pile of coal to make more room for Teresa's cast, Mrs. Parker instinctively hid Eddie and Teresa in the coal bin and closed the door. There was no room for herself or the others.

"Stay there and be quiet!" she whispered sternly. She held Sabrina's cold, moist hand, using the other to grope her way along the dampened walls as she led the way toward the furnace, with Miss Pearl tagging blindly along behind, holding onto Sabrina's waistbelt. The cracked wall became drier and warmer, the scent more familiar. She could feel the furnace. They were there. They crouched together behind its great stomach.

Sabrina tugged at her mother's arm. "Momma, I'm frightened," she whined, but her mother wasn't listening. She was trying to hear any noise from outside but the basement walls prevented any sound from penetrating.

There was a muffled panting followed a few seconds later by a chilling scream from Sabrina.

"Shut up!" Miss Pearl threatened. "Do you want them to find us?"

Sabrina tried desperately to control herself but no matter how hard she tried, whines and squeaks kept slipping out, echoing sharply against the barren walls.

Teresa clutched her brother to her bosom. She was old enough to understand their danger but Eddie thought it more like a game, although he remained stone quiet. Teresa's chest was hard against his face. It was bony and not as full as Sabrina's. He wished Sabrina was in the coal bin instead of Teresa. Sabrina's chest was always warm and comforting. He held his breath and tried to listen. Sabrina had stopped wailing, the only sound now being that of coal settling in the pile on which they sat as Teresa tried to adjust her leg to the uncomfortable position. It hurt almost as bad as when she fell off her bicycle, but she knew better than to cry.

Minutes passed; still no sound. No movement. Now it was Teresa who began to sob softly under her breath. Eddie knew his sister was frightened but couldn't understand why. He clutched her hand tightly and buried his head even deeper into her shallow cleavage, even though it hurt his cheekbone. "It's okay," he whispered. "I'm here. I'll take care of you, Sissy."

He sensed a smile as her fragile arms pulled him closer. "I love you," she whispered. "I love you."

The black silence was suddenly broken by a thunderous crunching sound from above their heads, quickly followed by a tinkling from bits and pieces of glass and debris shaken from the back door. Then footsteps. More noises. Voices, all over the house.

By the time George Parker reached his car in the plant parking lot there was no time to go back and phone his wife again. He had thought about telling her to call the police but the way things had been going lately he distrusted them as well and decided against it. Now he wasn't sure he had made the right decision.

It would take over an hour to get home. A lot could happen in that time, but he was betting against it. He had received threats before, but never directed toward his family. The man's voice over the phone bordered on hysteria, pleading for him to get home before it was too late. Who was it? He reasoned that it was probably just another of the union organizer's tricks to disrupt his business, but he felt he couldn't take the chance today. If the threat had been directed at him alone, he would have ignored it. He had conditioned himself over the past few months against such things. But this was more than that. It was a warning, a very alarming and realistic intimidation.

The low winter sun was beginning to fall beyond the cold western shore of Lake Michigan when he nosed his big car out of the lot and into traffic, pushing the accelerator to the floor. The car rolled faster and faster and his mind kept an equal pace. His whole world seemed to be falling apart. He began to question his past decisions to stay and fight for what he believed in.

His business was his life. It provided him with the wherewithal to care for his family. His past personal sacrifices and even today's dangers had always been outweighed by the rewards he enjoyed as a result of his own endurance and resiliency. But now his family was in danger and it was beginning to rip at his conscience. He shook his head clear of his thoughts and pressed on through the traffic. There was only one thought now, one concern: to get home as fast as possible.

The footsteps were directly overhead now, the noises coming from the kitchen. Mrs. Parker, Miss Pearl, and Sabrina were kneeling, still bunched closely together in tomblike silence, barely breathing even though their pulses raced and their knees were beginning to ache against the hard cellar floor.

Eddie tried to peek through a small crack in the coal bin door. "I can't see," he said loudly, squirming from his sister's grasp. He felt Teresa's hand press hard against his mouth as she pulled him back onto her lap, burying his head in her lap. He twisted his face free but made no effort to pull away again.

The noises stopped. A moment passed without a sound, then another. Slowly, methodically, the footsteps crept toward the pantry. A creak as the pantry door opened, quickly trailed by a few steps and a thunderous rattling of the locked cellar door.

A kick at the cellar door sent a chilling shiver down the backs of everyone hiding below. Everyone except Eddie. He was smiling, still playing the game. A stream of light from the kitchen pierced through the darkness and Mrs. Parker pushed the others down to the floor. The men's voices were clearer now. The door was open.

A voice bellowed down the stairs and echoed off the cavernous cellar walls. "Now what do you suppose we'll find down here?"

Eddie still couldn't see. He strained toward the crack in the door as Teresa released her hold on him but she was still in his way. There wasn't enough room for both of them. Suddenly she buried her face in her hands and began to pray. Eddie looked through the crack but could see nothing but the stairs.

Then a man, followed by another, began cautiously descending the stairs, their eyes searching. Teresa pulled Eddie away again, her eyes once more glued to the small opening. At first, all she could see was their legs but soon they were both in full view. One looked to be a monster, bigger than any man she had ever seen, the other, more her father's height but much stockier.

The larger man's arms were searching wildly overhead in the semi-darkness, blindly looking for the pull chain to light the bare globe that hung overhead. He found it and pulled, violently jerking the chain from its mounting but not before a harsh blast of light interrupted the cellar's darkened sanctity.

For a fraction of a second the two men stood still, suspended in their tracks, looking and listening for their motionless prey.

Teresa's strained eyes widened as both men surveyed the cellar and her heart pounded hard against her chest when they fixed their eyes on the coal bin door.

The smaller man, who looked to be barely out of high school, spoke first. "In there," he said nervously, pointing to the coal bin door.

Booming laughter bellowed deep from the mountainous man's chest cavity as he started toward the door.

A penetrating scream stopped him short of his goal. Miss Pearl straightened up and exploded from behind the furnace across the cellar floor with blinding speed. Teresa continued to peer through the doorway crack, her brother still fighting to see. She sucked in her breath and held it when she saw the kitchen knife reflecting brightly in Miss Pearl's right hand.

"Look out! She's got a knife!" the small man yelled. He instinctively backed away and reached inside his pocket.

With a curse the large man lunged head-on to meet Miss Pearl's charge, hammering against her with all the strength he could gather in just two short steps. Miss Pearl's rage and bulk momentarily matched the surprised behemoth's strength as he desperately struggled to keep the knife from reaching its mark.

Suddenly, without warning, a succession of roaring blasts came out of nowhere, reverberating against the cellar walls. The smell of gunpowder permeated the air. A glazed look came across Miss Pearl's face. She momentarily hung suspended from the intruder's treelike trunk, then, slowly, she slumped to the floor.

The young man alternately looked in disbelief at his victim and the small handgun in his palm while his companion casually stepped over her body, ruthlessly kicking her aside.

"I did . . . I didn't," the small man muttered incredulously. "I mean . . . shit!"

A voice yelled. "Bastards!" It was Mrs. Parker, cursing loudly, rushing from behind the furnace.

Almost without exertion, the giant's arm reached out and clubbed her across the head as she ran past him toward Miss Pearl. She collapsed across Miss Pearl's bloodstained body, a blank look on her face replacing the crimson rage displayed only a split second earlier.

Eddie was watching now, horrified, finally finding a small crack of his own near the lower hinge. The two men had their backs to him. Impulsively, he reached for the door to go to his mother's aid but Teresa managed to hold him back. It took all her strength. "Quiet," she whispered, grimacing to hold back her tears. Her fingers were like vises tearing into her brother's flesh but neither noticed. She pulled Eddie back and hugged him with all her strength.

"Let's get outta here!" yelled the young man nervously,

shoving the gun back into his pocket.

"Wait! Listen," the giant commanded.

They both stood silently. Muffled sounds reached them from behind the furnace. It was Sabrina crying. She scrambled to her feet, trying to run past the two men as they approached but she was easily caught around her waist by the giant.

"What do you want?" she screamed. "Let me go! Please!"

A broad smile crossed the giant's face. He wasn't an ugly man, but nevertheless terrifying.

Once again he bellowed with laughter. "This one's mine for a few minutes," he said slowly. "Then we can leave."

"Come on, let's get going," the younger man pleaded. "You got all the broads you can handle."

"Cut it!" the giant commanded, his black eyes turning back to the struggling girl. He jerked around and forced her to her knees while reaching with his free hand for the knife still clutched in Miss Pearl's stiffened fist.

Sabrina was facing him now, her head back and mouth open as she began to choke on her own tears. Suddenly he ripped the front of her dress, hesitating only momentarily at her bra, which quickly gave way. An involuntary scream stuck in her throat as she turned her head downward and saw a thin line of blood beginning to surface from her chest down to her waistline. Her cotton dress hung like an unbuttoned coat exposing her tiny breasts. Only her panties remained intact and the giant's eyes were riveted there, on the tiny swell that formed a V between her legs.

The younger man was scared, impatient. "I'm gettin' outta here!" he yelled, starting for the stairs.

"Stay where you are!" the giant demanded, not removing his eyes from the girl. "We're not finished here yet."

The young man momentarily considered ignoring his command to stay but thought better of it.

Slowly, the giant pointed the tip of the knife at Sabrina's throat and pressed lightly. He turned his head away and studied his reluctant companion who alternately returned the glare and kept an eye on the stairs. They had never worked together before, and the giant wasn't sure the boy could be trusted.

The giant challenged his younger partner. "So you want to run away before the job's done?" he tested.

An arrogant voice of dignity suddenly replaced the boyish trepidation of a few seconds earlier. "I've never quit anything I've started," the young man exclaimed proudly.

The giant smiled broadly. The boy could be trusted after all. He could feel it. "Then go upstairs and keep an eye out," he said. "I'll be up in a couple of minutes."

The giant watched as the young man ran quickly up the stairs, closing the door behind him. He could feel the heat building in his loins as he turned his attention back to the girl. Finally, Sabrina was able to emit a piercing scream. She tried to get away, but her struggle was futile. It only made her attacker laugh louder.

Teresa was shivering now, still clutching her brother to her breasts and covering his eyes as she watched. She wanted desperately to help but knew she would be defenseless. She knew what the giant was going to do. She had read enough books to understand rape. Her sister was standing now, her back turned toward the coal bin.

The giant ripped what remained of the shredded dress from her shoulders leaving her standing only in her panties.

"Take 'em off," he ordered, scratching the surface of her stomach with the knife point.

With a sudden reckless burst she tried to get away again, but it was insanity to think she could succeed. He quickly slammed her to the floor, grabbing her by the throat with one hand while tearing away with the other at her last remaining garment. She lay on the floor, naked and trembling. He stood on his knees and began to undo his belt. His pants fell around the base of his knees and his undershorts quickly followed. His belly was matted with hair and his massive penis already erect, protruding at an obscene angle from between his legs.

Even from several feet away, Teresa could see the wild and terrified stare of her sister's eyes as she lay flattened against the floor looking upward. Suddenly he was on her, pinning her down with a forearm buried across her chest at an angle that allowed him to hold her throat with his hand while he guided himself with the other.

Sabrina screamed when he forced her legs open with his knee but she couldn't combat his strength no matter how much she tried. For a moment, just a moment, he was still, his buttocks poised in an obscene upward motion. Then she felt the pain as he lunged forward, jamming hard against her. The pain subsided momentarily. His body weight lifted again but the pain became even more excruciating as he slammed into her again and again, her screams becoming louder and louder. Each thrust began to bury him deeper, tearing at her insides inch by inch, until he was fully inside her small cavity.

Teresa couldn't watch any longer. She could feel the uncontrolled hatred within herself but could make no effort to help her sister. Eddie began to cry again and she tried desperately to keep him quiet pushing her hand hard against his mouth. His game was over. His pants wet with urine, he clutched his sister tightly, too scared to cry. At four years old, he had learned the meaning of terror.

His sister's screams and her attacker's loud groans drowned out his tiny muffled cries even though Sabrina's wails and cries had now turned to a muted and tortured whimpering as the man continued his relentless pounding between her legs. Then, finally, a single protracted animal sound signaled the end as the giant man's body shuddered uncontrollably before coming to rest on top of her.

A minute passed, then another. The giant toyed momentarily, almost whimsically, with Sabrina's breasts before lifting himself up, tucking himself back in and replacing his trousers. His glazed eyes surveyed her limp and naked body one last time before he silently turned and clumped his way upstairs.

The young man was waiting, standing near the broken

kitchen window, nervously staring out into the darkened winter street. "Ready?" he asked anxiously.

The giant smiled and shook his head from side to side. "We haven't finished yet," he said without emotion.

"What do you mean?"

"Just what I said. We were hired to do a job. We gotta finish it."

The young man was trembling. He knew what his partner meant. "But we've already killed one person. Isn't that enough?" he asked, his voice cracking.

"You wanna get caught? There's two witnesses down there. It would be very untidy if we left them there to talk. The boys wouldn't think too kindly of that."

The giant stepped away from the pantry door, pointing to the stairs.

It didn't have to be explained. The young man knew he was being tested. "Why me?" he asked weakly.

Not a word of response came from the giant, only an indifferent grunt coupled with an unnerving cold stare. The young man's blood turned to ice. Beads of sweat broke out over his entire body as he sucked in his breath and inched his way through the pantry and down the stairway.

"No mistakes," commanded the giant, yelling from above. "Be sure they're dead," he added matter-of-factly.

Exactly twenty minutes later, Eddie Parker's father arrived home. Eddie's mother and his sister Sabrina lay dead on the floor, ceremoniously dumped across the bloodstained body of Miss Pearl.

But Teresa and her little brother were still alive. Their silence had saved them.

There had been a mistake.

Chapter 2

LOUIS CORDARO sat alone at his desk and reflected on his past. He had come a long way since he had organized his first union strike. Through the subsequent years he had had many victories but none could ever match the triumphant elation he had experienced thirty years earlier when he had transformed a small crew of fellow dock workers from a disorganized group of frustrated malcontents into what eventually became a powerful unionized body with one voice. By refusing to unload perishable cargos, they were able to force management to bargain for a better wage and improved working conditions. Although he had been younger than most of his fellow workers, he was able to polarize their discontent and frustrations and thereby proved himself a leader. He was on his way.

Now, he was president of the world's largest and richest labor union, the largest driving force in the lives of millions of Americans. He had fought long and hard over the years for his right to become president of his union. He wasn't about to lose that position without putting up an even tougher fight.

The fuse of his notorious temper grew dangerously shorter as he sat redfaced, staring at the morning's *Washington Post* editorial. While he would never publicly admit it to anyone, the words were disturbingly truthful and threatening.

Louie Cordaro can probably cope with Billy Hawk in his present capacity as a private citizen who just happens to be also legal counsel for the Senate Select Labor Committee. For that matter, he may well be able to control Hawk's more famous brother James who just happens to hold a more public position as United States presidential candidate as well as simultaneously holding down the job of Chairman of the Senate Select Labor Committee—"The Hawk Committee"—as so many around Washington prefer to call it.

There have been past investigations and committees upon committees that have come and gone after failing to prove the scandalous improprieties allegedly committed by officials of various unions. Whether or not Cordaro or any of his union's officials have misused union pension funds or if its ranks are filled with members of organized crime, as the Hawk Committee contends, are longstanding and burning questions that have surfaced many times over the years only to be routinely and quickly doused behind some closed Washington doors without any public explanations.

Under its present structure, it is doubtful the Hawk will fare any better against Cordaro's union in the long run than did the Kennedy brothers when they and the McLellan Committee aimed both barrels at Teamster boss Jimmy Hoffa years ago. While the Kennedys succeeded temporarily in stopping one man, Hoffa, they did not enjoy any of the spoils of that victory, which many had hoped would mark the beginning of the end to the same union corruption that has since spread like a slow cancer to other trade unions as well. Even with the reluctant support of President Jordan, who despite his denials, was forced by public opinion to create the committee, the committee lacks the strength to continue any long-term battle.

Some of Louis Cordaro's earlier energy began to drain. He sighed deeply, his eyes straining at the small print as he read on.

But if James Hawk succeeds in capturing the democratic

18

nomination for the U.S. presidency next summer and eventually becomes president, the committee will have investigative teeth never before experienced by any union. Couple a winning Hawk presidential bid with the strong possibility that brother Billy will successfully launch his political career with the senatorial race out in California and you'll get the attention and maybe even the cooperation of some key union officials. That would spell trouble for Cordaro's union and especially Cordaro himself.

While Cordaro has never been asked to testify, it's everybody's bet that the Hawk brothers eventually have that as their number one goal. Though they've given no new public hints as to what the overall scope and breadth of the committee's objectives would be should either of them become elected, it appears that all the vigor and strength of the committee is waiting for just such an eventuality. They appear to be awaiting a simultaneous attack and kill call not unlike that of a group of vigilantes throwing the noose around an accused's neck as the trial begins under a tall oak tree.

Louis Cordaro couldn't read any further. He slammed his fist into the paper, impatiently pushing the intercom simultaneously with his other hand. His secretary quickly answered.

"Get me Tom Wilson," he screamed.

He swiveled in his chair and flopped his feet on the window sill behind his desk, tilting the chair to a semi-reclining position and staring out the window up the hill toward the Capitol. He knew he had a lot of political friends, but if James Hawk became president there would be difficulty in using those friends to suppress the committee's investigations. The Hawk brothers were out to destroy him and the hard reality of that fact was sinking in. His position as president of the world's largest labor union was in jeopardy. Something had to be done.

As chief counsel to the union's legal department, Thomas Barrett Wilson III knew more about the union's affairs than any other man alive other than Louis Cordaro himself. Over the years Wilson had been a brilliant strategist in directing union litigation with incredible success. Today, Louis Cordaro was going to force him to accept the biggest challenge of his career.

The intercom buzzed. "Mr. Wilson on line one," the secretary announced. Cordaro's rage began to build again as he turned quickly back to the desk, accidently slamming his knee against the desk's side.

"Goddammit," he screamed, picking up the phone. His voice was quivering and loud. "Tom?" he yelled into the mouthpiece.

"Yes, sir," Wilson replied calmly. He had a habit of meeting frequent gruff loudness with a voice inversely proportionate to Louie's volume. He had found over the years that it was the only way to calm Louie down to a point where he could reason with him. To his knowledge nobody had ever won a shouting match with Louis Cordaro.

Cordaro was irate. "That son-of-a-bitch Hawk is using his position on the committee to get his fuckin' ass elected senator and I won't stand for it! Who the fuck does that snot-nosed asshole think he's taking on anyway?"

Wilson let him blow off more steam.

"You listening to me?" Cordaro demanded.

Wilson remained nonchalant. "Yes, sir," he responded.

"Then why the hell aren't you saying nothing?"

"Because we have an appointment tomorrow. We can discuss anything you want then in far more detail and with a little more privacy."

Wilson knew Cordaro would never call him to discuss any meaningful business over the phone because of his near paranoic fear of wire taps. Over the years Cordaro had become known as "Jingles" to many of his intimate friends because of his frequent habit of carrying pocketfuls of coins to use in public phones where he felt most comfortable discussing business. It didn't matter that there were sophisticated detection devices available to prevent anyone from listening in on his conversations. He neither understood nor trusted them.

Cordaro didn't know how to handle Wilson's practical response. Wilson's calm resolve and intelligence had always intimidated him but he always managed to cover his inward uneasiness with the same authoritative brashness that had helped him win many arguments over the years. Cordaro pushed back in his chair, his mind momentarily blank. Then without a word, he slammed the phone in its cradle. It didn't take any degree of brilliance for Wilson to determine their conversation was over.

Cordaro sat there, staring at the phone, allowing his mind to wander. His frustrations about Billy Hawk weren't centered around his getting free publicity for his senate campaign through his position on his brother's committee. What he feared was where Billy was leading the committee . . . where it was going in its investigation. Many people had been called to testify, yet no indictments had been issued. If formal charges had been meted out he would have an indication how close the committee was getting to their ultimate goal. Witnesses could be bought, even made to disappear, but those who had appeared before the committee to date had only offered what on the surface, appeared to him to be meaningless testimony. Billy Hawk was doing a masterful job of disguising his overall plan, and it was unnerving to watch a committee that seemed to be going nowhere with such calculated precision.

Cordaro sat alone in his office for another hour, his mind continuing to come back to the same inescapable conclusion. There was no avoiding it. What he feared most of all was being asked to testify. By then, Billy's trap might have already been set and it would be too late. He was desperate. He had to know what was going on within the committee. He had resources to do that . . . private ways of finding things out. He decided to use them.

Chapter 3

THE MORNING was clear and crisp. An April sky of unbroken turquoise framed the San Francisco skyline when Tor Slagle got out of the house, jumped in his Porsche, and sped toward the city across the Golden Gate bridge from his home high above the bay in Sausalito's wooded hills. He was operating, as he always did, like the highly tuned sportscar he was driving.

From his earlier memories, Tor had always enjoyed the company of people of accomplishment and Winston Sheffield was no exception. He couldn't remember the first time he had met his father's good friend, though he surmised it had to have been nearly twenty years earlier when he was still in high school and Sheffield's hair was still jet black without a trace of its current silver-gray.

Through the years, Tor had grown used to being surrounded by men from his father's business—men several years older than himself, with most of whom he shared a mutual distrust. But Winston Sheffield had always been an exception because in his youth it was Sheffield who accepted Tor as a coeval to be respected for his opinions and ideas. Mutual respect kept their friendship together despite the generation and geographic gap that separated them. Even on short notice such as today, Tor always had time for his friend.

Winston Sheffield headed the largest and most prestigious labor consulting firm in the United States, dealing mainly with large businesses in contract negotiations and labor disputes. While it was frequently rumored behind closed doors that his main function was really working as a silent partner for clients in developing strategies for antiunion campaigns, Sheffield always vigorously and emphatically denied any such shenanigans. In fact, his firm was businesslike and unsentimental about the persons or organizations it represented. Not stifled by any sort of morality, if the clients paid, Sheffield took them on.

Once through the toll gate, it was only a matter of a few seconds before Tor again exceeded the speed limit. A stoplight turned amber as he toyed momentarily with pushing the throttle to the floor and testing his luck with the local police before quickly and calmly braking.

It was 10:05 and he had already assumed his customary role of being late for an appointment. He often wondered why he was so predictable when it came to his tardiness and he always came to the same conclusion: he hated to waste time waiting for others. Better they than him, he thought. He tapped his fingers nervously on the steering wheel while watching a bedraggled old man and his dog cross the street in front of him. The old man's sun-leathered skin was almost dark enough to cover the broken capillaries in his maroon-tinted nose but the bright morning sun exposed his long tribute to the joys of alcohol. The gray-white stubble on his face and balding head seemed to glow with the morning sun as he led his limping dog across the street on a makeshift leash of pieced together bindertwine.

Scenes of poverty were becoming commonplace in San Francisco. It seemed that only the rich and poor remained and, given time, even the poor would eventually be squeezed out by high rents and even higher prices on the barest of essentials. Tor felt that there were a lot of reasons for that kind of injustice but in his opinion one of the primary forces behind the city's fast-changing face was the trade unions, a subject he felt sure Winston Sheffield would bring up this morning.

The old man tucked a wrinkled brown bag under his arm as he walked with awkward determination from the street to the curbside lamppost where the old dog promptly made a perfunctory sniff followed by a half-hearted leg lift. The old man used the post as a temporary resting point, staying only long enough to imbibe enough courage and warmth to start off again on an apparent destination-less journey. It was a sight Tor could never get used to nor understand. Human waste was a anathema to him. He couldn't understand, regardless of the circumstances, how any individual short of mental or physical incapacity could permit himself to lead a meaningless existence. He thought of the sign that hung over his office door, the same sign that used to sit on his late father's desk: "If it is to be, then it has to be me!"

The signal light changed. Tor's body pressed firmly against the leather seat of his Porsche as he pushed his right foot hard to the floor. A tight, high-pitched engine howl echoed loudly against the storefronts and apartment buildings as he sped down Lombard Avenue toward Nob Hill.

Disdaining an early morning chill and light wind, Winston Sheffield stood waiting impatiently outside on the hotel steps, his hair flowing with each gentle breeze. He was a tall and slender man, his face tanned from a recent vacation week in Florida.

Sheffield had never known Tor to be on time for anything but today he had hoped would be an exception. Though he had never been able to appreciate Tor's care-free life-style, he had come to respect the boy who had become a man so quickly. The name Slagle's in the ladies fashion industry was tantamount to what Tiffany's stood for in jewelry, and Tor had done a masterful job of assuming the corporate responsibilities after the death of his parents. Slagle's employees felt Tor had developed into even a better manager than his father because of his emphasis on putting the employees' welfare ahead of that of the company, something which his father would have had grave difficulty comprehending let alone implementing.

It had been six years since the funeral of Tor's parents

and the memory of how Tor's endearing youthful qualities
had suddenly turned to manhood within days after the
tragic accident was still vivid in Sheffield's mind. Overnight, Tor's boyish face grew more masculine. His jaw stiffened. His profile was transformed from that of a handsome young athlete to that of a seasoned hunk that made
women of all ages easy prey. The boy had taken charge
when the torch was passed. There was a job to be done and
he had asked no questions, just moved into his father's
office and attacked his duties with the same tenacity of
purpose and stamina with which he had pursued sports
and girls. The transition from racing cars and sailboats to
the executive office had not been difficult for Tor, although he possessed a determination to keep his business
life at arm's length from his social activities. From what
Sheffield had been able to observe, Tor had a remarkable
capacity to do exactly that.

The sound of tires screaming down California Avenue
broke into Sheffield's thoughts. He looked down the street
toward Grace Cathedral where the roar grew louder by the
second. A black Porsche thundered across the intersection,
overtaking several more hesitant and prudent drivers and
intercepted, by an eyelash, a Yellow Cab attempting to
enter the gated brick entrance to the Mark Hopkins Hotel.
The Porsche screeched to a halt just inches from the lobby
doors. The driver emerged, his blue eyes glistening as
bright as the sky as they searched for someone to park his
car. Tor Slagle had arrived.

A wide grin creased Tor's face when he saw Sheffield.
Sheffield cut him short before he could even say hello.
"Sorry, Tor, there's been an emergency. I need to go to St.
Mary's Hospital right away. Can you take me?"

"Get in!" Tor responded, asking no questions.

Within seconds they were on their way and had traveled
less than one block before Sheffield's calm turned to
terror. "Slow down," he pleaded. "It's an emergency but
not one in which I'm willing to part with my life!"

A stoplight on Van Ness Avenue gave Sheffield's pulse
rate a chance to slow.

"What's the problem?" Tor asked, still half amused at Sheffield's uneasiness and flushed cheeks.

"I had asked a friend to sit in on our meeting this morning. He flew in with his daughter on Saturday and apparently there was some sort of accident yesterday afternoon. The hospital just phoned me. They're both in serious condition."

"What sort of accident?"

"Hit and run, they said. Apparently over near the Marina. He just regained consciousness long enough to tell them where I could be reached. That's all I know."

The light changed and Tor edged the car forward, leveling out at a more subdued pace which suited Sheffield better.

"Who is this fellow?" Tor asked, still not sure exactly what Sheffield wanted to discuss.

"Up until a month ago he was conference president for the union in Illinois." Sheffield responded.

"Which union?" Tor asked.

"Is there any other union of any significance anymore?" Sheffield asked facetiously.

"Oh, *that* union," Tor responded with a grin. A moment later, the smile was replaced with a quizzical frown.

"I don't understand. I mean, it doesn't make sense. Why would you be having a meeting with a union official?"

"You didn't listen, Tor. I said that he *used* to be conference president. Technically, he resigned a month ago. He's on sort of a sabbatical. He's also a personal friend. I've known him since he was a little boy. His father gave me my first job."

"What in the hell does a conference president do? Is a conference a local or what?"

Sheffield was calmer now, his nervousness abated by Tor's saner method of driving. "Actually the conference is made up of all the locals in the state."

Sheffield went on, explaining how the union representation system worked even though Tor was well aware of a union's internal structure. Tor politely listened as Sheffield explained how an individual local, which frequently represented employees from several different companies, would join forces with other union locals from surrounding counties and form an even larger bargaining body called a joint council. Banded together, joint councils commanded considerably more clout at the bargaining table than individual locals and could threaten regional strikes. By affecting the profits of more businesses, the unions could force pressure on the primary target.

"Therefore," Sheffield added, "the Illinois conference is made up of the presidents of all the joint councils in the state. Together, they form union policies and approve or disapprove all strike votes and contracts. They have the last say for all the union's matters in Illinois."

"And your friend was president for the conference?"

Sheffield nodded. "Yes, it's a very lofty position in the union's hierarchy."

"How does the Illinois conference fit into the picture with the union's national organization?" Tor asked, humoring Sheffield's passion for union politics.

Sheffield explained, choosing his words carefully. "All the state conference bodies are subject to the rules of the national charter. They have autonomy only as long as the international body approves of their decisions."

"And from what I've read in the past, the international interprets the charter," Tor added.

"Exactly," Sheffield answered, "and the interpretation isn't always consistent. Louie Cordaro runs the ship the way he wants it run, so the rules aren't always followed too closely."

Tor looked curiously at Sheffield. "Cordaro has that much power?"

"More than you'll ever know," Sheffield said matter-of-factly.

Tor swung the car sharply around a slowing bus and crossed the double yellow line bisecting the road, narrowly missing an oncoming car before pulling back into the proper lane. A block later, they were abruptly stopped by another traffic signal.

"Nice ass!" Tor exclaimed appreciatively.

"What?" Sheffield replied, still not completely recovered from their narrow brush with the car a moment earlier.

"Over there," Tor answered, pointing to a young girl in tight jeans who looked to be about eighteen.

"A little young, isn't she?" Sheffield responded weakly.

A wide smile crossed Tor's face. "I'm only looking, Winston. I can't go to jail for that."

"I would have thought that you would have grown up a bit in the last six years," Sheffield joked.

Tor was quick to defend himself. "First of all, I'm only thirty-six. Second, when I am as old a war horse as you, I'll still chase a little pussy from time to time. It's in my blood —from my mother's side of the family I think."

Sheffield smiled. His mind was still very much on business.

Tor sensed his preoccupation. "Okay, I give up. Why don't you just tell me what this meeting we were going to have was all about."

Sheffield grew even more serious. "I'm not exactly sure."

"Come on, Winston! I know you're free spending, but I also know you wouldn't just jump in a plane and come to San Francisco without a good reason."

Sheffield began to explain, this time with more conviction. "I have a client here in town who's very concerned about the union movement within their organization."

Tor cut him short. "Not that again! We've been through all this before."

"Hear me out, Tor. This is different." Sheffield spoke in a monotone as if he were thinking about each word before he let it pass his lips. It was a habit that frequently tempted Tor to jump in and complete the thought before Sheffield finished talking.

Sheffield continued. "My sources are reliable and almost always accurate. I don't like what I hear. More than that, I don't like what I am *not* hearing."

Tor's curiosity was finally beginning to surface. For the first time, he slowed the car to nearly the posted speed limit.

Sheffield drew on an unlit cigar he pulled from his breast pocket. "I've heard that the city of San Francisco is a target city for Cordaro and the Retail Clerks Union to combine their unions' strengths in a total organizational drive to increase their membership. They want to be able to demonstrate a complete dominance of the city by proving that they could shut it down at any time if they're successful in this new drive. What I don't know and haven't been able to find out is just exactly why they want to do it. Nevertheless, the implications are scary. Since my client has stores here, naturally they are concerned."

"What's that got to do with Cordaro? All the retail stores are represented by the Retail Clerks Union."

"By tying in with Cordaro, the Retail Clerks Union can guarantee the trucking industry will cut off supplies. Without supplies, the stores can't stay open long. That's where Cordaro's support is vital."

"But unions always support one another by not crossing picket lines. Why do you think this is so unusual?"

"Because this time is different. Cross-support works, but if a strike lasts more than a week the nonstriking unions inevitably go back to work and cross the striking union's picket lines. When they have nothing to gain directly and it affects their pocketbook, the token support from unions that have no grievance doesn't last very long."

"And you think this time there's going to be more than token support?"

"Absolutely."

Tor didn't share Sheffield's concern. "It's the same old story. The union just wants to fatten their treasury. It's nothing new. They come in, butter up the nonunion store employees on the monthly dues list, then disappear. That's how the organizers get paid. I don't have to tell you that."

30

"It's different this time, Tor."

"But what does it have to do with me? There's no way a union can promise more than I am already giving my employees."

"That's just it," Sheffield countered. "You're a sore spot with them. They're getting a lot of pressure from the locals wanting to know why they can't get more money for their members to equal what you pay your employees."

Tor was unimpressed although still intently interested. "Simple," Tor answered. "I charge more for my merchandise. Most companies can't compete with my profit margin. It's the nature of my business. I have more bottom-line profit and consequently more dollars to pay my employees than any other retailer."

Sheffield shook his head. "But," he warned, "the average union employee doesn't understand that. All they know is they're paying dues and receiving less money than someone in your store who pays no dues and no initiation fees. That's the problem."

"The problem?"

"The Retail Clerks' city-wide contracts with the larger retailers will be up in about six months and they'll need the support of all their members if they're to win any major concessions in their negotiations with the employers."

"What's that got to do with Slagle's?"

"They plan to organize every conceivable retailer who is not yet unionized, regardless of how small. It only takes three or more employees in any one store to make that store legally eligible for possible organization."

Tor nodded and continued to listen.

"The Retail Clerks feel that if they can organize the smaller retailers before the city-wide contracts are up for the larger retail outlets, they'll have enough strength to gain major wage and retirement concessions by threatening to walk out of every store in town. Their organization of the smaller retailers is imperative before they can expect to increase their support of the larger existing members. Word is they'll be asking for the moon when the contract expires and they're going for total support from all their members, for a long strike if it's necessary. The enlistment of new members will help support and solidify that movement.''

Tor wasn't convinced of Sheffield's argument. ''But they've tried before. Besides, I am not a small retailer. I have over three hundred employees.''

''Believe me, you're included along with my client and the others in the drive,'' Sheffield answered coolly.

Tor didn't ask, but knew who Sheffield's client was. Hemp, Lathrop and Company were the world's largest retailer with over thirty billion dollars in annual sales and had over nine hundred department stores. They had two stores in San Francisco, both nonunion. Sheffield had secretly represented them in antiunion campaigns for years, a fact that Tor's father had let slip over dinner one evening when Tor was still in college.

''What makes you think it will work this time?'' Tor asked.

''Cordaro's support. The Retail Clerks have never had this kind of help. Cordaro's bringing in all his best organizers from all over the country. In a situation like this they normally would have ten people. I got word that over a hundred are on their way. If necessary, strike funds from locals in other states will be made available to support the Retail Clerks' drive.''

Tor shrugged. ''Why all of a sudden a big push in San Francisco?''

''The November elections,'' Sheffield offered emphatically. ''No doubt in my mind about it.''

''The elections?''

''Louie Cordaro would do anything to stop Billy Hawk from being elected senator. Remember, the union membership supports whomever Louie endorses,'' Sheffield added.

''Why would Cordaro be involved in this?'' Tor asked, still unclear of the significance of Sheffield's comments.

''The more union members Cordaro can muster in San Francisco before the election, the more votes against Billy

Hawk. Cordaro wants to show that Hawk is behind in the polls in his own home town which in turn will help his opponent's chances in the rest of the state. If the Retail Clerks pull this off, Cordaro will spare no expense letting the public know the Clerks could not have done it without his union, which will bring the rest of the Retail Clerk members in the state into a subservient attitude. They'll feel they owe Cordaro's boys a favor for helping their union, which really means the Retail Clerks owe Louie Cordaro. The union and Cordaro are synonymous. Even if Cordaro gets some grass roots support behind his campaign against Billy Hawk, I wouldn't be surprised if we see a lot of pressure from some of the elected and appointed officials as well to stop Billy Hawk. They don't want Hawk in as senator either.''

Tor knew why Cordaro would fight against Billy's senatorial bid. He read the papers like anybody else. If James Hawk were elected president, and Billy senator, the committee's power would be awesome. The Hawk brothers owed no political favors and the committee's investigation into Cordaro and his union activities would get even more support. What Tor didn't understand was why some of the state officials would be against Billy's election.

"Because it could become embarrassing," Sheffield answered.

"Embarrassing?"

"You are naive, Tor."

Tor said nothing as he continued to drive toward the hospital. He just waited for some explanation, which he knew Sheffield wouldn't be able to resist offering.

True to form, Sheffield didn't disappoint him. "A lot of our government and local officials owe their jobs to Cordaro's union. Without union voting strength, many of them would never have been elected. In exchange for that support, the union frequently gets concessions in contracts and judges sometimes look the other way when the union crosses the fine line between legality and unlawfulness.

"To put it simply, Louie Cordaro doesn't let anybody forget their debts. He helped put many of the politicians where they are today. If they lose Cordaro's support—and they will if Cordaro gets nailed by the Hawk Committee—many of them will lose their jobs in the next election. They're either stupid, imcompetent, or both. Most of them could never win reelection without some sort of blind support by an unsuspecting public.''

Tor was sure Sheffield was overreacting, off again in some abstract labor consultant's world. "I am beginning to see your point," he said kindly, choosing not to challenge any more of Sheffield's assumptions.

Sheffield persisted. "All I am asking is that you watch your store for signs of activity and let me know if anything looks suspicious. You know, employees who never talk to each other suddenly going to lunch together or strange people in your parking lot talking to the employees.''

"You said earlier it's what you don't hear that bothers you. What did you mean by that?"

"I'm not sure," Sheffield confessed, taking the cigar from his mouth.

"You're being evasive."

Sheffield was unable to keep the impatience from his voice. "No, it's not so. It's just that I have a gut feeling that something bigger than what shows on the surface is behind all this and I can't put my finger on it. Even my sources in Washington, D.C. tell me they feel something more than what appears on the surface. I just know it.''

Tor flashed his boyish grin and chuckled. "Well, it's been a pleasure talking to you, Winston. It's always good to hear from friends with good news.''

The car came to a sudden halt at the hospital. Moments later, both men were inside walking briskly toward the waiting room. Tor stopped abruptly, lightly grabbing Sheffield's arm. "By the way," he questioned in a low voice, "What's this fellow's name?"

"Parker," Sheffield responded. "His name is Ed Parker.''

Chapter 4

WHEN MIKKI PARKER awakened it was midmorning. The long flight from Paris the day before and her late meeting with Winston Sheffield at the hospital had nearly drained the last ounce of energy from her twenty-four-year-old body. Though she had slept for over ten hours, she still felt weak and confused over the events of the last forty-eight hours.

Outside, street noises from below her fourteenth floor hotel room filtered through a partially opened window along with a ray of autumn sun.

Beside her bed lay a crumpled Alka-Seltzer wrapper, the contents of which she vaguely remembered taking the night before to try to rid herself of a headache that still persisted, although now reduced to a more bearable level.

The evening paper was also beside her bed, a last minute purchase from the hotel gift shop before retiring. Propping herself up with pillows, her long brown hair cascading over them, Mikki unfolded the paper and scanned it, something that she had dared not do the night before.

On page three she found it. A sizeable portion of the page contained an all too graphic description of the accident suffered by her father and sister. She skipped most of the details and speculations about the description and whereabouts of the hit and run vehicle and went to the last paragraph that was now only half correct: "While both victims' injuries are listed as critical, they are expected to live."

35

Her father had been dead for over six hours when she reached the hosital. The burden of informing her had rested squarely on the shoulders of Winston Sheffield. She closed her eyes and thought about Sheffield, how kind and gentle and comforting he had been the night before. Though she had known him all her life, until last night she had never realized how close he had been to her father.

Mikki's thoughts returned to her father; because of Winston Sheffield's compassionate revelations a few hours earlier, she began to understand him far better in death than she ever had when he was alive. She had had little personal contact with her father, who had never told her of his own tragedy as a youngster. Thanks to Winston Sheffield, the nannys and tutors, the boarding and finishing schools all began to make sense. Her father's lifelong passion for revenge against those who he had seen kill his mother and sister when he was a small boy was matched by an equally unbending drive to protect both his daughters from ever knowing of his inner agony and suffering. The private schools and colleges were not, as she had believed, an unloving effort on his part to keep her out of his life, but his method of protecting her. And now the same little boy who had grown up with violence against his family permanently inscribed in his mind had died in another cruel act on the streets of San Francisco without ever fulfilling his life's promise to avenge his family.

Mikki thought about what her father had told her nearly a year earlier when she was leaving for her first year at art school in Paris. Suddenly the words took on more meaning to her: "You've a mind of your own and always have, so I won't oppose your going away just now. Maybe, in time, we can become as close as you have been to your mother. Even though I haven't shown it on the surface, you're always in my heart. I hope you believe that." At the time she thought it an empty apology for his lack of emotion toward her over the years. Although she was never disrespectful of her father, she carried a resentment toward him for not sharing with her as she had observed her friends' fathers doing. Something was missing from her life and she blamed her father for that. Now that she knew the truth, it was too late.

With an impatient, almost angry gesture, Mikki threw the newspaper down and pulled the bedclothes aside, sliding from the bed quickly. She felt a burst of energy, a need to get outside, to be with others who knew nothing of what was going on in her life, to be without responsibility and to breathe the same carefree air she had experienced during her first few months in Paris. She turned to the phone beside the bed, picked it up and dialed. A woman's voice answered. It was the hotel operator.

"Good morning, front desk."

She asked for the time.

"Eleven twenty, Miss Parker," the operator answered.

"Thank you."

A moment later it hit her.

"Christ," Mikki said aloud. She knew that what she felt versus what had to be done were imcompatible. She had to be at the hospital at one o'clock to meet with Shana's attending physician. There was no time to escape reality, a world closing in, a world she had never known or was prepared to face. She sat down. Covering her face with her hands, she began to sob silently.

Later, her face still wet with tears, she stood and walked to the bathroom to shower. There was a job to be done and she had to do it. She was going to face the real world.

Chapter 5

THE DOCTOR'S WORDS still rang mercilessly in Mikki Parker's ears. She sat alone in the hospital waiting room, staring out the window, trying desperately to fight back the tears that filled her eyes.

"She's resting now," the young doctor had said. "We've run tests for any possible internal injuries and they're negative, but there's a definite paralysis in her lower body. We're not sure just yet what's causing it but we'll know more tomorrow."

Tomorrow. Yesterday. For Mikki, they both seemed so far away now. Yesterday no longer mattered and tomorrow was unattainable. What had appeared within reach only days before—her career as a fashion designer, the chic apartment in Paris, her independence—had been stolen away only hours earlier by a hit and run driver. One moment there was joy and laughter, the next a grief she had never before experienced, not even when her mother had died.

"Paralysis . . . paralysis . . . paralysis." There was no escaping that word. What was before, was no longer; what mattered was now. Her little sister lay helplessly paralyzed in a room no more than forty feet down the antiseptic hallway.

A familiar voice came from behind. "Mikki . . ." It was Winston Sheffield. Mikki looked up, unable to respond immediately. Her face told a story that defied questioning. Sheffield kept silent as he embraced her with a comforting hug.

"I just talked to the doctor," Sheffield said at last. "He brought me up to date."

Tears began to trickle down Mikki's cheeks and she blinked several times, trying to check their flow. Then her swollen eyes focused over Sheffield's shoulder where Tor Slagle stood several feet away, being careful to remain unobtrusive. Embarrassed at his oversight, Sheffield quickly made the introduction.

"Thank you for coming," Mikki offered politely, shaking Tor's hand. "I'm afraid I . . ." She turned and walked away, unable to complete the sentence.

A momentary, uncomfortable silence fell among them. Tor sensed Mikki's uneasiness and excused himself. "I'll be outside if you need anything," he offered.

Sheffield turned to Mikki. "Is there anything we can do?"

Her quiet eyes went past him toward the window. She shook her head, her eyes still staring into the distance. "My father is dead," she said suddenly, "and now my sister has to be told that she'll never see her Daddy again and that she may never walk again. How could anybody help me tell her that?"

Just six months earlier, her little sister had endured what Mikki thought would be the biggest tragedy of her life when their mother had died. And now this . . .

Sheffield walked over to the window and quietly stood beside Mikki.

Mikki began slowly. "You told me yesterday that when my father was a boy, he watched two men rape and kill his sister and mother, and that two years later his other sister committed suicide because she could never adjust to what had happened. Last night I didn't really understand the significance of all that you said and what was going on in my father's mind during our years together. But I think I understand now, and I can honestly say that I'd go through everything my father went through if I didn't have to go in that room and tell Shana that she may spend the rest of her life in a wheelchair!"

Mikki fell silent, trying hard to blink back the tears.

Sheffield placed his hand on her shoulder. "You know, when your mother died a few months ago, your father decided to give up trying to vindicate his sister's and mother's deaths. After thirty-six years, he was no closer to finding out who those men were than when it first happened. The day of your mother's funeral he told me that Shana was already eight years old and that he hardly even knew her. He said he had been so preoccupied with satisfying his own inner needs that he'd managed to leave whatever love and affection he had for you and Shana buried deep inside. He said he couldn't even remember a time when he had ever shown any real emotion toward his family. When your mother died, he decided he wouldn't let Shana grow up without the affection he so desperately wished he could have shown you."

Sheffield turned away from the window and walked back to the sofa and sat down heavily. "Your father worked for over twenty years but not for the same reasons as other people. Instead of working to earn enough money to raise a family and to enjoy life, he'd been financing a damn manhunt. He even got married for the wrong reasons. He thought if he had someone else to share his agony he could keep going forever. Somewhere along the line he just lost sight of the part where it says you're supposed to share and enjoy life, take the good with the bad. He realized his mistake in the end. I think you should know that."

Sheffield saw the quiet tears creeping into Mikki's eyes again. She was no longer making any effort to stop them.

Sheffield went on, trying to strengthen her confidence. "You know," he offered, "in many ways you're not unlike your father. As a young boy your father experienced a great tragedy. He had a broken heart and it showed even though he lived long enough to see you grow into a young woman. I'd hate to think that Shana will spend her childhood experiencing the void you must have felt knowing your father was a beaten man. You owe it to her and to yourself to put your grief aside and not to let that happen again."

Sheffield stood, turned his back to Mikki and stared out the window, silently praying that his words wouldn't be taken too harshly. He thought about how long he had known her father. It was Christopher Parker who had given him his first job as a part-time maintenance worker when he was still in high school. He remembered being personally harassed by union organizers in Parker's manufacturing plant because he resisted their demands that he sign a pledge to vote for the unionization of the plant. He admired the senior Parker's guts for standing up and fighting for his employees' right to make their own decisions. He recalled all too vividly the day Christopher Parker came home to find his wife and daughter savagely murdered. Even though his son and younger daughter survived the massacre, he nevertheless had lost his own desire to live. Sheffield knew that Ed Parker hadn't gone to work for the union because of any strong belief in their constitution or goals. What motivated Ed Parker was a strong belief that somewhere in that union's organization lay the secret to the identities of his mother's and sister's murderers. Now with Ed Parker's death, four lives had been uselessly wasted in the last thirty-six years. Sheffield was determined to try and keep Mikki Parker from destroying her own life and dragging an innocent young child along with her.

Sheffield turned to look at Mikki who sat staring at the floor, her hands cupping her tear-swollen face. Suddenly she looked up and stared into Sheffield's eyes. They mirrored the confidence of a man who knew what he wanted and how to get it. She didn't necessarily like what she had just heard, but knew that Sheffield meant well. Actually, she thought, Sheffield was on target. She had no right to feel sorry for herself. She wasn't sure how she was going to pull it off, but Mikki was determined not to let Shana see or feel her true emotions. For that inner strength, she decided she could thank Sheffield.

Her eyes were dry now, but still reddened. "It's been a long time coming, but I think I understand my father now because of what you said," she said quietly. "I want to

42

thank you for having the courage to tell me.''

Sheffield walked over to Mikki's side. His voice lowered. ''If there's anything I can do, I want to help. You know that.''

Mikki nodded, smiling slightly for the first time. ''I know,'' she responded slowly, clearing her throat. ''I know.''

She looked toward the door that led to the hallway. ''Right now there's something I've got to handle alone.''

Chapter 6

EVERY INCH OF her upper body felt bruised and beaten when she awakened and Shana didn't understand why. She was in a hospital bed and didn't understand that either. There was a numbness below her waist and her body went cold when she realized there was no feeling in her legs. She wanted her father.

Shanalynn Parker was waiting impatiently when her sister walked through the door to her room. For a split second, her initial reaction was to get out of bed and run over to her but, when she turned back the covers to move, the smile on her pretty face was reduced to an instant frown. There was no movement. A confused and disgusted look quickly passed over her face.

Mikki's thin lips smiled as she watched her sister squint her eyes and brush back her curly blond hair so she could see her better against the sun's glare that was reflecting off the room's white antiseptic walls.

"Mikki," she whispered excitedly, "what are you doing here?" she asked holding her arms out wide. Mikki could feel a strange stillness of spirit in Shana that was foreign to her little sister's nature. Shana kissed her gently, holding Mikki's hand tightly, enjoying every second of her sister's comforting embrace. Shana had always had a prolific imagination but it had deserted her now. There were no games to play today. There was a void and she was confused.

Shana looked up into Mikki's face. Her older sister was silent and she watched her closely. There were grim lines she had never seen before and her face was pale. "What's wrong with me, Mikki?" she asked. Despite her eight years, her voice left no doubt that she wanted a straight answer.

Mikki gripped Shana's hand tightly. Her voice trembled slightly, but was soft and reassuring. "Sweetheart, you're going to be all right. The doctors are going to run some tests for a few days while you're in the hospital."

"To find out what's wrong with my legs?" she asked bluntly.

Mikki nodded.

"But they look okay," she retorted. "Why don't they move? Are they broken?"

Mikki kissed her sister gently on the head. "No, honey, they're not broken. The doctors don't know for sure why they won't move. That's why they'll have to run some tests."

"Is it cancer?" she asked abruptly. "Like what Mommy had? Am I going to die too?"

Mikki stared at Shana with shocked surprise. Shana had such a tremendous capacity to come in and out of her fairy tale world that she was sometimes an enigma. One moment her fantasies would have her riding carefree through the countryside with Sir Lancelot, and in a split second she could forsake her dream and be as pragmatic as a college professor.

Their faces were almost touching as they stared into each other's eyes.

"Am I, Mikki?" she persisted. "Am I going to die?"

Mikki shook her head and touched her fingers to her lips, still unable to respond. For a while, her mother's death had been pushed out of her mind. Now, there it was, staring her in the face again, put there by her own little sister's practicality. They clutched each other closely; tears stood in Mikki's emerald eyes. Mikki wasn't sure whether her grief was for her mother and father or for Shana.

Mikki's voice cracked as she spoke. "No, precious, you're not going to die. You're . . ." The words stuck in her throat. "You're just not going to be able to walk for a while. The doctors are going to help but it's going to take some time.''

Shana pressed closer to her sister, squeezing her slender arms tightly around her neck. "How long?" Shana asked matter-of-factly. "And where's Daddy? Is he okay?"

Mikki was still lost in her thoughts. "What?" she asked weakly.

"How long before I can walk again?" Shana asked again, temporarily forgetting the second half of her question about her father.

Shana's head was still buried in Mikki's shoulder. Mikki tried hard to think of an answer. The world was hostile, filled with invisible enemies for a little girl who had just lost her mother and, although she didn't know it yet, her father as well. For Shana's protection, Mikki decided to diffuse the actuality of what had taken place. The truth could come later.

"Look at me," she asked, softly kissing Shana's forehead.

Shana looked up, her eyes questioning.

Mikki's eyes became clearer now, soft and gentle as she spoke. "Remember," she began slowly, "last summer when we went to the theater to see *Camelot,* and how you began to cry when everyone thought Lancelot had killed Sir Lionel?"

Shana nodded, a smile beginning to creep across her trusting face. She had never been to a real play before her sister had taken her to see *Camelot.* Mikki had even read some of T.H. White's *The Once and Future King* to her before they went so she could understand and appreciate the play even more. Because of their age difference, it was the first time in her life that Shana ever really felt she had a big sister and she cherished those nights when Mikki read to her more than her big sister would ever know.

"I remember," Shana responded.

"What happened?" Mikki asked, with a confident smile.

Shana's enthusiastic response was quick. "Lancelot brought him back to life. It was a miracle."

47

"Mmmm . . . maybe," Mikki responded, with a trace of disbelief. "You know what I think really happened?" she asked, baiting Shana into another response.

"What?" Shana asked, beginning to play the game. Her confused mind was becoming clearer as she began to sink into the fairy tale she had been reliving over and over since seeing the play.

"I think Sir Lionel was really alive. The others just thought he was dead but Lancelot wouldn't let him die. He had faith that Sir Lionel was still alive. That's what brought Sir Lionel back to life."

"Lancelot's faith?" she asked.

Mikki nodded sagely.

"What's faith?" Shana questioned.

Mikki looked at Shana steadily. "Faith is something you believe and hope with all your heart. It's because of faith that certain things that sometimes seem impossible actually happen."

Shana was puzzled and her mind raced wildly. Suddenly she understood. The mystified stare disappeared, replaced by a discerning glow. "Then faith is what miracles are made of," she proclaimed proudly.

"That's it," Mikki answered encouragingly. "And that's what's going to help you walk again. Everyone has it. I have it. The doctors have it. But most of all, you have to have it. Without you, it won't work."

"Just like Lancelot?"

Mikki nodded. "Just like Lancelot."

Shana studied her sister for a moment. Her eyes began to fill with tears. "Do you really believe?" she asked, turning her face away. A sharp pain in her arms began to pierce her temporary escape from reality.

Mikki hugged Shana as hard as she dared. "More than you'll ever know," Mikki answered, her voice beginning to crack again.

The pain in Shana's arms subsided momentarily and she took a deep breath, sighing deeply. "Then I believe too," she finally responded, closing her eyes and laying her head against Mikki's shoulder. "I believe."

Soon Shana fell asleep in her sister's arms, thinking of King Arthur, Guinevere, Lancelot, and a magician called Merlin. Reality would have to wait until tomorrow.

That night Mikki lay awake, alternately thinking about how she would tell Shana about her father and trying to analyze the delicate line between her own grief and a new joy she was experiencing in finally understanding her childhood insecurities about her father's love. As each minute passed, she began to gain more strength. She was determined to lead her little sister out of their tragedy. Their life together as the remaining family unit was just beginning. At last, she thought, she had a purpose in life. She *had* been loved by her father, she just never knew it. Now she knew. For that, she was thankful.

Chapter 7

TOR SAT BEHIND his desk, his mind wandering as he stared out the window to the city streets forty-one stories below. It had been two days since his introduction to Mikki Parker and, despite their brief meeting, he couldn't get her out of his mind. She was slim, tall—nearly five-nine he guessed —and as beautiful as any woman he had ever seen. He remembered the pain he had seen in her eyes and the gracious manner in which she had carried herself despite the circumstances. He wanted to know her better, to help her through her crisis in any way he could. Deep down, he knew his motives weren't totally altruistic, nevertheless he had managed to convince himself that his considerations were pure.

World headquarters for Slagle's Incorporated occupied one entire floor of the Bank of America Building on California Avenue, and Tor's private office suite anchored the southwest corner affording him a peek-a-boo view of Slagle's newly remodeled store on Union Square. In all, there were five Slagle's retail stores but San Francisco's was his favorite. While those in Chicago, Dallas, New York City, and Paris were considered in a class by themselves, none in his opinion matched the opulence and grandeur exhibited in the newest Slagle's. Making the decision to tear down the decaying old building and start all over again had been difficult for him. His father had started the Slagle empire at that location and few citizens shared Tor's opinion that the city was losing its character far too fast with the transplanting of old historic buildings with faceless high-rise offices. It was for the nostalgia that Tor elected to keep the new building at six stories, the same as the original, and replace the fifth and sixth stories, that formerly housed the officers, with two more retail floors. By moving the offices, he was able to gain the much needed additional square footage of selling space and maintain the integrity of the new building by designing it much the same as the original structure. For the first time since he had ascended to Slagle's presidency, Tor felt part of the organization. The new building was his concept, his design, his tribute to his father. By his own choosing, Slagle's had never really been part of Tor's life. Only his father's death had made it so. Now the business had taken on a new meaning. It suddenly had his personal mark and for that he quietly harbored a fierce pride that only he truly understood.

Tor stopped daydreaming and unwrapped a cigar, lighting it with a mock formality. Perhaps he was finally becoming responsible, he mused. He chucked as he choked on the vile clouds of smoke that began to fill his office. Someday, he thought, he would learn how to smoke cigars like a proper tycoon, but tonight he had a more important priority. Billy Hawk was coming home, back to San Francisco, back to his old friend's house for dinner.

The day's brightness began to fade away from San Francisco, yielding grudgingly to the fast approaching evening as the water's dark blue hue deepened in the late afternoon sun. The towering city buildings glowed in an almost surrealistic, blinding whiteness behind Billy Hawk as he headed north across the Golden Gate Bridge toward Sausalito. Billy stopped momentarily, parking at the vista point on the bridge's north end. He never tired of the view from there, and the stark contrast of the city to the tiny tree studded hamlet of Sausalito on the other side had always been particularly enchanting for him. The beauty of the hilly, crooked, and narrow Sausalito streets lined with hearty oak and pine trees was accented even more, only a bridge away, by the city's denuded streets. He sat there enjoying the rare solitary tranquility that forever seemed to elude him. He was at home there, staring across the bay. There were no reporters, no cameras, no questions to answer. He wanted to move home again someday, back to San Francisco, but he was only thirty-six years old and a long career in politics still lay ahead. For now, Washington D.C. was where his life's goals would be met. The family Victorian house on Pacific Heights he used to call home would have to remain as vacant for the next twenty years as it had for the past five, inhabited only a few precious days a year. He sat for a long time before he reached for the ignition key and turned it. Slowly, he pulled away from his sanctuary, again pointing the car toward Sausalito.

A few hours later, Tor watched Billy's face closely as they were both alike, yet they differeed greatly. They were both from wealthy families. Their personal fortunes, while vast, weren't self-made and they shared a personal sensitivity to that fact. In their college days together they had frequently discussed what their roles in life should be. Certainly neither needed to work a day in his life if he chose not to, but their personal makeup wouldn't permit a meaningless and purposeless existence. Billy chose a lifetime commitment to community service in politics. Tor, while firmly entrenched in his capacity as chief executive officer and chairman of Slagle's, still wasn't so sure he was where he wanted to be, but was confident politics would not be one of his pursuits. He was simply not interested in answering to anybody but himself and chose to avoid political confrontations whenever possible.

Tor marveled over Billy's physical resemblance to his brother James. His face was fuller now and his sandy brown hair a bit darker and longer than his brother's. Even their voices were almost identical.

"I can't believe it's been over a year since I've been here," Billy said, sipping a glass of Chardonnay.

"It's an old cliche, but time flies when you're having fun," Tor replied, raising his glass to his lips.

Billy grinned. "So that's what it's been! I haven't been able to slow down long enough to decide whether that's really the case. I'm glad you told me. I was beginning to think what I've been doing is a lot of work."

"Politics getting to you already?"

Billy's response was quick. "No!" he said emphatically. "It's just that every time I come back to San Francisco I begin to question my priorities. And it doesn't help any to come to this bachelor's paradise you call home. This house, this view—I mean, what more could a man ask?"

"A man's got to live," Tor retorted in mock defense.

"You know a woman doesn't have a chance once she sets foot in that door. You should be arrested for premeditated corruption of unsuspecting females. It's rape by consent. There's nothing else you could call it!"

"A man's got to fuck once in a while. You should try it sometime. I bet Elaine would appreciate it."

"Leave my wife out of this," Billy laughed. "She's already mad as hell that I'm with you tonight instead of her. She knows what a bad influence you can be on my morals."

Tor shook his head. "The day I get you to stray off the reservation I'll go into politics myself. If I can sell you that program, I can sell anything to anybody, even an unsuspecting voting public. I could get myself elected. Just like you!"

Billy's boyish smile flashed across his face. He was comfortable with Tor. Theirs was a friendship that had begun when they met at Harvard Law School and had grown steadily stronger over the last sixteen years. It was nice to be home, even if it was only for one night. The city's lights sparkled and danced across the bay into and through the huge plate glass window that was the focal point of Tor's exquisitely furnished dining room.

Billy became quieter. Two bottles of Chardonnay shared during dinner had calmed his earlier tenseness. As they retired to the living room Billy became serious as Tor poured him a glass of sherry. "I hate to say this," he began, "but I have to admit I had more than one reason for wanting to see you tonight.''

A sheepish grin crept across Billy's tanned face as he waited for Tor's response.

"Not that again,'' Tor roared, shaking his head wildly. "We've been over this before. The answer is still no.''

Billy wasn't impressed with Tor's negative. "Hear me out, Tor. This time I really mean it. I need help and you're the only man I can trust to do the job.''

The resolution in Billy's voice made Tor listen rather than offer another negative response. Billy had been after him for over a year to join the Hawk Committee staff. Mostly, Billy maintained, because of Tor's nonpolitical inclinations. Billy had frequently argued that past commissions charged with investigating the various union activities were frequently stymied because of politically sensitive issues and past political favors that had to be repaid to the unions. It was for that very reason Billy wanted Tor to join the committee. Billy had handpicked the entire committee staff, consisting of both young personnel who had no political ties and seasoned veterans that were calloused to threats of any kind. Tor could never see why adding his name to the committee's staff listing would be of any benefit, always vehemently declining Billy's offers.

Billy was standing now, looking out the window, his back turned to Tor who sat comfortably in his favorite chair.

Billy watched the city below for a minute. "We're close, Tor, real close,'' he said slowly.

He turned and looked at Tor. From across the room Tor could see a look in Billy's eyes he had never seen before. They were cold and piercing, beaming a laser-sharp emotion. It was unmistakable. It was hatred.

Tor stirred restlessly in his seat. "How close?'' he asked.

"We're at the exact point where all the previous so-called governmental investigative bodies have mysteriously stopped their investigations by unilaterally declaring their tasks complete. I think I know why that's happened in the past but I don't have all the facts just yet. That's where you come in."

"Why me? From what I read in the papers your staff seems to be moving ahead just fine."

"They are! But I've purposely kept them all working independently of each other in different areas. Each knows their part of the puzzle but not how it fits into the overall picture. They all report to me weekly and I piece their information together."

"I still don't see why you need me."

"Jim's campaign schedule is getting so heavy he's not going to have as much time to devote to the committee as he has in the past. We've both discussed it and feel we need another mind to share the load. We think it's important that he remain in the forefront of the committees.

"Otherwise, it'll lose its impetus," Tor added matter-of-factly, allowing himself to play the straight man.

"Exactly. Especially now. We're too close to getting to the bottom of this mess to let it slip away."

"But what about your schedule? Running for the U.S. Senate isn't exactly a part-time job."

Billy nodded. "You're right. Our timing stinks. When this whole thing began two years ago I had no idea I'd be running for senator and Jim was only toying with the idea of running for the presidency. But we can't change that now. We have to keep moving—the committee, the campaigns, everything."

"Aw, come on, Billy, your schedule won't be any different than your brother's. Whether you're running for senator or the presidency, the schedule's the same. The territory might be a little closer but the time on the road won't be any less."

"I know, but it's more important for Jim to get elected than it is for me."

"What do you mean?"

"That I can cut down my campaign schedule if I have to. Jim can't. If he's elected, he can do far more good for this country as president than I could as senator. I sincerely believe that."

"You'd cut your campaign schedule and risk not being elected all for the sake of the committee?"

"If that's what it takes to nail that son-of-a-bitch, yes."

"You mean Cordaro?"

"Yes."

"Is that what it *is* going to take, your backing off on the senatorial campaign?"

"It is if I don't get you on our team."

"You bastard!" Tor protested, rising from his chair. "You've got plenty of men you could bring into the fold to share the load. What in the fuck do you need me for?"

Billy stared evenly at Tor, squinting pensively. "Call it instinct, friendship, trust, or whatever you want. I just don't want anybody but you."

A small disturbed smile broke across Tor's lips. "You make it awful tough to say no," he said.

"Then you'll do it?" Billy asked sternly.

Tor lowered his eyes. After a moment's thought, he looked back up at Billy. "I don't know," he said, shaking his head. "For the first time in my life I feel like my existence has a purpose. I own what I believe to be some of the finest retail stores in the world. Stores that are beginning to show my mark, my ideas, not just my father's. There's a sense of worth and responsibility in my bones that I've never felt before. It would be tough for me to abandon that right now, particularly when I still think you can do without me."

"I won't back off, Tor. You're the one I want," Billy persisted.

Tor suddenly felt a need for a drink, a stiff one. He fixed himself a Chivas rocks, his first hard liquor in years. Billy remained calm and silent, placing himself confidently in Tor's vacated chair.

Tor raised his glass to his lips, sipping a small swallow. "Do you really think Louie Cordaro is that big a menace to society?" he asked.

Billy's response was swift. "More than I could ever hope to tell you in one night. The man's as big a potential threat to our way of life than any we've ever known. Given

57

time and no restraints, he and his union could literally govern our lives without the least bit of public resistance. He's like a cancer. Catch it early and we stand a chance to survive. If we wait much longer it will be too late. I can guarantee it!''

Tor still wasn't convinced. Billy's convictions about social causes had always been stronger than his own and similar political discussions between them were usually forgotten soon afterward, at least as far as Tor was concerned. Just how serious Billy really was about his joining the committee staff was a subject Tor wanted to drop. He decided to break the pervading heavy air by proposing a toast. "Here's to our next U.S. senator from California. By way of Massachusetts, I might add, but who's keeping track anyway?''

A wide grin creased Billy's face. He joined Tor with a raised glass. "Thanks," he said laughing. "But if my critics are right, that may be a bit premature.''

"But the polls show you way out in front," Tor protested.

"It's a fickle public," Billy answered with an audible sigh. "They only remember today's headlines. They have a tendency to forget the overall picture. Next week will be the big test.''

"Next week?''

"The Hawk Committee reconvenes," Billy answered. "Up until now, we've been fairly low key in our approach against Cordaro's union activities. The public hasn't had much chance to react because there have been no specific charges or indictments, only some minor arrests of thugs and small-time racketeers. Public reaction has been favorable because we've exposed an element of corruption that the union can well do without. Nobody can argue with that. Even Louie Cordaro has had to publicly support us to some degree even though we damn well know he'd rather we pack our bags and fold.''

"So what changes the public's reaction next week?''

Billy brushed back his hair which had a habit of frequently falling into his eyes. His eyes glistened as if he had anticipated Tor's question. "Donald Peck will be in the witness chair on Tuesday morning," he said.

"You mean Cordaro's predecessor?" Tor asked. "I thought he retired."

"He has," Billy answered, "but Peck still sits on the trust that controls the health and welfare and pension funds. That's where we believe Cordaro is apt to be most vulnerable. The union is playing with other people's retirement and benefit money without too many controls. Almost no controls to be exact. We have a lot of questions to ask Peck about those two funds."

Tor's interest was increasing.

"So how's this going to affect your popularity in the Senate race?" he asked.

"The surface support of the union for the Hawk Committee's activities has been low keyed by their own design. They haven't reacted to anything we've done so far because they haven't had to. The committee simply hasn't done too much up until now. But when we go after one of their leaders, even a past leader, than the integrity of the union will be at stake. I think they'll come after my brother and me with both barrels. They'll try to discredit both of us as well as the committee."

Tor placed his drink on the table. "And you're going to hit Peck pretty hard?"

"With a cannon," Billy answered grimly.

"Is he vulnerable?"

"We think so."

"So how's that going to cost you votes? I would think the public would appreciate what the committee is doing."

Billy explained. "If we're on the right track, and I think we are, we'll be breathing down the necks of many leading union officials, including Cordaro. Rank and file union members have put a lot of trust in those people and my guess is they won't like their leaders being shot at. Hell, I have nothing against unions, only the corruption that happens to be going on in the biggest one in the world. But Cordaro and his boys will throw up a big smoke screen

59

and call me, my brother, and the entire committee anti-union. It's no big secret that the union packs a lot of political clout. It's tough to win any election without the support of labor, I know that. After we finish with Peck next week, Cordaro will be running scared. The anti-Hawk campaigns are sure to start. That's when my brother and I will start to fall in the polls. There's no avoiding it. It's a fact of life.''

A silence fell as both men looked out the window. The ticking of an antique wall clock over the fireplace became more audible. Tor thought about the Hawks. Their motor reflexes were always in force to play to win. They believed that men should work hard, got to bed and rise early, strive to the extent of their abilities, and be ruthlessly penalized if they failed in their responsibilities. Yet, they were simple men who could be moved by great emotions. Tor valued and admired Billy's friendship and was thankful that he wasn't in the shoes of any of Billy's adversaries, particularly Louie Cordaro.

Tor broke the silence. "I still have to ask why not wait until after the elections to go after the brass ring?"

Billy shook his head. "The committee is apolitical. It has no election timetable to govern its members or activities. There are two Republican and two Democratic senators and their staffs. I'm just the legal counsel. I couldn't stop it even if I wanted to. Besides, there's too much time between now and November. I don't trust Cordaro. I wouldn't stop now even if I could.''

"Why not?"

Billy's high-pitched tenor voice became higher, his irritation with the subject of Louie Cordaro becoming more evident with each word. "We have witnesses who for the first time in history are being cooperative with us. But, if too much time lapses before we ask them to testify, we could lose them. Cordaro has a history of mysteriously convincing people to see things his way.''

"Then you're going after Cordaro right away?"

"Not really. But he's the committee's ultimate target. Peck's just our logical stepping stone to get at Cordaro.''

"But going after Cordaro too soon will hurt your brother's chances of getting elected president. Isn't that right?"

Billy had no illusions about his brother's chances. "According to the polls, his lead over President Jordan is close to ten percent as of yesterday. If the committee runs its course and goes after Cordaro before the elections, the race will probably go down to the wire. Jim will win the democratic nomination in June easily, but he could still lose the November election."

"All because of the flak that will be raised by the committee?" Tor asked.

Billy shook his head. "Not flak from the committee. It's the union propaganda and antiunion accusations against Jim and me that we're sure will follow. Louie Cordaro is a master at that."

"And the committee has to start now if it is to keep from losing Cordaro, is that it?"

Billy nodded.

"And you think you have to get Jim elected to insure putting him away permanently?"

Billy nodded again.

"Sounds like a Catch-22 to me!"

"Your political acumen is beginning to show, Tor. Be careful, you may be headed for a life in politics."

"Why not go after Cordaro first? Get it over with before the election. Then you'll both be heros."

Billy hesitated. "Because . . . we don't have enough evidence to hang Cordaro on anything right now. We're still bluffing our way through this thing. Even if we had anything, there wouldn't be enough time to get him convicted before the elections."

A faint look of confusion crept across Tor's face. "So what in the fuck are you going after Peck for when what you really want is Cordaro? I mean, if you lie low right now until after the elections you might both get elected and then you can still go after Cordaro."

"Two reasons," Billy responded, pointing two fingers in the air. "Number one, the committee will die like all the others if we don't move ahead in an orderly manner and show fruits for our labors. If we can't show progress, the president can ask for its abolishment, which would be perfectly justified. We can't justify spending the taxpayers' money without results. As long as we show progress, we can keep it alive. Nobody can stop us, not even the president.''

''Would he want to?''

''Sure he would. He and the union have always scratched each other's backs. But the committee is a politically sensitive issue with the president right now because his opponent in the November election is heading it up. He has to keep hands off for the time being or it could make him look like he's trying to make the Hawk Committee a campaign issue. That could cost him votes.''

Tor looked at Billy inquiringly. ''You said there were two reasons.''

''Donald Peck,'' Billy snarled. ''Peck's not sure what we have on him right now, but word has it he's running scared. We've got enough evidence right now to throw him behind bars for years. But I need to get him in front of the committee first. He's our ticket to survival. He's our progress. By showing what we've uncovered about Peck's illegal activities when he was president of the union, we'll assure the committee's existence at least long enough to allow us to get at Cordaro. Peck's small potatoes, but I need him now to buy more time for the committee.''

Tor walked away and flopped casually on the sofa, draping his legs over one arm. Suddenly his earlier meeting with Winston Sheffield was more significant. Certainly the implications were now far more interesting and fascinating than a mere localized union organizational effort. He mentioned his meeting with Sheffield to Billy.

Billy's response was quick and his enthusiasm even more alive than before. ''Outside of Louie Cordaro,'' he began, ''Winston Sheffield probably knows more about the union's organization than any other man alive. He's a scholar on the subject. That's why he's been so successful in helping companies fight them off for so long. He always seems to be one step ahead of them. Hell, I tried to get him to work as a consultant with us but he wouldn't accept. He said he likes to work behind the scenes and he didn't need the exposure.''

Billy stopped talking, his mind weighing the possibilities of what Winston Sheffield's cooperation would mean to the committee. "What's Sheffield's interest in San Francisco?" he asked.

Tor went on to explain about his family's relationship with Sheffield. Billy's inquisitive eyes narrowed even more when Tor explained about Ed Parker's accident. "You mean Sheffield and Parker were openly going to work together?" Billy asked.

Tor shook his head. "Not officially, and not openly as far as I know. Sheffield just said that he had been an old friend of Parker's father and that Ed Parker was considering helping him out on this little union organizing problem we're supposedly going to have in San Francisco.''

Anxiety shot through Billy in a flash. Something about Parker didn't compute for him. "Parker would have been risking a lot by working with Sheffield. If Cordaro had found out, he would have kicked Parker's ass all the way back to Chicago. Why would Parker have risked that?''

"Winston told me that Parker was a 'former' union official. Apparently he had either resigned or intended to resign. I'm not sure which.''

"Christ!" Billy yelled. "This could be the chance we've been waiting for.''

"I don't understand," Tor replied, confused by Billy's continued exuberance.

Billy was up and pacing the floor, his mind racing far ahead of Tor's. "If Winston Sheffield really is your friend we might be able to convince him to help us gather information on Cordaro. He could be invaluable to us. I know he has inside contacts that would take us years to put in place. Ed Parker was a classic example of Sheffield's influence within the union. I'd bet a million bucks that for every Ed Parker, Sheffield has ten others just like him tucked away in his pocket.''

Billy was suddenly in a world of his own, thinking out loud. ''If my memory is right,'' he continued, ''Ed Parker was real close to Louie Cordaro, maybe even a personal friend. We need to find out why the sudden split.''

''What do you mean *we?*'' Tor challenged. ''I'm still a private citizen, you know.''

Billy ignored Tor's retort. ''Had Parker resigned?'' he asked.

''Like I said, I don't really know. At the time it was just a bit awkward to ask his daughter. I mean, the man was dead. Even you should understand that. In fact, even if Ed Parker were alive I'm still not sure I would really give a shit whether or not he had resigned from the fucking union!''

Tor's testy response and obvious sarcasm slowed Billy momentarily, long enough to recognize his enthusiasm over Ed Parker's relationship with Winston Sheffield wasn't being shared.

''I've been waiting for two years for a chance like this,'' Billy exclaimed. ''Your help with Winston Sheffield could be the key to a lot of unanswered questions. I've got to know if you can convince him to cooperate. I can't say it any simpler than that.''

Tor studied his friend's face. There was an expression he had never seen there before. Billy's confidence was weakening slightly, slowly giving away to just a trace of insecurity. For the first time in their long friendship, Billy was asking him for something that he could provide.

After a long silence, Tor responded, ''I'll try,'' he offered. ''I'll try.''

Chapter 8

WHEN PERCY TINSLEY arrived for his morning meeting with Tor Slagle, Tor had already been in his corner office for over an hour.

"Good afternoon!" Tor bellowed. Tinsley responded with a nonchalant smile as he casually ambled across Tor's huge office and sat himself in the single chair that faced Tor's desk.

Tinsley let out a deep breath, unable to resist responding to Tor's reference to the time. "It's not the afternoon. It's eight A.M.," Tinsley shot back. "If you wanted the damn meeting to start earlier then you should have said so. Don't ask for an eight o'clock meeting if you really want to start at seven forty-five. Just say the time, I'll be here. Not a minute before, not a minute after."

Tor couldn't hide the smile that crossed his face. "How's my best security director this morning?" he asked, his grin widening.

"You mean how's your only security director this morning," Tinsley corrected with mock disgust. "I don't recall your authorizing additional personnel for my department. I'm just the token nigger here."

Tor reached for a cup of coffee, fully immersed in the enjoyment of his usual banter with Tinsley. "Well, when you're colored, you've got to learn to stay humble," Tor shot back. "I keep your staff lean as a reminder for you of your black heritage. I've seen what happens when you jungle bunnies get a taste of authority. It's too damn close to anarchy. I mean, I gotta do my part to keep you assholes in line. You understand, of course."

"Yassuh, boss. I understand jus' fine!" Tinsley answered obediently, chuckling in a deep baritone.

The two men stared at each other silently, each respectful of the other. Tor smiled affectionately. "What do you hear on this union organization effort?" he asked abruptly, quickly getting down to business.

"I figured that was why you wanted to talk to me," Tinsley answered.

"Have you got anything?"

"I've nosed around a bit, but so far there's no sign of anything unusual. Are you sure Sheffield knows what he's talking about?"

Tor shook his head. "Hell, I don't know. We've all been through this before, but if what Winston tells me has an ounce of truth to it, we'll need to be careful. We need to know about anything unusual that happens around here, no matter how insignificant it may seem at the time."

Tinsley took a thin cigar from his coat pocket, placed it in his mouth, and lit it. Like many security personnel in private industry, he had spent several years in a city police force before changing from public to private service. For three years, Tinsley had capably controlled Slagle's entire security staff throughout the country, and he was enjoying every minute of it. While his imposing tall black frame lent credibility to his position, his greatest strength was his calculating mind and his ability to get people to trust him. The fact that his popularity and respect with Slagle's personnel was high helped make his job easier. He was fair, tenacious, strong willed, and totally incorruptible, virtues that had caught Tor's attention when they played football together in college.

Tinsley casually put his feet up on Tor's desk. "You planning on calling in Willie Ray on this one or you going to leave the strategy to Sheffield?" he asked.

Tor frowned. He had spent much of the previous evening thinking about Willie Ray. Ray was what many in the city euphemistically called a labor consultant. He had in the past frequently worked with Tor on various labor matters and, while he was invaluable for his local union expertise, Tor had always been a little apprehensive of using him because of his dubious business tactics and general lack of honor. As former president of the largest Retail Clerks's local in the city, Ray knew the union's defenses and strategies well, using his inside knowledge to help employers keep one step ahead of the unions in organizing drives and negotiations. Dirty tricks were not a small part of his arsenal. Tor didn't like them, but on the other hand he knew they worked.

"What would you suggest?" Tor asked.

Tinsley sat silently for a moment smoking his cigar. Then, without hesitation, responded. "Get Willie," he answered. "We need his contacts."

"I thought you'd say that," Tor said resignedly.

"I'm still a little confused," Tinsley said. "I can't see why all the big fuss over this organization drive as far as Slagle's is concerned. We've never had a problem keeping the union out before. Why do we need to even react? Just because Sheffield's involved?"

"Because I think we should this time," Tor answered.

"But it's Hemp Lathrop's ass he's trying to save. They're the ones that'll be paying Sheffield's fees, not us," Tinsley rebuttled.

"You have been snooping around, haven't you?"

Tinsley smiled. "I'm not without my contacts."

Tor began to explain his position. "I just don't think we can be too careful on this one. Sheffield's been around too long to be very far off on his assessments of what the unions are up to and he's definitely concerned about what might happen here. I don't want to take any chances. I don't want any damn union getting in the way of how I run my business."

"Come on, Tor, unionism isn't all that bad. I mean, if it happened we could still operate. It wouldn't exactly be the end of the world."

Tinsley was testing, Tor knew that. He wanted to know

how committed he really was to keeping the union out. Tor wasted no time in letting Tinsley know exactly where he stood. "Unions are a pain in the ass!" he began. "They have their place in history . . . in the sweat shops of the thirties! I admit that in some cases they perform a useful function in some of today's industries and businesses where employees might otherwise be taken advantage of by the employers. But they've turned the tables now. Unions are extorting exorbitant initiation fees and dues from employees, which go to finance thugs and high-priced union officials who do nothing to help the members when they have a legitimate complaint or question. Their retirement programs are ending up without funds and from what I hear they are horribly mismanaged. What really tees me off is that they portray management as the enemy to the employees. If my stores ever operate on the 'We-They' concept, I'll close up shop."

Tinsley thought for a moment, reflecting on Tor's comment. "I think I'd better get off my ass and get moving. Sounds to me like you mean business, boss."

Tor smiled slowly, realizing he had let his emotions slip. "Use the back door." He chuckled. "I don't want my neighbors to know you're working for me. It might bring the property values down around here."

Outside, a taxi pulled to the curb and Winston Sheffield exited quickly. Five minutes to nine. He paid the driver, left a small tip, and quickly entered the building clutching a large brown envelope closely to his chest as he rode the elevator. It was nine sharp when he was ushered into Tor's office.

Tor wasted no time coming to the point. "Frankly, Winston," he offered, "I don't like asking you to do this any more than you do. But, like I said over the phone, Billy is my best friend and he's asked me for a favor. I am going to do my best to fill it even though I'd rather stay the hell out of this mess."

"Then that makes two of us," Sheffield said flatly, sinking into a huge leather sofa that faced Tor's desk.

Sheffield's face was expressionless as Tor and he exchanged stares across the desk. Tor still wasn't sure how far he could push him into cooperating. Sensing Sheffield's uneasiness, he decided to ease the subject into the conversation. "How's Shana Parker?" he asked.

Sheffield didn't answer for a moment. Then a gradual smile inched its way across his face. "Thanks for asking," he answered, "She's doing much better but the jury's still out on the paralysis. Right now the doctors aren't willing to make any predictions."

As Sheffield continued to talk about Shana Parker's progress, Tor's mind mechanically organized the questions he was going to ask. He hated himself for being so calculating but he had a job to do. The sooner he got it over with the better as far as he was concerned. He took a long silent deep breath, then plowed into his first question. "I'd like to know more about Ed Parker," Tor began. "As I understand it, Parker resigned from the union. Would you mind telling me why?"

Sheffield forced a wry smile. "You're not exactly right. I said he hadn't officially resigned. He was on a temporary leave of absence."

"Temporary?"

"As far as the union was concerned, it was only temporary."

"And as far as you're concerned?"

"Permanent."

"Why was that?"

Sheffield looked at Tor for a long moment and displayed no visual emotion before responding. "When people start telling others what to do rather than asking, then it's time to move on. Particularly when what they're telling them to do goes against the principles they've believed in all their lives."

Tor looked into Sheffield's eyes. "You mean the union?"

Sheffield nodded.

"Would you mind elaborating?"

Sheffield's response was quick. "The ideals that

motivated the union as Ed Parker knew it are nonexistent today. Dishonesty and corruption are rampant among the union's leaders. It's sort of like waking up one morning and finding out your country's been taken over by the Russians.''

"That's how Parker felt?''

Sheffield nodded.

"It happened that fast?''

Sheffield shook his head. "No, he saw it coming. He just didn't want to believe it. The union has been a big part of his life.''

Tor leaned forward in his seat. "I take it Louie Cordaro is responsible for the corruption?''

Sheffield made no effort to hide his dislike for the man. "He's the worst.''

"But I understand Parker and he were friends at one time,'' Tor challenged.

"Where have you been getting your information?'' Sheffield challenged.

Tor smiled. "You know as well as I do! When Billy found out the two of us were friends, he leaned on me as hard as I've ever been leaned on. I can't hide that. He wanted to convince me to work with the Hawk Committee. When it became obvious over dinner last night that I wouldn't be able to, I settled for this meeting.''

"Like I said last night, this is all you're going to get,'' Sheffield reminded dryly. "I'll stay today as long as you wish. But, when I leave, our relationship goes back to normal. Strictly personal, no business.''

Tor nodded sagely. "So, shall we continue?''

"It's your show,'' Sheffield answered, turning both palms upward.

Tor was scratching notes on a pad on his desk. "I asked if Parker and Louie Cordaro were friends. Beyond their business relationship, I mean.''

"They were friends, yes. But I don't think Ed Parker was claiming that distinction before he was murdered.''

"Murdered?'' Tor questioned, his voice and interest rising. Sheffield recovered quickly, not wishing to speculate on a gut feeling he had.

"Slip of the tongue," he corrected calmly.

Tor considered challenging Sheffield's conjecture but thought better of it. He decided that he needed to know more about Parker's relationship with Cordaro before he could start chasing down wild accusations, even if they did come from Sheffield. Right now, he didn't even know why he should be interested in Parker except that it seemed a logical common ground to start his topic of conversation. "Was Cordaro the reason Parker decided to leave the union?" he asked.

"Partly."

"Did Cordaro know that?"

Sheffield's voice was cold. "It's not exactly healthy to be on the wrong side of that man. Parker kept his feelings to himself. Nobody really knows how he felt about Cordaro. Call it self-preservation if you want."

Tor stared at Sheffield. There was a question he wanted to ask but he was hesitant. Then, "What would Parker have done when Cordaro found out he left the union and was working with you?"

Sheffield's voice rose with an uncharacteristic anger. "Who said he was going to work with me?" he asked sharply.

Surprise echoed in Tor's voice. "But I thought . . ."

Sheffield cut Tor's response short. "It's not important," he said, waving his hands in the air. "I agreed to come here today because you asked a favor of me. I owe you and your father at least that much. I don't owe so much that I'm willing to risk my life. I'll answer any questions you may have as best I can but when I walk out of here today the favor's over. I'll disavow anything and everything I say here today. Not that what I say isn't truthful, it just won't do you any good to ask me to repeat it. Do I make myself clear?"

Tor tried not to let his disappointment show in his face. He had hoped he could still convince Sheffield to cooperate even further. "Then you're not planning on working on the committee?"

"Absolutely not," Sheffield responded flatly.

"But you will answer my questions today?"

"For as long as it takes," Sheffield answered cautiously. "But like I said, this is a one-time deal on this subject."

The conversation came to a halt as the two men exchanged glares for a moment. Within seconds, Tor broke the silence. "Well, as long as we each know where the other stands I guess we should get started," he said with a sigh.

A smile began to crease Sheffield's face. "I guess we should."

In an almost clinical voice, Sheffield began to answer Tor's rapid fire questions. After a series of seemingly innocuous inquiries, Tor became more specific. "Tell me what you know about Tom Wilson," he asked.

"He's Louie Cordaro's personal lawyer," Sheffield answered matter-of-factly.

"What's his relationship to the union?"

"He's their chief counsel. When Cordaro took over the union presidency, he felt the union needed to upgrade their image and Tom Wilson fit the bill. He's a public relations man's dream come true. He's educated, on the young side, tall, dark and handsome with a Clark Gable smile and knows his way around most of the power bases on Capitol Hill. Add to all that his golden tongue for oratory and you've got an instant touch of sophistication for the union that never hurts when female jurors begin to deliberate."

"Then you'd say he was pretty influential?"

"He's proud of his social status and friends in high places. His personal connections extend far beyond Louie Cordaro."

"Like throughout Washington?"

"And beyond! Don't underestimate what he can do. There's a brain and power behind all that glamour. He has a very distinguished record and he's proud of it."

"Then why would he want to get mixed up with Cordaro and the union when it's obvious there's a lot of shit about to be thrown around?"

Sheffield spoke softly. "Two reasons. One is a half-million dollar a year retainer fee he collects from the union and the other is he couldn't resign his position even if he wanted."

Tor sat forward in his chair, a raised eyebrow his only response.

Sheffield continued. "Next to Cordaro, Wilson probably knows more about the internal structure and affairs of that union than any man alive."

Tor rubbed his cheek reflectively. "Including the illegal activities, I presume."

"Particularly those," Sheffield answered, a smirk crossing his face.

"Would that include the pension funds?"

"I don't know how much he knows about them beyond monitoring the fact that employee and employer contributions are in compliance to the various union contracts. That's the only area he would be legally involved in. It's after the money gets to the union headquarters that the trail becomes a whole lot less auditable."

"Meaning some of the money disappears?"

"Meaning a whole lot of money disappears!"

Tor was scribbling as fast as he could.

"How does that happen?" he asked.

"Let's just say that a few of the union's leaders entrusted to administer the funds are guilty of a lot of indiscretions. That's what scares the hell out of Tom Wilson."

"Why is that?" Tor asked anxiously.

"Because the word has it that the trustees of the two funds have been taking care of themselves by making some questionable no-interest loans to themselves and a few other unnamed individuals. Donald Peck's a trustee and if the committee gets too far into Peck's dealings it could eventually lead to Cordaro."

"Wilson knows that?"

"He knows Cordaro's pockets are lined with the union's money through various personal loans. I don't know for sure that Wilson really knows where the money is coming from but the funds are a good place to start. Hell, I don't have to tell you that. It's pretty obvious the committee is looking into it.''

"How close is Wilson to Cordaro?"

"Meaning what?"

"Meaning do they like each other?"

Sheffield knew what Tor was driving at. Billy Hawk had schooled him well. "You mean could you get Wilson to cooperate with the committee?"

"Exactly."

"No way," Sheffield exclaimed emphatically. "You couldn't use anything Wilson could tell you in court even if you could get him to cooperate. Cordaro put him on retainer for that very reason. Wilson's the union's outside attorney. He's not on the payroll so the lawyer-client trust agreement keeps him from saying anything to anybody. Cordaro was very clever about that when he brought Wilson aboard. An employee could testify against an employer. An attorney can't testify against a client's confidence.''

Tor persisted. "I still want to know if they like each other.''

Sheffield shook his head. "They've never been bosom buddies if that's what you mean. The big retainer and the prestige of a big union account was what got Wilson aboard in the beginning. Now he's in so deep he can't get out although I think he would if he could. He tried resigning once but Cordaro wouldn't let him. He probably knows more than enough to put a lot of people, including some very influential politicians, behind bars for years.''

"Including Cordaro?"

Sheffield didn't comment. He merely nodded his head in agreement.

"So how would you suggest the committee proceed?"

"They're on the right track."

"Peck?"

Sheffield nodded slowly. "If they get Peck, they'll find a trail that leads straight to Cordaro. There is no question in my mind about that."

"Is Wilson involved in any of those deals?"

Sheffield shook his head from side to side.

"No way. He's above all that. He doesn't need the money anyway. He's got plenty."

"Then why would he defend Louie Cordaro?"

Sheffield held up two fingers. "Two reasons again. One, Wilson is willing to stick his head in the sand and save face in case anything embarrassing should come up. It helps to keep Wilson's reputation intact although I know it frustrates the hell out of him when Cordaro conveniently forgets to tell him certain things that come up later and causes Wilson to scramble in front of the courts. Even with all Cordaro's secrecy, Wilson's managed to pull him and several of his friends out of a lot of pretty touchy scrapes with the law. As long as he keeps winning, Wilson's not likely to jump ship. It's too good for his reputation and he's never been one to shy away from publicity. He eats it up."

Tor was intrigued with Sheffield's insight. "But I would think his reputation stands to go down the toilet if the committee gets past Peck and goes after Cordaro. From what I've been told, if the committee goes after Cordaro you can damn sure bet they won't go after him unless they're sure they can hang him out to dry. Then Wilson's reputation wouldn't buy him a cup of coffee."

"You're forgetting I said two reasons," Sheffield interjected. "Wilson's just like a lot of the others that have worked for Louie Cordaro over the years. They do what he says or pay the price."

"You mean force?" he asked.

"Exactly," Sheffield answered coolly. "Euphemistically, there are people on the union payroll as 'business agents' but they're nothing more than hired goons that do whatever Cordaro tells them to do. Louie decided early in his career he would always have more muscle than the next guy. The goons are his muscle and he's not afraid to send them out, even after Tom Wilson if he thought it would keep him in line."

"Would it?"

"It's pretty hard to argue when someone's just killed you," Sheffield added sarcastically.

Tor was incredulous. "They'd resort to that?" he asked. Sheffield nodded.

"Where's Cordaro get people like that?"

"The Illinois State Prison has been one of the main recruiting depots over the years. Cordaro's got a nephew that used to be an inmate there who has all the contacts. When someone gets out Cordaro can use, he's put on as a union business agent. Louie has a few select ones on special call to help keep any uncooperative people in line."

"Wasn't Parker afraid Cordaro would come after him if he quit the union?"

"There wouldn't have been reason for that. He'd never given Cordaro any trouble. He ran his area as clean as he could ever since he joined the union. He had nothing to be ashamed of. He was leaving because he could no longer control the outside influence from Cordaro's headquarters. They were asking him to do things his conscience wouldn't permit. He wasn't offering any trouble or resistance to Cordaro. He was just getting out of the way. He did his best. It's just that it got out of hand."

"What did they ask him to do?"

"Nothing different than what you're investigating," Sheffield answered.

"You mean the pension funds?"

"Right."

"They wanted him to extort the funds."

"In a manner of speaking."

"How's that?"

"Cordaro's always had a habit of working behind closed doors with employers, without witnesses, always trying to negotiate contracts that were as beneficial to himself personally as well as the employer. Under-the-table money frequently ends up in Cordaro's pocket in an agreed upon exchange for less dollar contributions to the pension funds from the employers. Realistically, that money belongs to the rank and file union members but frequently they never see it. Parker couldn't do that to his people.''

"They were asking him to do that?"

Sheffield nodded. "Telling him is more like it."

"Who?" Tor asked.

"Cordaro. He said Parker could take a cut for himself too."

"And Parker told him he wouldn't do it?"

Sheffield shook his head. "He hadn't told him anything. He just took a leave and went on vacation. He planned to resign when he got back."

Tor looked at Sheffield thoughtfully, saying nothing. "Tell me more about the pension fund," he asked.

Sheffield smiled confidently, the first time he had done so since stepping into the office.

"I thought you'd want to get into that," he said. "I spent most of last night and the early morning hours putting together what I've learned about it over the years and how I perceive it to be today. The problem is you need to know a little union history to fully understand how it got into the mess it's in now."

Sheffield opened the brown envelope he had been guarding closely and pulled out several typewritten pages. "I typed it myself," he explained, "in the hotel office. I couldn't take the chance on anyone else seeing it. I think you'll find the reading interesting."

A puzzled look crossed Tor's face as he shot a glance at the papers Sheffield threw on his desk.

Sheffield sensed Tor's dismay. "Call it a documentary," he said. "I figured there was less of a chance of leaving something out if I put it down on paper. It's noncommittal on my part. There's nothing in there that someone couldn't find out if they just spent a little time doing some legwork. This just speeds the progress up a bit."

"No confessions?" Tor kidded.

"Not even a signature," Sheffield shot back. "Like I said, when I walk out of here I won't even remember what we've discussed. What you have there is my parting shot. I have nothing more to say on the subject as far as what the committee wants to know. So, if you'll excuse me I'll be on my way."

"Won't you stay until I've read this?" Tor asked.

Sheffield stood up, shook his head, and offered no verbal response as he walked toward the door.

"What if I have some questions later?" Tor asked.

Sheffield shook his head but this time more vigorously. "I said this was a one-time deal. A favor. I've done what I was asked to. What you do from here is your problem, not mine. I'm sorry, but that's the way it has to be."

A frown spread across Tor's face.

"I'd be remiss if I didn't ask you to change your mind. I know Billy wants you to be part of the committee staff."

Sheffield was adamant, shaking his head. "Be realistic," he said. "Billy wants what I know. He doesn't want me. He doesn't even know me."

Tor had no defense. He knew Sheffield was right. "Well, if you ever change your mind . . ."

Sheffield smiled, nodding his head. "I know," he answered, starting out the door.

Tor called out, "Winston."

"Yes?" he answered, turning back slowly.

"Thanks. I know Billy will appreciate all your trouble. Let us know if we can return the favor."

Without another word, Sheffield was gone.

Tor thumbed through the pages nearly as quickly as Sheffield had exited. Black bold letters across the top of some of the pages segregated and identified five different sections of the meticulously typewritten pages.

The first three section headings were plainly familiar, LOUIE CORDARO, DONALD PECK, PENSION FUND HISTORY. The remaining two were nothing more than unfamiliar names, PETER DENNING, BARTIE BONANO.

He settled back in his chair and began to read the first section which was narrative about Louie Cordaro. There was little in the section that Tor hadn't already been exposed to but one bit of information offered him an insight about the union leader that couldn't be found in any objective outsiders' reports:

While Cordaro's union is made up of thousands of local unions throughout every city and township in the United States, one should never underestimate the power of Louie Cordaro to literally control each and every one. The officers of each local are elected by the individual rank and file local members but the more important elections in the larger locals are arranged to insure that Cordaro's personal choice is elected, particularly in the case of elections for the local's presidency. These "arrangements" can come in many forms including force, but in most instances it's in the form of promises of future unnamed favors for those who support Cordaro's candidate for elective office. Again, the promises can be in many forms but the most prevalent is the exchange of votes from certain individuals for a pledge from Cordaro of support in any future elections they may be involved in. By placing his best supporters in key positions throughout the locals, over the years Cordaro has been able to build his own empire at the grass roots level. He's now able to sustain that support by repaying past favors by declaring unsupporting local officials incompetent after surprise audits from union headquarters that inevitably recommend at the very minimum the replacement of the local's president. This is permitted by the union constitution and Cordaro uses it to his own advantage by replacing the president that has fallen into his disfavor with an appointment of his choice. Cordaro frequently repays past favors by handing over a local to a political ally and with that comes many privileges for the new local president including virtual unlimited and unaudited expense accounts and a handsome salary. Each time Cordaro makes a change, or his man wins an election, he strengthens his hold and influence. Personally, I don't ever see the process weakening. He can only get stronger as time goes on.

Tor slipped the Louie Cordaro section under the others and began to read Sheffield's comments on Donald Peck. It was the shortest of the five sections.

There are only two reasons Don Peck ever became union president. One was he was in the right place at the right time. When the former president retired, Peck was executive vice-president and the outgoing president's logical personal choice to succeed him. Unlike Cordaro, who at the time was president of the Midwestern Council, Peck was an uncontroversial choice (although many members were urging Cordaro to challenge for the presidency). Peck's eventual confirmation was virtually guaranteed when Cordaro elected to cast his vote for Peck after a secret quid pro quo agreement with Peck that elevated Cordaro to Peck's vacated executive vice-president's post after election. Peck respected Cordaro's strength enough that he didn't want to risk a defeat in an open election. That would have been devastating and as long as there was the slightest chance he could lose it, Cordaro didn't risk it. Cordaro leaves nothing to chance and by being named executive vice-president he was only one step away from his ultimate goal. He could deal with getting Peck out of office later and he did just that. I am certain there was more to Peck's early retirement than met the eye.

Tor reached for a tumbler and poured himself a drink of water from a pitcher on the credenza behind his desk. He turned to the section marked PENSION FUNDS.

The birth of the union's Midwestern Council brought with it the introduction of what was to become the largest independent pension retirement fund and health care plans in the United States, the union's health and welfare fund and the pension funds were simultaneously conceived and born. Cordaro never forgot his roots and his concerns for employees that were formed early on during his years on the docks of Chicago. As the ranks of his membership increased during those years at the local level, Cordaro's organizing and bargaining skills increased and he became more aggressive and creative with new labor contracts. His domain had spread to the neighboring mideastern states and he felt the need for an all-encompassing and uniform plan that would be supported by all firms organized under the union's contract. Every contract up for renewal as well as newly organized companies had the provision included. The two plans call for employers to pay into a general fund a set amount of money for each employee every month. In turn the plans are administered jointly by participating corporate represenatives and union members who act as a board of trustees. Cordaro always insured that the members of management elected to the board were on his list of friendly cooperating employers and the union appointees were of his personal selection. His board consisted of six employer representatives and six union representatives. Cordaro held the thirteenth or tie-breaking vote.

The successful implementation of the union's National Health and Welfare Fund and the Pension Fund marked the end of Cordaro's territorial career and helped start another as a National Union officer. The growth of the funds was so fast in the Midwestern Council, he was recognized for his contribution and elevated to the Vice-Presidency and named Chief Administrator of the funds and charged with the responsibility of implementing them into the union's contracts nationwide. The Midwestern Health and Welfare and Pension Funds were soon to become the union's National Health and Welfare Fund and Pension Fund and Cordaro became as powerful as any bank president.

But Cordaro's obsession had never been with administrating the funds, but with becoming the president of the union. He was impatient, a poor administrator, and he knew it. He decided to bide his time and go about the task to which he was assigned while watching for any internal political opportunities to advance toward his ultimate goal.

All the unions soon required employers to donate two dollars per week per employee into the funds. With the union membership swelling to just over three million, the funds stood to receive over three hundred million dollars annually. They were so loosely managed, that at no time were there any stipulations as to the amount of money that was to be allocated toward either fund or how either of the fund's were to be administered. If there's one thing the committee can do to serve the public, it's to correct the injustices that are going on within these funds. It's happening, I can't tell you who or how, but it's happening.

Tor laid the papers down in front of him and stared thoughtfully out the window. The more he read the more he wanted to drop the commitment he had made to Billy. A few days earlier his life had been full of positives and now as he sat consuming paragraphs the reality of life on the other side of the tracks was setting in. He felt sheepish about his lack of concern. Only his loyalty to Billy and a personal regard for his word made him read on. He searched for the sections headed with two unfamiliar names. The first one he found was headed PETER DENNING.

The formation of the Health and Welfare Fund required letting out bids to underwrite the insurance. Although his bid was not the lowest, Louie Cordaro selected Peter Denning over some of the nation's largest insurance companies who had also bid on the lucrative plan. What made Denning's selection so unusual at the time was that he had no license, no experience, and no office. Cordaro's power with the voting Health and Welfare Fund trustees was never more visible. Denning had been a major figure in Chicago's underworld for years and he knew his way around in both political and labor circles. Cordaro always felt he needed a contact with organized crime and Denning was his man. (Denning was a former union president of the sanitation union in Chicago having acceded to that position from the vice-presidency when the former president was mysteriously shot and killed.)
Sanitation districts have always been considered prime

contracts for any labor union in helping their organizing drives into other areas, especially food chains and restaurants. If employers refused to unionize, their garbage and trash pickups suddenly ceased, soon causing the health departments to shut them down. Forced with unionization or closing, nonunion employers normally agreed quickly to union contracts. With Denning, Cordaro bought an underworld association he had never been able to gain before. He also bought, he hoped, the allegiance of a man named Bartie Bonano (of whom he concealed a paranoic fear).

Cordaro's trade of the insurance for the gigantic National Health and Welfare and Pension Funds in exchange for his underworld introduction was quickly completed when Denning obtained his insurance license through hurried underworld expedition of his license approval through manipulation of old political favors. Cordaro now had another powerful tool in his arsenal.

During the following years, Peter Denning became a millionaire as a result of his new insurance company and the expansion of his underwriting to include the fund when it was formally expanded nationally. He has extracted exorbitant fees and commissions in excess of three million dollars, half of which was funneled to his underworld supporters in payment for their previous favors in helping him set up the underwriting business. Many states had tried to contest Denning's right to do business in their states but the inquiries inevitably fell on deaf ears. Denning's political influence is, along with his underworld friendships, proving to be a formidable foe for any state board of inquiry. He and Louie Cordaro have become one. Wherever Cordaro goes, Denning is never far behind.

There were several more pages on Denning. Tor was impressed with Sheffield's thoroughness as well as his ability to editorialize without pointing a finger at himself should the documents inadvertently find their way back to Louie Cordaro. There was a strange lack of emotion in the pages, as if Sheffield were merely reporting the score on a football or baseball game and, once completed, the task would be over. It wasn't until he came to the final page that Tor felt Sheffield had let his inner feelings show. There was only one page, headed with the other alien name to Tor, that of BARTIE BONANO.

While Peter Denning is a master of his trade, much of his strength comes from an animal of a man named Bartie Bonano who was his chief union organizer during the earlier years in Chicago. Bonano's a hulking six foot six, three hundred pound mountain with a chest and arms like a village blacksmith's. With a head half again the size of a normal man's and facial features that match, the man is Denning's enforcer, his muscle if you will. Just listening to Bonano's drill sergeant voice is enough to scare hell out of any man. One look at his body wraps up any lingering doubts among any dissenters. He towers over Denning's diminutive frame and together they worked the sanitation union more for extortion than for expansion of their union activities. They practiced terrorism with the smaller merchants. Louie Cordaro had always wanted the sanitation contracts when he was in Chicago but respected Denning's position with the underworld and never pressed his luck in that territory. He also showed a healthy respect for Bartie Bonano. An ominous glare from Bonano would freeze the coolest of individuals, including Cordaro who has known Bonano since their earlier union days together in Chicago. I don't exactly know why I've included Bonano as part of my notes except that you had best be aware of his existence. If you press on with your investigations, you're bound to cross his trail. Better that you look for him first and not the other way around. I wish you luck. Others have tried and failed to correct the malady that's infecting what started out as a good cause, a good union. Don't let a scum like Bartie Bonano stop you dead.

The report ended there. He looked at his watch; it was after one o'clock. He had been reading for over two hours, yet it seemed like only a few minutes. In all, Sheffield had left behind over fifty single spaced typewritten pages but the only one Tor could remember at the exact moment was the last. The implications of it all made him sick to his stomach.

Chapter 9

TOR SLAGLE WAS finding it hard to concentrate on his executive duties.

The chief executive officer of Slagle's had been deeply affected by the events of the past few days, not the least of which was his fascination with Mikki Parker with whom he had shared dinner the previous night at Casablanca, a small, intimate restaurant on Polk Street that remained uncommonly true to the spirit and atmosphere of Humphrey Bogart's film of the same name. It had been only a week since his and Winston Sheffield's rush to the hospital. Tor paced his office suite, seeking to place the recent events in true perspective. Billy Hawk's request for his help was different this time, more urgent than before and cause for reflection. So was his relationship with Winston Sheffield that had suddenly grown more pragmatic and less personal as a result of Billy's request for information. So, too, were the developments in his personal life that were growing more complicated by the minute because of the almost sophomoric infatuation he was having trouble disguising for Mikki Parker. Her beauty housed a magnetically proud personality that Tor found alluring. Even now, during a crisis when most people would be reduced to near chaotic desperation, Mikki Parker was demonstrating an immense storage of energy and determined perseverance.

Now, even though she was trying desperately to be decisive and unyielding to even the slightest quiver of emotion, her ability to do so was being taxed to the limit.

Tor continued to nervously comb the office from one end to the other, pacing back and forth. Once or twice he stopped to look out the window toward San Francisco Bay and sip from a cup of coffee. He was about to be drawn right into the middle of the Hawk brothers' struggle and he was going to do so willingly. Why he would submit to such an uncharacteristic act was for Tor beyond self-comprehension, so he abruptly decided to stop thinking about it, preferring instead to let his mind drift back to last night and Mikki Parker.

He looked out across the city toward where he knew Mikki to be. He wondered how she was, what she was doing. He wanted to know her better, to discover what made this twenty-four-year-old woman so fascinating to him. Although his intellectual curiosity was piqued, he was strongly aware of the physical reaction he was experiencing as he felt a swelling begin to press against the inside of his trousers. The sex they had shared the night before was spontaneous, tender and without expectation or apologies. Their bodies had communicated in a manner that words would have been incapable of expressing. Their sense of release and joy, in contrast to the grief and confusion of the past week, had been overwhelming. And they both knew their relationship was just beginning.

Tor reached for the phone and dialed a number he already knew by heart.

Chapter 10

QUICK INTELLIGENCE AND probing curiosity were Hawk traditions, inbred into the Hawk brothers by their father who studied at the Boston Latin School where great scholars were as common as clams in chowder. Descended from a family that migrated to America from Ireland just after the Civil War, Joseph Hawk passed through his early life taking in what he could of the country's history and wealth. A Harvard degree and a track record as one of the leading financiers in the country eventually led to an appointment to the post of ambassador to Great Britain. His two sons learned to see the world from the top but with a wisdom that began to surpass their father's shrewdness. In his own way, each brother learned that it was as important to give as to acquire. Over the course of a century in America, the family developed and passed down through the generations a unique sense of citizenship that told them they were responsible for what happened to their country as well as to their own lives. They were dedicated to making their homeland better for those who came after them as others had made it better for them. Today, Tuesday, April twenty-ninth, was no different. Donald Peck would be appearing before the Hawk Committee.

At stake was the pride of middle America. A blind faith had been invested in the various trade unions across the country by America's citizens. Their jobs, their futures, retirement plans, and to some extent their very existence depended on their elected union leaders. Today, they would for the first time be able to hear what Donald Peck had to say about the charges of corruption in the labor movement.

Louis Cordaro was no less interested than the public over Donald Peck's testimony as he sat alone in his office. He still had no feel for what the committee would ask Peck. An irritability that had begun at his first waking moment that morning increased as he sipped at a glass of milk and stared out the window and up the hill toward the Capitol. He worried about the loose ends he and Peck had carelessly left behind and whether they had managed to sufficiently cover up all the potentially embarrassing and damaging pecadillos of the past. Something inside told him that they had not.

The third floor of the Senate Office Building housed the Caucus Room and it lit up like a stage as the closed-circuit television cameras scanned the immense assemblage. Through a special hook-up secretly arranged and implemented by union electricians, Louie Cordaro was being afforded the same privileged view of the proceedings that was being privately televised to every House and Senate office. A huge gallery of reporters and private citizens sat patiently awaiting the committee's entrance. The gallery faced the committee members' elevated conference table, separated only by another long table and chairs that faced the committee members' seating area. This was reserved for the witnesses and their counsel.

Cordaro fidgeted as the cameras focused on the microphones in front of each empty witness chair. A moment later, the cameras panned the audience, quickly picking up Donald Peck. A telephoto close-up framed Peck's stone-white image on the screen.

Then, without fanfare, the Hawk Committee members began to file in through a side door, each reaching his respective seat with the obligatory period of paper shuffling, handshakes, and microphone adjustments.

One by one, Cordaro methodically and quickly reflected

on the opposition, assessing their strengths, their weaknesses.

James Franklin Hawk was without question his most serious concern. The possibility of James Hawk being elected president of the United States weighed heavily on Cordaro's mind. While he never stated it publicly, Cordaro knew that both the Hawk brothers privately held a strong dislike for him and had often boasted of devoting all their political strength to rid the union of his presence and influence. In twelve years in Congress, James Hawk had built a tight New England political machine which he operated with a merciless efficiency. He had a thorough understanding of American government and had become the unofficial shepherd of the powerful and influential northeastern politicos. Backroom democratic power brokers had been won over and the June Democratic convention was only a formality in handing the presidential nomination to James Hawk. He was handsome, educated, polished, wealthy, and an experienced speaker. He possessed all the ingredients required to flush President John Jordan from office. For Cordaro, it was imperative that James be prevented from being elected. The thought never left Cordaro's mind.

The next committee member, seated to James's left, was Harold "Harry" Truelson, Republican senator from Montana, a hard worker with a sense of humor that even Cordaro liked, despite his mistrust of politicians. Cordaro had watched Truelson cut witnesses to ribbons many times but always in a pleasant manner that somehow kept them at ease. Cordaro squirmed in his seat, knowing that under the senator's constant smile existed a shrewd and vigorously responsible man genuinely concerned with the course of American destiny. Playing politics above and beyond the call of duty was second nature to the senator and Cordaro feared that Truelson could possibly manipulate the public's opinion of his union.

Immediately adjacent to Truelson was Samuel Longley, the Democratic senator from North Carolina, who sat fidgeting with his tie while staring out across the gallery. Longley could destroy a witness simply by telling poignant and curt stories which would be more to the point than an hour-long speech or a full day's questioning from other less proficient interrogaters. He was an impressive two-hundred pounder with a slightly receding hairline and flowing white hair as well as an unkempt handlebar mustache. He wore gold spectacles that he was forever misplacing. His bulbous nose was a constant bother to him and he had a habit of sniffing a lot as he spoke while unconsciously scratching his head, ear, armpit, or whatever itched at the time. Such gestures were as natural to him as breathing. He was devastating with pompous or overbearing witnesses and his expertise in the Bible was legendary in the Senate. By drawing many of his anecdotes from the Bible, Longley made it difficult for most people to retort, feeling any response critical of his Biblical analogy would be tantamount to sacrilege.

James Hawk, Harry Truelson, and Samuel Longley were untouchables. Not even Louie Cordaro could possibly exert any influence on them and he knew it as he nervously watched the three men as they continued shuffling their papers. No amount of pressure or political support from his union would mitigate their intensity toward the investigation. That left the fourth member of the panel, Senator Benjamin Gregory of Ohio, who had not yet entered the room. Gregory owed his election to Cordaro because of the union's support two years earlier. It was Cordaro's shift of allegiance during the last few weeks of the campaign that allowed Gregory to win the election, albeit by a slim margin. The Cordaro personal seal of approval came just weeks before the election when Gregory was a Representative chairing a committee charged with investigating two of the union's organizers in Ohio. The organizers were consistently pleading the Fifth Amendment on questions relating to their income and eventually the hearings were recessed at the call of Chairman Gregory. Though the public was under the impression that they would be resumed with resultant contempt citations, the hearings never reopened. Only Louie Cordaro and Samuel Gregory knew why.

Gregory's position on the Hawk Committee gave Cordaro a slight sense of comfort. Gregory had never been strong or decisive and Cordaro knew the Hawk brothers had fought hard to keep him off the committee, rather because they suspected his possible indebtedness to the union rather than his general lack of ability.

James, tanned from a weekend campaign retreat to Palm Beach, grew irritable over Senator Gregory's late arrival while Cordaro, in the seclusion of his own office, privately delighted in the delay. A moment later, Senator Gregory casually strolled through the heavy oak doors that connected the Caucus Room with the private hallway that led to the Senate offices on the fourth floor.

James cast a disgruntled glance at his colleague and gaveled the meeting to order.

"During the past several months," James began, "this committee has interviewed literally hundreds of individuals concerning corruption and dishonesty in the operations of certain labor unions and labor-management affairs. I am not, nor are any of the members of this committee, an expert on labor-management affairs or on labor union practices in the United States. However, we believe that there are serious questions before us that need to have accurate answers. Mr. Peck, who is with us today, by virtue of his past position was an authoritative force during the time that many of the events took place about which we have questions. Until now, our questioning has by design been of a general nature, generating a broad spectrum of inquiries and investigations by our staffs throughout the country.

"Let me say now that we are ready to move forward to begin to rid the nation's unions of the racketeering and corruption that our investigations now suggest has infiltrated their ranks through the past few years. It is my opinion that many fine hardworking and honest union officers and union members are being devoured by a cancerous growth of corrupt leaders that are misleading them and misusing their trust. Specifically, our investigation now must turn to those leaders.''

Billy watched Don Peck's eyes as his brother spoke. They appeared to be lost in his large oval-shaped bald head, yet they commanded Billy's attention, shifting back and forth nervously as James spoke. Except for one empty chair, Peck was flanked on both sides by his lawyers who were intermittently whispering to him.

Billy's eyes shifted to the missing chair next to Peck. In an attempt to influence the committee, Peck had retained former Illinois Senator Duffy Johnson as his attorney. For no known reason, it had been announced that Johnson was unable to attend the morning session. An associate attorney sat in his stead which didn't appear to noticeably disturb Peck's concentration.

Billy paid particular attention to Peck when James stated that the committee would concentrate on the misuse of union funds. He knew that in the basement of the Senate Office Building his staff had gathered enough information and documents to force Peck to spend the rest of his retirement in prison. Peck's reactions were minimal. His face occasionally flushed and he frequently shook his head from side to side when his lawyers tried to converse with him.

James concluded his opening statement, followed by an audible rumble of low verbal speculation throughout the room, which soon ceased when James called Donald Peck to the witness chair.

Dressed in a brightly colored green shirt with a wide floral blue-green flourescent tie that was tied so short that it accentuated his portly torso, Peck began with a question.

''Mr. Hawk, may I read a brief statement for the recond before we begin the questioning?'' he asked.

''You may, Mr. Peck,'' James responded.

Peck put on a pair of small rimless glasses and began to speak pompously into the microphone. His voice was strong, the delivery rough and choppy. ''I am very happy to speak before this committee in my present official position as a trustee for my union's Health and Welfare and Pension Funds, and . . . ah . . . ah . . . as past president of the International Union. This . . . ah . . . committee and Congress itself will render a distinct service to the country as a whole and for labor and its individual membership, if you . . . ah . . . write into law an absolute compulsion for the . . . ah . . . accounting of union funds. If there has been any past misuse of those funds, I am here to say that . . . ah . . . I am not . . . ah . . . aware of it. Thank you.''

Billy could hardly contain himself from smiling at Peck's remarks. He couldn't imagine what Peck could possibly expect such a statement to buy him. Peck was actually enjoying himself. He was back in the limelight. While that fact amused Billy, it caused a cold sweat to penetrate Louie Cordaro's forehead.

"We intend to initiate your suggestion," James responded sternly, not nearly as amused at Peck's comments as Billy. "And I would like to remind you that you are under oath."

Peck smiled broadly. "I understand that, Mr. Chairman," he announced.

James wasted no time. "Mr. Peck, can you tell the Committee what your past relationship has been with a Mr. Frank Billings?"

It was a question Peck hadn't expected but it seemed harmless. "He is a personal friend and a labor relations consultant. The union frequently retained him for various projects," Peck answered, adjusting his glasses.

"Did you ever retain Mr. Billings' services for anything other than official union business?"

"I'm not sure."

"Not sure?" James questioned.

"I mean I don't know what you mean."

"Did you ever use his services personally?" Billy interjected, anxious to get to the point, fully realizing that the unofficial protocol called for James to ask all the initial questions.

Peck was still unconcerned about the line of questioning

and responded without hesitation. "Billings is a friend. We frequently have done each other favors but no payments were ever made to each other as far as I can recall."

"What kind of favors did he do for you?" James asked politely.

The attorney on Peck's left side immediately whispered into his ear. A moment later, Peck answered as he was instructed. "I don't feel that the committee has jurisdiction or authority to pursue this line of personal questioning and therefore I refuse to answer the question."

James countered immediately. "I believe the chief counsel has some questions to ask you, Mr. Peck, that will be relevant to this investigation and also clarify my previous questions. Mr. Hawk, the floor is yours."

As chief counsel, Billy had rarely prepared written questions, but chose to do so today. "Would you please tell us where you currently live?" he asked.

"I have a retirement home in Vail, Colorado," Peck answered calmly.

"Who owns your home?"

Peck once again conferred with his attorneys before answering. Then, "The union," he answered.

"How did the union acquire the property, Mr. Peck?"

Peck was suddenly defiant. "I sold it to them!"

"When?"

"About three years ago, I think."

"Do you pay rent?"

"No."

"Why did the union buy your home?"

"As part of the union's Pension Fund investment program. It's the Fund's investment."

Billy kept firing questions.

"For the record, Mr. Peck, would you explain what that investment program is?"

Peck hesitated momentarily then read from a paper handed him by his attorney. "The Health and Welfare Fund and the Pension Fund are two distinct entities. Since they are relatively new, . . . ah . . . receipts are greater than

96

expenses at this time. The . . . ah . . . trustees have set up a common investment program that is designed to . . . ah . . . conservatively increase revenues for the benefit of the union members by reinvesting excess cash.''

"How much did you sell your home to the union for, Mr. Peck?"

"Four hundred thousand dollars.''

"How much did you pay for it?''

Peck slammed his glasses on the table. "I don't see where this is leading us. What's your point?"

Billy ignored Peck's question, quickly asking another. "What is the union's Public Relations Account?''

This time, the question confused Peck. He didn't expect Billy to drop the question about his house so easily, although he suspected the connection with the house and Billy's last question. He wondered if the committee knew of his arrangement with Louie Cordaro where, in exchange for having the union buy his home in Vail, he had agreed with Cordaro to recommend to the union's board of directors that they endorse Cordaro's election to succeed him as president. In exchange for the endorsement, Peck was to receive lifetime free rent at Vail in his home sold to the union, a lifetime position as a trustee on the union's pension fund with an annual salary of one hundred thousand dollars. As far as he was concerned, it was a form of thanks given for his past service to the union. He couldn't understand why that would be a problem even if it were known publicly.

Billy's voice boomed over the loudspeaker. "Mr. Peck, are you going to answer my question?"

No response.

Billy was undaunted. "Mr. Peck, I'll ask again. What is the union's Public Relations Account?''

Peck huddled with his attorneys and then answered with an obvious trace of indignation. "It's a general fund, Mr. Hawk. One of many within the organization.''

"As president, did you have access to that fund?''

"Of course.''

"What did you use it for?''

97

"To pay bills for public relations services. What the hell else would it be used for?"

Billy smiled, paused a few seconds, then continued. "Did you use the fund to pay people such as Mr. Frank Billings?"

Peck and his attorneys were caught by surprise. They were not prepared for Billy's back-door method of getting back to the original line of questioning. To their chagrin, Peck responded before his attorneys could confer with him.

"He sometimes could have been paid through that account. I can't be sure," Peck muttered defiantly.

"Did you ever have Mr. Billings buy things for your home in Vail?" Billy asked.

"Such as?"

Billy smiled and opened a manila folder. He started reading from a typewritten list taken from the folder. "Such as draperies, carpeting, a swimming pool, a tennis court. Were these items purchased for your home by Mr. Billings?"

Peck pushed himself back from the table and slouched in his chair, pausing several seconds before responding. "Yes. He always got things wholesale. He did it for lots of people, not just for me."

"Did you pay him for these services?"

Peck straightened up in his chair again, his voice becoming higher. "Of course!"

"How did you pay for them?" Billy asked.

Peck's face flushed as he grew more impatient. "I don't get it!"

"Did you pay for these services by check?"

"I suppose."

Billy was incredulous. "You mean you don't remember?"

"I'd have to check my records."

"We've checked for you, Mr. Peck."

Billy's next move was swift and unexpected. "Mr. Peck, you're excused from the witness chair."

Peck's surprised eyes glowed with piercing contempt.

He could hear a rippling of noise from the gallery as an audible speculation as to what Billy's next move would be began to crescendo. The wait was short.

"I'd like Mr. Frank Billings to take the witness chair, please." Billy announced unceremoniously without looking up from his notes.

Frank Billings's testimony was quick and devastating. He told of his relationship with Peck and stated the facts clearly. He said he had received items from underwear to refrigerators. He had also arranged for construction work on Peck's Colorado home at the lowest possible prices. He indicated Peck had always paid promptly and that he had done only limited consulting work for the union. Union checks, all with Peck's signature, totaling $65,000 were presented as evidence.

Billy was calm, calculating in his approach. "Thank you, Mr. Billings, you're excused. Mr. Peck, would you please retake the witness chair."

The gallery became restless and loud but quieted when Billy resumed his questioning. "Mr. Peck, would you please examine the checks submitted by Mr. Billings and tell the committee if it is your signature on all the checks."

Peck was silent as he stared at the checks, refusing to confer with his attorneys, then speaking only after several seconds had elapsed. He again read from a piece of paper, this time from one he had taken from his breast pocket. "In the absence of my . . . ah . . . personal attorney, Mr. Duffy Johnson, I must . . . ah . . . decline to answer the question because this . . . ah . . . committee lacks jurisdiction or authority under Articles one, two, and . . . ah . . . three of the Constitution; further, I . . . ah . . . decline to answer because I . . . ah . . . refuse to give testimony against myself and . . . ah . . . hereby invoke the Fifth Amendment."

Suddenly it hit Billy why Duffy Johnson hadn't appeared with Peck. If the questioning got a little sticky, Peck would save face by invoking the Fifth due to his attorney's absence. That way it would be more palatable to the public. He would look as though he had been forced to take the Fifth. Not by choice, but because of matters beyond his control—his personal attorney's absence.

Billy quietly assessed the move as an intelligent one but refused to drop the issue. "Were union funds used to pay for improvements and maintenance of your home while you owned it?" he asked.

Peck answered in the same noncommittal words that he used before.

Billy persisted. "Did you use union funds to improve your property and then sell it to the union at a profit?"

Peck didn't answer. He purposely avoided conferring with his attorneys who were unaware that he had been instructed to do exactly that by Duffy Johnson. The silence continued. Peck stared directly at Billy who was returning the glare with equal force.

Seeking to hasten the process, James interrupted the silence. "Mr. Peck, did you understand the question?"

Refusing to buckle, Peck took the Fifth.

The questioning was at a standstill but the damage had been done. James knew there was sufficient evidence to convince the Attorney General to indict Peck for misuse of union funds, but he still wanted even more. The public would be watching the news on television tonight and he wanted to be sure there would be no doubt as to the result. "Mr. Peck, have you ever heard of the Freeman Trailer Company?"

Peck automatically started to plead the Fifth, then caught himself after he had uttered the first few words. He realized it would seem a harmless question to the general public and he would look foolish if he refused to answer. Every businessman in the country knew of the Freeman Trailer Company. "Yes, of course," he finally responded. "It's one of the major trucking companies in the country."

James shot back. "Did you ever borrow two hundred thousand dollars from them as a personal loan?"

"I have borrowed some money from them in the past but I don't remember the exact amount," Peck answered, his voice again pitching slightly higher.

"Why would the Freeman Trailer Company lend you that amount of money?"

Peck didn't answer.

James persisted. "Why didn't you go to the bank for a loan?"

Still no answer.

"What did you do with the two hundred thousand dollars, Mr. Peck?"

Peck rubbed his face with his hands, then broke his silence. "As I said before, that's a personal matter and the committee has no jurisdiction."

James snapped back, visibly irritated at Peck's lack of cooperation. "It does if you sold your house to the union's pension fund at an inflated profit so you could repay your personal loan bill from the Freeman Trailer Company!"

Suddenly forgetting Duffy Johnson's advice, Peck huddled with his attorneys, stalling for more time before answering.

James was relentless. "Do you feel that if you gave a truthful answer to the committee on your use of sixty-five thousand dollars of union funds and on the circumstances surrounding the sale of your house and the two hundred thousand dollar loan from the Freeman Trailer Company that that might tend to incriminate you?"

"It might," Peck answered sarcastically.

"Is that right?" James asked.

"It might," Peck snapped again.

James's response was terse. "I feel the same way."

The gallery's hushed conversation suddenly turned to a large, nearly thunderous roar as the two men's argumentative tone increased.

"We will have order, please," James commanded, his gavel coming down hard.

Rather than risk reducing the session to a pissing contest between himself and Peck, James called a thirty-minute recess which was then followed by even more intense questioning of Peck. Senator Longley took over the questions for the balance of the day but Peck remained unresponsive.

The following morning Senator Truelson resumed the questioning but Peck's earlier prepared statement about helping the committee with its investigation was as invisible as it had been the previous day. Senator Gregory continued to remain conspicuously silent as he had the day before, choosing instead to allow his allocated floor time to be used by the other committee members.

Peck continually declined to answer any delicate questions, offering only brief responses to the simpler inquiries. It had become all too clear that Donald Peck would shed no new light on the committee's investigation. James knew that Peck was not publicly finished but he had nevertheless been discredited extensively. By appearing before the committee he had unwittingly served as a stepping-stone to the ultimate goal James wanted so badly. There had been enough evidence presented in the last two days to insure indictments against Peck and any subsequent investigations of Peck's past were sure to provide the impetus and public support for the committee to continue to pursue the union's current hierarchy. And that meant a shot at Louie Cordaro.

With a voice that echoed thoughout the Caucus Room, James decided to close the hearing. "Mr. Peck, you have shown a flagrant disregard and disrespect for honest and reputable unionism and for the best interests and welfare of the laboring people in this country. Above all, you've shown an arrogant contempt for the two million laboring people in the union you once led."

The hearing, at least temporarily, was over. Donald Peck's problems were just beginning. He exited quietly, choosing to avoid the waiting reporters by using a side door.

Four blocks away, Louie Cordaro sat alone in his office. He slipped out of his chair, walked over to the television and shut if off. An internal rage that began the day before as only a small ember now glowed with a white heat, fueled by Peck's embarrassing performance over the last two days.

That evening, radio and television stations of the

nation's capital, decreed that Donald Peck's fate would be decided when he had his day in court with the right to cross-examination, stating that "only then would the truth about Donald Peck's activities be known."

Donald Peck would never have his day in court. Louie Cordaro wouldn't allow it.

Chapter 11

THE VIEW FROM Louie Cordaro's plush office in the marble mausoleumlike building that housed his union's headquarters in Washington, D.C. looked straight up Capitol Hill toward the old Senate Office Building. Cordaro stood at his window watching the rain begin to fall, reflecting on the previous day's Committee hearing and Don Peck's testimony, which had turned into self-immolation. The thought of Peck testifying further made him apprehensive and angry.

His fist slammed hard against his desk. "I don't give a shit about Don Peck, but for the sake of the union we've got to keep that bastard off the witness stand!" he yelled, his face flushed crimson with anger.

A noticeable hush filled the room as Borg Trenier remained silent, something he had learned to do long ago when his boss's humor was conspicuously absent. Through the years he had frequently listened to Cordaro's tirades and, while he never mentioned it specifically, he felt sure Louie had always appreciated using him as a sounding board.

Borg Trenier had paid his dues, both in service to the union and to Louie Cordaro. Past favors had been repaid when Cordaro promoted him to his own vacated position of executive vice-president when he was elected union president. Trenier understood the labor movement perhaps better than any other person within the organization and Cordaro respected that. He was a financial wizard, a strategist, but not necessarily a natural leader, something Cordaro covertly cherished. The idea of having someone in the number two position who wasn't ambitious was comforting. Cordaro never liked looking over his shoulder, and Trenier offered no potential threat to him.

Still mute, Trenier sat puffing on an oversized cigar. Cordaro's voice grew even louder. "That cocksucker has had his fingers into more pies than we'll ever know about and if we don't shut him up that fuckin' committee will start snooping around here!"

Cordaro was livid, his voice filled with contempt. "Can you imagine that stupid, senile old fart making a statement about pension fund accountability and then meekly sitting there and being eaten alive? What the fuck was he thinking of?"

Trenier ignored the question, scratching at his left calf which was comfortably crossed over his right leg. While he didn't dare say it, he knew that Cordaro's personal financial record was as spotted as Peck's regarding the use of union funds and that Cordaro's real fear was centered more on what the Committee could do to him once they got past Peck than what they could do to Donald Peck. Trenier knew Louie had some virtues, but altruism was not among them.

Trenier readjusted his large frame in the black plush chair. "They apparently know a lot more than they were willing to let out at the hearings," he offered casually. "Their charges were mostly conclusions. I doubt they'd do that if they didn't have the facts to back them up."

Cordaro rose, stretched, then walked to the window shaking his head. "Yeah, I thought about that," he said, his voice trailing off as he looked away.

The rain began to beat heavily on the window. Cordaro stood still, looking out, saying nothing.

Trenier hesitated a moment, then broke the silence. "You know indictments are going to follow and I just don't see how you're going to keep him off the witness stand. They've got him and the Committee knows it."

Trenier was testing. He wanted to see if Cordaro would offer any thoughts on how to keep Peck from testifying, but Cordaro didn't bite. For some reason unknown to Trenier, Cordaro always kept him at arms length from any union business that might be construed by outsiders as unethical. Trenier was sure that Cordaro had frequently stepped beyond the law in his personal and union business but he never asked about such affairs. In a way he was grateful, but since his appointment to executive vice-president he always felt on the outside. He didn't feel that he knew what was really going on within his own union. Cordaro would frequently make private arrangements with employers as well as union employees that sometimes made him look foolish to his peers because of his ignorance, and for that he wasn't grateful. While he resented Cordaro's autonomy, it was nevertheless proving to be a blessing in disguise. While the Committee might seek Louie Cordaro as a target for investigation, they would never come to him because it was publicly known that he knew little about any unscrupulous union affairs. He had never been asked to go on a picket line or to become part of any potentially violent or embarrassing union activity. The union had a longstanding unwritten philosophy prescribing that one individual of senior headquarter's management have a conservative history, completely free of any indiscretions that would make that individual vulnerable to public chastisement from the media or within their own ranks. Borg Trenier knew he was that man. The union had done him a favor and he was enjoying his position. He had it made and wanted no part of Louie Cordaro's job or responsibilities. He was sure of that.

Trenier fell out of his thought pattern, realizing that Cordaro was still talking. He hadn't understood a word for several minutes.

"If we just knew where the committee was headed," Cordaro continued, "we could concentrate on busting a few heads before they got their witnesses on the stand."

Trenier joined the conversation once again. "What about Senator Gregory? He owes us a favor."

107

"Jim Hawk has sat on him. Hasn't given him a fuckin' thing that'll help us. He knows Ben owes us so he's been tightfisted with information. That little bastard brother of his and him are like Fort Knox. They don't tell anybody nothin'."

"Well, we've had investigations before and we've always survived, so . . ."

Cordaro cut Trenier short. "But none of them ever got this far before!" he snapped. "That fuckin' Peck's gonna get hung by his balls at high noon with the whole town watching if we don't do something."

"Are you going to talk to Peck?"

Louie said nothing, sitting down disgustedly.

Trenier answered his own question. "You have to," he said matter-of-factly. "We need to know everything he may have done that would discredit the union. Once we find out, we should be able to clean up the records easily enough."

Cordaro was up again and walked to the window. He pushed an electric button activating a small motor that began to pull shut the draperies, muffling the noise of the spring rain. He looked around his office. He had always dreamed of such an office. The thick carpeting, plush furniture, and spectacular views gave him a sense of security he had never felt before. The thought of having to fight to save his position began to annoy him even more. His pulse rate quickened. He turned and stared at Trenier who did not return the glare.

Cordaro groaned aloud. "I know what has to be done!" he said, his voice rising with indignation. "I don't need you or anybody else to tell me what to do!"

"What's your plan?" Trenier asked softly, ignoring the impoliteness.

Cordaro thought for a moment, hesitated, then went on. "We'll step up the P.R. about the Hawk brothers' vendetta, about their antiunionism. We've got some people on Capitol Hill that better get off their butts and put some heat on Jordan if he expects our support in the November election. That asshole started this whole

108

fucking thing thinking he could keep it under control and buy himself some votes, but Hawk has turned the tables. He's shit all over him. He's bought himself a million dollars worth of publicity.''

Trenier put a match to a cigar. "But what can Jordan do now?'' he said, simultaneously exhaling a large puff of smoke.

"He could fire Hawk from the committee since he appointed him to it in the first place, but he won't. It's too close to the election and that would cost him more votes now than we could generate for him. The public wouldn't stand for it. Anyway, the son-of-a-bitch should've fired him before Hawk announced his candidacy. Now it's too late.''

Trenier, ever the pragmatist, persisted. "Like I said, what can Jordan do now?''

Cordaro waved a disparaging fist wildly. "He has to discredit the committee, particularly the Hawk brothers. We've got to get the public on our side. Tell 'em we're being made scapegoats for the sake of getting James Hawk publicity. Make 'em feel sorry for us.''

"But he's avoided the issue so far," Trenier said, exhaling another stream of smoke.

"He won't anymore, not if he wants the labor vote. I'll see to that.''

"What do you want me to do?" Trenier asked expectantly.

Cordaro stared quietly back at him, then forced a smile. "Sit tight for now. I'll get back to you," he said, suddenly standing at the door and holding it open.

Trenier looked at Cordaro in surprise, then left the room, trying hard to ignore his disquiet. Cordaro had managed to brush him aside without giving him any details for which he could help develop a strategy. From the beginning, he felt Cordaro really wanted to handle the matter alone and the only reason he was invited into the room in the first place was to perform his normal bullshit conciliatory function. He wanted to help. In his gut, he knew he could. But only if Louie would just give him a chance. Just once, he fumed silently to himself, he'd like to prove his worth. Someday, he thought, he would get that chance.

Cordaro watched Trenier walk through the outer office and down the marble hallway before closing the door behind him. He returned to his chair and sat behind his desk. It was quiet now and he sat motionless, studying his picture that hung on the wall facing his desk, the same picture that hung in every union hall in the country. It had been over two years since the picture was taken and he was proud that he still looked the same. His stocky five-foot-seven frame with slicked-back black hair made him look like he had no neck, but it made him look rugged and he liked that. A tough businessman that didn't take shit from anybody, he thought to himself proudly.

He looked about his enormous office. It was his shrine, his room, a place where he conducted union business and signed papers atop the leather-topped desk that was personally given to him by President Jordan as a gift when he was elected union president. He was convinced he could run the world from his office and it would only be a matter of time before he was the most powerful man in America. It was a dream he had nurtured for over thirty years and, if his plan worked, he was sure it would become reality. His timing was perfect, right on schedule. The only thorn in his side was the committee. It was a nuisance, but he was confident he could handle it in the same manner he had handled everything else that stood in his way over the years.

He swiveled quickly in his chair and turned his back to his desk, pushed the button to reopen the draperies, and stared at the rain again. He confessed to himself that in reality he was actually scared of James and Billy Hawk. Peck's weak performance on the committee witness stand would be enough to pique the public's interest as to other union activities and he couldn't have that. The questions about the Freeman Trailer Company particularly bothered him. There had only been surface questions about the Freeman issue but he couldn't be sure the committee wouldn't press it much deeper. If they did, all his dreams would be shattered . . .

That night, Louie Cordaro lay awake thinking about what had to be done, and he decided that an inside plant on the committee's staff had to be found and put in place to gather information. Electronic eavesdropping could be used as well but there was always the risk of detection. The committee's main private meeting room was in the center of the old Senate Office Building and security was tight there, especially when James Hawk was present because of all the added security for a presidential candidate. He had to find someone to gather information who would be trusted by the committee. That would be easy. For Cordaro, every man had his price. But first, he had to eliminate his primary problem and that problem was Donald Peck.

That would be easy too.

Chapter 12

IT FELT GOOD to be home. The engines of the DC-10 had barely shut down when Senator Gregory hopped out of his first-class seat and headed for the exit. Having spent all the previous day and most of Saturday traveling around the state making obligatory campaign appearances supporting Republican candidates for state offices, he was looking forward to an evening of pleasure in Cincinnati.

The senator used the campaign trail as an excuse to leave Washington hurriedly after Donald Peck's testimony before the committee. His personal performance as a committee member was of little or no help to Peck or the union and he didn't want to face Louie Cordaro to explain why. He hoped that a few days cooling off would dampen Cordaro's wrath.

Everett Richardson waited patiently as the senator walked down the deplaning ramp. The pudgy Ohioan took off his heavy black-rimmed glasses and held them in his hand as he stetched out the other to greet him. As general counsel for the Ohio Federation of Labor, he fequently met with the senator to discuss the state's labor problems and programs. He represented several of Cincinnati's union locals as legal counsel and was deeply involved in the union's affairs throughout the state. Today, however, was different. His meeting with the senator was unofficial.

"Welcome home, Senator," Everett offered enthusiastically.

"Thanks, Everett, it's good to be back. Is everything set for tonight?"

"You bet!" he answered, taking the senator's briefcase.

"Good. I need a little diversion. It's been one hell of a week with the hearings and the campaign and all. Where are we headed?"

"Campbell County."

"Kentucky! Good, I knew you'd be discreet."

"I have a friend who has a house in the country. We should be there in less than an hour."

The senator stopped walking for a moment, placed a cigarette in a long thin holder and waited for Everett to light it for him.

"Who else will be there?"

"The usual. Judge Morris, Judge Marconi, and a couple of my friends you haven't met."

"Marconi from Chicago?"

"Yes."

"God, I haven't seen him in years. I didn't think the old fart could still get it up."

Richardson smiled to himself. He was doing his job, something at which he had become expert over the years. Everett Richardson's unique specialty had evolved many years earlier when he had set up a tryst between a young assistant district attorney and a prostitute to further enhance his plea-bargaining negotiations for a union business agent who had been arrested for assault. He learned the value of such tactics and had practiced and fine-tuned them regularly through the years. Many of his past associates who had become judges or were now in elected offices or in politically influential positions continued occasionally to use his services. His friendship with legislators and officials throughout the state enabled him to perform his primary labor counseling duties with unprecedented effectiveness.

It was a few minutes past eight when their car stopped at the end of a long network of muddied and winding gravel roads that led to a large two-story red brick house, with a three foot high brick fence that completely surrounded it.

A simple wrought-iron gate opened automatically and the car pulled forward, the gate closing quickly behind.

The senator followed Richardson out of the car and up the steps. Before they had a chance to push the bell, they were greeted by a butler in full livery.

The sound of glasses clinking and muffled conversation filtered through to the entranceway from the end of the hall. They were quickly escorted down the hall to a drawing room where a fireplace provided the only source of light. Introductions, as always at such affairs, were on a first name basis. The rules on that issue were strict and any deviation meant never being invited again. Even though most of the men knew each other, care was always taken to insure that the women present personally knew none of the other female participants.

In all, there were twenty guests, each neatly paired in advance. The senator introduced himself to all in a manner befitting his political background. It was then that he noticed her—a diminutive young girl glided graciously down the stairs and walked directly toward him. With an air of confidence about her, she came closer, her eyes riveted on his flushing face.

The senator felt a brief and nervous discomfort. He looked about and quickly counted the people in the room. They were all paired. She was meant for him. The light scent of her perfume left him momentarily speechless and a swelling began to rise between his legs.

Everett Richardson took the initiative.

"Sheila, this is Ben who will be your host this evening."

"I am delighted you could make it, Sheila," the senator said, studying the cascading blond hair that framed her small, sun-darkened facial features. Her skin was without blemish and her radiant eyes, tiny upcurved nose, and full lips gave her an innocent, virginal appearance.

Sheila's deep blue penetrating eyes studied the senator as if she were a cat peering cautiously at a potentially dangerous foe. "How nice to know you," she said, politely offering her hand. She was unsure whether or not it was proper decorum to shake hands in such a situation.

The senator smiled to himself. She was not only slender and beautiful, she was young. About eighteen he guessed. Everett Richardson had always known his preference for young girls, but she was by far the youngest he had ever arranged for such an encounter. Her figure was delicate but quite shapely and she wore a white ruffled blouse and black satin pants.

Name cards written in old English style letters with the first names of all the guests enabled the couples to find their candlelit seats. An elegantly set table of fine china, ornate silver, and fine Danish linen complemented a huge centerpiece.

The pattern after dinner had always been the same and the senator became anxious with anticipation. The ladies would retire early to their bedrooms to await their hosts in order to allow the men enough privacy to enjoy an after-dinner drink with unencumbered conversation. Guests were always preassigned to their respective hosts, but even that was subject to change. Frequently the men would play a few hands of elimination poker to establish a pecking order, with the ultimate winner getting his choice of women to entertain in his quarters. Beyond that, exchange privileges could be bartered for and trades frequently were made. There was no doubt in the senator's mind that he would make no deals this evening.

Dinner was brief and boring. The cordials were served and Sheila, as instructed, excused herself and went upstairs to make herself ready. She could hear the men downstairs talking loudly over the blaring and insistent music coming from a stereo someone had turned on. The contrast between the subdued, formal pleasantness of the evening's meal and the raucous noises now coming from below seemed strange to her. She had never done anything like this before and, while it seemed exciting, she became apprehensive as she reflected on what she knew was her real purpose that evening.

She walked slowly into the bathroom, unbuttoned her blouse and shrugged it from her shoulders, laying it neatly over the shower stall door. She splashed hot water on her face, carefully patted herself dry, and stared at herself in the full-length mirror. She looked older than her sixteen years, certainly enough to pass for eighteen, and that pleased her. Her nipples were hard and she brushed them lightly with her hands before unfastening the snaps on her pants, stepping free one leg at a time, then letting them fall on the vinyl floor as she slowly moved closer to the mirror. She dropped her panties, stepped over them and stared down at the lightly matted blond triangle between her legs. It barely hid the soft vaginal crease and made her look even younger than her years. She worried about that because she had lied about her age and didn't want any unnecessary questions that could cause her to lose her job.

She hurriedly put on a white lace nightgown that, like her evening clothes, had been provided by Everett Richardson. It was so short it barely covered her pubic area. Goose bumps began to cover her arms and legs as a chill cascaded down her back.

The noise downstairs still showed no signs of letting up. She was uncomfortable, unsure of what to do next. She had never been in a position like this before. The idea of preparing herself sexually for a man's pleasure caused a wetness to form between her legs even though she was trembling with hesitation. A trace of embarrassment ran through her as she threw herself on the bed and arranged herself as modestly as she could. She waited.

Nearly an hour passed before the senator finally appeared. Her eyes were shut when she heard the door close behind him and when she opened them she saw him clumsily step farther into the room, bumping into the bureau as he passed by. He looked to be at least fifty, heavy through the body with sagging jowls and what appeared to be very thin legs. His exquisitely tailored suit gave off a quiet impression of success even though it appeared rumpled from the long day.

Suddenly he stopped just short of the bed. His long silent stare at her naked legs made her uncomfortable and she nervously offered him a glass of wine from a chilled decanter placed there only a few minutes earlier by the butler. When she reached for the bottle, the gown pulled up slightly toward her waist revealing traces of hair between her legs even though she held them tightly together. His eyes riveted to the blond triangle, his anticipation grew.

"Thank you, Sheila. Sorry about the late hour, but I had business to discuss," he said, breaking his trancelike stare.

She handed him his glass, wanting to make polite conversation and ask what kind of business he had been discussing, but knew that was impossible. He leaned over and kissed her on the neck, allowing himself a privileged peek down her nightgown at the material that clung to her breasts. Her nipples swelled, forming an obvious outline that the senator stroked lightly with his hand as he moved his lips upward from her neck to her ear. "I'm going to shower, won't you join me?" he whispered.

"But I've already showered," she blurted innocently, not realizing his intent.

He laughed and walked toward the bathroom, recognizing her uncertainty. While he would have given anything to take a shower with her, he decided that his sexual appetite could wait a few minutes more.

He showered quickly and alone; afterwards he walked slowly into the darkened bedroom. The bathroom light was still on, the door half closed. It provided just enough light for him to see across the room. She lay silently atop a blanket and turned-down quilted spread. She watched his naked body, never once raising her eyes to meet his. The skin on his paunch hung slack in small folds and it seemed to bounce as he inched his way closer to her.

It was depressing, she thought. She had hoped for a much younger man on her first experience at selling her body. She rationalized that at least he was clean and the money she was earning made it worthwhile.

He moved closer without a word. She held her breath then did what she had been planning all night. Deliberately and slowly, she spread her legs. He stopped beside the bed. He was within one foot of her but he did nothing.

A slight pinkness began to appear at her velvety orifice as her vaginal lips parted slightly. She raised her right leg a few inches, stroking the inside of his knee with a delicatae motion. Even in the dim light, she could see his response, slow at first, then more dramatic. She raised her hand and touched his hardness. Without looking at it, she looked up at him. He waited, looking down at her face. He began nodding his head. She knew what he wanted. Gently she took him inside her mouth. His fingers clutched the back of her head as she gradually increased the tempo. It had been years since he could climax that way, but the hot sensation excited him to a hardness he couldn't attain any other way.

He tugged gently at her gown and she released her oral hold on his penis. She felt the thin silk as he pulled it over her outstretched arms while he simultaneously motioned for her to lie down where he quickly joined her. She felt his hands go between her legs; they felt surprisingly gentle. His hardness rubbed spasmodically against her legs as his fingers probed inside her. The docile penetration began to give way to a rougher and deeper probing. Her tightness excited him more and more until he suddenly rolled over, positioning himself squarely on his knees between her legs.

His weight was oppressive and unappealing to her but she raised her legs high, parting them even wider to accommodate his wide body. His phallus was small and skinny but very erect and very hard. Again, he put his fingers between her legs. She could smell the tobacco and liquor on his hot breath as he fell on top of her, putting his hands under her buttocks. His face was against her cheek and she felt him slide deep inside, then deeper still. She turned her head and tears began to come to her eyes. As he continued to thrust uncontrollably, she tried to think of her first experience with her boyfriend and how wonderful it had been. She had been excited about having an experience with someone other than her boyfriend, she even looked forward to it, but now she was disappointed and scared. She wanted to get it over with. She put a hand over her mouth, trying desperately to hide her emotions. She squeezed her eyes tightly shut but traces of tears seeped through as he pounded into her repeatedly. A moment later she felt him explode, followed in a few seconds later by the semen that began to run down the inside of her thighs.

He stayed inside her motionless, his heavy breathing slowly diminishing until she could begin to feel his hardness softening. He slipped from her wetness gradually.

It was over. She had regained some of her composure but she dared not move. She hoped in a few minutes it would be over, that he would be gone, but she had to wait. He was hers for as long as he wanted. That point had been made clear to her by Everett Richardson. The man was old. She was sure he would not want more sex.

He rolled over, releasing her from his oppressive weight. She breathed easier. A minute passed, then another. His breathing subsided, turning to a loud snore as more minutes ticked peacefully away. An hour passed. She lay quietly at his side for another fifteen minutes before deciding to get up. Perhaps if she went downstairs she could find a ride back with one of the others. She dropped her right leg off the side of the bed and began to raise herself.

"Roll over," he said suddenly. His voice was quiet, but it was a demanding tone she had not heard from him earlier.

Dutifully she turned over, not knowing what to expect.

He reached for the drawer of the nightstand beside the bed. She could hear a muffled rattling as he rummaged through the drawer but she couldn't see what he was doing. She stayed motionless, flat on her stomach, her arms tucked beneath her chest.

Then she felt his hands begin to massage the back of her legs as he sat on his knees behind her, calmly working them upwards in a penetrating circular motion. She began to relax. It was a good feeling. She had never had a massage. She relaxed even more. Then, unexpectedly, she

120

felt a piercing pain in her backside. She tried to move away but he held her down firmly with one arm locked stiffly in the small of her back while his other hand dipped into the jar of lubricant that he had taken from the drawer. He slapped at her buttocks wildly.

"Spread 'em!" he demanded. "Spread your cheeks apart."

She hesitated. He slapped her harder, pulling her arms out from underneath her breasts. "Pull your ass apart. Now!"

She pulled at her buttocks, revealing her anus. She began to cry.

"Shut up and raise your ass," he demanded. "Put it up in the air."

She lifted her waist only slightly. He jerked her toward him, burying her face in the pillow which helped to muffle her crying. He rubbed her anus with vaseline and thrust his index finger inside, tearing at her tightness. She began to scream violently. When he pulled his finger out, she gasped. Then he jammed his thumb in her ass.

He repeatedly pulled his thumb in and out with a vengeance and purpose that seemed to fuel itself with more intensity with each thrust. Sheila's pain began to subside as her anus widened but her indignity made her screams grow even louder. He was oblivious to her objections; the pleasure she saw in his face as she tried to fight him off made her fear for her life. He appeared crazed. She decided to save her strength. She would need it to get away when the chance came. She would do whatever he wanted. Suddenly, he released her from his hold. The pain in her backside began to increase even though he was not now inside her. He knelt behind her, breathing hard. A warm trickle of blood began to stream down her leg from the torn tissues of her rectum. She began to move off the bed when one of his arms came out with a swift motion, flinging her back on the bed.

"Stop," she screamed. "I'll get you for rape! I'll tell the others!"

"Go ahead," he laughed grotesquely. "We're used to

it around here. It won't do you any good, you fuckin' whore." He could feel the heat building in his groin again as he moved toward her.

She saw the fist coming but was unable to move quickly enough to avoid it. It caught her in the shoulder, spinning her once again face down on the bed. She struggled to her knees and looked up only to receive another blow. Pain flashed into her left breast and radiated throughout her upper body. He laughed as he struck her again and again until she lay flat on her stomach and motionless.

She was sure he meant to kill her but she was too weak to fight or even scream. She thought her immobility might stop his fury and she was only slightly conscious when she felt his penetrating hand again. He was behind her, on his knees between her legs, masturbating. He dipped his hand into the vaseline again and made his final assault. Ugly, unintelligble sounds grunted into her ears as his body pounded against her buttocks again and again until she could feel an even greater pain as his gland swelled and tore at her even more as he approached his climax. An orgasm racked both their bodies, his of pleasure, hers of excruciating pain.

Later, she awoke. A knifelike pain shot through her as she struggled to get up to find her clothes in the darkness. She sat on the edge of the bed, shivering, trying to make sense of what had happened. Her head began to clear. She could hear water running. She walked toward the bathroom door, leaning on it to listen. Then, with small backward steps, she slowly retreated. The shower was running. He was still there. She looked around the room. His suit hung neatly on a valet stand next to the bureau. Next to that lay his jewelry, and next to the jewelry, his wallet. She went over and picked it up.

It was still dark and she had difficulty trying to read the driver's license through her swollen eyes that now held no fear, only an all-consuming hatred as she moved toward the light by the crack of the bathroom door. The water stopped running. Quickly, she replaced the wallet and got back into bed, nearly screaming as the sharp pain returned.

A few minutes later, the bathroom door opened. Her eyes were closed. She pretended to be asleep. She could hear footsteps. She hoped he was leaving.

Chapter 13

BILLY HAWK LEANED across the dinner table and lit his brother's pencil-thin cigar. For the first time since last Christmas, they were sharing a rare moment alone over dinner at L'Etoile, one of San Francisco's finest restaurants. Separate campaign schedules kept them apart, their only communication during the last four months being a few brief days while working together on the committee. Even now they couldn't keep from discussing politics and even more so the committee. Personal and family matters would have to wait.

Billy smiled as he watched his brother savor the cigar.

"Word has it that Cordaro's steaming over Peck's testimony," he offered enthusiastically. "He feels we've made a fool of the union and he doesn't like it a damn bit."

"Don't get overconfident," James warned somberly.

"We've still got to get him to court and convict him. Right now if I had my way I'd rather slow that process down. I didn't expect you to be so damned efficient with your facts."

Billy ignored his brother's concern. "The Attorney General said he expects indictments to be handed down against Peck within two weeks. I think we've given him everything he needs. I dropped off our entire file personally the day before yesterday."

"Grand larceny?" James asked.

Billy nodded.

James sat uncharacteristically still, flicking his cigar in the ashtray.

"I thought you would be pleased at our progress," Billy said, his face tightening with a sudden seriousness.

James thought for a moment, his brow beginning to wrinkle. "It's just that the indictment creates a complication on how to handle it for the rest of the campaign. What could get you elected senator may cause me to be looking for a job in November."

"Why not make it a campaign issue?" Billy offered. "I can see the headlines." Billy captioned some weakly humorous headlines in an effort to add some levity to the evening.

James was unconvinced but laughed anyway. He could always laugh at himself in a serious moment; it helped to relieve the pressure. "It sounds so elementary. I just may have to adopt your strategy. Who's your campaign manager?"

"I'll introduce you sometime. There isn't anything he can't do," Billy said while getting to his feet. "Except one."

"What's that?" James asked.

"Take a piss for me! I'll be right back."

James laughed as he sniffed his barely smoked cigar. He brushed aside some ashes that had fallen on the tablecloth and watched his brother make his way toward the restroom. He knew Billy was excited about the success of the committee, but it was causing his presidential campaign manager headaches. It was going to be tough to win the election without the support of organized labor, which was something he had always had on his side in his past campaigns. Now he was about to lose that support because of the committee's success in exposing some of the union's racketeering and mismanagement. He knew that Louie Cordaro's reactions could be blueprinted. He would try to discredit the committee and, worse, would cast his support to the incumbent president, encouraging all union members to do the same. The power of such a move would be close to insurmountable in a close election. Making union corruption a campaign issue was something he wanted to avoid but it appeared there would be no other choice but to meet it head-on. The basic issues and differences between himself and president Jordan would be overshadowed by the sensationalism sure to be created if the union scandal was brought before the public. He tried to think of how he could clearly present his views on the union investigation in order that his intent not be misconstrued by the media or the public. He wasn't out to destroy the labor movement, but he would be portrayed as antiunion. Votes would definitely be lost. It was hard to calculate exactly how many but it was clear his current lead in the polls would be narrowed significantly.

"Damn," he said aloud to himself, coming to no conclusions. He realized the secret service agents who were anchoring the tables on either side of his own were staring at him.

He grinned broadly. "Just daydreaming," he answered to no one in particular, smiling.

The maitre d' approached, bowing obsequisously. "Will there by anything else, Mr. Hawk?"

"I'd like to wait a moment until my brother returns," James responded, ordering coffee in the meantime. He wasn't sure, but it seemed that Billy had been gone for a long time.

Two minutes later, Billy walked back to the table, obviously deep in thought.

"Where in hell have you been?" James asked in mock anger.

"On the phone. I've got some bad news," Billy answered. His earlier spirit had diminished noticeably.

"Are you going to keep me in suspense or would you care to share it?"

"Peck's flown the coop," Billy answered somberly. "He's in Europe."

"How do you know that?"

"We haven't let him out of our sight since he testified last Thursday. He boarded a plane headed for Geneva an hour ago. There was nothing we could do to stop him. He hasn't been charged with anything yet."

James sipped his coffee. "You must be thinking the

same thing I am.''

''Yeah, we can't subpoena him if we can't get him back in the country.''

James gritted his teeth. ''I was afraid of that. We may have tipped more of our hand at the hearing than we should have. Do you think he'll come back?''

''Who knows? He listed his trip as travel for health reasons. He's had some trouble with his heart in the past. It may be something as simple as that but I wouldn't bet on it.''

James nodded. He knew that if Peck didn't return, the committee's approach would have to be altered. Their plans to pursue more witnesses to back up the claim of Peck's illegal activities before concentrating on Louie Cordaro would have to be altered. Without Peck, there was no other choice.

''Do you suppose Cordaro's trying to force the issue?'' James asked.

''What do you mean?'' Billy asked.

''Well, it's not exactly a secret. Cordaro knows damn well we're after his butt. We can prove Peck is guilty but we'll never get him to trial if he doesn't come back. With Peck out of the way, we'll have to concentrate on Cordaro now, before we really want to. The public will demand proof about Cordaro or tell us to get off his case. We can't just sit and wait.''

''You mean we're at a dead end?'' Billy asked.

James sighed hopelessly. ''Exactly! Without Peck, we have to go after the big cheese now or disband the committee, being satisfied with a handful of indictments for some of the small fish that don't mean shit to the overall picture.''

Billy's gaze met his brother's challengingly. ''Why should Cordaro want us to come after him now instead of later?''

James shrugged. ''Why not? He's probably hoping we'll drop the matter for a while. It could buy him some time. He knows it could do nothing but hurt my campaign to go after him right now. He's banking on our campaigns keeping us from being as prepared as we'd like to be. If we don't produce and throw his back against the wall, he'll use the witness stand as a soap box and scream antilabor. Either way, he comes out ahead.''

Billy completed his brother's thoughts. "And he knows he'll end up testifying before the committee anyway so why not before we can dig any deeper. I can see your point.''

Both men's minds began to calculate all the ramifications of the unexpected change of events. Louie Cordaro had to be subpoenaed. There was no other choice. Neither man felt they were ready for that challenge but they accepted reality. They always had in the past.

It had been exactly two weeks since Don Peck had taken refuge in Europe. It was Monday morning, and Louie Cordaro was about to take his place in the witness chair in front of the committee.

Thomas Barrett Wilson III watched quietly as Louie Cordaro stormed into the committee room with his entourage of friends and bodyguards. Wilson had the toughest job of any lawyer in the country. As the union's chief counsel, his responsibilities for administering the complex national and local contracts were enough to tax any person's energies. Dealing with Louie Cordaro's unpredictable demands made the job almost unbearable. In a few minutes he would be directing and coaching a man who he knew would pay little attention to his advice.

Cordaro stopped to shake hands with many of his friends in the gallery who were offering brief words of encouragement as he continued slowly down the aisle toward the long row of tables in front of the committee members who were awaiting his arrival. He was over a half-hour late for the scheduled ten o'clock starting time and he made no effort to hasten his movement to the front of the room. He had arranged to have the Caucus Room filled with supportive friends and he wanted to be sure media cameramen saw them all as they recorded his every move.

129

He slowly inched his way closer to the front of the room, taking care to linger while shaking hands with supporters long enough to afford everyone behind a camera sufficient time to get a clear short of his smiling profile. Only when James gaveled the meeting to order did he stop his grand-standing and take his seat next to Wilson. Senators Longley and Truelson were visibly enraged over his contemptuous tardiness. They went on record stating their point while Senator Gregory predictably refrained from any comment whatsoever.

It was customary with all major committee witnesses for James to make the opening remarks. He swiped at his brown hair which, like his brother's, had a habit of falling in his eyes.

"Ladies and gentlemen," James began, "We have asked Mr. Cordaro here today to allow him to speak publicly before this committee. As most of you know, this committee has been in existence for over thirteen months, meeting regularly during that time. Over ninety-three thousand man-hours have been spent interviewing witnesses, both publicly and privately, both cooperative and uncooperative."

James stopped momentarily to refer to some brief notes he had written on a small pad. He put them down again and continued. "We must always be reminded that Mr. Cordaro's union is perhaps the most powerful institution in this country aside from the United States government. In most of our metropolitan areas, its members control all our transportation. They drive the mother to the hospital for the birth of her child and, at the end of that child's life, it is usually they who drive the hearse to the cemetery. Between birth and burial, they drive the trucks that clothe, feed, and provide the vital life-blood necessities for all Americans. They control the pickup and delivery of all foods, delivery of general merchandise, newspapers, air-freight, and travel, rail express, and sea cargo. Our nation can no longer remain insensitive to the injustice and mis-management of an organization so essential to our very existence. As president of the union, Mr. Cordaro is in a position to do this nation a great service by correcting the errors that we believe exist and ridding his union of the corruption that has been brought to light by this committee."

Jabbing his index finger at no one in particular, James continued his opening speech.

"We have specific questions to ask Mr. Cordaro concerning many areas regarding his union's past and present activities as well as his own personal involvement in other areas for which we hope he will further enlighten the committee. We have, as our final goal, a commitment to propose legislation to Congress that will, once all the facts have been defined, prevent future deviations from sound management practices and set up a monitoring system that will preclude any future repetition of past mistakes. We have not assembled here, now or in the past thirteen months, to purposefully or expressly defame anyone's personal character. However, as in any investigation of this type, that is inevitable; and subsequent indictments have and will continue to be meted out as the United States district attorney sees fit. What we have found is not only deplorable, it is frightening. Mr. Cordaro, if you will be sworn in, we'll get started."

James studied the fact sheets in front of him as Cordaro was sworn in. He waited silently for a moment, then turned to Senator Longley. "I'd like Senator Longley to begin the questioning. Senator, the floor is yours."

The senator leaned toward the front of the table, adjusting his microphone, causing a loud crackling noise over the public address system. "Mr. Cordaro," the senator began, "it's a miserable thing to live in suspense, and I, for one, feel like I've been living the life of a spider these past few months because answers to our questions have been greeted with less than spectacular reaction. I sincerely hope you can help us out of our dilemma."

Cordaro smiled broadly and answered with authority.

"I'll do my best, Senator," he offered.

"Thank you, suh," the senator drawled, his Southern accent thickening. He decided to get right to the point.

"Mr. Cordaro, it is on the record that several of your union's employees that have testified before this committee have done nothing more than plead the Fifth Amendment during their entire stay here. Do you have any idea why they would do that?"

Cordaro's response was quick, terse. "I do not."

"Did you instruct them to do it?"

"I said I didn't know, Senator."

"Do you think they have anything to hide?"

"I can't very well answer that when I don't know who you're talking about."

"Come now, Mr. Cordaro, there have been so many. The most recent was Mr. Peck. Surely you're aware of Mr. Peck's testimony?"

"I still don't know," Cordaro answered.

"Maybe I can be a little more specific!" The senator reached for a leather-bound brief, opened it, and pulled some papers from it. He replaced his glasses that had been hanging around his neck and continued. "Mr. Cordaro, it's no secret that your union employs some characters that have questionable backgrounds. However, just for the record, I'd like to mention a few and then maybe you would like to comment on them."

Cordaro remained silent as the senator proceeded to read from the papers he had pulled from his brief. It was a list of union officials and Cordaro sat sideways in his chair wearing a crooked smile listening to the senator's list.

"Henry Desilve, twice convicted on narcotic charges and once for murder is a trustee in Local 197 in Detroit. He's in charge of preserving union funds.

"Mr. Shorty Fielding has been arrested sixteen times and convicted five times for burglary and has served time in San Quentin. He is in charge of Local 290 in Chicago and the committee has found that eighteen of his officers, business agents, and organizers have long police records. After he took the Fifth Amendment before the committee concerning misuse of local union funds, you appointed him a union trustee."

The senator stopped for a moment to sip a glass of ice

water and clean his glasses. He polished them on his handkerchief, fogged them with his breath, and polished them again, all the while returning with equal force the same scowling glare he was receiving from Cordaro.

He returned his eyes to the list and continued to read.

"Jack Phillips took the Fifth Amendment before the committee when questioned on the use of strong-arm methods in a recent union election. After his testimony, you made him organizing director of a major union drive on the east coast.

"Abe Jackson, vice-president of Local 906, publicly is an admitted close friend of yours. Our investigations have shown that his Local office is frequently used as a meeting place for Johnny Gurzi and other underworld figures. Jackson spent eighty-five thousand dollars of union welfare funds to purchase a piece of property from his cousin that we determined was worth only twenty thousand dollars at the time. Afterward, he renovated the property with nonunion help and has used it frequently as a private resort for his family. While he is under indictment for this, you keep him in charge of Local 906.

"Fred Marschullat is a convicted perjurer, yet you've appointed him as one of the International Union's trustees charged with the responsibility to administer union funds.

"Tony Polanski is president of Local 650 in New York and was elected last year as president of Joint Council 71. He has known underworld connections and is under indictment from this committee for taking payoffs from a number of employers."

The senator's pace quickened, his temper shortening.

"Jim Threader is currently an officer in Local 366 in Flint, Michigan. He has a record of fourteen arrests and five convictions, including a conviction for armed robbery and arson. He is currently out on parole."

Cordaro tried to interrupt, but the senator was reading so fast his objection went unheeded. The senator wanted to make sure the point would be made and wanted no interruptions.

"Gus Tryson stated before this committee that he had

been arrested so many times that he couldn't get a job in Chicago. Frustrated, he finally went to Indianapolis and became an official in the Indiana Joint Council Number 32.''

The senator finally stopped reading, took off his glasses and began cleaning them again as he stared at Cordaro, who was now conferring with Tom Wilson. He waited for a response but Cordaro offered no retort, choosing instead to drop his scowl and reinstate his earlier smirk.

The senator was furious, his voice grew loud. "Mr. Cordaro, this committee has interviewed over fifteen hundred witnesses and three hundred ninety of them have pleaded the Fifth when asked about their activities in your union. Many of them are under indictment as a result of our investigations while some have already been, and others probably will be, convicted. What this committee would like to know is what steps are you taking to rid your union of these people.''

"As of now, none," Cordaro responded, smiling nonchalantly.

"Why?" the senator demanded. .

Cordaro's smile vanished as quickly as it came. He slammed his hand angerly against the table. "Many of these cases are on appeal, Senator. Surely you don't expect me to act before these people are proved guilty?''

"Mr. Cordaro, I don't think you're interested in cleaning up corruption in your own union," the senator shouted back. "It should not be difficult to do with your extensive powers. These people who have come before us are notorious crooks yet you take no action.''

"There will be action taken in due time, Senator!" Cordaro snapped.

The senator was unimpressed. "It is not the disease but neglect of the remedy which generally destroys life, sir. I hope you remember that.''

Another voice bellowed over the P.A. system. "Mr. Chairman!" It was Senator Gregory demanding recognition.

"Senator Gregory," James responded, nodding recognition to the senator.

"Will all due respect to the senator, this line of questioning is a bit premature. Mr. Cordaro has indicated that action will be taken if necessary. Surely we can't prejudge these people until they have had their day in court."

Senator Gregory's retort was not entirely unexpected. James knew the committee had no right to ask for specific action against the people singled out by Senator Longley, the timing was premature, but Senator Longley's point had been made. The senator's line of questioning could probably be defended with some degree of success but James chose not to do so. The fact was that Cordaro's union was infested with officers with long police records and the public needed to be made aware of that fact. Senator Longley's presentation had gone a long way toward that cause.

In spite of Senator Gregory's interruption, James found himself smiling, forcing a warmth into his voice he did not feel. "Senator Gregory, I believe you've made your point."

James turned his head to look at Senator Longley who sat to his right. "Senator, if you'll confine your questions to any unanswered areas of concern that have yet to be reviewed by this committee I believe we can move forward with no further objections from either the committee members or from Mr. Cordaro and his counsel."

Senator Longley couldn't have cared less about his censure. Both he and James couldn't have planned it better, which was exactly what they had done the evening before. It went against the senator's grain for James to use the committee for political gain but he had no choice. He was enough of a politician to realize that total honesty didn't always work. By exposing Louie Cordaro's obvious lack of concern over who occupied key union management positions, the presidential campaign of James Hawk stood to gain by weakening some of the antiunion publicity he had been getting from the press. At a minimum, the public had to recognize that there was at least some substance to his attacks on the union and Louie Cordaro in particular.

The humid heat of an unseasonably warm May afternoon poured into the hearing room as the questioning went on without recess. Senator Gregory continually tried to come to Cordaro's defense whenever possible but he was largely ineffective, and Cordaro grew more irritable at what he considered to be trivial questions.

The senator persisted for over two hours in asking but receiving no explanations from Cordaro as to why the union found itself with such a large percentage of officers with police records.

When James finally recessed the hearing for two days, the room suddenly buzzed with a new-found energy. Cordaro's friends quickly crowded around him. But Cordaro only scowled at the well-wishers and turned stiffly to catch James's eye across the room. He nodded, James reciprocated. The results of the day's hearing were not unexpected, nor did they reveal anything that wasn't already a matter of public record. It only synopsized what had gone on before and perhaps helped the public better understand some of the results of the previous hearings. But that wasn't the committee's ultimate goal and Cordaro knew it. He exited hurriedly, avoiding any comment to reporters.

Billy Hawk waited alone outside in the marble hall for an elevator which had been reserved exclusively for participants of the hearings. He could hear a high-pitched sound created by metal-capped heels coming from behind him. The noise grew louder and Billy looked over his shoulder for the source. It was Cordaro. Despite his discomfort, Billy managed a smile and stepped into the elevator flanked on one side by Cordaro and on the other by Thomas Wilson.

The three men exchanged glances, nodding at each other as if they were gladiators giving silent salute before a fight to the death. Billy was amused at the silence. Everyone assumed the typical elevator stance, looking straight ahead, as if looking at fellow elevator passengers would produce some sort of radical instant retaliation. Only when the elevator stopped and the doors slid open was the silence broken.

"Billy," Cordaro said amicably, stepping aside, allowing Billy to get off first.

"Thank you," Billy said. "See you in a couple of days."

"I'll be there," Cordaro answered, his voice gruff. He stood and watched Billy go outside and trot quickly down the long row of steps to the parking lot. He and Wilson followed without a word to each other, walking silently at each other's side. Wilson noticed a curious expression cross Cordaro's face as they chatted together in the parking lot. Cordaro was up to something, Wilson was sure of that, but he'd never tried to understand his mercurial disposition and he wasn't about to try now. His job was done for the day. Cordaro's wasn't.

That evening, Louie Cordaro sat in his office alone. His feeling of distress and confusion grew, pressing against his gut in an unaccustomed manner. Despite the committee's publicly exposed intentions to purify his union, he felt that their ultimate and primary goal was to immolate him in the process. It was a matter of hate. The Hawks versus him. It was as simple as that.

He rhythmically tapped at his mouth with a clenched fist. "Damn," he said aloud, suddenly standing up. He slammed his chair against the desk, causing a small lamp atop the desk to teeter.

Cordaro had had fights before, and he almost always won. His own reluctance to recognize the committee and the Hawk brothers as just another fight puzzled him. He was being thrown into a frenzied state he'd never before experienced.

He sat for over an hour, watching the darkened sky. His mind raced through potential solutions that were discarded as quickly as they came. Later, he sat laughing quietly to himself. When the chuckling stopped, he picked up the phone and dialed.

A man's voice answered and Cordaro identified himself.

"Be here in the morning, ten o'clock," Cordaro ordered, hanging up the phone without any further comment. A few minutes later he was still smiling broadly as he walked outside to his waiting limousine for the ride home.

He had found the solution. Marshall Tucker could help him solve the problem. He was sure of it. He wondered why he hadn't thought of it sooner.

Chapter 14

THE NEXT MORNING, as requested, Marshall Tucker walked slowly down the wide, plushly carpeted corridor toward Louie Cordaro's office. His walk was no longer spry. He was over sixty and had limped badly ever since he'd slipped on some ice and broken his hip several years ago. The surgeons had placed a pin in it and, because of his sudden lack of activity, he had gained far too much weight. Aside from the added pounds and his unnatural gait, his every gesture was the epitome of fine breeding. He was a thoroughbred put out to pasture, but his keen mind and political influence still commanded national respect. He had grown gray and paunchy but that didn't bother him so long as he could stay in the middle of American politics; and that was exactly where he was.

As editor of the *New Hampshire Globe,* Tucker was a driving force in presidential politics every four years because his state traditionally hosted the nation's first primary election and he controlled the only newspaper with statewide distribution. Endorsement by his paper for a presidential candidate was a coveted jewel and he took great pride in his editorial role. Even in nonpresidential election years, his stinging editorials were well circulated throughout the country through reprints in virtually all major newspapers. Every four years, during the weeks before the primary elections, he was in his real glory. Every word printed by his newspaper concerning the election would be picked up by the media and spread around the world. He acted as a broker with unlimited access to the television stations and to publishers. An endorsement from his newspaper meant a political candidate would have a handle on the media, a weapon to go over the heads of the public he or she represented. Republicans and Democrats alike were losing the ability to choose their own candidates. The journalists and the newspaper and magazine editors were the people creating and destroying candidates and Marshal Tucker was the granddaddy of them all, a fact he never let anybody forget.

Louie Cordaro was reading the newspaper when Tucker entered his office. He quickly stood and walked around his desk, courteously offering a chair. Tucker pulled the chair closer toward Cordaro's desk and greeted his friend with a warmth that had grown steadily over the years. Cordaro was an enigma to Tucker and the magnetism of such a force in the United States always made him available whenever the union boss wanted to talk.

Cordaro appeared nervous and fidgeted with some papers on his desk before leaning back in his chair and plowing ahead, explaining what had been on his mind all night.

"Marshall, I've got a special favor to ask," he began . . .

It was ironic to Marshall Tucker. Within minutes of his meeting with Louie Cordaro he found himself at the White House just in time for his appointment with the President. When he came to Washington that morning he had no idea that his meeting with the President would make it a point to visit with the President but he wasn't Cordaro. During his Washington trips he always tried to make it a point to visit with the president but he wasn't always successful in securing an appointment. It was not surprising to him that the President's availability suddenly improved today. In an election year, it was always easier.

But even in an election year, it wasn't unusual for him to be kept waiting in the outer office. Tucker adjusted himself in his chair and lit a cigarette. He sipped at a cup of coffee provided by a secretary, leaned back, closed his eyes and let his mind wander.

Tucker remembered the last time he had seen the President, nearly six months earlier. He had looked tired and had put on weight. His bushy black hair had begun to recede and the lines on his face from nose to chin were deeper, more furrowed than before. Never an athletic person, the President always looked somewhat pale, with an oddly shaped body with gangly legs and arms and large feet that made him appear awkward and uncoordinated. His public relations staff always took great pains to insure he was photographed and televised from proper angles to minimize his physical unattractiveness, but in person it was all too obvious and there was no way to hide it. It always amazed Tucker how the President had ever been elected to any office with such features, even though he knew that an expert public relations and advertising firm out of New York were primarily responsible for doing a superb marketing job in the last election by keeping his personal appearances to a minimum and maximizing his strengths on radio and television. Now that he was up for reelection, he faced a much sterner test in James Hawk than when he had won four years earlier over a greatly divided Democratic party.

The *New Hampshire Globe* had supported the President throughout the last campaign, and the President was a great believer in the spoils system. He always repaid political favors, and Tucker's newspaper was frequently provided with preferential presidential press releases.

The secretary politely interrupted Tucker's pensiveness. "The President will see you now, Mr. Tucker," she announced quietly, ushering Tucker into the Oval office.

"Marshall, how are you?" the President said, stretching both arms high, temporarily framing the personal purple-and-gold presidential flag behind him.

Both men headed straight for two small sofas in front of the huge fireplace. Tucker nodded, smiled, and sat down. Tucker had sensed from their phone call the day before that the President would be in a hurry and it was obvious he was only meeting him out of election-year courtesy.

"John," Tucker said, "I didn't drop by just to say hello this time. Although I must admit that my editorial comments after my conversations with you do help sell my newspapers."

The President smiled, lit a cigarette, and readjusted his position on the sofa. "Sorry, Marshall," he apologized. "With the campaign getting so much more of my time, the days are getting shorter and the schedule longer."

"Then I'll get right to the point. I've just come from a meeting with Louie Cordaro."

The President was silent for a moment, suddenly interested.

Tucker smiled wryly. "I thought that might get your attention."

The President began to grin. "You know me too well, Marshall."

Tucker wasted no time coming to the point. "We had a long discussion about the election and the question of the importance of union support for the right candidate."

The President stared at him with interested eyes. "And?"

"You know it's been a long time since the Republican candidate for the presidency has enjoyed union support. According to the polls, you're behind James Hawk by over six percent of the vote. You're going to need all the help you can get and the labor vote is, in my opinion, going to be the pivotal issue in this campaign. The simple matter is it's extremely difficult to win any election without the support of rank and file labor and you're fighting an uphill battle as far as I can see."

Tucker still had the cigarette he had lit in the outer office. It became distasteful and he butted it, brushing aside a few ashes that had fallen on the coffee table. "Cordaro has a lot of respect for you, John. He says you both have a lot of things in common. He says, with a great deal of pride, I might add, that you're both hated by experts, both self-made men, and you're both dedicated to your respective fields. He says you both have a lot of guts. Now I know that's a rather long description, but

Louie made me memorize it. He wanted to be sure I got it right.''

President Jordan tried to hide his pleasure at the flattery but was doing a poor job of keeping the smile off his face.

Tucker cleared his throat and continued. ''Louie feels the Hawk brothers are harassing him and that the large number of investigators and attorneys who have been assigned for special duty in connection with his union's activities are working up nothing more than nuisance suits.''

The President shook his head. ''I have no control over the committee. Cordaro must know that.''

''He realizes that, John, but you were the person who initiated the mechanics that got the committee funded. Louie's not expecting any special privileges or special treatment.''

''Then what does he want from me?''

''A few words privately to the right people to get some of the heat off, that's all.''

''That's all?''

Tucker shook his head. ''Not exactly,'' he answered. ''He'd like a public reprimand to certain committee members for their vindictive tactics.''

''But they've just now sat Cordaro on the witness stand. What the fuck's he complaining about?''

''Cut the bullshit, John!'' Marshall's tone became unexpectedly impatient. ''You know as well as I what the Hawk brothers are after. They want Louie's ass out in the street and they won't stop until that happens.''

''Unless someone invervenes?'' the President offered.

''Exactly! Look, these nuisance suits are costing the union a great deal of money. Getting a grand jury indictment against Cordaro or anybody else for that matter would be easy, but a conviction is another thing altogether.''

''Does Cordaro believe the committee or a grand jury would recommend that an indictment be issued against him?''

''Who knows what those bastards will dream up!

Nobody's perfect. Shit, if they followed any of us around long enough they could come up with something."

"And if they indict, what then?"

"Louie says that as far as he is concerned, he has absolutely no worries. He says he leads a clean life, pays his taxes, and obeys the law."

The President shook his head. "But what about the union? It's pretty obvious that there are problems there. That's why I was forced to name a special commission to investigate in the first place. I had no choice."

Tucker nodded with an understanding smile. "Look, Louie knows you can't condone what's been going on in the union. He can't either, but it's going to take time to clean up some of the things that have been going on long before he ever became president. He's trying to clean up the union as rapidly as possible. He just doesn't want to be treated as a scapegoat. He says he needs more time. He's convinced the committee will drum up something and try to get him into a lengthy court trial. He can't afford that kind of time and effort to defend himself if they want him to clean up the union, too."

"Marshall, I can understand his position, but he's a pretty sensitive political issue right now. I don't think it would be real smart for me to jump in the middle of all this right now. You must know that."

"I realize that an outright endorsement by Louie Cordaro for your reelection would probably do more harm than good, considering the investigation and all. But an open endorsement of you by local union officials in certain major cities just might be to your benefit and the work of individual union members throughout the country won't hurt you either."

The President was skeptical. "All this for simply talking to a few people?"

"Don't be naive, John. Louie wants the Hawk brothers stopped. You do whatever you have to. He doesn't care how you do it, just do it."

Tucker didn't have to elaborate on his last comment. President Jordan knew what he meant. The powers of the president of the United States were far beyond the comprehension of most people. He suspected what Tucker was really asking but chose not to discuss it. "How do I know Cordaro's serious about all this?" he asked.

"Do you want to talk to him yourself?" Tucker challenged.

The President looked away. "No, ah, no. That wouldn't look right in view of the hearings and all."

Tucker shrugged his shoulders nonchalantly. "Look, Louie will put the word out to the rank and file on knocking Hawk. You can count on it. There's nothing to worry about. He's also starting a political action group within the union that will use the union newspaper. It's mailed to every union member weekly and it's going to urge everyone to wage a political war at the polls against the Hawk brothers. It's one of the most powerful political weapons in the country."

The President was visibly pleased. If he could get the support of labor without getting deeply involved with the sensitive political issues that surrounded Louie Cordaro, he could start his move toward chipping away at James Hawk's lead. It was the only way he could win, he knew that, but he didn't want to let Tucker see his elation at the sudden turn of events. "Of course, you realize I'll have to study the matter a little further before making any commitment to this proposal," the President said casually. "I mean, this is a ticklish bit of politics we have on our hands."

Tucker knew he had Jordan where he wanted him. "I understand, Mr. President," he said politely, getting up to leave.

"Sit down, Marshall," the president insisted. "There's still another matter we need to discuss."

Marshall Tucker left the White House hurriedly a few minutes later. His meeting had gone very well, but the last subject brought up by the President was unexpected. He considered going directly back to Louie Cordaro's office to discuss it, but thought better of it. Never in his life had he expected to be placed in such a precarious position. He needed to get away for a few days, to provide himself time to think. He couldn't believe what was happening. He had to be sure what he was about to do was right. If he did what the President had asked him to do, he would have to live with it for the rest of his life.

Chapter 15

SID BONNAM SAT quietly staring at the money feathered neatly on top of Louie Cordaro's desk, his fingers tapping nervously on his knee. Cordaro sat calmly across the desk staring at him, awaiting an answer to his offer. Bonnam was not a foolish man, but ten thousand dollars in untraceable one hundred dollar bills was tempting him beyond a point he thought possible. If he accepted Cordaro's proposal, it would mean jeopardizing his career. It could even mean jail. His law practice hadn't exactly flourished since he'd left the Secret Service, but it was paying the bills. On the other side of the coin, the competition was keen and there was no sign of any relief.

Cordaro waited confidently, content to let his proposition mature a while longer. Bonnam had not suddenly become a friend of Louie Cordaro just because he was an ex-Secret Service agent who happened to have a law degree along with a few inside connections with some of Washington's backstage bureaucrats in the Attorney General's office. What it was was bribery, pure and simple.

Bonnam looked and stared directly into Cordaro's eyes.

"What if I can't get on?" he asked, swallowing hard.

"Then keep the ten grand for trying," Cordaro answered magnanimously.

"And if I get on, then I get two thousand dollars a week for every week I stay on the committee staff?"

"You got it. But I need information about what the

Hawk brothers are up to. You supply it, I supply the cash. No other strings.''

"How will I get paid?"

Cordaro jumped to his feet. "Then you accept?"

Bonnam's head rose as if he were thinking it over.

Cordaro became impatient. "Yes or no," he demanded.

Bonnam had already made up his mind, but Cordaro's jugular approach for a quick answer made him uneasy. He spoke slowly, almost afraid of the words that were coming out. "I'll try my best," he answered.

Cordaro bounded around his desk to shake Bonnam's hand.

"Great," he said, enthusiastically pumping Bonnam's hand. "Now, there's someone I'd like you to meet."

Cordaro pushed the intercom and asked his secretary to summon Borg Trenier.

Bonnam reached for a cigarette to steady himself. He had just accepted an assignment he felt he really wasn't in a position to refuse. He had been more apprehensive of what would happen if he declined than the potentially troublesome waters he would encounter by accepting. At least this way Cordaro would be temporarily on his side.

"There's just one question," Bonnam announced hesitantly drawing a deep breath.

"What's that?"

"Why me? I mean, how did you get my name?"

Cordaro opened a silver cigarette case, pulled out a cigarette, snapped it shut and dropped it back into his pocket, all the while considering Bonnam's question. He decided there was no need to tell Bonnam that the union kept a computer file on all known ex-Secret Service and F.B.I. agents, a complete dossier and character study that included their current occupations, political contacts, bank account balances, credit histories, marital status and any other bits of useful information that would point to a potentially cooperative individual. Bonnam's profile was near the top of the list and he was local. It was as simple as that.

"Let's just say I took a chance," he answered.

"Is it wise for us to be meeting here in your office?" Bonnam asked.

"I purposely wanted to meet here. There's so many visitors going in and out of here each day it's impossible for anyone to keep track. We won't be meeting here again. Once you get on the committee staff we'll make other arrangements."

A heavy knocking at the office door preceded Borg Trenier's entrance. He didn't bother to wait for a response and Cordaro ignored Trenier's informality. "Borg, there's someone here I want you to meet."

Trenier was cordial during the introduction but kept looking over Bonnam's shoulder at Cordaro, waiting for some sort of explanation as to whom he was meeting and why.

Cordaro was all smiles. "Borg, Sid is going to work with us awhile in a special assignment that I want known only to the three of us." He leaned between the two men referee-fashion and placed each of his arms on their backs. "I just wanted you to meet Sid for a moment. We can discuss the details of his assignment later this afternoon."

A look of annoyance crossed Trenier's face but he quickly disguised it.

Arms still on their shoulders, Cordaro steered Trenier and Bonnam toward the door. "Sid, I want you to call Borg every day from here on out and report your progress. He'll know what to do and if necessary he can relay any information from me."

Trenier was silent as they all entered the outer office. He still didn't know what role he was to play, but Louie Cordaro always had reasons for everything and they were invariably expertly calculated. Trenier decided to try to talk with Bonnam alone.

A huge cloud of smoke from Trenier's cigar spewed into the hallway when he opened the double walnut doors from Cordaro's outer office that led to the main corridor. Trenier silently motioned the way and Bonnam followed.

After Bonnam left, Trenier sat alone in his office, fuming. Bonnam's assignment to spy on the committee and relay his reports through him placed Trenier in a position he had not been extended the courtesy of being asked to accept or reject. For the first time in his career he felt he was being used and, worse, he felt betrayed. Today, for the first time, he realized he was no longer the same person who began his union career as a loyal servant to his fellow man years ago. He had become something else, someone else. He felt dirty, undignified. That had to change. There had to be a reason for his being.

Chapter 16

MAY 25 . . .

"Could you tell the committee the whereabouts of Don Peck?" Senator Truelson asked.

"I believe he is in Europe on vacation," Louie Cordaro replied, a bored expression on his face. It was Friday, the first day after the recess, the hearings had started exactly on time. It was another warm day and the lights required for the television cameras made the room temperature approach a stifling ninety degrees. Cordaro had been answering questions for over an hour.

The senator persisted. "Do you have any idea why he would leave the country so suddenly?"

"No."

The senator was becoming increasingly short-tempered and his questions quicker. "It wouldn't have been because of the fact that he faces indictments from the grand jury, would it?"

"I don't have to comment on that," Cordaro challenged.

"Did you tell him to go?" the senator asked.

Cordaro disgustedly waved his hands in the air and turned sideways in his chair. He said nothing, choosing to sit and stare at the floor.

"Mr. Cordaro," James interjected, "there is a question on the floor that requires a response."

Cordaro let several more seconds pass, then conferred with his attorneys. "No comment is the response, Senator!" he replied tersely.

A voice bellowed over the public address system. "Mr. Chairman. Mr. Chairman!" It was Senator Gregory.

James recognized the senator.

"I fail to see the relevance of this inquiry by Senator Truelson about Don Peck. Mr. Cordaro obviously can't speak for someone not here to defend himself and, furthermore, we're here today to discuss Mr. Cordaro's activities relative to his duties and activities within the union, not Donald Peck's. If we can't do that, then I suggest we adjourn so we can all get on with more important matters."

James knew the senator's point had to be addressed. He looked at Billy, then smiled as he began to speak slowly and deliberately. "I can see your point, Senator, but I can't say that I necessarily agree with your assessment that there are more important matters than the primary purpose of this committee. However, in order to move forward I'll ask Senator Truelson to complete his questioning within his prescribed time allotment. Senator, Truelson, you have another fifteen minutes."

Senator Gregory was doing his job. He was Cordaro's secret voice on the committee, frequently taking poorly disguised hand-signals from Thomas Barrett Wilson that silently instructed him when to object to a particular line of questioning. The signals did not go unnoticed—both Billy and James had recognized them early on. Wilson's right hand rubbing lightly over his right brow indicated an objection was in order. The left hand rubbing the back of his neck during a conference with Cordaro meant he wanted the senator to stall for time by asking a question, any question that would buy a few more seconds.

The day dragged on with seemingly mundane questions and even more mundane objections from Senator Gregory until James became impatient and interrupted one of Cordaro's meaningless answers to a question from Senator Gregory.

"Mr. Cordaro, do you know a Mr. Harold Weisbrod?" James demanded.

Cordaro hesitated, then answered. "Yes."

"Where did you first meet him?" James fired back.

"He was once a union representative."

"He's not anymore?" James asked.

"No, I don't think so. He's in the real estate business I believe."

"Have you personally ever had any financial transactions with the man?"

Cordaro didn't answer, stopping a moment to listen to Wilson who was tugging on his arm. Wilson appeared surprised at James's question. After a brief exchange between the two that appeared to be less than cordial, Cordaro finally answered. "He loaned me twenty thousand dollars once."

"Why?"

"Because I asked him!" Cordaro snapped, his eyes narrowing to a brilliant icy blue.

"What did you use the money for?"

"That's none of your business."

"When was it that you borrowed the twenty thousand dollars?"

"I don't recall exactly. But I believe it was last year."

"That has been your only financial transaction with Mr. Weisbrod or any companies associated with him?"

"No."

"Do you know where Mr. Weisbrod's real estate business is now?"

"In Florida, I think," Cordaro answered, obviously upset.

"Does Mr. Weisbrod have any relationship, and by that, I mean any business relationship, with the union?"

"Only so far as the fact that union members can buy lots in Florida at a discount from Mr. Weisbod."

"Do you mean that there is no other relationship?"

"He's not an officer in the union, but I think without a salary he might be a special agent."

"Special agent for the union?"

Cordaro shrugged. "He might be—on certain incidents. We may need him to do something, and he may have the capacity to advise, but I don't think, Senator, that he is presently an officer or presently paid a salary.''

James turned in his chair and reached for some papers that Billy was handing him. "Do you know when Mr. Weisbrod went into the real estate business?" he asked.

"About a year ago, I think, but don't hold me to that," Cordaro answered.

"I have here a copy of some loan papers taken out by Mr. Weisbrod for a loan in the amount of fifty thousand dollars. Do you have any idea why this committee might be interested in this, Mr. Cordaro?"

Cordaro was defiant. "Why don't you tell me?" he demanded.

"According to the records, you countersigned Mr. Weisbrod's loan papers and the note."

Cordaro was unimpressed. "I have nothing to hide. That was personal business and it had nothing to do with the union."

"Why did Mr. Weisbrod borrow the money?"

"To go into the real estate business."

"Where did Mr. Weisbrod borrow the money from?"

"You obviously have the record!"

"For the record, Mr. Cordaro, I'd like to know if you recall. You countersigned the note. Surely you must know where you borrowed the money."

Wilson was furiously taking notes and Billy watched him closely. It was obvious that Wilson had no knowledge of Harold Weisbrod and James's questions had caught him by surprise. Wilson kept tapping Cordaro on the shoulder but Cordaro waved him off with flicks of his wrist. Cordaro was warming up to his battle with James and he wanted to fight one-on-one. Cordaro hesitated momentarily before answering James's question. "I think he borrowed the money from a bank. One in Florida, I think," he answered.

James was losing patience with Cordaro's slow memory. He knew that Cordaro would never plead the Fifth Amendment. He would simply use his "forgetfulness" to avoid answering questions directly. "Surely you can be more specific," James demanded. "It's been less than a year!"

Cordaro continued in his deliberate mode. "Mr. Weisbrod originally borrowed the money from First National Bank of Detroit, which I co-signed. I think he paid that off and now has a loan from a bank in Florida."

Billy felt increasingly confident as he listened to Cordaro answer the questions. Months of investigations, of analyzing records, of interviews, and of taking affidavits were about to pay off. Cordaro didn't know it, but he was playing right into James's hand with his answers.

James became methodical, like a Wall Street analyst. "Mr. Cordaro, I am submitting for the record a memorandum obtained from the records of the First National Bank of Detroit. It was written in the loan file of Mr. Weisbrod. I am having a copy sent to your chair and would like you to read along as I read this into the record."

The copy was quickly placed in front of Cordaro and Wilson. James began to read from the bank's notations. "About a year ago we lost a union pension fund account of nine hundred thousand dollars through some misunderstanding. We are trying to get this account back and if we don't accommodate Mr. Weisbrod's loan no doubt they will get it elsewhere and we may stand to lose even more union deposit accounts." James took off his glasses and stared at Cordaro. "Mr. Cordaro, do you have any idea why the bank approved this personal loan of fifty thousand dollars for Mrs. Weisbrod?"

Cordaro's answer was casual, without concern. "It was a legitimate loan. They would have had no reason not to approve it."

"Did you promise that you would reinstate the union's pension fund account to First National Bank of Detroit if the loan was approved for Mr. Weisbrod?"

"I can't make a positive statement on that until I have talked to the bank officials. I simply can't recall just now."

"Our records show that the account was reinstated."

Wilson whispered something into Cordaro's ear. This

time Cordaro listened. "There's nothing illegal about that arrangement," Cordaro responded.

James changed the subject. "What kind of real estate business did Mr. Weisbrod go into in Florida?"

Cordaro knew James already knew the answer. "You have the record. Why don't you tell me?" he asked with a trace of belligerence.

"Was it the Sky City project?"

"Yeah, I think that was it," Cordaro answered slowly.

"Did the union have at that time any connection at all with Mr. Weisbrod's Sky City project?"

"From a sponsoring situation only," Cordaro answered, matter-of-factly.

"How was that?"

"We sponsored it on the basis that our members could have the first opportunity to buy lots at reduced prices, I think for five thousand dollars. I am not quite positive. I'm told those same lots today are worth over ten thousand dollars."

"How many lots were involved in this project?"

Cordaro hesitated momentarily. He wasn't sure where James was headed. "Around two thousand, I think," he answered.

"At the time, that represented about ten million dollars worth of property. How did Mr. Weisbrod finance a project of that magnitude with only a fifty thousand dollar loan?"

Cordaro's patience wore thin. "Why don't you ask him, Senator?" Cordaro's eyes met James's head-on. A penetrating expression of intense hatred crossed his face then disappeared as quickly as it came. Cordaro now had little remaining doubt about the trail James was following.

"Why would Mr. Weisbrod first lend you twenty thousand dollars, and then go out and borrow another fifty thousand dollars from First National Bank of Detroit?"

Cordaro didn't answer.

"Mr. Cordaro, could you tell the committee if you ever repaid the twenty thousand dollars to Mr. Weisbrod?"

"Of course! I always pay my debts, Senator."

"Can you prove the repayments?"

"I always pay my expenditures in cash. I have no records, and, if I did, it wouldn't concern this committee."

The question Cordaro feared came. "Mr. Cordaro, did you charge Harold Weisbrod twenty thousand dollars to co-sign his loan of fifty thousand dollars and use your pension fund influence to guarantee the loan to the First National Bank of Detroit?"

"If you've got something to prove, then prove it. Otherwise let's stop wasting time," Cordaro demanded.

"That is our intent, Mr. Cordaro," James answered.

Cordaro's rage began to escalate noticeably. James continued his questioning. "We've looked into Mr. Weisbrod's financing of this Sky City Florida project and found some very interesting things. Would you like to know what we found?"

Without waiting for a response, James began to read a lengthy chronology that told of how Weisbrod financed the Sky City project. The investigation showed that the manager of the First National Bank of Detroit, after getting the union pension fund account reinstated by Cordaro, wrote a letter of introduction for Weisbrod to the Florida City Bank of Sarasota. The bank manager than accompanied Weisbrod to a barbecue where officials of the Florida bank were also invited. Weisbrod used $30,000 of the original $50,000 loan as a down payment on the Sky City acreage but he needed much more money to develop the property. The records showed that Weisbrod told the bank officials at the party that he and Louie Cordaro were the actual owners of the Sky City property and their plans were to develop it into a retirement village. Weisbrod then asked for substantial loans from the Florida bankers with the assurance that a union pension fund account would be opened in their bank that would guarantee a minimum average balance in excess of or equal to the amount loaned to the Sky City project. Based on those representations, the records James provided showed that the Florida bank approved the loans and funded the Sky City project. James presented records that showed that on the same day the loan was finalized into the Sky City account the union opened a pension fund account in the amount of $900,000 and that currently the Florida bank had advanced the project in excess of $6,000,000 and, under the same unwritten agreement, the union pension fund account was also in excess of $6,000,000 which made the loans totally secured.

"Mr. Cordaro, do you have a financial interest in Sky City?" James asked.

Cordaro's response was monotone, as if disinterested.

"I have an option to buy an interest in Sky City, yes. But I have never exercised that option," he answered deliberately.

"What does that mean?"

Cordaro grinned defiantly. "Exactly what I said."

"What percentage?" James asked.

"I can't tell you at this moment. I don't recall exactly."

James motioned to an assistant seated nearby who proceeded to set up a series of display easels with copies of Sky City advertisements pasted on matte board. Each had a series of slogans: "Every detail of your business transaction can be handled by your local union business agent" . . . "Stake your claim in the model city of tomorrow" . . . "Your investment has every safeguard."

James continued. "Mr. Cordaro, do you recognize these signs and advertisements?"

"I've seen some of them, yes. So what?" Cordaro answered, persisting with his habit of ending an answer with another question.

"Did you set up the program to promote Sky City through different union locals?" James asked.

"I approved the program, yes," Cordaro answered.

"Did you tell your members that you personally had an option to buy a percentage of the Sky City project?"

"I certainly did not! That was my private and personal business."

"Did you approve the initial nine hundred thousand dollar deposit and subsequent deposits in the amount totaling six million dollars from the pension fund into a noninterest-bearing account at the Florida City Bank of Sarasota?"

"I can't say that for sure, we have so many accounts. I'd have to check the record."

Cordaro suddenly turned his attention to Billy. His eyes became transfixed with an evil stare lasting for several seconds. It was as if he could destroy the man if he stared long enough. Billy noticed Louie's gaze and smiled faintly.

"Why would the union put a large amount of money into a noninterest-bearing account?" James asked.

Cordaro's eyes were still on Billy's. He answered. "Like I said, I'd have to check."

"We have checked. The bank officers at Florida City Bank of Sarasota have stated that that was their agreement with Mr. Weisbrod. The interest-free deposits were to be loan collateral for the Sky City project."

Cordaro quit looking at Billy, then stood in front of his chair. Suddenly he began yelling. "I never signed anything like that! Show me in the record," he demanded, slamming his fist to the table.

"Mr. Cordaro, whether you signed anything or not will be brought out in court," James answered tersely. "Wouldn't you say the use of the union pension funds in an interest-free account as collateral for a loan in a company of which you have an option to buy would constitute a misuse of union funds?"

Cordaro didn't answer the question and the gallery grew restless.

Cordaro sat down, conferred with Wilson, then began to speak into the microphone he was clutching in his left hand. "To the best of my recollection I have tried to answer the committee's questions. I must rely on my memory and I can't remember all of the facts surrounding the matters brought up here today. I simply can't recall

159

everything and request the Chair to grant a recess until tomorrow in order that I can research these matters further and provide more specific answers to some of these questions. I want to do my best but under the circumstances, I need more time.''

Cordaro had turned on his most sincere facial and vocal expressions and James knew it would be difficult to turn down the request without appearing harsh and uncompromising. He was tempted to press on but decided against it. He was sure there was nothing Cordaro could do overnight that could change the facts.

The hearings extended not for two more days, as most had expected, but for four more days with only Sunday as an off day.

As the committee uncovered more and more evidence of apparent corruption, Cordaro's genial television mask of amiability began to erode. He became aggressive as the hearing dragged on and excessively contemptuous whenever he knew the cameras were off. The hearings were tedious, a physical and mental strain for everyone involved. Billy watched Cordaro closely and saw his deterioration as the days went by. The man began to appear morose, his facade cracking. At the end of the fifth day, Louie Cordaro appeared beaten.

But on the last day of the hearings, Billy noticed a significant change come over Cordaro. His stamina returned and he bounced back, as forceful as he had been the first day. His glaring stare once again became uncomfortably noticeable.

When James at last gaveled the hearing to a close, it was obvious to all that a subsequent grand jury investigation of the committee's charges was sure to result in indictments against Cordaro. For that reason, Billy couldn't understand the look on Cordaro's face at the end of the hearings. It was the expression of a man that had scored a tremendous victory. The committee members were tired, exhausted. Cordaro wasn't. It was as if he regarded the hearings as a sort of endurance contest—a game of arm wrestling on a national scale that he had just won. It was as if he knew something the others did not.

Chapter 17

MIKKI OPENED HER eyes. The room was dim and only vaguely familiar. She rolled over on the bed and looked at Tor who was sleeping at her side. It had been three weeks since she had last seen him and made love with him for the first time. Their lovemaking this time had been less spontaneous, almost preplanned to the point where each had known the other's needs and desires without being told.

She closed her eyes and lay her head back on the pillow, reflecting on the night before.

"This might sound crazy," she had told him, "but I've wanted you to make love to me ever since the first time I saw you at the hospital."

"That makes two of us," Tor said, smiling.

"I'm glad. And now I want to make love to you," she whispered. She lowered herself between his legs. Her mouth opened wide, ready to receive the hardness she held in her hands. Her mouth was warm, almost unbearably so as her head moved up and down, slowly at first, then faster as the swelling grew even more firm.

As Tor's legs began to stiffen and his back arched spasmodically, she released her hold and with one motion raised herself to her knees and straddled his maleness with her back to him. She lowered herself, guiding him into her with one hand. She began to move, slowly, then faster, her body slamming down on him. She knew it would be quick this time . . .

Tor opened his eyes and looked at Mikki who was still deep in thought.

"Good morning," he said.

"Oh, good morning," she replied apologetically, a startled and embarrassed look crossing her face. "I was just daydreaming, I guess," she said, yawning.

"You looked so peaceful I wasn't sure I should say anything."

"Oh, that's all right. I've been awake for a while. I have to get up anyway," she answered.

Mikki got out of bed, picked up her clothes that were scattered about Tor's bedroom and started for the bathroom. "See you in a few minutes." When she returned, she was wearing Tor's bathrobe she had found in his dressing room. She sat on the edge of the bed facing him. "Got a big day today?" she asked.

Tor shook his head. "The usual bullshit. How about you?"

She leaned forward and cupped his face in her hands, her eyes beginning to brim with tears. "I was afraid you might want to know that," she answered, kissing him gently and burying her head in his chest. Her tears began to flow heavily.

He took her in his arms and held her. "Hey, young lady, I just asked a simple question. What's the matter? What's going on with you?"

After a long moment of silence, she gained control over herself and looked up. "I—I'm leaving San Francisco today. Shana and I are leaving for Washington, D.C. This afternoon, as a matter of fact."

Tor was confused. "I don't understand. What do you mean you're leaving? What's that supposed to mean?"

"Just what I said. We're leaving—or moving I should say. I've taken a job there. Shana's rehabilitation program will be administered by George Washington University. She'll be better off there, I'm sure of it."

Tor still couldn't understand Mikki's emotion. "Then why all the tears?" he asked.

Mikki's head pressed hard against his chest, her eyes tear-filled again. He held her tightly, saying nothing.

"Oh, Tor, so much has happened. I'm not sure I'm doing the right thing. I don't even know if I'm capable of raising an eight-year-old. I'm so confused, I just want to go away and hide," she cried.

"Okay, okay, babe, I'm here," he said, tightening his embrace. After a few minutes of silence, he felt her tension release against his touch. "Let's get up and have a cup of coffee," he said, helping her up.

He quickly grabbed another robe from the bureau drawer and walked her slowly out into the brightly sunlit atrium next to the kitchen where he sat her down.

The bright morning sun touched her skin with a welcome warmth as Tor prepared coffee. She had grown fond of him and right now she felt he was the only person in her life she could turn to for comfort. She dearly hoped her insecurities wouldn't scare him off. She had tried her best to hide her perplexity but, for the first time since her father's death, she could no longer contain her emotions.

Tor returned with a small tray of croissants and coffee and sat next to her on the loveseat overlooking the bay far below. "Now," he began, "tell me about this new job you've taken on."

She took one of Tor's hands, squeezing it tightly as her confidence began to grow. "I'm going to work for Louie Cordaro," she announced proudly.

Tor set his cup of coffee down hard, taken aback by her statement. "*The* Louie Cordaro?" he asked incredulously.

Mikki nodded.

"Why?" he asked with a trace of annoyance.

Mikki became defensive. "Why not?" she asked.

Tor suddenly realized his insensitivity. He knew he had no right to place his own judgments on her decision. Ed Parker and Louie Cordaro had been friends for a long time. Winston Sheffield had told him that much. To demean Louie Cordaro to Mikki would be tantamount to pulling the crutches out from under someone with a broken leg. He didn't agree with her decision but wanted to know more about it without appearing to meddle. He eased up on the Cordaro issue. "What made you decide to go to D.C.?" he asked, picking up his cup.

Mikki watched him closely. The faint feeling of hope she had earlier felt was beginning to erode but she was determined not to show it. "Louie Cordaro has been an absolute angel since the accident," she began. "He's sent roses to both Shana and me every day and he's called at least once a day. Even all of the hospital bills are going to be paid for by the union. When he asked that I come to work for him while Shana's undergoing her treatments, it seemed like the best thing to do for now."

She looked at Tor for some sort of validation for her decision. He didn't disappoint her.

"Under the circumstances," he sighed, "I'd probably do the same thing. Shana's rehabilitation is the most important issue right now."

"Then you approve?" she asked.

"I didn't know it required my approval," he answered, smiling.

"Well, it doesn't. I mean . . . well, you know, I just want to be sure."

"How well do you know Louie Cordaro?" he asked casually.

"He and my father were close when I was a little girl. I used to see him a lot. He used to come over to the house and I would call him 'Uncle Louie.' But it seems like Daddy and he weren't as close during the last few years. In fact, Daddy never really talked much about him since I went away to college. Maybe it was just because I haven't been around, I don't know."

Tor remembered Sheffield's comments about Parker's disillusionment with the union and his intent to resign. It seemed strange that Cordaro would know Parker was in San Francisco at the time of the accident.

"How did he know where your father was?" Tor asked.

Mikki shook her head from side to side. "I don't know," she answered slowly. "When I got to the hospital there were flowers there already. I called him a couple of days later to thank him. Maybe Winston told him. Why do you ask?"

"Just curious," Tor answered, disguising his distrust. "What will you be doing for Cordaro?" he asked.

Mikki's face began to brighten. "He said I'll be his executive secretary. I'm not much on that type of work so he'll have to put up with me for a while. It's nothing permanent, I'm sure. He's just being kind. When Shana gets better, the two of us will pick up the pieces and move on."

"Back here, I hope," Tor said sincerely.

Mikki shrugged her shoulders. "Who knows?" she responded wistfully, "Maybe we'll move back to Paris. I think it would be good for Shana, and I could continue my studies too. But right now, that's a long way off."

Tor didn't want to bring the subject up but for him there was no way to avoid it. He didn't want her to go but couldn't really convince her not to, he knew that. But somehow, without appearing to be callous, he wanted to be sure that she was fully aware of what Louie Cordaro was all about.

"You know Cordaro is up to his ass in hot water with the Hawk Committee, don't you?" he asked, trying to remain casual, almost distant from the subject.

"Oh, that," she said, shaking her head. "That's just the same old stuff that's been going on for years. Even my father went through some of the same kind of thing from time to time."

"But your father was different," Tor added quickly.

"What do you mean?"

"I mean that any investigations your father went through were routine. If he was clean, he passed the test. I don't think Cordaro can pass the test."

"And what makes you an expert on Louie Cordaro?" she asked defiantly.

Tor looked at her seriously, wishing he didn't have to respond. "Like you said a little while ago, I was afraid you might want to know that," he answered.

For the next half-hour, Tor spoke without rancor, fully explaining his friendship with Billy Hawk, his new role as investigator for the Hawk Committee and his conviction that Louie Cordaro would eventually be indicted and removed from office. A painful depressed look settled onto Mikki's face as Tor gently tried to explain.

Tor's attempt at changing her mind about joining Cordaro was not convincing enough. For the second time in two months, Mikki felt betrayed by someone she liked. She held no animosity for Tor, or even Winston Sheffield for that matter, but her feelings for Tor she now felt had been premature, perhaps even wrong. "I think I'd better be going," she said, suddenly standing.

She realized she was still in Tor's robe. Embarrassed, she quickly moved toward the bedroom, emerging only a few minutes later fully dressed but without makeup. "I have to go now," she said. "They're releasing Shana from the hospital in an hour."

She turned and walked toward the front entryway. Tor walked after her, touching her arm to turn her around to face him. "Look," he began, "I don't think we . . ."

"Please," she said quietly, "I really don't want to discuss this right now."

He saw the genuine hurt in her eyes. Suddenly he wished he hadn't said anything about Louie Cordaro. "I'm sorry. I didn't mean to sound like I was preaching."

She shook herself free from his grasp.

"Look, I really am sorry," he said, apologizing once again. "I like you a lot, more than I ever thought I would. You've got to believe me. I don't want you walking out of here with us on opposite sides of the fence."

She held the back of her hand to her nose and sniffled, looking up at him. "I know," she said. "But for now, that's exactly where we are."

She turned, opened the door, and left.

Chapter 18

LOUIE CORDARO'S SLICKED-DOWN patent-leather hair glistened in the early morning sun as he stood in the international union's parking lot watching Senator Gregory walk slowly away from him. The federal grand jury was moving swiftly and the senator had just told him that he should expect an announcement sometime later in the morning that an indictment would be handed down against him for misuse of union funds. It had taken the grand jury only three days to reach their decision and the senator indicated that according to reports he had heard the evidence against him was apparently overwhelming.

Cordaro's fury at Gregory's ineffectiveness in squelching the investigation had not subsided when he returned to his office and viciously slammed the door behind him, something Borg Trenier, who occupied the office next door, couldn't help but hear. Trenier had awakened slowly that morning, around six A.M., and agonized for over three hours what he must do when he arrived at the office. His mind had alternately faded from one subject to the next but centered mostly on thoughts of his family and what would happen to them should he be forced to leave his job. He had always considered himself a good provider and he spared no expense when it came to his wife and three daughters. There were some savings, perhaps enough to get him by for a year without any noticeable change in lifestyle, but that was all. If Cordaro fired him, he wouldn't know where to turn. The union was his life, his career. In his mind, he had worked things out: go to the office, prepare some notes about last night's meeting with the executive board, wait for Cordaro to come in and tell him first thing what he had learned about the board members' feelings. There was no other way, he was sure of that. Cordaro had a right to know.

Whatever confidence he had built up quickly exited when Cordaro slammed the door. Trenier looked at his family's portrait that hung over the credenza behind his desk, took a deep breath, stood, then walked slowly into the inner office that separated his office from that of his boss. He hesitated a few seconds, then swung Cordaro's door open and walked in unannounced.

"I've got some bad news," Trenier announced. He stood still, standing framed in the doorway while Cordaro just sat at his desk staring back at him. "Louie, there's a movement within the executive board to throw you out of office."

Cordaro had been writing on a tablet in front of him. He stopped and dropped his pen on the tablet, his eyes suddenly narrowed. "What the fuck are you talking about?" he demanded.

Trenier avoided Cordaro's eyes but pulled no punches. "A lot of them are concerned. They're afraid you're going to be indicted and they're getting a lot of flak from some of the rank and file about carrying some of your friends on the payrolls."

"What friends?" Cordaro asked tersely.

The words stuck in Trenier's throat. "Well," he said, hesitating, "to put it in their words, they say your friends are a bunch of crooks and that they're giving the union a bad name. The board wants you to either get rid of them or resign."

"And they sent you in here to tell me because they didn't have the balls to do it themselves, I suppose."

Trenier shook his head. "They don't know about this," he said. "I'm telling you this as a friend, not as an emissary."

Cordaro stood, restlessly moving to the window near his

desk. He turned to glare at Trenier. "I don't give a shit what those pricks are saying. They might be talking a lot, but by the time they get enough balls to do anything they'll all be ready for retirement. Most of the board members are growing old and pretty fuckin' tired. You can damn well bet they'll trade their uneasiness and self-respect for the pot of gold that I've got waiting for them a few years down the road. Eighty grand a year pension for sitting on the executive board isn't exactly something they want to mess around with. If I decided to fire their asses, they won't get a nickel of it. Their fuckin' talk is cheap."

Trenier refused to sit, the tension finally taking total control. He worried. His conversation with Cordaro might be considered foolhardy by many and he couldn't hide his nervousness. There was more he had to say, but he didn't know where or how to start.

Cordaro sensed Trenier's dilemma and pressed. "What else?" he demanded suspiciously.

"There have been some secret meetings among some of the board members. They're testing their strength for election to the presidency if you should be thrown out."

Cordaro walked quietly toward him. "Ha! So they're testing their constituency. I suppose you've been included in these meetings?"

Trenier was defensive, standing nearly nose to nose with Cordaro. "I felt I had to. It's the only way I could get the information I'm giving to you now."

Emitting an audible sigh, Cordaro turned away. He was perturbed and regretted having found a new enemy within his own ranks. "What's the verdict?" he asked.

"It appears that there are two groups," he began. "Neither trusts the other or even themselves. They can't even agree whether to vote to throw you out. One side says yes, the other no. Those that don't want to vote can't agree who your successor would be so they see no point in voting on whether or not to fire you. They're hopelessly deadlocked."

Cordaro's face was uncommonly solemn, but his tone urgent. "So where do you think they'll take this?"

Trenier was feeling more comfortable. He bit off the end of a cigar and lit it. "These guys are mature, intelligent men. They won't try anything rash. Besides, I think too many of them are afraid of you."

"You mean they're afraid of my friends, don't you?" Cordaro corrected.

Trenier nodded. "One of them said he didn't want to go out feet first in a box."

"Now what?" Cordaro asked, a smile beginning to appear.

"The consensus last night was to wait and see what happens at the trial. There doesn't seem to be any other choice right now. If you're convicted, they say they'll kick you out."

Cordaro became furious, his mood changing with almost every comment. "Those lily-livered bastards! They don't have the guts to stand up and say anything now. They think that if I go behind bars that'll protect them from me. I've got news for them, if that happens and they throw me out, none of 'em'll be safe!"

Cordaro snatched up a scratch pad from his desk and began writing. "Those cocksuckers got a long way to go before they'll ever get me out of this office or behind bars. You can tell 'em that, too!"

Cordaro handed Trenier the piece of paper he had written on. "Call this guy and tell him to find Joe Avery. I may need his help and I want him ready."

"Joe Avery?"

"Yeah, Joe Avery!"

"The ex-heavyweight champion?"

"Yeah. Just tell him what I said about standing by if I need him. He'll understand what I mean."

Cordaro pushed past Trenier, opened the door, and walked out while Trenier let himself out, wondering about Joe Avery. He breathed a sigh of relief. He still had his job.

Three hours later, Thomas Barrett Wilson got out of a taxi and headed straight for Louie Cordaro's office.

Cordaro was at his desk, the telephone receiver caught between his ear and shoulder, waiting for the switchboard operator to locate Borg Trenier. He looked at a piece of paper Wilson pushed in front of him and after reading the first few lines slammed the receiver on the cradle. His day had not changed. "Those bastards don't give up, do they?" he yelled.

The paper provided by Wilson was a press release from James Hawk stating that while Cordaro was under indictment for misuse of union funds, the committee would continue to investigate other areas of interest regarding the union and Cordaro in particular. In short, Wilson explained, the committee was continuing its investigation.

Wilson sat down, calmly tugging up his socks. There was work to be done and he came prepared to do it. "I have some concern over who the presiding judge might be at your trial. I've made a list of those I consider acceptable and unacceptable."

"Christ! Now they've got *you* on the run. They haven't even issued an indictment yet and you've already got me going to trial. This whole fuckin' thing's turning to shit. I can't believe it."

Wilson remained calm. "We've got to be realistic, Louie."

"What do you mean? Those bastards can't prove shit."

"I believe they can," Wilson countered.

"You son-of-a-bitch! Get the fuck outta here! I don't need you to come in here and feed me this line of bullshit. Why are you doing this?"

"Because unless you open your eyes, you'll never survive this trial. I believe the committee has finally laid all their cards on the table. They had to or else they would never have gotten the grand jury to recommend the indictments. Once we've got the specific charges in front of us we can attack them one by one. Up until now we've been operating in the dark. Now we'll know what and who they're after besides you. After we get you cleared of these charges we can take measures to insure any future investigations by the committee wind up on dead-end streets.

But, first, we've got to start moving on your trial. There's going to be no avoiding that.''

Cordaro made no attempt to disguise his annoyance. "What do we have to do?"

"First, we'll request a change of venue if any accommodating judge isn't named to try the case. Since the trial will probably initially be assigned close to Washington, D.C., the chances are good that we can get the trial moved to a more neutral territory if necessary. I'm fairly certain that the Hawk brothers will push for the assignment of a judge who would be to their liking, one they know already. If that happens, our defense would be to claim an unfavorable climate for a fair trial because of the proximity of your home and office to the trial site. We can say that would allow for the possibility of a prejudiced jury which we can't accept. They'll have to move the trial. Either way, I think we'll eventually get the judge of our choice but I'm sure it will be somewhere other than around here.''

"So what happens once we get a favorable judge?"

"We get a P.R. firm.''

"For what?"

"Once the trial city has been selected, their job will be to initiate a hype, an anti-Hawk campaign to discredit the committee. They'll be charged with instilling subconscious prejudice within the local citizens against the indictment before the jury selection process even begins.''

Cordaro shrugged and sat down. "Hell, we can use our own P.R. people for that.''

"I'd rather not. We shouldn't take a chance on that backfiring on us. If some nosy people did some checking they could probably trace it back to us. We should use another firm, one that we've never used before.''

"Who then?"

"I have a former associate, his name is Bob McCallum. He started his own firm a few years back. He'll do anything we direct him to do.''

"What are your plans?"

"I want him to play on the public sympathy, concentrating heavily in whatever city the trial gets assigned to.

He'll be charged with presenting the public with an image of an able leader being an innocent victim. We'll claim that the past poor management practices of certain union officials shouldn't be brought down on you and that you should be given a chance to lead your union out of this mess. We'll go all out. Newspapers, magazines, the media. He can hire some of the best to speak out in your favor. Slip 'em enough money and we can buy anybody we want.''

Facing the powerhouse forces of the United States government was a formidable task even for Louie Cordaro. The two men stayed together until darkness had set outside. Wilson left no doubt in Cordaro's mind that he had the entire scenario completely and thoroughly thought out with enough contingency plans to patch up any unforeseen problems. They were an effective combination. Their organizational abilities complemented one another and they worked well together. Neither particularly liked each other but their business relationship had always been mutually beneficial. Today hadn't been any different.

It was after nine P.M., when they walked out of the office together. Wilson noticed a smug coolness from Cordaro not exhibited earlier during their lengthy discussions. Cordaro stopped for a moment, chatted briefly with Sammy, the janitor who was about to clean his office, then continued on out the front door. A smile, a mere twitch of his lips, crossed Cordaro's face. Wilson couldn't understand the transformation. Then an old feeling, a familiar one, suddenly hit him. Cordaro knew more than he was willing to tell him and, as usual, there was nothing he could do to find out what that was. He was sure that would come later. It always had before.

Chapter 19

AMERICAN AIRLINES FLIGHT 562 from Chicago set down ten minutes late in San Francisco. Louie Cordaro exited up the wide carpeted ramp and then down the hallway to the escalator and outside to wait for his limousine. The wind blew hard to his back and his trousers ruffled violently but he paid it no mind. He was at peace with the world.

He had just spent four grueling days traveling around the country personally negotiating final contract settlements with some of the country's largest corporations. It was important for him that he continue to exhibit his strength and powers in the shadow of his impending trial.

Major but separate contract stalemates in the airline and railroad industries had been bogged down for months in futile, hot-tempered negotiations that were going nowhere. Much to the chagrin of the individual local union presidents, threatened strikes were averted when Cordaro came in and subjugated their authority, quickly conceding many contract demands to management in exchange for a common contract expiration date that lengthened the normal two-year contract life of the airlines by more than six months and shortened the railroads' contract by almost a year. He had swept in on the negotiations without warning but not without great public fanfare. In each instance he quickly disappeared behind closed doors with management to effect covenants that would be consistent with his personal master plan, regardless of the concessions required by the locals to obtain the agreements. To have nearly identical contract termination dates for the major industries throughout the United States was a personal objective that obsessed him far beyond what would be considered by his peers as pragmatic union management principles. His habit of selling out the subordinate union management by stepping in and agreeing to less than the original union demands and then exiting as a hero to management and the general public was becoming quite common and was beginning to anger his own organization. What went unnoticed by the separate arms of industry and by the union hierarchy itself was that many of the contracts throughout the different industries that he personally settled were scheduled to expire within a few weeks of each other. Only Cordaro knew of the importance and significance of those moves and in private he delighted that such an overt plan could be put into operation before the public eye without observation.

While he took great pride in the settlement of the air and railroad disputes, it was an undeclared prize that furnished the most pleasure for him as he stood calmly watching the hectic airport activity around him. Taxis honked and people rushed in and out of the automatic doors behind him. He paid no attention to the exterior distractions. An unexpected victory the day before occupied his thoughts. By signing Amalgamated Grocers to a new contract he had won a victory over the nation's largest food chain. More important, he had conquered a company with over two thousand stores that now had union representation for the first time in history. With the exception of a small and ineffective Meat Cutters and Butchers Union, Amalgamated had fought off drives to organize their clerks many times over the past thirty years. They had only one weak union and management had wanted to keep it that way. A few weeks earlier, when a competing chain of grocery stores signed a contract with another union that guaranteed a work week reduction to forty hours from their current forty-five hour week, Louie Cordaro recognized a weakness in Amalgamated's defense. He knew that at the expiration of Amalgamated's Meat Cutters and Butchers Union contract the union would also demand a forty-hour week. The meat cutters and butchers would then be working forty-hour schedules leaving the rest of Amalgamated's nonunion employees working forty-five-hour weeks. The doors to a union organizing drive were bound to be opened and Cordaro made sure Amalgamated's management knew it as well when he sat down with them the evening before. That was when the representatives of Amalgamated secretly agreed to stop fighting future organizing drives, virtually guaranteeing ten thousand new members for Louie Cordaro. In return, Cordaro guaranteed Amalgamated a five-year contract that called for the same forty-five-hour work week they already had. The company got what it wanted because the move would save them over two million dollars over the five-year period in overtime salaries, and Cordaro got what he wanted—ten thousand new dues-paying members. The employees would get nothing but the obligation to pay dues for representation for a contract that had already been agreed upon, one that would prevent them from attaining a forty-hour work week for at least another five years. For Cordaro, it meant one thousand shares of Amalgamated Grocers stock worth over forty thousand dollars at the current prices. Cordaro thought of the shares as a private negotiating fee. For him it was all in a day's work.

A shiny dark-blue Cadillac limousine pulled up along-side the curb and stopped. The rear door quickly opened and a powerful and massive hand reached out to shake Cordaro's hand. It was Bartie Bonano.

Bonano had been in San Francisco for two days, sent there personally by Cordaro to meet with the San Francisco district attorney. Like many others, Richard Jackson owed his position as district attorney to the union. He was a union-supported representative to the government and Cordaro had come to privately discuss some form of repayment for Jackson's support, something which Jackson had already been briefed on by Bonano.

Cordaro was barely in the car when it pulled from the curbside and Bonano reached for a newspaper that lay on the jump seat in front of him.

"Did you see this morning's paper?" he snorted, rubbing his enormous nose.

"Why?"

Bonano pushed the paper toward Cordaro and pointed to a small article on the lower right-hand side of the front page. It told of a threat on Billy Hawk's life if Cordaro were eventually sentenced to prison. It had been made by a man named Armando Muniz, head of the union's local in Puerto Rico.

Cordaro slammed the paper to the floorboard and motioned for Bonano to push a button that raised the glass partition between their driver and the back seat. He was livid, his face suffused in deep crimson. "You call that bastard and tell him for me that anything like that would destroy any chance I have to stay out of prison or ever get out if I have to go in! If I hear any more of that kind of shit he'll be the one who gets it, not Hawk!"

Cordaro remained silent for the balance of the ride to the Stanford Court Hotel on top of Nob Hill, where Richard Jackson and Borg Trenier were already waiting in the Cordaro suite.

Jackson had been in office for over two years and until now few favors for the union had been asked of him, never any from Cordaro himself. He was nervous but attentive as he sat and listened to the proposals. Bonano's intimidating presence as he sat slumped in his chair staring out the window added a mental discomfort to his physical nausea caused by the smoke of Trenier's cigar. He tried to ignore the cigar but it was impossible to shut out Bonano's occasional grunts which were laced with intermittent farting.

Cordaro was wasting no time in telling Jackson what he wanted, stating that a new pin-ball distributing company would be coming into San Francisco and they would immediately sign a union contract. Existing major pin-ball and electronic game distributors that were not organized would not be allowed to join the union. Union pickets would then be sent out to bar and arcade locations that had equipment from nonunion distributors, which in turn would force the owners to sign contracts with the new unionized distributor; otherwise the union pickets would keep them from getting deliveries of food or spirits from organized truck drivers who would not cross the lines with their deliveries.

Jackson's job was to see to it that the union pickets would not be harassed. He didn't need to ask who was backing the new distributing company; it was a familiar tactic. Organized crime frequently moved into a city in that manner. Once established as a legitimate business with a working base throughout the city, the next step would be to set up prostitution rings, usually with one or two discreet houses that would have to be protected by the police. Card rooms and horse books would soon follow.

There would be problems and Jackson knew it. He had to tell Cordaro. "Commissioner Hardy is an old hard-nosed puritan," he offered. "I don't see how the long-range plan will work in this city. The pickets are easy to handle, but protection for organized crime will be impossible with Hardy directing the force."

Cordaro had anticipated Jackson's response to his proposal. "That's were you come in," he said.

Jackson was hesitant, cautious. "Do you mind explaining in what way?" he asked.

"I want you to visit the mayor and tell him to get rid of the commissioner. We already know Hardy could be troublesome and we can't live with that."

"Why would the mayor agree to that?" Jackson asked in an incredulous tone.

Cordaro smiled. "The same reason you'll cooperate. He'll lose our support in the next election if he doesn't and he can't afford that. He likes his job and he barely won last time out even with our support. Without us, he's a dead fish."

Jackson looked at Trenier who was avoiding his glance by staring off toward the window. He looked back at

Cordaro knowing full well he had no other choice but to cooperate. Even if he didn't care about retaining his job, the potential repercussions if he didn't accede to the demands were unthinkable. It was as if he were selling out to the devil.

Cordaro broke Jackson's private thought pattern. "One more thing. We're planning an organization drive here that could get a little sticky. I'll be expecting your help in that too!"

Once again Jackson found himself maintaining a passive role as listener as Cordaro continued. "The retail employees in many of the stores throughout the city have indicated a desire to organize and we mean to help 'em. Some of the companies around here have shown a reluctance to listen to us but we're going to get their attention this time. We're going after this city with both barrels, pulling out all the stops. We don't want any unnecessary harassment from the police."

Cordaro's gaze met Jackson's challengingly, but Jackson merely shrugged, resigning himself to reality. "I'll do whatever you ask," he said quietly.

Later that night, Louie Cordaro opened his suitcase, took out a green canvas merchants' bank bag filled with change, loaded his pockets with quarters, and left the hotel. Minutes later he had Marshall Tucker on the phone. Tucker's voice was unusually stern. "Where the hell have you been?" he asked. "I've been leaving messages everywhere!"

"This is the first I've heard of it," Cordaro answered casually.

"Are you somewhere you can talk?"

"Yeah, public phone."

"The president is deeply concerned, Louie. He's convinced that Billy Hawk is an evil force, a rebel in the network of American government. In the president's personal analysis, Billy Hawk's presence could possibly be a threat to the nation's security."

Louie was incredulous. "How in the hell did he come to that ridiculous conclusion?"

"I don't think that should concern you. What *should* concern you is the president's offer."

"Which is?"

"He thinks you're in serious jeopardy of being convicted if you got to trial, something he feels is a certainty as long as Billy Hawk is assisting the prosecution. Now he wants you to know that he's very appreciative of your offer for support in the election and he accepts it graciously."

"So what's the catch?" Cordaro asked skeptically.

"The president's just shrewd enough to know that the union has offered discreet personal monetary support payments to other politicians, including himself, in the past and he sees no reason why he shouldn't suggest a counter-offer to your original proposition for support."

Cordaro paused a moment, then asked, "What's the deal?"

"He is concerned about the national security issue which in this case centers around Billy Hawk. He's suggesting that the Hawk problem be handled in exchange for your original pledge to election support plus a million dollar campaign contribution to be laundered into his account whenever he asks for it."

"What about the trial? Getting rid of Hawk won't stop that!"

"The president has agreed to personally handle any complications that you might experience in the upcoming trial including any subsequent sentencing. He said that the committee has gone too far to stop it now and that your offer of election support is good but not alone worth what it will take to save your ass."

"That's were the million dollars comes in?" Cordaro asked.

"Exactly."

Cordaro was unconvinced.

"How do I know he'll follow through?"

"I know for a fact that he's already had Hawk's house electronically bugged and the phone has been tapped. I was in his office when he ordered it done."

"So what's that supposed to mean?"

"That he's serious about his offer."

"How serious?"

"I think it's better not to ask what he's planning. He's the president, he can probably do just about anything he wants."

"You don't think he'd have him put away, do you?"

Tucker's answer was matter-of-fact. "Like I said, he's the President."

"Christ!"

"What's the problem? I thought you'd be delighted to have the president on your side."

"I said I wanted Hawk out of the way, not six feet under. Why can't he just get him fired or something?"

"Louie, settle down! I don't know what he has in mind. It's best to leave it up to him. Let's keep our end of the bargain and let him worry about how he handles his. It's out of our hands. We can't be responsible for his actions."

There was no response from Cordaro.

Tucker broke the silence. "Louie?"

"Yeah."

"Do you agree?"

"When does he want the dough?" he asked.

"Within a week."

"Christ! That's a pretty tough order. It'll take more time than that to scrape it up."

"One week or no deal. The president was adamant about that."

"And if I don't come up with it?"

Tucker's voice was emotionless. "You'll probably go to prison."

Cordaro was terse. "I'll get back to you," he said, hanging up the phone. His hand gripped the receiver tightly against the cradle for a few moments and his hands were still shaking as he dropped more coins into the receptacle. After three rings, a man answered on the other end.

"Paul?" Cordaro questioned.

"Yes," the voice answered.

"It's Louie."

Paul Denning looked at the clock beside his bed. It was two A.M., in Chicago, two hours later than San Francisco.

"Where are you?" he asked.

"It doesn't matter. Just listen and don't ask questions because I can't answer them right now."

Denning could hear the strain in Cordaro's voice. "All right, Louie," he said. "Whatever you say."

"Get me a million dollars. Put it into a general fund where only you know where it is and can get it whenever I tell you I need it."

"Louie . . ."

"Cut it! Just get it."

"How?" Denning asked incredulously.

In the space between two calls, Cordaro had already devised a plan. "Hide it in the Health and Welfare Fund insurance premiums. Raise your premiums by one dollar a head to the union and we'll raise the dues to the employees by that amount to cover increased costs from your firm. I'll approve the increase, but I'll need the million whenever I ask for it. Within a week. Understand?"

Denning closed his eyes and shook his head. He was silent for a moment, then responded, "I'll handle it."

Cordaro hung up without another word and walked slowly back to his hotel.

The next morning, he awoke with renewed vigor. Life during the last year hadn't been as much fun for him as it had been in the past. But today was different. He had reason to believe the president would be true to his word and that made him feel good. For the first time in months, he felt so totally alive that he found it hard to fix his mind on the problems at hand.

That afternoon he walked across the street to the Fairmont Hotel to deliver a luncheon speech to over one thousand members who had gathered in San Francisco for the annual western states joint council convention.

His earlier strength and vitality had not diminished as he spoke. "Big business and government are out to divide and conquer us," he admonished. "I implore you not to be fooled by editorials and trumped-up news stories about your headquarters management team. They're trying to weaken the very thread that binds us together, our brotherhood. They've tried it before and failed. They'll fail again if we stay united, fighting for the same common causes and principles that have made our union the most powerful workingman's voice in the world! I ask you now, do I have your support?"

Thunderous applause broke out throughout the room. One by one, a few people at the front began to stand, followed quickly by others at tables behind the front row until nearly everyone in the room was standing, applauding wildly.

Upstairs, Bartie Bonano was packing his bag preparing to leave for an assignment Louie Cordaro had given him at breakfast that very morning.

He put the last item, a Nikon 35-millimeter camera, carefully into his bag and surrounded it with undershirts for extra protection. He snapped the case shut and walked downstairs carrying his bag as if it were a toy, dwarfed by his huge body. A waiting limousine quickly hastened to San Francisco International. It was nearly one P.M. At precisely 2:05 P.M., he boarded a plane destined for San Juan, Puerto Rico.

Chapter 20

JUNE 13, TWO HOURS before an unseasonably rainy Los Angeles dawn, a telephone broke the silence in room 702 of the Century Plaza Hotel.

A man stirred in the darkness, reached for the phone and acknowledged the four A.M. wake-up call.

Outside, the rain continued to fall making loud noises as it splashed atop a patio table that rested on the balcony. A stiff wind tugged at the collapsed outdoor umbrellas, making intermittent fluttering noises as it vibrated with an irregular rhythm against the table.

The man turned on the light and with rigid militarylike precision he rose, urinated, brushed his teeth, dressed, and fixed himself a cup of instant coffee. He opened a brown hard-covered suitcase, pulled a smaller briefcase from inside and inspected its contents exactly in the same precise manner he had done the night before. Satisfied, he locked the case, placed it back inside the suitcase and locked it inside. At 5:35 A.M. he left the hotel, his suitcase at his side.

Nearly fifty miles away, Billy Hawk stirred under the covers, rolled over, and lay quietly for a few more minutes. At 6:05 A.M., he, too, was out of bed preparing for the day ahead.

While Billy showered, Elaine Hawk was already laying clothes out on the bed as she always did for her husband when he was on a tight schedule. Billy frequently relied on her tasteful, appreciative, and keen eye for appropriate clothing and he was becoming increasingly dependent on her for such things during his senatorial campaign.

Their rare night together in their Newport Beach home wouldn't be experienced again for at least a week as he intensified his campaign in the northern and central parts of the state before returning to Washington, D.C., to continue his work on the committee.

In the downstairs dining room, Elaine lit a fire in the fireplace and Billy's voice trickled downstairs as he talked on the bedroom phone upstairs. A moment later he joined her in the dining room after gathering the morning paper.

He was in more of a hurry than she had expected. He hurriedly sipped his coffee and chewed half an unbuttered English muffin. It was already 6:45 A.M.

"Why the hurry?" she asked, marveling at his ability to eat while not taking his eyes off the newspaper. His endless capacity for work never interfered with his passion for the morning sports section of the *Los Angeles Times*.

"My aide was supposed to drive me to the airport, but he's running late. I'll be picking him up instead," he explained.

"I can drive you," she offered.

"Thanks, but I don't know when we'll be back. I need to leave a car at the airport."

Billy looked at her for a moment, then leaned over the table and kissed her gently. "You're being a real sport about all this."

"About what?" she asked.

"Well, I haven't been home much lately and the prospects for improvement aren't going to get any better."

"Maybe you'll lose the election. Then I'll see you all the time."

"Maybe," Billy responded. They both smiled affectionately. Losing the election was something neither of them expected or wanted.

"I have to run," he said, pushing away from the table and disappearing upstairs.

Elaine was in the corridor waiting when he bounded

down the stairs with his bags slung over his shoulder. "I'm sorry I have to run like this, but . . ."

"So what else is new, Mr. Hawk?" she asked, and smiled reassuringly.

Billy wasted no words, leaving with a simple, "I love you."

Before backing out of the driveway, he sat in the car for a moment, staring back at the house. He had a strange feeling inside. He always disliked leaving her like this but for some reason today was different. Less than a week ago they had had a long discussion centered around her depression at being alone so often. It was nearly six months before the November election and the schedule was sure to become more hectic. By his standards, six months was by no means the eternity she imagined but he recognized her point of view. She was thirty-six years old, the same age as he, and they hadn't yet started their family. It was time, he decided. She had been so patient to have waited this long. She shouldn't have to wait any longer. He wanted to go inside and tell her but he was running late. He would call her from the airport. It seemed he always called her from airports, but this was one call he was sure she would welcome. It wouldn't be a delay, a schedule change, or a quick hello between planes. Today was different. He was sure of that. It was a beginning Elaine had waited for far too long. He couldn't wait to get to the airport. It was time he began repaying her for all her sacrifices. It was time to become a real husband.

Two blocks away, just over the short bridge that connected the rows of exclusive waterfront homes of Lido Isle to the Newport Peninsula, a meticulously dressed man waited for his prey with exacting patience. He had been there for over thirty minutes, listening to the silence broken only occasionally by the warbling of an assortment of small birds overhead and an occasional passing car. An open briefcase lay empty at his side and he clutched the small rifle he had taken from it to his breast as he sat behind the wheel of his parked car. The same look of intense concentration that had been on his face many

189

times before froze his stone-cold features as his eyes never moved from the stop sign at the foot of the bridge. He had already paced it off—exactly twenty-two feet from his car door to the center of the right-hand lane where every car coming across the bridge had to stop. From that range, he couldn't miss. His finger tensed on the trigger as he looked across the bridge toward Lido Isle. First he heard a noise, then he saw what he had been waiting for all along. A car approached, stopped.

Billy Hawk was right; today was different. It was the last day of his life.

Chapter 21

JAMES HAWK WAS sitting at his home on the New England coast, preparing a speech when he first heard the news.

He always had the radio on when he was working alone even though he rarely could recall anything he heard. It was nearly one A.M., Eastern Standard Time when the classical music station he had tuned in broke the news about his brother's death. A thousand thoughts flashed through his mind within a few beats of his heart. His initial doubts about the veracity of the announcement were quickly erased when he punched the remote control device and activated his television. A moment later the picture came on and he quickly scanned the channels. Within seconds, there was an interruption to one of the soap operas on CBS. "And now, ladies and gentlemen, from the CBS newsroom in New York—a late-breaking story."

The scene dissolved from the CBS letters logo to the face of a daytime news commentator. There was a look of seriousness on his lean face as he began.

"Good afternoon, ladies and gentlemen." His impressive, smooth, voice flowed. "This is Robert Cochran, CBS News. We are interrupting our normal programming to bring you this late-breaking news bulletin from Orange County, California."

The commentator continued, "Billy Hawk, Democratic U.S. senatorial candidate from California and chief counsel to the Hawk Committee headed by his brother, presidential candidate James Hawk, was found shot to death in his car this morning a few blocks from his home in Newport Beach, California.''

James was numb with disbelief. The world which he and his brother had shared so enthusiastically was shattered. He slumped in his chair, continuing to watch as the commentator described Billy's background and how he was found slumped behind the wheel of his car.

The phone began to ring but James ignored it. He felt a deep guilt, a personal sense of tragedy that went beyond that of losing a brother to an assassin's bullet. The sudden pressure and warmth of tears pressed hard against his eyes as he thought about the reasons behind Billy's death. He knew that if Billy hadn't been involved with the committee he would be still alive, yet he refused to label his brother's death a tragedy. To him, tragedy meant waste, and he was determined his brother's life and work would not be reduced to such a level.

The phone stopped ringing, then began again. James pushed the remote button, shutting off the television. The phone persisted. Reluctantly, he picked it up.

"Jim?" the voice asked.

James's voice cracked. "Yes," he answered.

J. Robert Wallace was the director of the F.B.I., and had become a close friend over the last two years while assisting with some of the committee investigations. "Have you heard?" Wallace asked.

"A few minutes ago," James replied slowly.

"I want you to know that every available agent in the Los Angeles office has already been assigned to investigate this thing. It's top priority."

James's voice was barely audible. "I appreciate that, Bob."

A few minutes later, James hung up the phone and started to cry. It lasted for only a few minutes. The phone rang again. He picked it up without answering and replaced it in the cradle before unplugging it from the wall. He wiped the tears from his eyes. There was no time for them now. His parents would have to be told.

The Hawk compound consisted of eleven acres with four large houses, one each for him and his brother, a guest house, and the fourth and largest for his parents. He walked downstairs, put on a jacket and stepped outside. His parents traditionally walked along the private beach that protected the compound at midday and today was no different. He walked slowly at first, his pace quickening when he sighted them nearly a half mile ahead.

That evening, numbers of stricken visitors soon became a crowd. Outwardly, James was more collected than his callers, most of whom had rushed to his home on impulse and found upon their arrival that they really didn't know what to say.

Inwardly, James was torn apart, bleeding in agony, but he joined the crowd in front of the television. The networks had all begun to interview or broadcast prerecorded quotes from all the major public figures concerning Billy's death.

President Jordan called Billy "A true American, struck down in the prime of life by a heinous act of crime by some despicable person who will be tracked down and prosecuted to the fullest extent of the law."

Louie Cordaro made a statement as he stood on the steps of his union's headquarters. "While we had our differences," Cordaro sympathized, "I liked the boy. He was bright. A real comer. It's tragic to see such a thing happen to one of our country's finest citizens. The hearts of all union members everywhere go out to the Hawk family in their hour of grief."

Still somewhat dazed, James stood, shook his head and shut off the television. He turned to face his parents and the few close friends who still persisted in trying to help.

"Maybe this will help reduce some of the hate in this country," a voice offered.

James turned to his right. It was the local priest. James looked at him kindly and shook his head. He knew better. "In a few months, the public will have forgotten," James answered bitterly. "It's a sad thing to say about someone's life and work but I've seen it before. Billy's death will only be a brief sensation, soon dropped and forgotten. Another sensational headline will come along and that will become the day's topic for discussion. The public won't rush to heal the wound that caused Billy's death."

James was suffering deeply, but he struggled to overcome his emotions, determined, as he always had been in the face of adversity, to move forward. He was alone at the helm now when he needed help more than ever before. He walked upstairs, closing the door behind him. He wept for over an hour before he called Tor Slagle.

Chapter 22

IT WAS A depressing morning. James's taut and drained face reflected back at him through the glare of the window as he sat quietly alone in the back of the police-escorted limousine that carried him from Los Angeles International Airport southward to his slain brother's home in Newport Beach.

He tried to formulate what he would say to Elaine when he saw her and for a moment wished he had had his mother and father accompany him on the same flight rather than waiting for the next day. Somehow their presence always made him more at ease when he became tense.

He watched the dawn through bullet-proof windows as he thought about the enormity of the tragedy, its impact on Elaine, the blow to himself and his parents, and the uncertainty of his own future. It was ironic that his brother's death, less than twenty-four hours earlier, would find him on a dual mission that morning: one strictly personal, and the other the continuing political battle that could not be compromised by Billy's death.

A muted voice from the front seat broke into his thoughts. "We're here, sir."

He looked out and saw that Billy's home had already been surrounded by police and secret service agents anticipating his arrival.

In less than a minute, James was inside, knocking lightly at Elaine's bedroom door.

"Elaine," he said quietly as he entered. "I'm here."

Elaine was startled momentarily—her brother-in-law's voice sounded so much like her husband's.

"Oh, Jimmy!" she said, throwing herself into his arms, simultaneously bursting into tears.

James looked into her haunted eyes, holding her hand reassuringly. He felt as though a great weight were pressing on his chest. "Let's only remember the happy things," he said.

Elaine was weary. She had not been able to sleep since learning of Billy's death. Now she wept freely. She had been unable to break down until now and it was comforting to finally share her grief. Being with James somehow made her feel as if Billy weren't really so far away.

The doctor had given her an injection of Amytal just before James' arrival to help her sleep and the sedative soon began to take effect. For the first time since she had kissed her husband good-bye the day before, she was finally asleep.

James sat beside her as she lay quietly on the bed. Only after an hour had passed did he go back downstairs to Billy's den and close the door behind him. He sat at Billy's long polished mahogany partner's desk, reminiscing to himself about the past while at the same time plucking at the ragged fragments of the disordered present.

There was a soft knock at the door before its opening. James looked at his watch. It was eleven A.M. Tor Slagle was precisely on time for his appointment.

For Tor, it was a strange feeling to be in Billy's den without his friend. He closed the door noiselessly behind him. He could still picture Billy sitting at his desk framed by tall bookshelves on both sides. He had spent many happy hours there with his old friend, casually discussing a wide range of subjects.

While he had met James several times before, today Tor felt uncomfortable and rigid in his presence. The room was different with James at the desk instead of Billy. Billy had been dead for over thirty hours, but the tragedy was just now beginning to register for him. In a way it was similar to when his parents were killed in a plane crash. It was several days before the reality of their loss hit him.

A moment of silence followed; then James motioned for Tor to sit down. They sat staring at each other for a few seconds before James smiled faintly and broke the spell. "Thanks for coming on such short notice," he began. "I'd like to think we would have gotten together soon anyway but under happier circumstances."

Tor looked down at the carpet and then back up at James. He could see the pain in his eyes but there was friendliness in his face. "Jim, I don't know what to say. I want to help in any way I can."

James leaned back in his chair. "I'd like you to attend the funeral. It's going to be strictly a family affair, but I know how close you and Billy were. You've a right to be there."

The bright mid-morning sun blazed behind James's head and silhouetted him. Tor half squinted as he answered. "Thank you, I appreciate that. I know how you must feel."

"That's precisely why I asked you here this morning," James declared. "To tell you how I feel and to ask you a favor."

A quizzical expression crossed Tor's tanned face, but he said nothing. James was operating just as Billy used to. Tor simply nodded and stared back.

"Tor, I'm in one hell of a quandary. Besides our family's personal sorrow, Billy's death brings up a long list of unanswered questions beyond the most obvious one of who was responsible for the assassination." James leaned forward and reached out, slapping his hand on the desk. "I've given this a lot of thought but first, I'll tell you out front, I need you help. I think you'll see why after I've explained."

Tor forced a smile. "As I said, I'd like to help in any way I can."

"Don't act prematurely," James cautioned, pointing his finger. "Hear me out first. This gets a little more complicated than you might think."

Tor scratched his head nervously. "I appreciate your candor. Please, go ahead."

"I believe you're aware of the work Billy was doing for the committee."

"Yes, we had discussed it fairly frequently. In fact, I had just agreed to help on a limited basis."

"I can't let the tragedy of Billy's death interfere with that work. My first gut reaction yesterday was to get the son-of-a-bitch that killed him, but I'm confident that will come in due course. Vindication will come if we keep our heads, but it can't be our primary objection. I occupy a very precarious position. If I lash out at the forces that I suspect are responsible, it will only add fuel to an already raging fire."

Tor looked puzzled.

"Let me explain," James said. "The Democratic convention is only two weeks away. My nomination is guaranteed because of the primaries. In order to carry on Billy's work, I must be elected president in November. That has to be my primary objective."

"You mean Billy's work on the committee."

"Exactly. The best insurance I can get to insure the committee's success is to win the election. That has to come first. It's the necessary means to an end. I can't let myself get involved in any name-calling contests about who killed Billy right now, but I'll say to you that, to me, the most obvious answer would be that Cordaro put out a contract on him to try and stop the investigation."

"Is that what you think?" Tor asked, appalled.

"I'm not really sure, but I can't accept or reject that thought at this time. Without any hard evidence, I shouldn't take a stand either way and I won't. Billy's primary concerns were for the country and, despite what others think, that's what drove him to fight Louie Cordaro and what he stands for. The real enemies of this country won't fall with the elimination of Cordaro but he'll be a damn good start."

"But where do I fit into all this?"

"Billy's murder will be old news within a few weeks,

I'm convinced of that. While that may sound cold to you, that's the way it is. But I can't take a campaign stance on the committee's work or the Cordaro issue without being criticized by the media and the union for trying to capitalize on Billy's death. If I try to push hard against Cordaro, I'll be accused of mounting a personal vendetta. It would cost me the election if I go after this thing the way I really want to, and the only way to clean this mess up is to go about first things first and that means winning the election."

"So you want me to take up the fight where Billy left off," said Tor.

"That's it."

Tor stood up and walked around the desk toward the bookshelves. "But I don't see how," he said. "I know nothing about the investigation. I wouldn't even know where to begin. Besides, there must be hundreds of others more qualified than I am."

James raised his hands above his head and stretched. "You're wrong. There's no one else I would trust with this assignment."

"Trust? You mean you can't trust the others on the staff?"

"Billy's work on the committee was mostly communal; the information he had was available to all the committee members. But there were some areas that he personally uncovered that were highly sensitive. Mostly unproved, I might add. Those were kept strictly between the two of us."

Tor sat down again, his interest piqued. "Go on."

"Billy's judgment of character was uncanny and you happen to have been his best friend. To me, that speaks for itself. I want you to replace Billy as chief counsel to the committee. I'll help direct you, but it has to be strictly behind the scenes."

Tor's mind was racing. He was flattered by the offer, but was caught totally by surprise, an experience he did not often have. "I don't know, Jim. It seems like there must be a better way. Shit, I've spent my life as a businessman, not in courtrooms. I wouldn't know where to begin.''

James readjusted himself in his chair. ''Dammit, Tor, I've got an election to win! I want Billy's death to mean something and that's the only chance we've got. This country has major problems that are devouring it from within; if they go unchecked, they'll spread to an incurable cancer. I can't be sure it's not already too late.''

Tor felt a sense of guilt at his own hesitancy. He admired James's strength. Here was a man who had just lost his only brother to an assassin, yet he was able to push personal emotion aside to keep clearly in sight the objectives he and Billy had shared. Others might call it selfishness, but Tor knew better. The Hawk family didn't operate that way. ''What about your position as chairman of the committee? Won't that hurt you if you remain?'' Tor asked.

''We'll cross that bridge if and when it's necessary. Meanwhile, I'll just keep a low profile. I'll even miss some of the meetings, which is inevitable anyway because of my campaign schedule.''

''What would my role be?'' Tor asked.

''We'd need to review the upcoming trial. Most of that could be done between the investigative staff and you. I don't have any information that they don't have.''

''What about the other areas you mentioned?''

There was a noticeable seriousness in James's eyes as he began to speak. ''Billy had evidence of political bribes and payoffs against some pretty high government officials,'' he began. ''Those we need to pursue, but they'll take time and I don't mind telling you it'll be explosive when they come out.''

Tor paused for a moment before speaking. ''What about Cordaro? What do you have on him?''

''We haven't even begun to scratch the surface on what that man's been doing. This trial is only a small sample of what we think we can eventually convict him on. That's why the committee has to stay intact, keep pushing forward. Will you help?''

Tor was still standing, leaning against the bookcase, his ash-blond hair reflecting brilliantly in the sun. "I've no experience as chief counsel. My law degree has dust on it," he challenged.

"I'll be your experience," James answered.

There was a long silence as the two sat staring at each other.

Finally Tor spoke. "Where do I begin?"

For the next two hours, James briefed Tor on subjects of which Tor had never before dreamed. He also told of a personal diary which Billy kept concerning the investigations. While James had never seen it or asked where it was, it had been an agreed-upon precaution in case something should happen to either of them.

"Have you looked for it?" Tor asked.

"Only here in the den, but not thoroughly. No one knows of its existence except you and me so there's no urgency to find it today, but we need to track it down. Billy usually briefed me weekly on what was in it but our schedules over the last two weeks prevented us from getting together. I have no idea what his latest entries were."

James's calm expression suddenly changed. He had a concerned, worried look on his face. Tor watched him closely but said nothing while James shifted uncomfortably in his chair. James was still somewhat unsure of his new relationship with Tor and was debating with himself whether or not to burden him with too much information too soon. He had hoped to cover the next topic at another time but decided it couldn't wait. "Billy called me Sunday and told me that he had some new information which was too sensitive to talk about over the phone. We were to get together Friday."

"What kind of information?"

"It concerned the president. He seemed pretty upset about it."

"Do you suppose he put in in the diary?" Tor asked.

"Let's hope so," James answered slowly. "Let's hope so."

Tor used the two days before the funeral to organize his staff at Slagle's in preparation for his prolonged absences. He was concerned over the potential union organizational activity within the city and decided against totally divorcing himself from his business responsibilities. He would try to come back for at least one day every other week to keep an eye on things.

The funeral was, as James had said, strictly a family affair at San Francisco Presidio. Billy's parents, a few close friends of the family, and some of Billy's staff sat quietly around the closed coffin, each preoccupied with their own private thoughts and grief. James delivered the eulogy with unbroken strength. Only at the end did his voice begin to falter and crack. "Billy was controversial," James concluded. "He was loved by most who knew him. To be sure, he disturbed some politicians, but fought his battles lustily, and gave his adversaries as many hard knocks as they gave him. In doing so, he lived his life the only way he knew how, the way our parents taught him, as a proud and honest man. He gave all of himself to the burning interest of the moment and his fire was usually directed at situations or ideas he found intolerable rather than at specific individuals. He dedicated his life to serving people less fortunate than himself and to exposing and destroying corruption wherever it might be found."

James hesitated a moment, blinking back tears. "We all loved him; the void in our hearts can never be filled. We must strive to move forward, attending to the unfinished tasks Billy leaves behind, using our fond memories of him to fuel our personal motivational furnace with the same desires and goals he would have completed had he been allowed to live. In that way, Billy will always be with us and his death will not have been in vain."

Chapter 23

"HOW COULD YOU do it?"

Frank Billings looked down at his coffee cup, then pushed it aside and leaned back in his chair. He stared directly into Mikki Parker's eyes as she sat patiently across the table awaiting an answer. "You mean testify against Peck?" he asked.

Mikki only nodded. It was difficult for her to be there even though Frank Billings had been one of her father's best friends. His testimony for the Hawk Committee against Donald Peck seemed to her totally irresponsible and a blatant twisting of the real facts. Now that she was employed by Louie Cordaro, she feared her meeting with Billings today might be misunderstood should they be seen together. The only reason she was there at all was out of respect for her father. When Billings had asked to meet with her, she had agreed reluctantly. The harshness of her decision never to see an old family friend again over a matter that only months ago would have meant nothing, weighed heavily on her.

Billings looked her straight in the eye. "I know what you're thinking," he began. "You think I was a damn fool for cutting off my livelihood by testifying against Peck."

"Something like that," Mikki agreed.

Billings made a gesture to the waitress who quickly topped off his cup with more coffee. The restaurant in a quaint out-of-the-way area in Alexandria's Old Town

203

district was extremely busy. For the first time since his testimony six weeks earlier, Billings was feeling comfortable in a public place. His eyes dropped a moment, then raised again. "I guess it's a little hard to explain," he answered, staring out the window.

"Try me," Mikki insisted, a faint trace of sarcasm in her voice.

"I can't say that I really know for sure," he answered, sipping his coffee. "I guess I just got tired of playing errand boy for Peck and some of the others. I started out in this business as a labor consultant. Somehow over the years I began prostituting myself by doing favors for some of the boys. Pretty soon, that's *all* I was doing. Hell, in the last three years I haven't done one lick of work that would even remotely resemble that of a labor consultant. I've been too busy chasing down everything from women to booze to new swimming pools for the union's brass. That's not what I want out of life. There's got to be more than that."

"But you could have quit without jeopardizing your career."

"You mean by not testifying?"

"Exactly."

"I was subpoenaed, Mikki."

"So?"

"So I had to testify! I was under oath. They asked me some questions, I told the truth. That's the way the law reads. I've had it with selling my soul to save my ass. My conscience won't allow it any longer. Some things are more important than fast company and a quick buck. I want to hold my head high when I come home to my wife, not crawl through the door like some damned whipped dog afraid to share my day's experiences with her for fear of losing her respect. I mean, how do you tell your wife you just spent the day arranging for a bunch of teenage hookers to entertain at some damned union party?"

Mikki looked across the table at him thoughtfully. "What are you going to do now?" she asked, her voice softening.

"Get out. Washington is too hot for me to hang around

here. I love it, but I'm no fool. Peck still has a lot of friends who would like to see me disappear even though he'll probably never come back for a trial. I heard by the grapevine that he may have put out a contract on me before he went to Europe. That's why I wanted to talk to you. I'm on my way to Hawaii. I need to stay out of sight for a while.''

Mikki studied his face. Her family had enjoyed Frank Billing's company for over fifteen years, ever since her father had first met him at an annual union convention in Miami. She could see pain in Billings's eyes. What a difference a year makes, she thought. Both their lives had taken an irrevocable turn and now each had to try to put the pieces together again.

''Why did you ask me to meet you today?'' she asked.

Billings sipped his coffee before answering.

''Get out,'' he warned. ''Before it's too late. Don't get caught up in it like I did and find yourself facing a decision like the one I had to make.''

She laughed. ''You mean about the union?'' she asked.

Billings nodded.

He was warning her against the very thing that she and Tor had argued about. Both men were asking her to turn against the hand that had fed and clothed her family all her life. She couldn't understand how Billings could have testified against Peck and the union. His life had now been shattered. Despite Billings's vague schemes to pick up the pieces and start over again somewhere else, she knew his life would never be the same. He would always be looking over his shoulder, unable to enjoy life without fear of reprisal. She admired his courage and convictions in speaking out against what he believed to be injustices, but she wasn't willing to believe his accusations or to jeopardize her job. She could still reshape her own life with her sister. Shana was more important than anything in the world to her and she needed her job to help with the expenses at the hospital. She couldn't afford to quit now even if she had wanted to.

Billings interrupted her concentration. ''I mean it,

Mikki, get out. You've still got time. There's no future with Cordaro.''

"I'll give it some thought," she said, smiling slightly. "I can't say that making the union a career is my goal in life. It's just that it makes sense at this time in my life."

"It's terrible, isn't it?" Billings said, looking about the restaurant at the crowd.

"What is?"

"All these people—here, outside, everywhere. Their lives are being flagrantly manipulated by people who will dictate how they'll live their lives and they go about their business as if they didn't have a care in the world. If only they knew how they were being used, maybe something could be done."

"Oh, come on, Frank! I've heard enough about how bad the union is. Can't we change the subject?"

Either Billings didn't hear her last comment or chose to ignore it.

"Why do people have to spoil everything? It was so beautiful before," he rambled. Tears began to well in Billings's eyes. He tried to blink them back. "I better go," he said, trying not to look at her.

"Is there anything I can do?" Mikki asked.

Billings shook his head. "No. I just want you to know how much your family has meant to Debbie and me. I can't explain it so I won't even try."

"Will Debbie be joining you soon?"

"I think so," he answered. "Right now I have to get out of here for a while. We can work out what to do with our lives later."

"Can I drop you at the airport?"

"I'd rather not. I can get by unnoticed a whole lot easier alone. As much as I like you, I don't need to be seen walking the streets with Louie Cordaro's secretary. That kind of attention I can do without."

"Where will you be staying?" Mikki asked, trying to be polite.

"At the Ilikai in Hololulu. Tomorrow, I'll go to Maui. I've got a friend with an old house on the south end of the island far enough away from the tourists that I shouldn't be bothered. I'll be safe there.''

They stood and shared an uncomfortable embrace. Billings turned and began to walk away, then turned back. "Mikki," he began, "there's something else I feel I should tell you. I feel I owe it to your father." He stopped himself and thought a moment before continuing. "No," he corrected, "I owe it to *you* . . .''

The next day Mikki Parker went for a long drive. She had to get away, had to have time to think. After an hour, she slowed the car and stopped on the shoulder, staring numbly at the highway that extended for miles ahead. She thought of Frank Billings. He had never made it to the house on Maui; the news of his death had been announced over the radio several hours earlier. His body had been found in an alleyway behind the Ilikai Hotel, twenty-one stories directly below his room. Officials called it suicide, but she knew better. Frank Billings's death less than twenty-four hours after he had told her about her father and Louie Cordaro almost convinced her that he had been telling the truth. Yesterday, she was sure that Billings's stories were the ramblings of a frightened man. Now she wasn't sure. She had to find out the truth.

That night the phone rang at Tor Slagle's home. It was Mikki Parker.

"I've been thinking about what you said about Louie Cordaro," she began. "I'd like to try and help." She sounded cold, determined.

"I'm not sure what you mean," he answered.

The sharpness in her voice began to subside as Mikki explained as best she could, telling of her conversation with Frank Billings and her concern over the circumstances surrounding his death.

What she was offering to do was beyond anything Tor could have hoped for, accelerating even his most optimistic timetables. She was offering to act as a spy for the committee—it was as simple as that. But Tor was enough of a lawyer to attempt to explain exactly what she was letting herself in for. He told her that any information supplied to the committee had to be voluntary, and that the committee could not directly authorize any payment for her services because to do so would be equivalent to an illegal wiretap. Any testimony she could provide would be inadmissible as evidence in a courtroom. It was a final legal line that had to be followed, but if done properly, Tor was convinced it would work. If she came up with enough information, the committee could probably compile enough evidence to convict Louie Cordaro without ever having to reveal the source.

"I understand," she repeated intermittently as Tor talked. Hearing his voice again was good as he methodically went over what would be expected of her and the dangers she might face.

"Do you understand everything we've discussed?" Tor asked.

"Yes, I think so," she replied.

There was a long pause as both waited for the other to speak. Tor broke the silence. "Mikki, about the last time we were together—I want you to know I'm sorry we parted in anger. I mean, I picked up the phone several times to call you but I never had the guts to stay on the line. I want you to know you haven't been out of my mind for one minute since I last saw you."

"That makes two of us," she responded warmly.

Chapter 24

TOR WAS ALONE. It was a few minutes past ten when he turned off the bedroom light and went to bed. As he lay in the dark, Tor looked out his window at the dancing lights of the city reflected on the bay toward Sausalito.

The fatiguing events of the past few days jumbled in Tor's mind as he tried unsuccessfully to fall asleep. Billy Hawk's death continued to dominate his every waking moment. The tragedy had altered the course of his entire life.

James Hawk's prediction had come true; public apathy was already apparent. There were no cries of outrage, no real demands for action and, as yet, no indication as to who was responsible for his murder. The public had read the headlines and moved on. The politicians were back at work, the world continued to revolve, unnoticing and unresponsive.

Tor's gaze shifted to the lights from the pyramid-shaped Trans-America Building that stood tall among the other buildings across the bay. It was there that he was to meet with Winston Sheffield in the morning. It was a meeting he didn't want to attend but knew he had no choice. He was anxious to get on with his committee work. Suddenly his personal affairs seemed insignificant, even unnecessary.

The next morning, the wind gusted from the sea, lightly brushing the eucalyptus trees against the exterior of Tor's bedroom wall, waking him only a few minutes before the alarm which he had set for seven.

An hour later, he was in San Francisco, listening to Winston Sheffield.

"I'll concede that if these words were spoken publicly by any of you distinguished gentlemen they would be unpopular," Sheffield announced. "I will even say that I personally would never say them in any public place. But between us, I consider what I've said to be realistic."

Sheffield puffed his cigar as he awaited a response from his audience. Tor fidgeted with his pen, first looking at Sheffield, then at the others. Everything Sheffield had said ran against Tor's own convictions, but he was particularly interested in hearing what R. Dalton Smith's reaction would be. As executive vice-president of Hemp, Lathrop and Company, he was their official spokesman and had flown out expressly to attend the meeting from his company's headquarters in Chicago.

Smith assumed the role of leader by addressing the issue. "What you're saying, Winston, I agree, is highly unethical," he began, "but speaking from past experience, I happen to know it has been done successfully before. The key, however, is approaching the right people within the union. And you say you have the contacts?"

Sheffield smiled thinly. "Gentlemen, I have been in this business on both sides of the fence for over thirty years. I know how to handle these situations. Believe me, there are people on the union's payroll we can buy if the money is right."

David Crocker was the only other person present besides Tor's labor consultant, Willie Ray. As president of the Small Merchant's Association for San Francisco, he represented the balance of the other nonunion retailers that would be affected by an organizing drive. He had been content to remain quiet for most of the morning but now his voice was strained. "I'm not sure that bribing union officials and organizers is the way to go," he protested. "In the first place, where will the money come from? Our association certainly doesn't have that kind of cash. Most of the small retailers I represent are barely breaking even and an assessment for funding is out of the question. I'd have to tell them what the money is for and then it would only be a matter of time before it would leak. I'm sorry, but I just don't see how it would work, at least not from our standpoint.''

''Money is no problem, I assure you,'' Smith interjected, leaning forward and rapping his knuckles sharply on the table. His pink, balding head seemed to turn an even deeper red.

Tor couldn't believe what he was hearing. He reasoned Smith must have considered the magnitude of what he was proposing but he couldn't be sure. The sole representative of such a prestigious corporation offering corporate money to bribe the union's own organizers was incomprehensible to Tor. He thought of the Taft-Hartley Act which outlined the governing authority for all labor-management disputes. It was precisely that Act that was on his mind as Smith continued to pledge his company's support in going along with Sheffield's bribery plan.

Tor decided to speak out. ''Gentlemen, I presume you're all aware that if we followed this course of action, we would be exposing our companies to potential damage suits by the NLRB,'' he announced.

Crocker was the first to respond. ''I admit that on a pragmatic financial basis, our association would have to back out on such a proposal since we simply don't have the money. But, if Mr. Smith's proposal to help solve the money problem is genuine, then I'm sure my group would go alone. By not spending any of the association's money, there would be less possibility for embarrassing questions; and the fewer people we'd have to involve in the matter, the less chance for any slip-ups. I, for one, don't see any other way. I believe it'll work, providing the finances are arranged, of course.''

''Damn right!'' Smith concurred. ''We all know that those bastards only use the NLRB when it's to their advantage. The union has never followed the rules, so why in hell should we?''

"Why not try it another way first?" Tor said calmly.

"What way?" Crocker asked.

"Look," Tor protested, standing up. "The only way a union can get into our organization is to fill a need for our employees that we're currently not providing for. The driving determination of the majority of people today is to improve their quality of life. Because of this, industry and business have the responsibility to meet these demands as long as they are reasonable. If we meet the employees' demands, what can a union card offering nothing more than monthly dues offer them that we aren't already supplying?"

Smith sat up straight. "It's easy for you to say that. You already pay more than the union contracts currently call for!"

"But I get it back in productivity," Tor retorted. "My employees like working for Slagle's so they push a little harder without my having to ask for it. I don't have to hire two slow people to do the work of one good one."

"Then you're not willing to go along with us, is that it?" Smith asked.

Tor pushed his chair back to allow himself a few extra feet of free movement. "The NLRB has authority to prevent employers from engaging in certain specified unfair labor practices," he began. "If bribery isn't listed, then I'm sure they'll amend the Act."

A voice came from the end of the table. "You're talking like a lawyer, Tor." It was Sheffield who had managed to remain silent for several minutes.

"It's because I am," Tor responded, his voice becoming louder. "And for a fellow member of the bar, I'm surprised to hear you make such a proposal. I didn't agree to this meeting just to see how we could bend the rules in our favor."

Willie Ray stirred and removed his hat, a straight stiff-brimmed leather model that matched his boots and vest. He shoved it back, allowing it to hang loosely from an attached gold-braided cord, his slicked-down auburn hair outlining his freckled bullet-shaped head. Willie Ray's expertise in local union activities in the City of San Francisco was as broad as Winston Sheffield's experience on the national level. Everyone listened when he spoke. "It appears," he began, "that at least for the moment, Winston's proposal is, to say the least, controversial. Why don't we consider the alternatives before settling the issue, if indeed we *can* settle the issue?"

Tor glanced at the others. There was no response. "You have the floor, Willie," he said.

Willie took off the rimless glasses that he had been wearing and continued. "I wouldn't dignify the union movement with a response right now. Wait until the subject comes up from the employees. That's when we make our move. Call the union organizers bastards or hoodlums—bums, if you will. Ridicule the union leaders. I say we have to fight fire with fire. They've got their organizers, so we should get out own organizers, people with no more scruples than theirs."

"What's your plan?" Smith interjected.

Willie wasted no time in explaining. "Find an employee in each of your stores who would be willing to work secretly with an appointed representative attorney to set up a secret antiunion propaganda group. The attorney can arrange to have defamatory materials given to the group indirectly through the American Legion or somebody like that."

"What kind of materials?" Smith asked.

"Anything! Communist claims about the union, or the fact that they are destroying our country with their inflationary demands. Attack their national leaders. We can weaken the union's credibility from within by using our own employees to our advantage, not theirs. It's no big deal, it's done all the time. Just go out and find yourselves a friendly employee to start the ball rolling. But be sure to use an attorney as intermediary who can't be traced back to your different companies."

Crocker and Smith looked at each other, each waiting for the other to comment. Neither did.

Sheffield combed his fingers through his flowing hair,

leaned forward in his chair with one elbow on the table and began to speak. "The way I see it, Willie's plan or the one I originally proposed or even a combination of the two could be adopted effectively. But we need a collective effort. We can't all be going off in different directions." Sheffield looked at Tor.

Tor was still standing. He paused, took a pace away from the table, then swung back abruptly. "Gentlemen, I see nothing wrong in seeking counsel and employing legal experts in labor-management relations . . . but it looks to me like we are talking about developing a strategy that amounts to nothing more than a payoff to union officials; or, if I read Willie's plans correctly, to pay off our own employees to have them influence the rights of the workingman. It's simply illegal and I can't in good conscience go along with either plan."

Tor glanced around the elliptical table to meet the eye of each of the others. Sheffield was at Tor's right and took the lead as mediator. "Gentlemen, this meeting is only a preliminary informational one that we set up based on some pretty reliable information about a union organizing drive in this city. You all have your own separate thoughts and legal counsel and are free to handle the situation in any manner you wish. But, in my opinion, a collective effort, regardless of the strategy, will work best. You must consider that before finalizing your plans."

The debate continued, lasting through the remainder of the morning. Tor steadfastly held to his convictions while Sheffield, Crocker, and Smith held to theirs. The meeting ended with Willie Ray concluding that the pay was the same for him whether it was legal or illegal while announcing that he would adopt whatever strategy Tor decided upon.

Chapter 25

"THERE'S A CALL for you on my private line. I think you better take it," Borg Trenier announced through a large cloud of white smoke he had just exhaled from his cigar.

Louie Cordaro was annoyed by Trenier's uninvited intrusion into his office. "Not interested," he bellowed.

"It's your man, checking in," Trenier announced.

Cordaro stood up, briskly brushing by Trenier's portly frame as he headed down the hall to Trenier's office.

Cordaro picked up the phone. "Yeah," he answered cautiously.

The voice on the other end quickly responded. "Mr. Cordaro, this is Sid Bonnam. I thought I'd better check in and Borg suggested I talk with you personally in case you had any special instructions."

Sidney Bonnam had been on the job for over two weeks. Until today, he had called in routinely and talked to Trenier every other day but, for the first time since accepting Cordaro's offer, he was speaking with him personally.

Cordaro was abrupt. "Any news?" he asked.

"I'm afraid not much. The Hawk assassination has stopped everything. The entire staff just disappeared when it happened. Our first real meeting is tomorrow. I hope to get more involved then."

"What about the new guy? Where in hell did they dig him up?"

"You mean Tor Slagle?"

"Yeah."

"I know he was a friend of Billy Hawk when they were in college together and that he's out of San Francisco. The announcement caught everyone here by surprise. Nobody seems to know much about him or what to expect. We don't even know yet when he's coming out from the coast."

"What's his background?" Cordaro quizzed.

"Harvard Law School. Graduated fourth in his class, but word has it that he's always effectively concealed the fact that he has much upstairs. Never got involved in politics. That's what doesn't make sense. He's stepping into something he knows nothing about at a very critical period. He's never even practiced law."

Cordaro changed the subject. "Who do you think dumped Billy Hawk?" he asked.

Bonnam paused before answering. He wanted to ask the same question of Cordaro but didn't dare. "Well, ah, they're still trying to find that Puerto Rican guy that threatened to kill him. That's about all I know and I heard that on the radio."

"You mean Muniz?"

"Yeah, I think that's his name."

"Bullshit!" Cordaro retorted. "Those cocksuckers would just love to find him and pin the rap on him to make me and the union look bad. Well, they won't get the chance because I know Muniz didn't do it. I don't know who did, but I know for damn sure it wasn't him. This union didn't have shit to do with Hawk's death."

Bonnam tried to ignore Cordaro's soapbox oratory, wishing he'd save it for the reporters. He took a deep breath and sighed quietly before responding. "Will there be anything else, sir?" he asked.

"Yeah!" Cordaro shot back. "I want information. You're getting paid plenty for it. I want action. That fuckin' trial is about to begin and I don't know any more now than I did four weeks ago. I expect results when I'm paying this kinda bread. Do you get what I mean?"

"Yes, sir," he answered.

Cordaro slammed the receiver in the cradle but it didn't

sit properly. He started to walk away, then thought better of it and turned to put it in its proper place. He turned back again and started toward the door, then stopped and looked at Trenier and pointed to the phone. "You sure that thing's not bugged?" he asked.

"Positive," Trenier said. "It's an illegal line I had put in especially for this contact. It's registered to a fictitious name in an apartment I rented over in the ghetto area. Our own man worked it so it only rings here. The phone's already been pulled at the apartment. They can never trace it to us."

To be on the safe side, Cordaro decided he would never use the line again, informing Trenier that he would have to relay any future messages. A few minutes later Cordaro was still fuming over Bonnam's remarks about Muniz. He knew he had lost his temper, more out of his continued shock at what he felt sure was the real force behind Billy Hawk's death rather than anything Bonnam had said. It was hard for Cordaro to believe that the president of the United States was no better than a common murderer.

The following morning Tor Slagle sat in his San Francisco office hunched in his chair, sipping his third cup of coffee. He was talking to James Hawk over the phone and had just told James of his arrangement with Mikki Parker.

James was skeptical. "I don't like it, Tor," he cautioned.

"Why not?" Tor asked. "I considered all the legal angles. We haven't planted her there."

"Hiring her to spy on the very institution that put bread on her family's table for most of her life is hardly what I'd call a good idea. How do we even know she's really on our side? She might change her mind and turn around and spy on us. How can we control such a thing? It could blow up in our faces."

Tor tried to explain Mikki Parker's background thoroughly and the reasons he believed she could be trusted, leaving out his personal feelings toward her. He assured James that his instincts were correct. He was positive that she was no longer loyal to the union because he had had enough conversations with her over the past few days to identify hatred of either the union itself or someone within the organization, he couldn't be sure which. She was willing to help, at least for a while, and Tor asked James not to question her.

"Tor," James said, "I'll go along with you on this but under one condition."

"Which is?"

"Don't tell her anything! Point her in the direction you want her to go and send her off. Take all the information you can get but don't give any out. We'll be less vulnerable that way. She's to know nothing about what the committee is up to."

"I understand."

James quickly jumped to another subject. "What about the Muniz investigation? Did you call my contact at the F.B.I.?" he asked.

"I called him. He said there's nothing the F.B.I. can do until they find Muniz. Every state in the union's looking for him. We'll just have to wait. He said they're going as fast as they can but nothing has broken loose yet."

"Damn!" James yelled. "I don't want Cordaro to go to trial with this thing about Muniz still hanging in the air. It needs to be cleared up. We don't need any outside influence about my brother's death to affect Cordaro's trial. If the public thinks that we're going to use Muniz to make Cordaro and his union look bad it could work against us."

Tor speculated, "But what if it *was* Muniz who killed him?"

"First, I doubt that Muniz did it. I think he's just scared because of what he said about killing Billy and he's holed up somewhere. He made an untimely threat, that's all, and the sooner he's found the better. Second, if Muniz *did* do it, he probably acted independently. I can't believe Cordaro would authorize Muniz to kill Billy after Muniz had already made the threat. Cordaro's too smart for that."

"I still don't follow what you mean about how this can affect the trial," said Tor.

It could wind up costing us a shot at Louie. If Muniz isn't found and his involvement cleared up one way or the other, we may have trouble getting enough impartial jurors together to bring Cordaro to trial right away."

"Do you really think that could happen?"

"It can and will if Tom Wilson thinks he can get a delay that will help Cordaro's case."

"Does Wilson want a delay?"

"Who knows! On one hand it could provide him more time to produce a defense, yet the same delay would provide us with an equal amount of time. My guess is they'll go with it as scheduled. They probably think we're not as prepared as we'd like to be and they sure as hell don't want to take the chance of going to trial after the elections. I could be president then and that sure as hell wouldn't help them any. Their troubles would just be beginning because I'd support the committee's work ten times over what Jordan's been offering."

"So they'll press on as scheduled?"

"I think so."

"Even with the Muniz thing still in the air?"

"It can only help them. They'll look like martyrs if we play up the fact that Muniz works for Cordaro, even if he's innocent. If he's guilty and acted independently of the union, they'll wash their hands of him. It'll just be a whole lot better if we find Muniz and get this thing out of the way. The sooner the publicity dies the better."

Tor thought for a moment. He wasn't sure, but he had a feeling James's concern over the unsettled Muniz situation was aggravated by the potential problems it could cause for the November elections. It was difficult for James to separate his feelings between what was needed to be done to carry on the committee's work and what was needed to win the election. The two responsibilities were beginning to oppose one another.

"There's not much time before the trial," Tor offered.

"I know, I know," James sighed. "When does the jury

selection start?'' he asked.

Tor checked his calendar. "Monday, the twenty-third."

"That's the day after the Democratic convention starts in Los Angeles. I want you there."

"In Los Angeles?"

"No. At the jury selection. Just observe. Watch for anything unusual. I don't trust anybody at this stage of the game."

"I'll be there."

"And, Tor."

"Yes?"

"We must find Billy's diary. I've got a feeling there might be something in there that could help us. I looked all over Billy's office in Washington. It's not there."

"Where then?" Tor asked.

"Probably at his house, in Newport Beach. Elaine's looked for it but I hate to ask her to look again. It's hard enough for her without asking her to spend more time scrounging through his den."

"You think it's there?"

"It has to be. It's the only place I haven't looked thoroughly. Would you mind going down there?"

"Any idea what it looks like?"

"Your guess is as good as mine. Elaine doesn't know either because she never heard about it until I asked her about it a few days ago. Billy apparently never said anything to her. You'll just have to go through every piece of paper in his den until you find it. It has to be there. It's the only place."

Tor finished his coffee, picked up the phone and called Elaine Hawk. He was unsure just how to approach her about coming down to go through Billy's office and was pleasantly surprised when she answered the phone in her usual positive and assertive voice. Her cheerfulness made him feel more at ease. She even invited him to a party on the Sunday following the Democratic convention at her home to celebrate James's nomination, which was already assured.

When Tor hung up the phone, he admired Elaine's

strength and resilience. Hosting a party so soon after Billy's funeral was her way of showing she was in control, carrying on as he would have expected her to.

A moment later, as Tor sat silently lost in his thoughts again, the phone rang. A man's voice, deep, and heavily muffled to a point Tor had to strain to hear, offered some strange advice. "If you want Cordaro," the voice mumbled, "get to Peck. Do you understand? You have to get to Peck."

A click of the phone, and the voice was gone.

Chapter 26

MONDAY, JUNE 23 . . .

For two days, Tor sat in a small Fairfax County Courthouse in Virginia and watched the jury selection process. As chief counsel for the committee, his presence was strictly as a spectator with no authority in the legal proceedings either at the jury selection or at the trial. The committee's investigations were to be continual. Once indictments were handed down by the grand jury, all documentation concerning the specific charges and the individuals involved would be transferred from the committee to the prosecuting district attorneys. The committee's official interest beyond that point would be strictly advisory as official investigations into other union matters continued.

The close of the second day found the prosecution and defense agreeing on twelve jurors plus two alternates. The trial was to begin in just six days in that same courtroom, and it was announced the jurors would not be sequestered.

As a handful of spectators filed out of the courtroom, Tor glanced over but was careful not to acknowledge the presence of Mikki Parker who had phoned him earlier in the morning. She had been personally sent by Cordaro to observe the second day's jury selection. They had arranged to meet that evening.

It was past eleven that same night and Tor sat in his hotel room, waiting for her call. He took a tape recorder from his briefcase and ran a recording he had made of the day's jury selection. He played it, ran it back again, and played it once more. He listened for a while longer, then shut it off and lay back on the bed, his eyes closed, thinking. There was something about Wilson's questioning of the selected jurors that bothered him but it didn't reveal itself on the tape. He didn't know what it was, but he was confident that Wilson had gotten the jurors he wanted by design, certainly not by the luck of the draw.

It was almost midnight when the phone finally rang. Without identifying herself, Mikki directed Tor to a parking lot behind an all-night theater a few blocks away where, after a brief embrace, they huddled in the front seat of Mikki's rented car while she explained why she was at the jury selection proceedings.

Tor was incredulous. "You mean he's actually going to try to bribe one of the jurors?"

"Not just one; probably two," Mikki answered calmly. "Louie has never believed in taking chances. That's why he sent me down to get a background check on each of the jurors."

"Jesus, I still don't believe it! What's more, I don't understand why he would involve you in this. He's really exposing himself."

"I don't think he had a choice. He's not particularly close to Wilson, at least not close enough to ask him to do what he asked me."

"Why you?"

"Up until the last few years, my father had blind faith in that man. Louie knows that. He thinks I'm the same loyal friend my father was all those years."

"Does he really think he can get away with this?"

"Louie gets what he wants. He believes every man's got his price."

"Who else knows about this?"

"No one. He just asked me to come down to get the profiles. He hasn't actually committed himself on it yet, but my guess is he will. From what I've heard, he's used bribery before, but always to get others off the hook. He's never had to use it to get himself out of a jam."

Tor was slouched low in the seat. He pushed himself up. "When will you know if he really plans to pull this off?"

Mikki shrugged. "When Louie Cordaro decides. I have no way of knowing when that will be."

"Who do you suppose he'll get to handle the bribe?"

Mikki could guess what Tor was thinking. "We'll just have to wait and see. I haven't forgotten what you said about my not participating in anything I could be arrested for. I'll just have to figure out a way of getting out of it if he asks me to do it."

"Anything else?"

"Nothing—except that Louie has become very nervous. It's not like him to be so edgy all the time. He's always had temper tantrums, but now they're getting out of hand. I honestly believe he's really scared. I've never seen him this way. Even Borg Trenier has commented on it."

"He ought to be—we've got him on the run."

Mikki tempered Tor's enthusiasm. "Louie is a stretch runner," she cautioned. "He's been behind before, so don't count him out because you never know what he's going to do. History should have taught you that."

Tor's generous grin spread across his face. "That's what you're there for, remember?"

Mikki nervously looked around in the dark surrounding them. "I can't help remembering," she replied sarcastically.

"One more thing," Tor added. "What do you know about Armando Muniz, the union official from Puerto Rico?"

"Only that half the country's looking for him."

"Have you heard where he is?"

"No. Louie wants to know too. He says it makes him look bad because of the threat to Billy Hawk. I'll let you know if I hear anything, but Louie doesn't know anything. I'm sure of that."

Tor told her of the anonymous call he had received advising the committee to get at Cordaro through Donald Peck but, like the Muniz situation, Mikki knew nothing of it nor could she offer any ideas as to who the caller could have been.

Once the subject of Louie Cordaro had been exhausted, they just sat there enjoying each other's company for a while. Mikki seemed different than she had their last time together. She appeared somewhat distant as if she were harboring some intensely private worry inside. Even their embrace earlier when he first entered the car had seemed perfunctory to Tor.

They looked at each other without talking for a moment, then exchanged a brief embrace followed by a kiss that, at least for Tor, showed a bit more warmth than her earlier reception. All too quickly, he was out of the car and around the corner nearly a block away and Mikki had pulled out of the shadowed parking lot, headed in the opposite direction.

It was exactly two A.M., when he got back to his room. He turned on the television just in time to see the Tennessee delegation at the Democratic convention cast the deciding votes that gave James Hawk the Democratic nomination for the presidency of the United States, followed by the usual hullabaloo with balloons falling from the ceiling and a sea of sign-waving delegates cheering loudly as the music blared.

Too soon, Tor's short night's sleep made the next morning an unwelcome reality. He was up at seven A.M., dressed, packed, and out of his room by eight on his way back to Washington, where he planned to spend two days working with the committee investigators before flying home on Friday in time for Elaine's victory party for James.

But a news item on the radio as he drove to Washington detoured him to National Airport. He would be going to Miami instead. Armando Muniz had been found murdered there.

Chapter 27

JUST OVER A month since her great tragedy, Elaine Hawk stood in her living room greeting guests, her proud head held high, her familiar wide smile in place.

It had been her idea to give the small private party for her brother-in-law and she was doing it the way she wanted—the way she thought Billy would have wanted it.

She looked stunning in a simple, yet elegant, embroidered white sundress that accented a healthy California tan as she circulated among her guests. She was aware of their mixed emotions so like her own, and somehow managed to encourage her guests to laugh, even to enjoy themselves. Her desire to fill every moment with fun, even when she didn't feel like it, had always been contagious. Since Billy's death she had been running at an even more hectic pace than when he was alive. It was her way of dealing with the tragedy, her way of coping.

As the guests awaited the arrival of the guest of honor, Tor slipped away and secluded himself in Billy's den. He pored over Billy's files and records for over an hour, looking unsuccessfully for Billy's private diary. He was disturbed to find Billy's safe unlocked. When Elaine delivered a refill for his empty wine glass, she told him that as far as she could tell after a cursory review of the contents, there was nothing missing. Elaine reasoned that Billy might simply have forgotten to turn the dial when he last used the safe, something he had done before. Perhaps there was no cause for suspicion, but Tor wasn't totally convinced of it.

Muffled applause filtered through the den door as Elaine's guests acknowledged the arrival of James Hawk. Elaine was out of the den in a flash.

It was the end of a beautiful day; the sun's crimson rays were beginning to fade on the horizon while the winds, gusting earlier in the day, had subsided and the bay waters had become still.

James seemed at ease, enjoying these brief moments between the convention and the final campaign surge which lay ahead. Tor watched him circulate through the crowd with a determination every bit as firm as Elaine's to help make the guests feel welcome. He looked strong and vigorous. From a physical point of view, he appeared to be ready for the arduous campaign.

When the last guests had departed, Elaine retired to her bedroom, leaving James and Tor in Billy's den. The melodic chime of the Austrian mantel clock had just struck ten.

"I've looked at that damn jury list for hours," Tor said. "I can't find anything wrong with it, yet I'm not comfortable with it. There's just something about the roster that I don't like."

"Have you checked their backgrounds?" James asked, throwing his suit coat over the back of the desk chair.

"As thoroughly as I could in the time I had. I'm still waiting for the police record check on each juror. All the other things check out. There are no radical union members on the jury, although there are two card-carrying members." Tor pulled a list from his pocket and studied it for a moment. "They come from all walks of life. Three are self-employed, two are housewives, one is a retiree, and the others are employed in various unrelated jobs."

"What about relatives?" James suggested. "Sometimes that'll give you more insight."

"I hadn't thought about that," Tor answered, rubbing his eyes. "I'll get on it first thing in the morning."

James smiled, looking at Tor closely. "You've gotten

your feet wet fast in just a matter of days. How do you feel about all this?'' he asked.

There was weariness in Tor's voice. "Ask me in November, when it's all over." He stopped rubbing his eyes and looked at James. "That *is* what you said. November, right?"

"Did I say that?" James answered, feigning ignorance.

"Damn right you did, and I'm holding you to it! This job is going to cut into my social life; in fact, it already has!"

James nodded, striking a match. He held it to his cigar. "Social life. What's that?" he asked.

"As a fellow bachelor, I thought you'd understand my predicament."

James began to laugh. "If you knew how long it's been since I've had a piece of ass you'd think your four weeks was a small sacrifice. Hell, I don't think I'd remember what to do even if I had the chance."

Tor began to feel more at ease. James was known to be a womanizer, not prone to long periods of celibacy, but the campaign was occupying his time and attention to a point where there was little left for any private social activities.

"Next time you're in San Francisco I'll see to it that your horns are clipped," Tor offered.

"Discreetly, of course," James added.

"Of course."

They sat talking for over an hour, polishing off two bottles of wine between them. They found it easy to communicate with one another. Because of Tor's friendship with Billy, they were on common ground and each felt more comfortable with the other as the evening wore on.

James took the news of Louie Cordaro's potential bribery attempt surprisingly lightly, saying that there was nothing that could be done until an actual attempt was made. He warned that to act too early would jeopardize Mikki Parker's already precarious position. For the moment, James appeared more interested in Armando Muniz. It wasn't until he raised the question that Tor realized he hadn't heard the news.

Tor picked up a half-filled glass of wine, walked over to the window and looked across the bay toward the houses that lined the other side, then back at James. "You mean you haven't heard about Muniz?" he asked incredulously.

"What do you mean?"

Tor turned from the window. "They found him murdered in Florida two days ago. I thought you knew. I flew to Miami when I heard about it. I just got back this afternoon."

"Christ!" James shouted. "I can't believe it. Why wasn't I told?"

Tor shrugged. "You've been busy. I guess your staff members assumed you already knew."

James was even more furious than he let on but was careful not to let his emotions show. He would deal with the communications breakdown later. "What did you find out in Miami?" he asked calmly.

Tor looked away, then back again. The memory wasn't pleasant and he had a difficult time bringing himself to an unemotional explanation. "The man's throat was nearly ripped out," he said, his voice cracking a bit.

"I didn't say this was going to be an easy assignment," James answered.

"It's not that," Tor went on. "It's just that I've never been so close to such a brutal crime. Muniz was obviously killed by a professional. I found it a little strange to look at pictures of a man ceremoniously laying on his stomach with his head turned 180 degrees to the sky and his cock stuck halfway down his throat. I mean, whoever did it wanted to leave some sort of message. He even took pictures after he killed the poor bastard."

"*Pictures?*"

Tor nodded. "When they found him, there were two empty packages of film right around the body. Footprints all around, like someone wanted to get different camera angles."

James held his cigar thoughtfully. "My sources told me Muniz always traveled with a gun and bodyguards. How could anybody get to him?"

"There was a gun still on the body. His bodyguards said they left him in his room around midnight and went next door to their own room through an adjoining door. They didn't hear a thing. They think he probably got up to take a walk. They said he rarely slept well and frequently sneaked out for early morning walks."

"What about the bodyguards?"

"They check out. Alibis, polygraph, everything. There's nothing to hold them on. Besides, the local police don't think they had anything to do with it." Tor paused and looked at James. "There's something else," he said.

"What's that?"

"The local police verified that Muniz was in Miami at the time Billy was shot."

James was skeptical. "How do they know that?" he asked.

Tor was matter-of-fact. "The coroner said he was dead at least one day before Billy's death," he explained.

James snuffed his cigar, leaned backward in Billy's chair and closed his eyes for several seconds. He still couldn't believe he had been isolated from such important information for two days. The demise of Armando Muniz solved his earlier concerns about the issues complicating the beginning of Cordaro's trial but now he had even more questions in his mind. He reasoned that the Muniz murder and the threat he'd made against Billy's life were un-related, but he found that difficult to believe, even though he could find no reason why someone would kill Muniz simply because he had threatened Billy's life. It was a question that would be resolved eventually, he thought, but right now he had no time for it.

He opened his eyes. Tor was patiently staring at him. "The trial starts on Wednesday. How well prepared are we?" he asked bluntly.

"I spent all day yesterday in Washington with the D.A. and I think they'll have everything they need." Tor hesitated a moment. "But . . ."

"But what?" he asked.

Tor brought up the bribery subject they had discussed

231

earlier. "This bribery thing bothers me. I mean, how do we know Cordaro hasn't gotten to some of the jurors already?"

"We don't," James responded coolly.

"Then why don't we ask the judge to sequester the jury?"

James shook his head. "We can't do that, not just now anyway. We'd have to tell the judge and the defense attorney that we suspect a possible bribery attempt and why we suspect it. That would give Mikki away because we'd have to tell them how we got our information. Now that she's in there, I don't want to pull her out just yet. We'll just have to sit tight for a while. Without anything concrete to go on as to how Cordaro plans to go about bribing a juror, or even if he's going to go through with it, we can't do much but sit and wait. That's why we have to keep Mikki in Cordaro's back pocket for a while longer. Until she gets something we can sink our teeth into, I want to leave things just as they are."

James thought for a moment, then continued, "We also are going to be faced with the problem of how to protect your young lady when it comes time for her to get out of there. If she's discovered, she could end up the same way as Muniz."

"I've thought about that and so has Mikki," Tor said. "The government can provide protection, can't they?"

"That can be arranged, yes."

There was a look in Tor's eyes that James had seen before. The two men had never discussed Tor's personal involvement with Mikki but James could read it in Tor's face and his voice when he spoke of her. She could be in grave danger and James felt sure Tor knew the severity of her situation. For now, it was a subject both felt should go undiscussed.

"There's one more thing," Tor added. "I received a phone call about a week ago and don't know what to think of it."

James rocked back and forth in Billy's chair, listening intently as Tor told of the anonymous call concerning Don

Peck. The committee's investigative staff was grossly overworked and understaffed. The fact that Don Peck was now tucked away somewhere in Europe made it even more difficult. He shook his head. "I agree," he began. "I'd like to get Peck back to stand trial too, but Cordaro has to be our number one priority. Right now, he stands to hurt this country more than any other person alive. We don't have the time or resources to go after Peck. We have to concentrate on Cordaro. We're too close to let him get away now."

"But what about the call?" Tor persisted.

"It was probably just a crank. I wouldn't worry about it. But . . ." James paused, toying with his cigar.

Tor pressed the issue. "But what?" he asked.

James shook his head again. "I don't know. This whole Cordaro thing bothers me. I want the presidency so badly I can taste it, but what keeps me up at night isn't the uncertainty of the campaign—it's Cordaro. Sometimes I have the feeling that if I don't devote full time to stopping him now, I may never get the chance again, even if I become president. I don't know what it is. My instincts tell me one thing and my campaign manager tells me another. Believe it or not, I seriously considered dropping out of the race just before the convention and letting someone else try and unseat Jordan."

"Just to get Cordaro?"

"Damn right! I rarely go against my instincts. When I have, I've always regretted it."

"And you think you're going to regret your decision to run for the presidency?"

"Like I said, I'm going against my instincts."

Chapter 28

Tor Slagle sat quietly in the back of the courtroom at the start of the Louie Cordaro trial. It was early, only eight-thirty, one-half hour before the scheduled start, and the room was already half-full. He sat motionless, thinking about the brief phone conversation he had had with Mikki Parker only a few minutes earlier. She had told him that she feared for the safety of Senator Gregory because Cordaro was infuriated at Gregory's ineffective support during the committee hearings. What bothered Tor most about the conversation was the fact that Cordaro had told her the night before that Gregory would be "taught a lesson." It was how severe a lesson Gregory would be taught that concerned Tor and he hesitated to speculate on Cordaro's intent.

Nine o'clock drew nearer and the gallery filled rapidly. As people poured into the courtroom, Tor noticed that a majority of the spectators were black, which seemed somewhat peculiar to him as it was not consistent with the makeup of the union rank and file, and especially not consistent with their elected officials. A front row seat that had been kept vacant by two spectators on either side was soon filled by another black, a large man with a gray-white beard. Tor recognized him immediately. It was Joe Avery, the ex-heavyweight champion boxer who had won the hearts and respect of most Americans during his nearly ten-year reign as King of the heavyweights.

When the jury began to file in, Louie Cordaro stood suddenly, turned from his chair, and leaning over the railing into the first row of spectators behind him, embraced Avery. He returned the bear hug while adding an enthusiastic smile and handshake. They lingered in the pose long enough to be sure that each juror saw them. Then, by order of the bailiff, they sat down in unison. Apparently Avery's mission had been accomplished.

It was only then that Tor finally realized what it was about the jury that had bothered him earlier. Interviewed individually during the selection process, it hadn't been obvious. But it was now. Eight of the twelve jurors were black. Cordaro had salted the audience with black supporters to play to the jury, and Joe Avery's public demonstration of brotherly love was simply the icing on the cake. Thomas Barrett Wilson, looking fresh and vitalized, had even done his part by bringing two black assistants, male and female, who sat on either side of him at the counsel's table.

Cordaro hadn't missed a trick. He was playing the cards to get the best draw. That he had clearly won the first hand before the opening comments were made was obvious. Wilson's quick dismissal of some of the prospective jurors during the selection process with only a few questions was now equally obvious to Tor. They had all been white. Cordaro and Wilson were playing the percentages by betting that at least one of the jurors wouldn't vote for a conviction for someone who was obviously so well supported by the black community, one of the jurors' own.

At least the judge, a man named Clinton Athers, was a hard-line veteran of thirty years on the bench. Tor derived some comfort from his presence.

After an uneventful day of opening remarks by both the prosecution and the defense, Tor labored later that evening over the profiles of each juror as well as those of their relatives well into the hours of the next morning. He was looking for anything that might give him some hint as to the potential vulnerability of any of the jurors to any outside influence. He felt it was clear that the black jurors were almost certain to be the target for any bribery attempt, and he concentrated on their backgrounds, ignoring for the time being the four white members of the panel. Employment records, past voting preferences, church affiliations, trade memberships, political party support contributions—all had to be reviewed. He made a list of every name, followed by a series of questions after each one. He decided to assign one committee staff member exclusively to each of the eight black jurors. Their job for the next forty-eight hours would be to research and answer all the questions he had scribbled by their names. From that he hoped to produce a clearer picture as to which juror or jurors would become Cordaro's most logical target. It would be easier to monitor the activities of one or two rather than all eight and even then he wasn't sure he had enough personnel at his disposal to do an effective job. Surveillance of all the jurors was physically beyond even the committee's budget—even eight was out of the question.

While Tor pored over the profiles and scribbled profuse notes along the way, a rented limousine parked less than two miles away from his hotel room provided shelter from the evening chill for yet another meeting.

"Have you found him yet?" Louie Cordaro asked.

"No, sir, but I know he's got an apartment in Geneva."

Cordaro eased forward in his seat and looked out the limousine window at the driver who was stationed fifty yards away, watching for anything that moved. Cordaro was uneasy and shifted uncomfortably in his seat, not enjoying what Sidney Bonnam was telling him.

Bonnam had been assigned by the committee to find Don Peck. Cordaro wanted to know why they still wanted Peck. "Are you still looking into that Freeman Trailer problem?" he asked.

Bonnam shook his head. "All I've been asked to do is to help find Peck, nothing more. It's the first real assignment I've had since I've been on the staff."

There was a rapping on the car window. It was the driver.

"There's a car coming down the road, sir. It looks like the one you're expecting."

Cordaro nodded and the driver resumed his post. A cloud of dust cascaded across the road and dropped lightly over the limousine as the approaching car pulled to a sudden stop. Mikki Parker got out and joined Cordaro and Bonnam in the back of the limousine.

After a brief introduction and an explanation by Cordaro about Bonnam's activities, Mikki listened quietly as Bonnam detailed his committee activities over the past several days. Bonnam's presence was surprising and she hoped her initial response to Cordaro's explanation about his undercover activities had been sufficiently disguised. Cordaro sat across from her, stone-faced, offering no indication as to what he was thinking. From what she was able to gather, Bonnam was offering no new information about the committee.

Initially, Cordaro took the lack of information with an unusual coolness. There was no anger, no frustration, as if he were preoccupied with something else. Then, without warning or explanation, Cordaro began a monologue describing each juror in his upcoming trial with uncanny detail. One by one, he began to select the targets. "The way I see it," he explained, "we go after that lady whose husband is a highway patrolman. She'll be our first target. Her husband's been up for promotion for over a year and he's anxious. A few words to the right people on the patrol and we can help him get his promotion. But he has to cooperate with us. We'll even throw in a little money if necessary."

"He?" Mikki asked. "I thought you were going after the lady juror."

"No. We'll go after her husband. That way we don't get too close to the lady juror. First we talk to the husband who just happens to agree to offer a few favorable opinions to his wife when she comes home at night. But we gotta move fast, do it no later than tomorrow."

Mikki sat back.

At least one of Tor's questions had been answered. Cordaro had not yet gotten to any of the jurors. She peered covertly at a piece of paper in Cordaro's hand on which he had scribbled all the jurors' addresses. If Cordaro was going to ask her to talk to the patrolman, she had to get out of it. Her mind raced to think of an excuse, but a second later, Cordaro unceremoniously appointed her as the courier. The worst had happened.

It was then that Bonnam saved her. "As an attorney," he interjected, "I'd advise against having her contact the patrolman. She's too close to you. If it blows, you'd be in a fix that would make this trial look like small potatoes. Jury tampering doesn't sit well with the public. You won't stand a chance if she gets caught."

Mikki said nothing but breathed easier when Cordaro agreed to Bonnam's assessment and suggested that the assignment go to a local union organizer who could approach the patrolman using an assumed name, thereby removing any potential problems should the patrolman resist the bribery attempt. Bonnam seconded Cordaro's new proposition.

Cordaro was still holding the list of jurors in his hand as he looked at the two people in front of him. "There's more," he cautioned. "We can't take the chance that this patrolman Patterson will cooperate. All I need is a hung jury, or a mistrial. Wilson doesn't think the government will try the case again if that happens. He says it would be too costly. So, we gotta win this one. That means I can't take a chance on just one juror cooperating. I don't want no last minute slipups with some son-of-a-bitch gettin' cold feet." He pointed to the jury list again. "This guy here, Trabert. He lives next door to a friend of one of our boys who says the man's always strapped for cash. We're gonna pass Trabert twenty grand to convince him he should vote our way. Trabert's neighbor thinks he can convince him to take the cash. I want one of you to take it over to our man in the morning. He'll pass the cash on to Trabert's neighbor. The rest will be up to Trabert and the neighbor.''

Cordaro tore off a sheet of paper and scribbled an address. This time, Mikki volunteered, rationalizing to herself that carrying the money would not involve her directly in the crime because the cash would not be passed directly to the juror. She also felt that doing so might solidify her somewhat ambiguous position with Cordaro. Until now, she had acquired little information not already public knowledge. She didn't know why Cordaro had asked her to come to Virginia tonight. She hadn't asked any questions when he had called her at the office earlier. She stopped by the hospital for a brief visit with Shana, then went home to change and await the limousine Cordaro had ordered for her. For the first time, he had asked her to do something other than accompany him on coffee breaks or to offer meaningless excuses over the phone to people he didn't want to talk to. She had to do something to gain his confidence. Perhaps, she reasoned, tonight would be a beginning.

She avoided Cordaro's eyes by staring down at his feet. ''Anything else?'' she asked.

''Yeah. I want you to get a line on some of our black business agents, some local boys we can trust, to make it a point to stop by and have a friendly chat with all the black jurors at their homes. You know, just a folksy chat, brother to brother. That might buy us a little more support. Those niggers usually stick together. You can get a list of our agents back at the office. Ask Trenier for it.''

''Buy?'' she asked.

Cordaro drew a deep breath. ''You know what I mean,'' he answered tersely.

Later that night, she lay awake in bed gazing at her bedroom ceiling. She needed to contact Tor about the evening's events but decided not to risk it so soon. She didn't trust the phone in her apartment. She'd have to wait until morning to call from a more secure phone. She wished she could be with him, share her frustrations and fears. With Shana still in the hospital and her work day so long, she felt empty and wanting. Tor always helped fill the void, but they had agreed to stay apart during the trial despite being less than an hour's drive away from each other. So far, they had managed to keep the agreement, but she found it more difficult as each day passed. For now, phone calls would have to suffice.

When Amos Westland awoke and prepared himself for the second day of the trial, he was about to share a common experience with seven of his co-jurors, all of whom were also black. He, like the others, found a copy of the current week's issue of the *American Afro Journal* tucked tightly into the doorjamb of his front door. The *Journal's* cover was unusual for a totally black political journal; Louie Cordaro's near life-size portrait was spread across the cover.

Westland thumbed through the magazine without closing the door of his twelfth-floor apartment. He frequently read the *Journal* because he believed it deserved its reputation as an unbiased political magazine and supported its frequent championing of black rights. He hesitated when he found the article on Louie Cordaro, remembering something from his juror instruction pamphlet about not being allowed to read about accounts of the trial once it had started. He wasn't sure if he should read the article but found himself already into the third paragraph where it was quoting Louie Cordaro:

James Hawk has spent over eight million dollars in tax-payers' money by having twenty-one grand juries investigate the union as well as myself. He has been using our government and thousands of F.B.I. agents, Treasury and Labor Department agents, local police, and prosecutors to get at me. His desire is not to rid unions of injustice, which I have been steadily doing since being elected president, but to buy himself publicity for the upcoming presidential election. I promise to you, my black friends, that his wishes to make our union subservient to anything he wants will never be fulfilled. He has a personal vendetta against me that has tinted his eyesight. He's blaming me for the

241

past indiscretions of some unscrupulous union leaders that
are no longer with us because I personally got rid of them.
I just want to be left alone so I can go about my job of
building a stronger America through the representation of
the workingman which includes over 200,000 of your
fellow black members.''

Westland finished the article before he finally closed the
door and walked outside to his patio. He watched as two
small boys played basketball in the park below. His mind
wandered away from the article to the innocence of the two
young boys. He thought about the world and its troubles
and wished the two youngsters could grow up in a world
free of the frustrations he had come to know too well. The
trial bothered him. He didn't feel he had the time to
devote to what he felt would be a lengthy ordeal but he
had already resigned himself to his responsibility. He
would try to do his best.

Later that morning, the second day of the trial began
without the fanfare of the first. It also began without the
prosecution's knowledge about the early morning deliveries of the *American Afro Journal*.

For the second consecutive day, Tor was sitting in the
first row of the gallery. At lunchtime, he received a phone
call from Mikki Parker.

"You've got a friend of Louie's working on your staff,''
she began.

Tor listened intently as she filled him in on Sid Bonnam
and Cordaro's proclaimed intention to influence the jury.
Their conversation was brief and perplexing for Tor. He
couldn't let the trial go on without passing the information on to the court, but to do so would have to divulge his
source. If he did, Mikki Parker would have to be identified
and forced prematurely out of her position as a Cordaro
confidante prior to insuring his conviction. If that
happened, Tor wasn't convinced there would be sufficient
evidence to link Cordaro directly with the bribery
attempts. The fact that Mikki had personally carried the
cash to juror Trabert's neighbor was also a problem that

would have to be dealt with. He hurried back to the court-room and still had not resolved his dilemma when Judge Athers unexpectedly recessed the court until the following morning. The judge's face was grim as he requested that Tor meet with him in his chambers. When Tor entered, he found the prosecuting attorney already seated.

The judge was visibly upset as he closed the door behind Tor. "Tor, I've been informed that one of our jurors has been approached with a cash offer intended to influence his voting decision in this trial."

Tor sat down, remaining silent. He wanted to hear more before deciding how much more he should add to what the judge had heard.

Judge Athers wasted no time in bringing Tor up to date.

"I've already dismissed juror Trabert and I want you to work with the F.B.I. in interviewing Trabert. We need to get to the bottom of all this."

Tor had a sudden fear that his efforts to keep Mikki clear of any involvement or publicity would be futile, even though he appeared calm as he spoke. "Would you mind giving me a few more details?" he asked.

It only took the judge a few moments to outline the story as Trabert had related it to him earlier that morning. The judge said nothing of any other bribery attempts.

Tor continued to probe. "I appreciate Trabert's honesty, but how do we know he's the only one that's been approached?" he asked.

"We don't!" the judge blurted, obviously still angered. "That's why I want his neighbor arrested and questioned immediately by the F.B.I. I won't permit the trial to continue if there's any other evidence of tampering."

The prosecuting attorney asked what Tor perceived to be a logical question. "Why not sequester the jury?" he asked.

The judge shook his head. "I can't do that just now. I've already replaced Trabert with one of the alternate jurors and the press is going to ask me why. I think I can control that but if I suddenly sequester the jury I'll have to answer the jury as well as the press and I don't think I want to blow the thing all out of proportion before we really know what was behind the bribery attempt. We're not even sure Trabert was offered the money. We're only going on his word.''

The problem with the patrolman still existed and Tor was compelled to speak out. ''Judge, as chief counsel to the committee, I know I have no jurisdiction, but I'm afraid I must insist that you reconsider the issue of sequestering the jury. There are some other matters affecting this trial that I think should be aired.''

Tor had no choice. He knew that now. The judge and prosecuting attorney sat quietly taking notes as Tor restructured the events that had led to Mikki Parker's delicate assignment and the possibility of yet another juror being influenced.

Judge Athers picked up his scratch pad and looked at his notes over the top of his glasses. Mikki Parker's presence in Louie Cordaro's camp as an agent for the government disturbed him. ''You know her credibility will have to be verified by the F.B.I.,'' the judge said sternly. ''And we cannot use the F.B.I. for surveillance on Cordaro or his attorneys. It's illegal and it would only jeopardize this case if Ms. Parker is ever asked to testify.''

''I understand, Judge,'' Tor answered.

The judge shook his head in wonder. ''Here I am sitting on one case trying to insure a fair trial and watching another crime unfold in my own courtroom. I never thought anything like this could happen.''

The judge told Tor he would hold a closed meeting with Cordaro's attorneys and the prosecution in the morning to determine if Mrs. Patterson had been influenced by her husband.

Tor insisted that the defense not be told about Mikki's precarious position even though both he and the judge knew that if the defense found out about her they would ask for a mistrial. The only reason the judge agreed was his concern for his primary responsibility, which was to try Louie Cordaro fairly for misuse of union funds. To do that he was taking what action he deemed necessary.

The next morning as Tor ate breakfast at a coffee shop near his hotel, he anxiously tapped his foot, thinking about the upcoming day's events and where they might lead. The sky was gray and overcast, the weather dank and humid. He was afraid his day seemed doomed to the same fate.

Shortly thereafter, he was sitting in an empty courtroom watching Patrolman Ed Patterson being ushered into the room for questioning by the judge. The patrolman had been brought in quietly through a back door and through the judge's chambers so he would not be seen by the press and spectators who had not yet been allowed into the courtroom. Two small windows in the doors leading to the courtroom from the public corridor were covered with newspapers held up by masking tape, insuring further privacy.

As always in such cases, both the prosecution and the defense were present for the interrogations. Louie Cordaro sat next to Thomas Barrett Wilson as Judge Athers began questioning Patterson.

Patterson nervously denied that anyone had talked with him about the trial. Then, when it was apparent he wouldn't change his story, Judge Athers motioned to the bailiff. The door to his chambers opened and a small man with thinning blond hair dressed in a flourescent green suit and unshined brown loafers walked in, escorted by a police officer who was holding his arm.

Wilson exchanged glances with Cordaro but said nothing as the man sat down in the first row of the emptied courtroom. The man identified himself as Bob Kane, saying that he was employed as a union organizer. He was the same man Tor told the judge would contact Patterson, according to Mikki Parker.

The judge looked at Patterson who was staring down at statement, Mr. Patterson?'' he asked.
statement, Mr. Patterson?'' he asked.

Patterson looked up slowly, staring at Kane. He pursed his lips and looked cautiously around the room. Then, slowly and deliberately, he began to relate his story. He admitted that he had talked to Kane, who he said had identified himself with another name. He said Kane told him he was anxious to help him get a promotion but denied that the trial was ever mentioned during their conversation or that he had been asked to influence his wife. He said Kane told him that his motivation in helping him centered around his desire to gain Patterson's support for a unionization drive to organize the state's highway patrol. Patterson insisted that there was nothing more to his story and continued his adamant denials about being asked to influence his wife.

Patterson was nervous and frightened. Judge Athers recognized that and excused him, simultaneously calling on Kane to take the witness chair.

Cordaro sat grimly silent, watching. Kane sat down, and for the first time, looked directly at Cordaro.

With his hand over his face, Cordaro flashed a quick five-finger sign that was noticeable only by Kane. Kane had gotten the message, continually taking the Fifth Amendment when questioned by Judge Athers.

After hearing Kane's continual and increasingly monotonous statements about not incriminating himself, Judge Athers dismissed the witnesses and sat back in his chair. He thought about what Tor had said about Cordaro's plans to have all the black jurors contacted by black business agents. Now another union official had refused to testify. There was no question in his mind that there was enough evidence to seriously question the advisability of leaving the jurors susceptible to what he knew —but could not openly admit or prove—was a conspiracy to bribe them.

After excusing himself and spending several minutes in his chambers alone, the judge reentered the courtroom and advised both the defense and prosecution that the jury would be sequestered. Mrs. Patterson was to be dismissed, leaving the jury with no more alternates. There was no argument from either side as Judge Athers explained in detail most of the reasons for his decisions, carefully avoiding the subject of Mikki Parker. The trial would resume tomorrow. If they lost one more juror, a mistrial would be declared.

A visibly angry but inwardly pensive Louie Cordaro filed out of the courtroom behind his attorneys. A moment later he was raging at Wilson who, in turn, was equally as furious at Cordaro for not telling him about Kane or the attempt to approach juror Trabert, a subject Cordaro categorically denied any knowledge about, all the while threatening to fire Wilson for questioning his integrity.

"Shut up, you motherfucker!" Cordaro yelled. "I own you and I don't want any shit out of you! Just keep your fuckin' nose where it belongs . . . defending me! I pay you plenty for that and don't ever forget it."

Wilson was controlled but became even more resentful at Cordaro's humiliating verbal barrage in front of his assistants. He simply turned and walked away.

The anger in Louie Cordaro's face was still plainly visible an hour later when he returned to his office from Virginia where he locked himself in. He began drinking martinis and stayed alone until late in the evening. The fact that Trabert would not accept the money from his neighbor and would tell the judge about the attempted bribery was a chance he had had to take and it had backfired. He had to move on, to make sure that his mistake wouldn't be too costly. If the neighbor wouldn't—or couldn't—tell who had offered him money to pass the twenty thousand dollars to Trabert, then the bribery attempt could never be traced back to the union or to him. He could probably buy off the neighbor with enough cash to more than compensate for any time he might have to spend in jail, if he were convicted. Whatever it took, cash or threats, he would keep the neighbor quiet. As for Kane, Cordaro knew he would be no problem. It was the Cordaro way of doing business and a frequent union strategy for a member to contribute jail time while at full salary in exchange for silence, disdaining any testimony that might prove embarrassing to the union. Sometimes, their salaries would be doubled for time served.

Cordaro kept reflecting.

It bothered him how Kane's identity had been discovered in the first place. Kane had used an assumed name when he approached Patterson. Something was wrong and he was determined to unlock the puzzle, but he would have to start tomorrow. Tonight, even though it was past midnight, he had other things on his mind.

He picked up the phone and called Mikki Parker.

"Hello?" she answered, half asleep.

Cordaro sounded drunk to her, which he was. "Mikki, this is Louie," he slurred.

"Yes."

"I need you here in the office . . . now. Can you come? It's important."

"But, Louie . . ."

"Can you come?"

She paused for a moment, then answered, "I'll be there in thirty minutes."

Chapter 29

THE BARRIER BETWEEN Tom Wilson and Louie Cordaro
grew thicker as the trial grew longer. Wilson sensed that
Cordaro's mental presence was somewhat other than in the
courtroom but he paid no heed to it. He continued to do a
masterful job of questioning witnesse while ignoring
Cordaro's unpredictable moods. Unlike Cordaro, Wilson
didn't let his emotions get in the way of his effectiveness.
The prosecution was intent on proving that his client not
only condoned illegal disbursement of union funds, but
that he was directly involved in personal gain from those
disbursements as well. Wilson's job was to shoot holes in
the prosecution's case.

The jury knew nothing of the bribery attempts or why
two of their fellow jurors had been replaced by alternates.
They listened attentively as Wilson continually hammered
away at the credibility of the government's case and
emphasized what he called a personal crusade by the Hawk
Committee to dump Louie Cordaro from the union
presidency.

Tor was irritated at the prosecution's weak response to
Wilson's more professionally calculated defense. The
district attorney was Ed Watson, a gentleman that Tor
guessed to be around sixty. He was a big man, six feet
two inches in height, heavily built but without fat. His
imposing physical appearance was in direct contrast to the
weak performance he was demonstrating as a prosecutor.
He appeared confused, disorganized to a point where Tor

found it hard to believe he was responsible enough to hold his position as district attorney. In this case, Tor surmised that competency had somehow been superseded by seniority. Watson frequently dismissed witnesses who could have enhanced his case simply by answering only a few well-directed questions, and frequently failed to call witnesses who would further support previous testimony. What had begun as a solid case for the government was dissipating as the trial went on. Wilson's effectiveness was continually highlighted by Watson's contrasting casualness and loosely organized approach.

At the close of the trial's fourth day, Tor had had enough. Closing arguments were scheduled to start after the July fourth recess, and he began coaching Watson over the holiday. He spent nearly twelve hours in what seemed, after it was over, to be a futile attempt to teach an old dog new tricks. Tor was sure seniority and incompetency had finally gotten the best of him and was more troubled than exhausted when he finally returned to his hotel room and went to bed.

The fifth trial morning began, as had the others, with the early arrival of the defense attorneys, followed a half hour later by the defendent, who offered no words to the reporters who tried to question him when he brushed them aside to enter the courtroom.

Ed Watson had not yet arrived.

Tor was tired but nevertheless felt somewhat refreshed from an earlier cold shower and was one of the first spectators to take his seat. He noticed a huge black man two aisles in front of him, wearing a neatly pressed long-sleeved white shirt and a black armband made out of a piece of torn cotton material wrapped around his right arm. The courtroom doors opened behind him and more spectators filed in. Two more men, one white and one black, entered. They also wore white shirts, also with black armbands. They calmly walked down a few rows and took seats on the end of the aisle.

More spectators, an equal sprinkling of men and

women, black and white, walked in similarly attired.

By the time the spectators' gallery had filled, Tor had a fairly complete if confused chronology of events that were about to occur. As a spectator, he was helpless to try and stop it. A moment later, the jury filed in, getting a clear view of the spectators' black armbands.

It was too late. Ed Watson scampered in at the last minute looking disheveled as ever, one minute before the judge entered.

"All rise," the bailiff announced.

Judge Athers entered ceremoniously after the bailiff's introduction and took his seat. He quickly took notice of the sudden uniformity of the gallery but made no mention of it. He fidgeted with some files, delaying while he contemplated his course of action. He started the trial precisely at 10:05 A.M., without comment about the armbands that were on three-quarters of the spectators. When he began to speak, the large black man Tor had noticed earlier suddenly stood up and unrolled a brown paper sign that was nearly the length of his arm span, and huge white letters that read: "Stop Louie's persecution— The People's Friend."

The damage had been done. Judge Athers acted quickly. "Bailiff, arrest that man for contempt of court," he ordered. "The jury is instructed to disregard this incident. Also, I'd like to dismiss the jury for a few minutes until I recall them. All others are to remain in the courtroom."

The jury were quickly escorted from the room.

Still visibly upset, Judge Ather's voice cracked as he spoke. "I want every person in this room wearing a black armband to remove it from sight immediately or leave the courtroom. It's your choice. Stay without the bands or wear them and leave. Whatever you do, do it now!"

Tor slumped in his seat. Despite the judge's actions, the harm was irreparable. What Cordaro couldn't do to influence the jury privately, he had done publicly and cleverly. The theme of the unwilling and persecuted martyr portrayed so vividly by Wilson throughout the trial had now been expertly punctuated.

Closing arguments were heard throughout the remainder of the day without further incident. Following instructions by Judge Athers, the case was finally given to the jury and deliberations began precisely at 3:35 P.M.

Tor sat in the empty courtroom flipping a dime in his hand, mentally equating the chances for Cordaro's conviction to the flip of his coin. Even without the attempted jury influence, Cordaro stood better than an even chance of getting at least one acquittal vote that would stick and cause a hung jury . . . all because of the weak case presented by the prosecution. Cordaro's use of union funds to finance the Sky City project that would eventually be owned equally by himself and Harold Weisbrod should in itself have been enough to convict him. The fact that many of the lots were misrepresented, some underwater and others without roads, was certainly cause for empathy for the bilked owners of the property, but it had nothing to do with Cordaro's misuse of funds, something Wilson had been quick to point out. His argument that there were no laws governing the use of union funds and how the money was invested was also convincing even though in Tor's opinion it had to be obvious to the jurors that Cordaro clearly benefitted personally from the loans to the project.

Two days later, July 7, President John Jordan was nominated at the Republican party convention to run for reelection against James Hawk. The Cordaro jury was still deliberating and Tor had spent all the previous two days briefing two F.B.I. agents on the jury bribery attempts as well as advising them on the position that Mikki Parker occupied within Cordaro's organization. The possibility of a hung jury became increasingly evident as each hour passed. Despite Tor's pessimistic feelings about the trial's outcome, he felt a sense of relief. Cordaro had overstepped his bounds by trying to bribe the jury. It was a federal offense and if this trial failed to put Cordaro behind bars, another jury and another charge surely would.

Word came late that day. Judge Athers summoned the

jurors into the courtroom. Tor hurriedly ran the two blocks from his hotel to the courthouse, arriving as Judge Athers addressed the jurors.

"If any of you thinks a verdict can be reached with further deliberation I want you to raise your hand," the judge asked politely.

One juror raised his hand. The judge continued. "Any juror who thinks the jury is hopelessly deadlocked, raise your hand." Tor watched dejectedly as the remaining eleven jurors raised their hands. A hung jury. A victory for Cordaro.

"There comes a time," Judge Athers began, slowly raising his hands in resignation, "when members of a jury cannot agree, and if they cannot agree, then that is it."

Tor felt a sick feeling in his stomach as Cordaro and his followers relaxed from the tension that had gripped them only seconds earlier. Cordaro turned, smiled defiantly at the prosecution's table, then turned back to face Judge Athers.

Suddenly, the stirrings ceased as Judge Athers turned from the jury and stared menacingly at Cordaro whose grin promptly disappeared. Wilson was watching the proceedings closely. He knew what was about to come.

The judge looked at his notes then back at Cordaro. "I have a statement to make which I will read for the record and it will be made a part of these proceedings. While I am reading this statement, I ask that no one leave or enter the courtroom and that no one stand up or get out of their seats. Bailiff, you are to enforce my request."

A hush engulfed the small courtroom with deadening silence. Only the bailiff's ruffling of some papers could be heard. All eyes centered on the judge.

With a furrowed brow, he began to read the statement he had completed the day before. "The trial of this case having been concluded, I feel that it is my duty to make a statement as to the unfortunate events that have occurred. First, I wish to make it very clear that I have no reason to question the integrity or honesty of any member or alternate member of this jury. The people who rendered this service are entitled to the gratitude of the court and the public they served. Early on, it became necessary to have the members of this jury sequestered and the remarks that I am about to make are not intended to reflect in any way upon these splendid people.

"It has been apparent from the outset that improper contacts and overt coercion have been made toward certain members of this jury. In one instance, the court was required to excuse a juror who had been approached with bribe money to vote for acquittal. That juror commendably made this gesture known immediately. In another instance, a session was held in private without the jury present in the presence of the defendant, his attorney, the prosecuting attorney, the official court reporter, Mr. Slagle of the Hawk Committee, myself, and witnesses that were called to testify. At that session, evidence was presented to this court indicating strongly that an illegal and improper attempt was being made by close labor associates of the defendant to contact and influence certain members of the jury."

The judge paused and adjusted his glasses. The jury members sat still, stunned by the sudden turn of events. He turned the page and continued. "In the public interest and to protect the court as an institution of government, I have decided that certain steps must be taken by the court at this time. First, I have signed orders to convene another grand jury as soon as possible to investigate fully and completely all the incidents surrounding this trial that would indicate illegal attempts to influence jurors by any person or persons and to return indictments where probable cause exists. I have also instructed chief counsel Tor Slagle of the Hawk Committee to oversee investigative actions by the United States attorney for this district which will be assembling all existing evidence on this matter for the grand jury when it convenes."

Judge Athers paused again, poured a glass of water from the pitcher behind his chair, took a small sip, and exchanged another penetrating glare with Cordaro. He sustained his attack. "I am now directing that the entire record of the closed door hearings that were held during this trial remain sealed, subject to a grand jury investigation of these matters. Should the grand jury see fit to pursue these charges further, the record will become public at any subsequent trial.''

Another pause, another stare by Judge Athers at Cordaro. Without reading from his prepared text, he delivered his final words. ''The right of the defendant in a criminal court to be tried by a jury of his peers is one of the most sacred of our constitutional guarantees. However, the system of trial by jury becomes nothing more than a mockery if unscrupulous persons are allowed to subvert it by improper and unlawful means. I do not intend that such shameful acts to corrupt our jury system shall go unnoticed by this court. I am now declaring this a mistrial. The jury is excused and court is adjourned.''

It was over. Thomas Barrett Wilson exited briskly, sharing no further words with his client. He brushed aside waiting media reporters and hurried to his limousine. He had done his job. He had achieved his objective, but his reputation had been tarnished by the jury tampering investigation and he was manifestly furious. His ubiquitous smile had disappeared, his composure conspicuously absent.

Tor also had no comment for the media as he exited through a rear door. Two hours later, he boarded a plane and headed for San Francisco.

That night, exhausted from the time change and the long flight, he lay quietly in bed thinking of the irony of the trial. Because of the ineffectual prosecution, Louie Cordaro had stood a good chance of getting a hung jury even without his extracurricular activities. Now there was a strong possibility that he would be convicted of a much more serious felony.

Still unable to sleep, Tor sipped a glass of wine in the darkened bedroom, watching the eleven o'clock evening news. Tucked between an excerpt of President Jordan's acceptance speech and a local news story about two men who had attempted to scale the Trans-America Building was an interview with Louie Cordaro that had been taped a few hours after the trial's end.

Cordaro attacked Judge Athers as "prejudiced and one of the most vicious judges who ever handled a criminal case for the Department of Justice."

Tor sat up and watched intently as Cordaro continued to degrade Judge Athers. "It's a disgrace that he would make a statement that I tampered with this jury. I have done absolutely nothing to warrant such an attack. Let them prove it in court."

Tor became lost in thought as he sat and watched the two daredevil climbers try to scale the pyramid-shaped Trans-America Building. Finally, he shut off the television, lay back and stared at the ceiling. He was determined to carry on Billy's fight despite his painful realization that the corruption Cordaro had spread throughout the union might not stop even if he were convicted. The cancer that was spreading throughout the country without a ripple of concern from the general public weighed on his mind. Someday, he knew society would eventually have to pay the price for its apathy.

Chapter 30

MIKKI PARKER DIDN'T know how much longer she would be able to stand it.

She had been almost ill for the last few days. The recurring memory of Louie Cordaro's half-naked body about to come down on her caused a physical sickness matched in intensity only by the abhorrence she carried inside. The same man she used to affectionately call her uncle had lured her to his office and raped her in a venomous attack that was now haunting every minute of her life. For three days, she had been a virtual prisoner in her own home. Today, it seemed, would be no different.

The shades, as they had been since she returned that dreadful night, were drawn. The house was quiet. Her first waking thought was of the attack, and terror swept through her. She looked at the clock; it was 9:00 A.M. Her eyes focused on the phone that lay on the floor, unplugged for the past two days ever since Louie Cordaro had called to apologize. She didn't know why she hadn't told anyone of the attack. Shame, fear, she couldn't be sure.

She could feel an energy today that had been absent before, an energy that grew as each hour passed. Her depression began to turn into anger and determination, a determination that made her want to know more about Louie Cordaro. Revenge wasn't part of it, she felt that. There was something more she needed to know about this man, something beyond his physical and emotional being. She wasn't sure why she had decided to stay on and accept his apology and excuse that it was the liquor that had made him violate her that night. For whatever reason, none of that was important now. She seemed to possess a strange courage that was forcing her to go on, to see it through, to defy her natural instincts.

She plugged the phone back into the jack and called Louie Cordaro. She was going back to work.

"Mikki," Shana cried.

Mikki's face glowed with anticipation as she hurried down the polished hospital hallway toward her sister who was standing unaided in the doorway of the therapy room. Tears welled in her eyes as she clutched Shana tightly and Shana's tiny arms hugged back as strongly as they could.

It had been nearly three months since Shana's accident and this was the big day. For the first time since then, Shana would be spending the night outside a hospital. Fitted with new leg braces, she stood unaided and watched as Mikki smiled with silent approval and jubilation over Shana's triumph. Shana was going home. Better, she was *walking* home.

Mikki could no longer control her tears as she helped Shana take her first steps slowly down the hall toward the elevator. The child possessed the same confidence, the same radiant blond hair and delicate blue eyes as their mother. Shana's long lashes were blinking, fighting back her own tears of joy. Like their mother, she was fighting adversity without flinching and never once had she asked for sympathy.

Mikki reflected on the past few weeks. So many nights at the hospital, holding back her own tears, holding Shana in her arms while trying to ease her pain as she cuddled closely at her side. Shana's courage had drawn them together into a powerful and unbreakable bond of love, of which Mikki had never thought herself capable. They were so far apart in age that until now she had never really known her little sister and she was ashamed that it had taken such a tragedy to bring them together.

They were met at the elevator by an elderly, heavyset

nurse pushing an empty wheelchair. Mikki pressed her hand on Shana's shoulder slightly, silently indicating that she would sit down in the chair. Shana sat herself down proudly, bringing her ankles neatly together and smiling self-consciously as her leg braces made a loud metallic clank. She folded her hands together and lay her head back in order to look up at her sister who pushed her inside the elevator.

"Are we going back to California now?" she asked excitedly.

Mikki shook her head. "No, not now, honey. We're going to our new home," she answered.

"Oh . . ." Shana replied, her soft voice trailing off.

The steady hum of the elevator that carried them down from the seventh floor to the lobby whirred noisily and Mikki remained silent. She knew what Shana wanted, what she needed. It was something she had never been able to give her sister and she was still unable to provide. Shana needed her love on a full-time basis. Mikki hadn't told her about her new job and she agonized for over an hour before bringing herself to do it. Shana took it much as Mikki had expected, with no tears, no real emotion, only an understanding nod and a large hug and kiss.

"Will it be much longer?" Shana asked.

"I can't say for sure, honey. I hope not."

"Who's going to take care of me when you're away?" she asked, a worried look creeping into her face.

"There's a lady, a hired lady. I used to call them nannies. She'll be living with us most of the time. She's a nurse too. She'll take care of you when I'm away."

"Like Mommy used to?"

"Kind of."

"I'd rather have Merlin. He'd take care of me. He'd take me to the woods and let me be a bird or a butterfly or whatever I wanted."

"Now you know we can't arrange that."

"I know, but it's nice to dream."

"Don't ever stop dreaming, sweetie. Without our hopes and dreams we'd only be living day-to-day with nothing to

259

look foward to.''

"Do you like her?" Shana asked.

"Who?"

"The lady that's going to take care of me?"

"She's a nice lady, yes."

"Will she be my mommy?"

Mikki shook her head and held her tightly, fighting back her tears. There was no time for them now.

Later that day, an image remained in Mikki's mind as she rode in the back of the limousine with Louie Cordaro and Borg Trenier—the sight of Shana clutching her new teddy bear in one arm while holding the hand of her nanny as the two of them watched her go down the front steps toward the car. An acidlike hatred began to eat away at her gut for what she was doing. It had to stop. It had to stop soon.

The limousine pulled up in front of an abandoned and dilapidated warehouse on the fringe of Washington, D.C. and waited a moment. Then a large wooden door slid upwards on metal rollers and the car pulled inside. The door closed quickly behind them and a man approached from a side warehouse office, entering the car through the rear door. It was Sidney Bonnam.

Cordaro had the driver step outside, ostensibly to keep watch but in reality to get him out of earshot of the conversation.

The smell of Cordaro's strong cologne and Trenier's cigar filled the stagnant air. Mikki sat uncomfortably between the two men as Bonnam faced all three of them from the jump seat.

"The whole thing looks pretty serious," Bonnam began. "The F.B.I. is interviewing every juror and alternate from your trial. It looks like they're going to concentrate heavily on cracking Kane and Trabert's neighbor to find out who approached them."

"I still can't figure out how the fuck they found out about Kane!" Cordaro snapped. "He didn't even use his real name. Patterson couldn't have led them back to Kane if he'd wanted to."

"That's got me stumped too, unless . . ." Bonnam hesitated.

"Unless?" Cordaro asked.

Mikki struggled to remain calm, a sick feeling surfacing in her stomach. Keeping her head down, she tried desperately to hide her nervousness.

"Unless Kane or Patterson for some unknown reason turned themselves in. Then, either one of them could have done it," Bonnam continued, explaining his theory.

Mikki quietly exhaled, feigning a yawn.

Trenier interrupted. "Why would either one of them do that?" he asked.

"Who knows! How else could anybody have known about Kane? Right now, it just doesn't make any sense at all."

Cordaro didn't like what he was hearing. He didn't believe either man could have been motivated to turn himself in. He reasoned with himself that he might have misread Patterson, who could have tipped the authorities after Kane's first visit and Kane could have been followed after their second conversation on the following day. It was possible, but Cordaro thought it highly unlikely. Patterson was hungry for a promotion. Cordaro was sure he wouldn't have turned himself in. And Kane had been in the union long enough to know what happens to troublemakers. That was sufficient reason for any man to keep quiet.

"What about Trabert's neighbor?" Cordaro asked. "Is he talking?"

Bonnam shook his head. "Nothing yet, but I think it's only a matter of time. He's scared. But that's a tougher line to follow back to you. Even if he tells who gave him the money to offer to Trabert, it probably won't lead back to you. There are too many people in between. But it would be an arrow."

"Arrow?" Cordaro snapped, his eyes questioning.

Bonnam chose to look at Trenier when he spoke, ignoring Cordaro's glare. "Yeah," he answered in a low voice. "The general direction of the investigation is to develop a series of incidents that would build a believable case of intent to influence a jury. If the black jurors all tell about their little chats with the union business agents or if Patterson or Kane break and tell of their meetings, all those things would lead directly back to the union in one way or another. Combine that with the delivery of the *American Afro Journal* to all the black jurors during the trial and you begin to get a whole lot of arrows going the same direction, which would build up a pretty convincing case for the prosecution.''

The smell of Cordaro's cologne was beginning to be overcome by the foul scent of Trenier's equally offensive cigar. The combination of the two began to make Bonnam nauseous. He stared at Cordaro, then Trenier, both of whom seemed locked in thought.

Cordaro broke the silence. ''Where's Kane now?'' he asked.

''Holed up in his house. He hasn't been charged with anything yet, but the F.B.I. told him not to leave town.''

''And the neighbor?'' Cordaro asked, glaring at Bonnam. ''Where is he?''

''Released on bail two days ago. He'll be arraigned in a few days, charged with passing money to Trabert. Trabert's testimony will insure his conviction for jury tampering. He could be a problem. If he talks and tells where he got the money, the trial will lead back to the union and that could evolve into one big arrow even though you didn't pass the money personally.''

''And Patterson's scared shitless, I suppose!'' Cordaro said, rolling down the window, much to Bonnams' relief.

''You got it,'' Bonnam answered, inhaling the fresh air.

Trenier interrupted again. ''Can the other black jurors hurt us? I mean, was there any money passed to them?''

Not knowing the answer, Bonnam could only look to Cordaro for a response.

An affirmative nod told the story.

''I feel like I may be polishing brass on a sinking ship,'' Bonnam offered in a fleeting moment of uncharacteristic levity.

Cordaro scowled, then leaned his head back on the seat

and stared up and out the rear window as he spoke. "We gotta get to 'em. All of 'em. Patterson, Kane, the neighbor, the whole fuckin' bunch. Give 'em enough money to keep 'em all quiet. We can't take chances on anyone talking. Scare 'em if we have to, just keep 'em quiet."

Trenier exhaled a large puff of smoke. "Who can we trust to do that?"

Slowly lifting his head, Cordaro jabbed his index finger into Bonnam's chest. "You're closest. They won't know who you are. I want you to do it. I can't take a chance having any of my people try it. Just tell me how much money you need and you'll have it whenever you need it."

Bonnam looked at Trenier, who nodded approval of Cordaro's suggestion. Bonnam meekly agreed even though he wanted no part of it. He decided to wait and talk to Trenier privately before actually refusing the order.

"One more thing," Cordaro said, as Bonnam opened the door. "What about Peck?"

"Now that the Sky City trial is over, my guess is they'll concentrate on him again. But it's only a guess."

"Find out!" Cordaro yelled, motioning for the driver to return. "And another thing. I want to know exactly where his apartment is in Geneva."

Chapter 31

BORG TRENIER ALLOWED a faint smile to cross his face. He sat comfortably at his desk studying a neatly arranged assortment of cancelled checks in front of him which were made out to two different people that until now he had never heard of. There were several different checks in varying amounts, from $20,000 to as high as $50,000. He quickly calculated the total, which exceeded two million dollars. Louie Cordaro's signature was easily recognizable on some, while Don Peck's more scribbled mark adorned the others. The account number penciled in on the back of the checks indicated that they were drawn against a special union advertising account set aside for public relations. Trenier knew a new billboard advertising program had been delayed and he knew of no other goodwill advertising programs that would require dollar expenditures anywhere near two million dollars, so he had had the bank deposit records checked where the checks were actually cashed. Eight months of painstaking investigation piqued by his own insatiable curiosity was nearly over.

His smile grew wider as he toyed with the checks and thought of the bank teller he had personally bribed to provide him with the bank's records. Now he knew why Cordaro was so concerned about the committee and its interest in Don Peck. Checks drawn against the account where the checks were deposited were all made payable to a stock brokerage firm to purchase stock in the Freeman Trailer Company and were assigned by a M.A. Hansen and

A.R. Phelps, who had become major stockholders in the Freeman Trailer Company by using the funds from the union checks authorized and signed by Cordaro and Peck to purchase Freeman Trailer stock. Together, they held the majority of the outstanding Freeman stock. It was now obvious that it was the majority stockholders of Freeman Trailer, Phelps and Hansen, who were Cordaro's concern. The committee's concern over Don Peck's $200,000 loan from the Freeman Trailer Company was sure to come up again if Peck returned to the United States for questioning and Trenier was convinced that if that happened, it would lead to Cordaro's destruction. It was so obvious he laughed out loud for not having recognized the situation earlier.

An hour later Trenier sat in Louie Cordaro's office smiling contentedly to himself as he watched Cordaro, who was on a telephone conference call with union leaders who had become uneasy over his latest brush with the law. The day before, the same people had called Trenier, demanding Cordaro's voluntary resignation. But instead of confronting Cordaro with the same demands, the union leaders were simply asking for a personal reassurance that Cordaro had done nothing wrong. Cordaro promptly provided them with their encouragement, then slammed the phone down.

He swiveled around to face Trenier. "Now, where were we?" he asked.

A cloud of cigar smoke surrounded Trenier's puffy cheeks. "You were talking about the anti-Hawk campaign," he answered.

"Oh, yeah. I authorized a no-interest half-million dollar building expansion loan to the *New Hampshire Globe*. Marshall Tucker said that if he got the loan he'd see what he could do to get his *Globe* editorials reprinted by some of his publishing buddies across the country. He said he'd use the money the *Globe* would normally have to pay in interest to get me some favorable attention."

Trenier stared at Cordaro's strained eyes. While he appeared to the general public to be unchanged by the events of the past few weeks, there were signs of stress perceptible only to those who saw him daily. His temper, forever short, had grown even sharper and he appeared tired from lack of sleep. Yet Cordaro's mind seemed to be thriving on the stress and grew even more acute and calculating.

There was an uneasy silence in the room as Cordaro rose from the heavy leather chair, walked over to the bar and fixed himself a drink, something Trenier had never seen him do during office hours. Louie usually drank only occasionally and never in his office. The bar had always been used only when entertaining guests and always only at Cordaro's suggestion, which was seldom.

Cordaro turned away from the bar slowly, looked down at his glass of Scotch and then back to Trenier, silently pointing to his glass, gesturing for Trenier to join him. Trenier needed no further invitation as he opened a bottle of Cabernet Sauvignon.

Allowing the wine to breath, Trenier swirled it about the glass, raising it to his nose several times to sniff its bouquet. Cordaro continued to stand, staring out the window, saying nothing.

Then Cordaro mechanically turned, walked back to his desk, sat down and began to write. "We got to make plans," he said.

"Plans?"

"Yeah, plans. If something should happen and I go to the slammer, we gotta be prepared."

Trenier sipped his wine and listened.

"I want to rewrite our constitution at the annual convention, to provide for the establishment of a new office. We'll call it general vice-president. He would run the union in the event I go to prison." Cordaro stopped writing and looked up. "I don't need to tell you who I want that to be," he announced.

Trenier nodded, letting Cordaro ramble on. "While I plan to nominate you as general vice-president, I would retain my own title as president even if I go to prison. Any major decisions on union matters would still be made by me even though it would appear to the public and other union officials that you're the chief administrator."

Trenier was deflated. The union's convention was only weeks away and he had hoped that it would pass without any such reorganizational efforts. Under the present constitution, he would automatically succeed Cordaro as president if anything should happen to him before his term expired. By creating the office of general vice-president, his powers would still be governed by Cordaro even if he were in prison. "So why bother to create a new office?" he asked sarcastically.

"The delegates will have to approve any change to the constitution. If I tell them I'm elevating your position, they'll go along with it. They all like you and that'll help get the amendment through without any hitches. They'll approve your promotion."

"Hitches?"

"Yeah. I don't plan to tell them about the part where I still run the show if I go to prison."

"How are you going to get around that?"

"We'll spring the vote as a last minute announcement. We'll pass out the written amendment proposal to a few key people and only give them a few minutes to review it and then ask for a voice vote. On the surface, it'll look like what we're tellin' 'em it is. But it'll be written in a manner vague enough that it can be interpreted to continue my powers if I go to prison."

Trenier was still silent, although his mind was considering his options. Within moments, he had been ushered from Cordaro's office. Cordaro was going somewhere, on his way outside with a pocket full of change.

Cordaro hopped a Pennsylvania Avenue bus and rode about a mile before spotting what he considered to be a suitable public phone. The phone rang twice. Peter Denning answered. Cordaro came right to the point. "I got some things I want you to arrange."

Denning responded without any formal pleasantries. "I'm listening."

"Where's Bartie Bonano?" Cordaro asked.

"I don't know, but I can find him quick enough."

"I got problems with those jurors. I want one of 'em taught a lesson. It might help quiet down some of the others if we show some muscle. Get Bonano on it."

"How much convincing are you talking about?"

"As much as it takes! It may take a lot. Make sure Bartie knows that."

"Anyone in particular?"

"No. Any one of those nigger assholes will do. There's something else, too."

"Something else?"

"Yeah. That fucker Gregory needs to be taught a lesson."

There was a long pause before Denning could bring himself to speak. "Wait a minute, Louie, that's a United States senator you're talking about. You can't go around bumping off people like that!"

"I'm not talking about bumping anybody off! Just rough him up a little. He owes me plenty ahd he's not comin' across. I don't want anybody goin' around thinkin' they can let me down when I ask 'em to return a favor. Gregory owes me plenty of favors and as far as I'm concerned he's never paid a fuckin' one of 'em back. It's time we settle the score."

Denning heaved a deep sigh.

"Whatever you say, Louie," he answered.

"How's the money coming?" Cordaro asked.

Denning had expected the question.

"It's been arranged. Just tell me when and where you want it."

Cordaro hung up the phone without another word and walked over to the bus stop. Then he changed his mind, deciding instead to walk back to his office. He had a renewed sense of power as he reflected on the million dollars Denning had arranged. Not many men in the world could accomplish such a feat with such short notice. He felt good. He walked down Pennsylvania Avenue with his head high.

Chapter 32

TOR GAVE HIMSELF a moment's pause as he sat in James Hawk's senate office. With every passing minute, his life was becoming more complicated. For the first time since he could remember, events were beginning to control him rather than vice versa, and he didn't like it. There was a thin line between what was becoming reality and what he thought reality should be and he was as determined as the man sitting across the table from him to change the feeling in his gut.

James sat quietly, outwardly expressing nothing. But inwardly his mind was methodically sorting out what Tor had just told him. Mikki Parker's discovery of Sidney Bonnam as a union spy, Louie Cordaro's continuing effort to bribe the original jurors by assigning Bonnam to visit them with money in hand, and the failure to convict Cordaro were all serious concerns. Even the union's campaign to discredit him by trying to show him to be ruthless and vindictive appeared to be working. His once enormous lead over the president had slipped nearly five points to 48 percent. Jordan's 43 percent and the 9 percent undecided made it the first time since Hawk had announced his candidacy that the undecided element was shown to be a factor that could possibly swing the election in the president's favor. The race was expected to become tighter, but the union's lobby against him was making it closer than anyone had expected.

"Bonnam's position on the investigative staff of the

committee has to be terminated immediately,'' James said. "We won't press charges or indicate why he's being released. I don't think we have to, at least for now, and we have to protect Mikki. Meanwhile, we'll let her stay put.''

"Is it really smart to leave her exposed?'' Tor asked.

"The committee stands a far better chance of convicting Cordaro if we wait for him to make a mistake. The potential information Mikki could provide is still worth the risk.''

Tor's voice was hard. "A risk that involves putting her life on the line,'' he cautioned.

James continued as if he hadn't heard Tor's comment. "You can cover Bonnam's release by releasing two other investigators as part of an announced decrease in the workload. Then use the two released investigators as undercover agents to keep an eye on Bonnam. If Bonnam goes after the other jurors, we can backtrack and nail him and Cordaro on tampering charges.''

"What if he's already gotten to them?''

"That's something Mikki will have to find out. If he has, we're screwed. There won't be any way we can document what went on between Bonnam and the jurors unless somebody talks. If that's the case, then Mikki becomes our key witness.''

James suddenly changed the subject. "What about the diary?'' he asked.

To Tor, James seemed more preoccupied with the still-missing diary kept by his brother than the current events. He was sure there was something in the diary that James either knew about or suspected but, for some reason, wasn't willing to share. The course of their conversation always seemed to come back to the diary.

Not until Tor described a second anonymous phone call he had received the day before did James temporarily drop the subject of the diary.

"You mean that all he said was 'Get Peck' again?'' James asked.

"Yes, but he was very insistent. He kept repeating it over and over this time.''

"Was it the same person who called the first time?"

"I'm sure of it."

James took a deep breath, his mind once again preoccupied, this time with the caller. "Do you think this is legitimate?" he asked.

"Who knows?" Tor answered. "But somebody's going to a lot of trouble to make us believe he is."

James raised his head and looked at the clock over Tor's shoulder. "It's getting late. You better get on out to the airport."

Tor was startled. "Where am I going?"

There was a moment's pause that served as a cushion for James's response. "To Switzerland," he said matter-of-factly.

Chapter 33

LOUIE CORDARO LOOKED out the window after hearing the news about Sidney Bonnam's dismissal from the Hawk Committee. Borg Trenier stood waiting for the explosion which never came.

Finally, Cordaro turned to face him. "Where's Bonnam now?" he asked.

"In my office."

"What did he say the committee is going to do about Peck?"

Trenier looked casually at his cigar. "He says they're going to try and extradite him."

Cordaro's world was in danger of coming apart at the seams and Peck looked to be the weakest link in his defense. Even with all his other problems, Peck was the only man who he felt could eventually bring about his removal from the throne he so cherished. "We got to get to Peck before the committee does," he said.

Trenier listened closely as Cordaro began to explain. He briefly related the story about how he and Peck actually owned the Freeman Trailer Company and how it would look bad if it came out that he owned one of the nation's largest trucking companies. Cordaro was careful to leave out the fact that the latest Freeman Trailer union contract, which he had signed only one month earlier as union president, called for slightly less pay and benefits than competitive union contracts negotiated with other trucking companies.

Trenier took the cigar out of his mouth and let his breath out slowly. He could make a guess at what Cordaro's plans were but decided to ask point-blank. Cordaro's frankness shocked him.

"I'm going to have Peck hit. I want you to handle it," Cordaro responded coolly.

At that precise moment Trenier understood why Cordaro had confessed his dealings with Peck. If he refused to follow orders, he wouldn't last an hour before Cordaro fired him and his fate wouldn't be any brighter than Peck's. Cordaro needed an ally. By telling him why Peck needed to be destroyed and enlisting him as the intermediary for letting the contract on Peck's life, it would cement a bond between the two. Neither would be able to turn on the other without destroying himself. Now, even if Cordaro went to prison, he would do so knowing that his position as union president would be safeguarded.

Cordaro leaned on the desk with both arms stiffly outstretched, awaiting Trenier's answer.

Trenier smiled weakly. The tension was like an immense knot in the pit of his stomach. Finally, "How do you want it handled?" he asked.

If what Borg Trenier felt as he walked back to his office could have been translated into actions, he would have cried. In retrospect, he knew that he should have found a way to provide the committee with the information he had discovered several months earlier about the Freeman Trailer Company. Now Cordaro had him where he wanted him.

By the time he reached his office he had already begun to devise an alternate plan, something he planned to discuss with Sidney Bonnam over dinner.

That night, without relating to Bonnam his earlier discussion with Cordaro, Trenier mapped out a plan that he hoped would put him back on the path to the peak of the union hierarchy.

"I want you to testify against Cordaro for the

committee," Trenier announced calmly, acting as if there were nothing unusual about his request.

Bonnam didn't see it in the same light. "You're out of your fucking mind!" he answered incredulously.

Trenier continued calmly, "Look, it's easy. The fact that Cordaro hired you to spy on the committee will be enough to get him thrown into prison for years."

Bonnam was unconvinced. He knew enough about Louie Cordaro to know better. But he was out of a job with only the prospect of picking up his law practice, which was not very exciting to him and even less lucrative. With over three thousand attorneys in the District's surrounding area, the likelihood of getting his bills paid in a hurry were dim. He decided to play along, to test the water. "Suppose I do testify," he asked. "What's in it for me?"

Trenier swallowed the last drop of wine in his glass. "A half-million dollars," he said.

Bonnam sat quietly in a state of shock. The amount of money being offered was staggering.

"Money is no problem," Trenier continued. "I've been approached by several of the board members asking for my support in a move to get rid of Cordaro. They know it won't be easy, and frankly, they're not sure how to do it. Most of them don't have the guts to do it themselves anyway. If I ask for the money, I'll get it. You can count on it."

"Up front?" Bonnam asked, still not convinced Trenier could pull it off.

"Half up front. The rest after Cordaro is locked up."

Bonnam gave him a penetrating look. "I don't know. It's not exactly a safe thing to do. I mean, Cordaro's got a lot of friends out there."

Trenier looked at Bonnam with a smile of serious amusement. "It's not exactly safe if you don't."

"What do you mean?"

"Do you think Cordaro doesn't know what you could do to him if you testified? You're not on the committee's staff any longer and as soon as you finish your round of persuasive talks with the rest of the jurors you'll be of no use to him. In fact, if you think about it, you'd be better off dead as far as Cordaro is concerned.''

That harsh reality was something Bonnam had not thought about. He became uneasy, suddenly losing his appetite. ''What about the government?'' he asked. ''There's no guarantee they'll give me immunity from prosecutive if I testify.''

''Believe me, you can count on it. They've been after Cordaro for a long time. That can be arranged.''

Their discussion continued until after midnight. Bonnam was no match for Trenier, who continually managed to beat down his every objection. Finally, he reluctantly agreed. They decided he should contact Tor Slagle. If the government could provide him with protection and a new identity plus immunity after testifying, Bonnam said he would consider the offer. ''I'd like to discuss this with my wife,'' he said at the end of the evening. ''I'll have to get back to you.''

Trenier watched Bonnam walk slowly out of the restaurant. He picked up a pen and signed the check with the flair of a millionaire. He was enjoying himself for the first time in years.

Chapter 34

MARSHALL TUCKER LIMPED adroitly into Louie Cordaro's office. He sat down in front of his desk, placed his cane between his legs and rested his chin casually on his hands that were folded around the top of the case. "You called, sir?" he asked facetiously.

Not reading the humor in Tucker's voice, Louie Cordaro responded sharply, "Yeah. I've been meaning to talk to ya about the deal we discussed some time ago."

"I thought that's why. Do you have the money?"

"It's all set, but something's been buggin' me about it. I mean, how do I know *he* kept his part of the bargain?"

Tucker knew Cordaro wanted to avoid using the president's name, even though his office was checked regularly for eavesdropping devices. "You don't," he responded, "but then again, you don't know he didn't either, do you?"

"But we never finalized anything. There was no formal agreement."

"Come now, Louie. A week after the offer was made, your little problem was eliminated. Now how else would you read that?"

Cordaro didn't accept Tucker's answer, shaking his head from side to side. He was still unsure.

Tucker continued. "Look, this man has a history of stepping on people at the slightest hint that it would help further his career. It only took a slight hint for him to set the wheels in motion. He wants the support of your union.

His part of the deal has been completed, albeit somewhat distastefully to me personally.''

Cordaro took a handkerchief from his pocket and blew his nose. ''What if I don't pay up? I mean, what would you do? The job's already been done.''

''You're kidding yourself and you know it,'' Tucker said, shifting his weight to one side of the chair to relieve the pain in his hip.

''Why?''

''The man's more powerful than you'll ever be and don't you forget it,'' Tucker responded sharply, his voice beginning to rise.

Cordaro sat looking at him, his piercing eyes shifting from side to side.

''Look,'' Tucker said, ''I'm in this with you, even if by chance. You don't pay that money and he'll have you and me behind bars faster than you ever thought possible. Even if you threaten to tell anyone about his part in the deal, he'll just claim it was all a part of the CIA surveillance plan and that you're the one who arranged to have Hawk put away.''

The two men sat silently looking into each other's eyes, each waiting for the other to acquiesce to his point of view. Neither did for the next twenty minutes as their conversation became even more heated.

Then Cordaro took the lead. He decided he had no other choice. 'All right,'' he said. ''How do we pass the money?''

Chapter 35

TOR PARKED THE car in front of her hotel. He sat there a moment not knowing what to expect, since he had only known the lady a few hours. The flight from Washington to Geneva was long and tedious and she had helped him pass the time playing backgammon in between her flight attendant duties. He reached across to open the door for her.

"Trying to get rid of me early?" she asked.

"Trying to be polite. I thought you had a four A.M. wake-up for the return leg of your flight."

"I do, but that doesn't mean I have to sleep from now til then. I've worked on short hours before. I would be delighted to do it again, particularly tonight."

"What did you have in mind?" Tor asked, teasing.

"Care to come in for a nightcap at the bar?" she asked.

He switched off the motor.

The nightcap in the lobby bar was short, the elevator ride to her room even shorter. She was beautiful, with long legs, straight brown hair that fell to her waist, and a face that reminded him of one he had seen only the day before on the cover of *Vogue* magazine. His hands lightly touched her back as they rode the elevator, both silent, both tense with anticipation. The elevator door opened and they walked across the hall to Room 902, entered, and closed the door behind them. A lamp glowed in the far corner of the room, providing no more light than that of a large candle. She was even more beautiful than the girl he had admired in the magazine.

He held her close, so close that her breasts were hard against his chest as he kissed her. His arms went around her and his hands slid up her back under her sweater. She responded quickly, thrusting her lower body rhythmically against his.

His fingers unsnapped her bra, freeing her full breasts. Quickly, his searching hands cupped them, brushed lightly on the hardening nipples and causing a marvelous sensation to shoot through her body. She pulled away, surprising him.

"Undress me," she murmured seductively, fastening the hook on her skirt and pointing to her zipper. She stared at him, waiting, closing her eyes. His fingers reached for her zipper and pulled.

Her skirt dropped to the floor and she stepped free of it, one leg at a time, then raised her arms as he tugged at her sweater and pulled it over her head, coaxing her bra along with it. She stood there, half-naked, wearing only her bikini panties while she churned with an inner passion she had not yet shown him.

He touched her again, this time stroking the crease in her panties before his fingers pulled them aside and extended themselves high inside her warmth. She wriggled, opening her legs awkwardly to allow him even more room to probe deeper. She pulled herself against him and pressed her lips against his. She experimented, opening her mouth, then closing it, then darting her tongue in and out of his mouth, pretending that it was his penis entering her vagina.

She could feel him now, through his pants. She reached for his hardness.

"Do it for me," he said, pressing on her shoulders. "Suck on it."

She went down to her knees, her hands fumbling with his belt and then the zipper. "I want you to come in my mouth," she said, taking his cock between her lips.

"No, later," he said. "I want to fuck you first."

Her head moved feverishly, feeling the explosion about to come.

"No," he said, pulling her head back. "Lie down."

She crossed the room to the bed, removed her panties, and watched him as he took off his clothes. He was almost embarrassed by his size as he stood naked beside the bed. The throbbing continued.

She reached out for him, guiding him between her legs that spread open automatically.

"Make love to me," she said. "Do what you said you wanted to do. Fuck me. Fuck me all night if you want."

He stayed rigid, hammering between her legs, her warmth feeding his hardness for over an hour. Then, he tensed. She arched her back, pressing her heels to the mattress in anticipation, awaiting the explosion that would fill her with his fluids. An orgasm began to rack his body and she thrust herself against him, matching each convulsion, until finally he lay still, the tension gone.

She could feel him beginning to subside inside her, the semen beginning to trickle down the side of her leg.

Later, they lay side by side, each minute bringing them closer to more arousal, more passion.

"I'm still wet," she said, reaching to touch herself. "I must have come at least ten times."

"Women always get the best deal," he jested. "Just once I'd like to be able to come every five minutes for as long as I wanted."

"I'll trade you anytime for your male superiority that lets you stand up and pee wherever you want," she challenged. "The inconvenience a woman goes through, having to sit down and get halfway undressed every time she wants to go to the bathroom would be well worth the price. You can have my monthly period, too."

"No thanks. On second thought, I'll stick with what I've got—one big explosion."

"Only one?" she asked, reaching for him again.

"I suppose with proper coaching, I could try for two."

"You mean like this?" She slowly began licking the underside of his penis, flicking her tongue intermittently on the velvety smooth skin while her hand began to move up and down the shaft, gradually at first, then faster until he grew so hard she couldn't resist trying to take him entirely into her mouth.

He pushed against her, feeling an obstruction at first as he reached the base of her throat. She relaxed, he pushed again, her head going all the way down against his pubic bone as she buried him deep inside her throat cavity. She held still, holding her breath while simultaneously relaxing her throat muscles. She pulled up, sucked in some air, and started the deep thrusts downward over his penis that seemed to be tearing away deep inside her throat. He pushed harder, faster. She timed each thrust with her own until the spasms were uncontrolled and the end was near.

She held him rigid with one hand, until she could feel him explode. She swallowed, continuing to suck his glans until he couldn't stand the sensitivity any longer. He pulled lightly on her hair and she drew away as he fell from her mouth.

She looked up, traces of white liquid still lingering on her chin. "Care to go for three?" she asked.

He sighed heavily and dropped his head back on the pillow. She was good, the best he'd ever had when it came to sucking him off, but three times was out of the question. Maybe in the morning, he thought.

The bed moved as he felt her move away from between his legs but he lay quietly, still savoring what she had just done.

"Open your eyes," she said.

He did as she asked, looking up without raising his head from the pillow. She was over him, her legs spread, only inches away. She wasn't finished.

"Eat me," she said, lowering herself on his mouth. "Eat me until I come."

Golden streamers of sunlight from Switzerland's nineteenth July morning crept through the cracks in the shutters as Tor blinked his eyes open for the first time that day. His mind was momentarily blank he had had difficulty remembering where he was. Then he remembered. He had been in bed only a few hours after dropping his flight attendant friend off at the airport. He had had one night stands before, but he couldn't remember ever having a more enjoyable one. There was some mystique that surrounded being out of town when such a thing happened. Two strangers in the night. No strings, no qualifiers, no recriminations. Simply raw sex for the pure fun of it. He didn't know whether he would ever see her again but he did know he would never forget her.

He dragged himself out of bed, ambling toward the window where he pushed the shutters aside. The crooked streets of the Quartier Saint-Gervais below and the view of the Rhone River reminded him of home. He felt a desolate loneliness, a kind he hadn't experienced very often as he stared at the city that had long ago become his favorite. He thought about the exact feelings he had when he last talked to James Hawk. James could look to him for hope, for relief, and for a renewal of courage to carry on his own battles but he, in turn, had nobody to seek out for such strength and encouragement. He felt empty but he told himself to forget his emotions, to go about his business. Tonight, he was having dinner with Don Peck. That took priority over everything else.

As they had agreed, Tor called Peck's suite one-half hour before their scheduled eight o'clock dinner reservation to get the name and location of the restaurant. Peck instructed him to wait in the lobby of his hotel where he would be picked up by a driver within the half-hour.

It was exactly at 7:55 when an old but impressive Rolls Royce Silver Cloud limousine glided effortlessly to a stop in front of the hotel. The glass partition between the back seat where Tor sat and the front of the car was up, affording no conversation with the chauffeur, who offered no hint as to where they were going. Resigning himself to go wherever the driver wanted, Tor sat back and enjoyed a chilled glass of wine from the bar, which was conveniently located in the back of the front passenger seat.

Twenty minutes later he sat alone in a private balconied booth above a small restaurant located in the old quarter of town, awaiting Don Peck's arrival. The restaurant was crowded yet it appeared to be the safest of places for intimate conversation. The constant murmur of voices, the rattle of silver and glass, and the passing of the busy waitresses would assure them of no unwanted eavesdropping. Two large tables directly below the balcony were filled with young Swiss Army officers at one and a group of five pretty young Swiss girls at the other. Both tables were equally boisterous as they started to become better acquainted.

Suddenly, without warning, a voice came from behind. "Your first night in town?"

Tor looked to his right and recognized the approaching figure. It was Donald Peck. He had never seen Peck in person and the television and newspaper photos he had seen hadn't done the man justice. Peck appeared to be much slimmer and better-looking than Tor had expected.

"I flew in late yesterday afternoon," Tor said, rising to shake hands.

Peck slid to the rear of the table, his back to the windowless wall. He pulled a cigar from his breast pocket and, after licking it, lit it from the flame from one of the two candles on the table. He looked about. "I see we've got quite a crowd tonight," he said, glancing at the tables below.

"Must be a local hangout," Tor responded. "My favorite kind of restaurant. My compliments. You have excellent taste."

Their waitress was an elderly woman who looked to be in her sixties, the wife of the proprietor. She swiftly took their meal and wine order and promptly returned with an opened and chilled bottle of Neufchatel wine.

Peck lifted his glass. "Here's to an enjoyable trip for you."

"And to your improved health," Tor added.

Peck began to laugh heartily.

"I'm afraid I don't understand," Tor said.

Peck's laugh slowed as he became more serious. "Tor, you look like a bright young man. I've never felt better.

Surely, your investigations have turned up the fact that I am not sick.''

"But I thought you were having problems. With your heart, I mean.''

Peck stopped laughing. "I thought so, too. It wasn't until I came to Switzerland that I found out I didn't have a heart condition. No trace of a problem.''

"What about our reports that say you're too ill to travel?''

"Nonsense," Peck boasted.

"What about the doctor who recommended you resign the union presidency?''

"All fakes.''

"Fakes?''

Peck became more serious, but still somewhat casual. "The doctors in the States, two different ones, for some reason came to the same conclusion. They said I was courting disaster by remaining with the union. They said the job was creating more stress than my heart could take. It was all bullshit. I stupidly fell for it.''

"How do you know the reports were inaccurate?'' Tor challenged.

Peck drew his brows together and gave Tor a fierce look, his voice suddenly bitter. "I had a complete check-up when I got here. I hired the best doctors money could buy and spent a whole fuckin' week in the hospital going through so many tests I felt like a damn guinea pig. There's not a thing wrong with my heart. I was railroaded out of the union presidency by a conniving son-of-a-bitch!''

"Cordaro?''

Peck nodded.

"You're sure of that?''

A smile touched Peck's lips. "Yeah, but there's nothing that can be done about it now, so I've retired to a life of leisure.''

Tor didn't have to ask about the Swiss doctors' reports that had declared Peck too ill to travel. The same money that had induced the American doctors to falsify statements about Peck's heart in the first place was now being used to keep him from being extradited to the United States.

"Look," Peck continued, "I don't give a damn what you know about me now because I'd never admit it to anyone publicly. I already know you don't have a recorder because the car you were riding in had detectors, so I know what we say here isn't going beyond this table."

"So why did you agree to talk to me?"

"All I want from you is to get that bastard."

"I was hoping you would help us do that," Tor offered.

Peck shook his head. "I can't help you. No way."

"Why is that?"

Peck smiled again. "You think I'm stupid? If I go back there, you guys will make life miserable for me. Life's too short to go through any more of that bullshit. Besides, I've got a few friends who might go down with me if I sink and I don't think they're too anxious for me to return."

"Are you aware there may be a contract on your life?" Tor asked.

The Swiss officers at the table below became noisier, and their newfound girlfriends followed their lead, making it impossible for Tor to hear Peck's response. Peck stared down at his hands, gripping his fork and knife as if they were struggling to get away from him.

"Are you all right?" Tor asked.

Pride and anger filled Peck's red face. "After all I did for that bastard and he repays me with this! A life in exile, afraid to go around the next corner for fear of what's ahead!" Peck was nearly shouting now. A woman at a table directly across the room began looking curiously at them before turning to whisper something to her companion.

Tor reached across the table and gripped Peck's arm. "We can help you if you'll let us," he urged.

Tor released his grip and Peck looked back at him starting to calm, smiling slightly as he looked over Tor's shoulder around the busy room below. A look of thoughtfulness returned to his eyes. "Look down there," he said. "All those people, the guests, the servants. All of them appear so happy and unconcerned. They don't know what they have because they've never lost it. I come to a restaurant escorted by a bodyguard and have to sit with my back to the wall. I pretend I'm free, but it's simply not true. Even if I came back to the States it would be the same. I'd either go to jail or I'd live in even more fear than I do here."

Tor sat still and waited a few moments before speaking. "I have been authorized to offer you immunity from prosecution if you'll testify against Cordaro," he said.

"And then what?" Peck asked derisively. "Sit around and wait for someone to kill me?" He shook his head violently. "At least I'm not as accessible in Switzerland! Besides, I have no interest in hurting my friends by testifying. I'd be doing just that if I testified against Cordaro."

Tor watched Peck closely. His original impression of a brash and cocky union leader who feared no one had disappeared into a bleached stare of fear that had estranged Peck from the rest of the world. He was shaking and there seemed to be some desperate, almost superstitious quality in his sudden terror.

Tor elected not to press the conversation any further. He was convinced that no amount of persuasion would induce Peck to return voluntarily to the United States.

They parted company the same way they had met, only in reverse order, Peck leaving first. Tor waited, paid the check, walked downstairs, removed his overcoat from the coat rack and stepped outside to the cobblestone walkway that led down a crooked pathway to the street where his limousine was still waiting.

When he neared the sidewalk at the end of the walkway, he stepped away quickly to avoid bumping into another pedestrian who had suddenly appeared from around a blind corner of the building. The man was huge, with thick thighs and calf muscles, a bulky frame with heavy shoulders and a short powerful neck. He carried a 35 millimeter Nikon camera. The man's pale skin seemed to

289

glow in the dark as he walked by and Tor stood momentarily in awe as he watched him glide quickly by and disappear rapidly around the next corner.

The next evening Tor stood in the customs area of San Francisco's International Airport. After what seemed to be endless unnecessary delays, he completed his perfunctory statements and baggage inspection and began to push his way through the crowd.

Outside, a strange sensation ran through his mind. He felt sure that the same man he had almost collided with on the street in Geneva had been in the customs area just moments before. He started to walk back towards customs but then thought better of it.

"Couldn't be," Tor muttered to himself. He turned and walked briskly away.

Chapter 36

IT WAS A bright sunny day in San Francisco but Tor didn't notice. Something about the report in front of him was bothersome as he read it over and over. It had been only two days since the bodies of Don Peck and his chauffeur had been discovered in a bullet-ridden limousine on a seldom used country road between Geneva and Lausanne, and just one week since he had dined with Peck in Geneva.

The official police report was sketchy and without any apparant clues to the identity of the assassin or any motive. Peck's wallet contained over a thousand Swiss francs and an expensive camera had been left untouched in the back seat of the limousine.

Tor looked at the photographs that accompanied the report. Both Peck and the chauffeur had been shot several times at close range with a powerful 357 Magnum handgun and their bodies ceremoniously spreadeagled over the car, Peck's across the hood while the chauffeur's lay face up across the roof.

The Swiss police theorized that the two men had strayed from the main road to take pictures of Lake Geneva and had been followed there by another car. Two different sets of tire markings were found nearby. Tor shook his head, wishing he could just toss the subject out the window and be done with it. The news of Peck's death was carried by the national wire services in the United States but had failed to warrant any additional coverage beyond the first day, which bothered Tor immensely. It was as if Peck had died of a heart attack one day and been buried the next. The public didn't care what was going on around them as long as it didn't affect them personally.

Frustrated, he put down the report and sat still for a long time. He rested his head on the back of his chair and closed his eyes, trying to allow his mind enough time to slow to a more effective and practical pace.

Then, as if someone had switched on the lights, he picked up the four-page report and rifled through it again. In the middle of the third page he found it. Almost as an aside, the report mentioned that there were several outer wrappings of 35mm film packages strewn about on the ground beside the car.

Tor's fingers tapped nervously on his office desk as he reread the line about the film wrappers. He wondered why someone would take that many pictures of the same view of the lake. The film came in exposures of thirty-six for each roll and if several wrappers were found that would mean that over a hundred pictures had been taken. It didn't make sense.

He remembered another police report he had read about the Puerto Rican union official that had been murdered in Miami, where the assassin had apparently taken pictures of his victim. The Geneva police report didn't indicate whether they had checked the camera found in the car for any exposed film. He needed to know if the film wrappers were from film taken by Peck. If not, there had to be a missing camera from a third party. He knew it was conjecture but he still had to know. He quickly scribbled a note with his unanswered questions and instructed his secretary to wire them to the Geneva police requesting an immediate response.

An interior excitement began to churn as he thought about Peck's murder. First Billy, then the Puerto Rican, and now Peck. If the deaths were all related in some way, and it seemed possible that they were, he couldn't make the connection.

His impatience, mixed with anxiety and frustration, soon turned to incomprehension and a sense of futility.

The telephone began to ring incessantly, reversing his unconscious confusion. It was Mikki Parker, calling on his private line.

"Where the hell have you been?" asked Tor. "It's been over a week since I last talked to you!"

"Traveling with Louie's dog and pony show," she explained. "Right now, I'm back in D.C. Something's come up. I'm afraid I've got some bad news."

There was a long pause as Tor waited for her to continue.

Mikki sounded tense. "It's about one of the Cordaro jurors, Amos Westland. He's dead. He was thrown out of his apartment window early this morning."

Tor was incredulous but managed to keep his composure. "How do they know he was thrown out?" he asked.

"A couple of kids were witnesses. They were necking in a car below and saw a man throw him off the balcony. No sign of anyone around by the time the cops got there, though."

"How did you find out about it?"

"It just hit the papers. I thought I'd better call, in case you hadn't heard."

"I suppose asking who did it would be a dumb question but I'll ask anyway. Any ideas?"

"No, nothing directly. My guess is as good as yours— but something tells me we're probably thinking the same thing."

"I can't believe the bastard would go that far!"

"Believe it," Mikki answered tersely.

Tor sat quietly, sorting out what he had just heard. What he feared most about the juror's death was what it would mean to the bribery investigation by the grand jury. Westland was one of the eight black jurors. Sidney Bonnam had had instructions from Cordaro to bribe the blacks into silence and, if Bonnam had already made his rounds, Westland's death would have a sobering effect on the others. It was possible that they would either be incensed at their fellow juror's death and want to expose the corruption or; more likely, they would be frightened into total silence. "We've got to get out and talk to the rest of the jurors before anything else happens," Tor said. "Has Bonnam been around to talk to the rest of them yet?" he asked.

"I don't know for sure, but I'd be surprised if he hasn't," she answered.

"Try and find out."

"If he has, what then?"

Tor felt a cold shot of guilt through his spine. If Bonnam had already gotten to the jurors and they refused to testify, then the only way to prosecute Cordaro would be through Mikki's testimony as an undercover agent. She was headed on a direct course into deadly quicksand for which Tor had a profound sense of responsibility. He had to be candid. "You know, Mikki, there may come a time in this whole mess when you're going to have to come out to the closet and help us tie this thing together."

Mikki wasn't naive. She didn't need any explanation, having thought about it constantly for several weeks. It concerned her, not for her own safety but for what it would do and was already doing to her relationship with Shana. That had become her most important goal—to insure her sister's happiness. It had even superseded her own objective to start her life over again. Ridding the union of its infectious disease didn't even come in a strong second. She just wanted out. "I know that," she answered.

Her resignation to what might have to be done was a relief to Tor. There was no sense talking about it anymore. Nothing could change the facts. "How's Shana?" he asked.

Mikki's voice became more exuberant, transformed effortlessly from pessimism to optimism. "Great! She's walking without crutches and her braces should be coming off in a few months." There was a long pause as she collected her thoughts. "Tor, she's showing a lot of courage. She hasn't complained a bit, and I'm so damned proud of her I can't begin to describe it, but . . ."

There was another silence.

"But what?" Tor asked.

"Well, it's just that I don't see her as much as I should. Louie's got me coming and going at all hours and . . . well, this is just not the way to bring up a kid. The sooner I get out of here the better."

"I know, Mikki, I know. It's tough, but you've got to stick it out. Hell, all my key witnesses are beginning to drop like sprayed Med-flys. You're all we've got going right now. This whole damn thing stinks to high heaven. The more I get into it, the more I see why Billy wanted to nail that asshole. Corrupt is too kind a word for him. You've got to stay with me. We can't quit now. There's too much at stake."

"I know, I know. I said I'd do it and I plan to keep my word. It's just that it's hard to explain to Shana, that's all. I don't know what to say to her anymore when I leave."

Tor paused, trying to find words he could use to encourage her. He thought of the tenderness they had shared and the many times over the past few weeks he had come so close to calling her despite their agreement that it would be unsafe to do so. He wanted her badly and the thought that she was often so near was maddening. He admired the special quality that made her sacrifice her time at a point so critical in her relationship with Shana. Words couldn't express his appreciation for her during a time when he felt a loss of direction himself. It was the blind leading the blind. Neither one of them wanted to be where they were. Given the choice again, he wasn't sure he would have made the same decision. He was sure Mikki wouldn't have. But it didn't matter now.

For more than four hot Virginia days, Tor and three other investigators interrogated all the members of the Cordaro jury as well as the alternates for any piece of evidence that would indicate any attempted illegal influence. The remaining seven black jurors denied emphatically that they had ever been approached by anyone, much less a black union representative. Even Robert Trabert, who had voluntarily provided information about being approached with money by his neighbor, was suddenly beginning to question his memory, saying he may have jumped to conclusions. To make matters worse, Patrolman Patterson and his wife had bcome equally unresponsive.

As tragic as it was, to Tor it was simple. The death of Amos Westland had its consequences. The jurors were afraid for their personal safety and no amount of national pride or sense of duty would eliminate man's greatest emotion. The urge for self-preservation was Louie Cordaro's strongest weapon. The investigation was at a dead end and Tor knew it. He flew home for the weekend, using the five hours on the plane to formulate yet another plan. The grand jury had gained some testimony before Westland's death that could lead to indicting Cordaro, but their case was weakening daily because of the sudden lack of cooperation by the witnesses. A positive point was that the jurors weren't even talking among themselves. Tor knew the jurors' silence could possibly be the key to success because each juror might individually be thinking that he was the only one holding out. It was around that point that he devised his plan.

If he could convince each juror individually that his fellow jurors were, behind closed doors, admitting being approached by either Bonnam or a union business agent, it might force each one into offering testimony for fear of perjuring himself on the witness stand. It was a devious scheme and Tor had a personal distaste for such tactics, but Cordaro's actions left him no choice.

When Tor's plane arrived at San Francisco's International, Percy Tinsley's tall frame towered over the others that had gathered around the deplaning ramp. It was past ten P.M., one A.M. Eastern time, and Tor was fatigued by a day that was approaching its twentieth waking hour, but he managed a broad smile and picked up his step when he spotted his old friend. "Percy, how are you?" he asked, shaking his hand vigorously.

"Better than most!" Tinsley replied. "I thought I'd better catch you down here before you ran off again."

"How did you know where I was? Even *I* don't seem sure anymore."

"I have my ways," Tinsley responded sagely.

"What brings you down here, Percy?" Tor asked, his face skeptical. "If you're trying to prove to me you're worth your salary again, you know long hours don't mean shit to me. It's performance that counts."

Tinsley turned his dark eyes on Tor and smiled, extending his hand to take his briefcase. "There's a meeting Monday in your office at three. Willie Ray requested it. I thought you might want to be there," he answered.

Tor slung his flight bag over his shoulder and began to walk. "You came all the way down here to tell me that?"

"Well, not exactly," Tinsley hedged.

"What then?"

Tinsley was uncharacteristically nervous and began to fidget, scratching at his broad nose. "It's just that I've got some time on my hands. I'd like to help you out wherever I can, you know."

"You mean on the Hawk Committee, don't you?"

Tinsley's face brightened, the smile broadened, displaying his abundant white teeth. "Yeah, that's it," he said sheepishly.

"You're a frustrated cop. Is that what you're telling me?"

Tinsley nodded, the wide smile continuing to crease his face.

"Percy, I appreciate that, I really do. But you've got your hands full with the union problem and I can't afford to have you out of the stores right now."

"That's just it!" Tinsley protested. "There's not that much going on, at least not in the store. We've had no problems so far."

"So far! That's the problem. Don't count on it. From what I've seen in the past two months of how these guys operate, we don't want to be lulled into a false sense of security. They're capable of anything at any time and they don't give a damn about the law. If I've learned anything in the past few months, it's that."

Tinsley sighed. "Well, it was worth a try anyway."

Tor sensed Tinsley's disappointment. "Look, if anything comes up, I'll consider your offer. Not because you're a friend, but because I respect your ability—and more important your honesty."

"Honesty?"

"Yeah, there doesn't seem to be a whole lot of that around these days."

Chapter 37

COMMISSIONER DANIEL HARDY jumped from his chair and disgustedly flung his newspaper to the floor to join another stack of papers he had discarded earlier. Willie Ray sat with his feet on the commissioner's desk, ignoring his outrage.

"My God, if we let those bastards represent our police force there's no hope for us, absolutely none!" Hardy yelled, seizing a coffee cup from his desk. He raised it to his mouth, ingested a small amount, then wiped his face with his shirt sleeve.

Hardy was a tall man, lean, with a body like a strong, thin tree branch, making him look deceptively frail but with rugged features. His movements were quick and his voice often impatient.

Willie Ray was dressed in his summer attire of faded blue jeans and open-necked shirt, which framed a gold-plated medallion, and leather sandals on his otherwise bare feet. He was outwardly emotionless and it seemed to steady the commissioner. Ray's voice had a soothing monotone twang. "There's talk by union officials of a coast-to-coast organizing drive. They say they want to get a national master contract to cover all the police forces," he offered.

Hardy sighed. "If the police are unionized by Cordaro's bunch of hooligans, I'll advise the people not to waste their money paying police commissioners a salary because Louie Cordaro would be their local police commissioner."

"But they're already unionized, Commissioner," Willie reminded him.

"You know what I mean!" the commissioner countered. He looked out the window and watched the activity, seven stories below on the steps of City Hall. "Look at those idiots! Every cop in the city must be down there. The poor bastards don't know what they're doing."

The commissioner dreaded the events that had led to the day's picketing. Many police forces throughout the United States were organized but most by different public employee unions, many of which were ineffective and fragmented. The government employees' union that the San Francisco police were affiliated with, the San Francisco Policemen's Association, was locked in an impasse with the Board of Supervisors over their new contract. As usual, higher wages were the key issue. Only two weeks earlier, the Policemen's Association had reached an agreement with the Board of Supervisors and recommended ratification of the new contract by their members, but the union leaders had been shouted down when they presented the contract to the rank and file members.

A slow frown wrinkled Willie's forehead. "My boys tell me Cordaro's boys have been hanging around for weeks just waiting for the Policemen's Association to stub their toes in the negotiations. It looks like they're going to get their chance to look like heroes. After what happened down in San Diego, it doesn't take a wizard to see why your men would turn to Cordaro."

The commissioner struggled to place Willie's comment on San Diego into some perspective but failed. "What do you mean?" he asked.

"Two years ago the San Diego police officers were receiving a flat eighteen hundred dollars a month. They were being represented by a public employees union much the same as we have here. Then they voted to go to Cordaro's union for representation and immediately received about four hundred bucks a month increase in salary. Now their wages are averaging as much as twenty-seven hundred a month and they're gonna go higher. The city is already struggling with an overextended budget. Now they've got the fire department asking for parity with the police officers.''

The commissioner was confused. ''I didn't think the San Diego officers were affiliated with Cordaro,'' he said.

Willie shook his head. ''They aren't,'' he answered.

''Then you've lost me.''

''They didn't actually become members of Cordaro's union. They kept their assocation with the public employees union but increased their dues to provide two hundred thousand dollars a year to hire Cordaro's union as an outside bargaining force. My figures show that Cordaro's bunch represents over two hundred different law enforcement units throughout the United States, either in an advisory capacity like San Diego, or as the sole and exclusive bargaining agent. You're just another rung on the ladder.'' Willie stopped talking momentarily and watched the commissioner who was becoming even more tense. He leaned forward and spoke in a low flat voice. ''Maybe if the ante was upped a little we could avert the whole problem and . . .''

Hardy cut him short, shaking his head. ''Willie, it's not the money that's the problem. As far as I'm concerned, you can't pay these guys too much for putting their lives on the line every time they walk out on the street. Money is a factor, sure, but we can't let that get in the way of our thinking. What the public has got to understand is that we've got to put a stop to Cordaro representing our police forces. That's the whole damned issue! If we don't put up a stand, we've got no chance. We have to stop this shit somewhere and it might as well be here.''

The commissioner was just warming up. Willie sat and listened, letting him blow off steam. ''Look, if lawmen joined a clean union I wouldn't give a damn, but Cordaro's union is another matter. What would happen if a union official, for whatever reason, is under government investigation and the detective assigned to work on the case belongs to the same union? I'll tell you! If the detective doesn't nail the bastard, people are always going to wonder if some other union official influenced the detective. There's the whole fuckin' problem. If the public begins to question their own law enforcement agencies because of their association with Cordaro—and I have to believe it would happen—then there will be no respect for the law. Cordaro's union is loaded with people who have open alliances with organized crime. Look at Cordaro, for Christ's sake. He's a prime example. How in the hell can a good cop honestly say he belongs to the same organization as a bunch of crooks and then go out and expect to get the public's respect to help him do his job?"

Willie started to speak but the commissioner interrupted and answered his own questions. "I'll tell you how. He *won't* get it! The public will tell him to shove it up his ass. Crime will become rampant because the people will see the union and the police as one thieving bunch of hypes. They'll all be one big happy family—the mob, the union, and the police. I can't believe it, but it could happen."

"What do you want me to do, Commissioner?"

The commissioner sat back down in his chair and stared across at Willie. "Talk to 'em. Try and reason with them. Tell 'em there's no need to throw in with those crooks. Anything! Just don't let it happen."

"I'm afraid we're too late. They've already voted to dump the Policemen's Association. Cordaro's boys are already talking with them. All I can do now is nose around and see what they expect them to do for them."

The commissioner leaned back in his chair and tried to deal with facts he couldn't change. The more he thought of it, the more he became prey to gloom and uncertainty. "What about trying to get them to come back to work?" he asked. "Half the force called in sick this morning and from what I can tell, it looks like the other half are all down there on the steps. Hell, I can hardly run this city on a full force, let alone half of one."

"I'll see what I can find out," Willie said, getting up to leave.

"Willie," the commissioner said.

Willie turned to look back, his hand already on the door knob.

"Be careful."

Willie nodded and walked out, slowly closing the door behind him.

Though it was difficult for him to keep his mind on local issues, Tor sat in his office and listtened quietly along with Percy Tinsley as Willie Ray related the events of the morning. "You think our police force is going to go along with Cordaro's bunch?" he asked.

"Seems like that's a safe bet," Willie answered. "More and more of the police, sheriffs, prison guards, even some command officers are ready to vote them in or at least hire them in a consulting capacity. In the minds of the cops I talked to today, the higher wages and bargaining clout they're offering seem to outweigh any concern about the union's history."

Tinsley interrupted. "What do your spies say?"

"That they'll cancel the sick call after today if the negotiations are reopened. If not, they say they'll give the commissioner a little taste of what the new union is all about."

Tinsley stared at Willie, a curious look on his face. "What do they mean by that?" he asked.

"Who knows? But I wouldn't put it past them to try a city-wide shutdown. I think they could pull it off. Everything would be shut off. Trucks, police, ambulance drivers, the whole ball of wax."

Tor was impatient. He changed the subject. "What about Slagle's? What have you found out about the organization drive there?"

"That's why I wanted to talk to you," Willie answered. "I've been told that your employees have been contacted and promised the moon if they'll just sign the organizing cards. If that happens, it would force an election for union representation."

Tor wasn't impressed. "That's nothing new, they've tried that shit before and my people have never fallen for it. Why should it work now?''

There was no answer. Tinsley and Willie stared at each other, then back at Tor.

"I guess I can answer that," Tinsley offered reluctantly shifting in his chair uneasily.

"Well?" Tor asked impatiently.

Tinsley hesitated, then began. "A lot of people think things have changed around here in the past few months. They miss the personal touch. You've been gone so much they think you don't care anymore. I've heard talk they even think you might consider selling the company and go into politics.''

"Where in the hell did that shit get started?" Tor demanded.

Willie provided the answer. "The union doesn't necessarily have to tell the truth when they talk to prospective members. They'll use anything to get those cards signed. They're starting the rumors. They only need thirty percent of the employees to sign the enlistment cards in order to call an election and my guess is they'll have no problem getting them.''

A silent fury crept over Tor's face. His smile had long since disappeared. He remained silent, wondering why the same workers who always seemed to understand him had suddenly become so blind.

The three men stared momentarily out the window to the city below, the only noise being that of Tor's fidgeting with the clip on his Cross pen. Tor's face was strained, every muscle taut.

"Why would Richard Jackson want to meet with me tonight?" Tor asked, once again changing the subject.

Willie looked surprised. "The D.A.?" he asked.

Tor nodded. Tinsley shook his head while Willie merely scratched his nose with his finger and shrugged.

"I'm meeting him tonight," Tor said.

It was the result of his anger that Tor couldn't sleep that night. Richard Jackson's request that he convince the committee to ease up on its investigation of Louie Cordaro in exchange for Cordaro dropping his organizational drive against Slagle's was disillusioning as it was infuriating to him.

He was exhausted but wide awake. He opened a book and read one sentence several times without comprehending a word. He looked about the room, then switched off the light and lay flat on his back staring at the ceiling, his mind still wandering. Then he remembered a paper he had found tucked in among several other documents in Billy's den while he was looking for the diary. He switched the light back on and rummaged through his briefcase until he found it.

It was simple and to the point! "Crime and corruption have spread through almost every structure of our society, sheltered by the terrible apathy displayed by the average American citizen. Gambling, theft, narcotics, and prostitution are linked through criminal conspiracies coast-to-coast. Citizens' reactions usually take the form of fascination, even shock, but the scandals soon become watered down and forgotten. Instead of getting angry or flashing into vigorous action, our citizens figuratively shrug their shoulders and turn to the next sensation that comes along. They have their own concerns. They feel they must get ahead in the world and devote their attention to making a better living and more money, acquiring material possessions and enjoying more expanded leisure. All this has dulled the responses of a large percentage of the American people. Sharp questions about morality, spiritual values, and good citizenship are no longer evident. The cancer is spreading. Without the support of its citizens, our government cannot succeed as it has in the past. We need our citizens to win this battle, or all will be lost."

The events of the day couldn't have been a more graphic depiction of what Billy Hawk had written. Tor shut off the light, climbed back into bed and rolled to his side, trying to fall asleep. His mind kept coming back to Billy's words. It was true. The cancer was spreading. For the first time, he began to think that it might be too late to stop it.

Chapter 38

ANOTHER DAY, ANOTHER CITY. This time it was San Francisco and James Hawk paused momentarily before deplaning and buttoned his denim sport jacket. The weight of the campaign, which still had nearly ninety days to go, weighed heavily on his mind despite his outward appearance. The latest Gallup Poll, released that morning, showed his once seemingly insurmountable lead over President Jordan shrinking rapidly, and Louie Cordaro's anti-Hawk campaign was just beginning to get rolling.

Speaking before a group of influential businessmen in Los Angeles and then again the next day in New York City, Cordaro had accused James of distortion and prostitution of the committee. Several congressmen and state senators, indebted to Cordaro for their own elections, had been giving similar speeches throughout the country describing James as a millionaire who could not understand the problems of the working man.

President Jordan was not immune to union pressures. He had offered a prepared statement earlier that morning that subtly intimated his support for Cordaro by attacking the committee's strategy of exclusively concentrating on Cordaro and stating that more important union issues lay unresolved.

James knew the reporters waiting outside the plane for a brief statement would want to know his reactions to the president's statement.

He decided to cut his statement short and limit the

questions and answers to five minutes. He wanted to see Tor Slagle as soon as possible.

Ironically, his arrival at Tor's home that evening was scheduled to be by way of helicopter in order to save at least forty minutes drive time from the peninsula airport in Burlingame. At the time the helicopter was chartered, there was no way of knowing that on this particular day, it would be the *only* way to get across the Golden Gate Bridge.

Tor waited for James's arrival and watched from his living room at the chaotic traffic on Highway 101 which stretched across the Golden Gate Bridge. He wondered if the people below had any real idea as to the significance of what was going on in their city. Traffic was at a standstill both north and southbound, a direct result of the union's demonstration which had begun earlier that morning, when a union labor organizer, frustrated at Commissioner Hardy's refusal to recognize them as the bargaining agent for the police force, decreed a general strike. Louie Cordaro's union was giving the commissioner and the city a taste of its economic force and pressure. Taxis suddenly disappeared from the city's streets. Municipal buses completed their morning runs and headed for the storage barns. Bridge toll operators on the Golden Gate Bridge and the San Francisco Bay bridges walked off their posts leaving them severely undermanned. Police cars became disabled for no apparent reason while trucks clogged all the major traffic arteries by slowing to a snail's pace and, in some instances, parking in the toll gates for hours at a time, backing up traffic in and out of the city for over twenty miles in all directions. The city was virtually shut down by eleven A.M., and the mayor issued a state of emergency notice shortly before noon pleading for everyone to stay home and off the city streets.

Commissioner Hardy was livid, ordering every off-duty police officer to report at once. He met with only limited success, as most officers were conveniently staying away from their telephones. Acting as an intermediary for the Board of Supervisors, the mayor quickly ordered a caucus with the union representatives to determine what could be done to alleviate the pressure while at the same time attempting to save face for the Board of Supervisors, who were following Commissioner Hardy's recommended hard line against representation for the new union.

Behind closed doors, the board reluctantly agreed among themselves that their attempt to keep the union from representing the police had been met by a force far more formidable than their own. They agreed to bargain and, shortly before 5 P.M., the demonstration was declared over.

The rumbling of the helicopter's blades slicing through the thin evening air became louder and louder. It was exactly six o'clock when it set down in Tor's backyard and James bolted exuberantly out of the cockpit. Tor greeted him at the door with a bottle of freshly popped champagne.

For James, the warmth of Tor's den was a welcome sight. The redwood walls and overstuffed leather lounge chairs facing an enormous plate glass window framing the bay below all combined to make the room a pleasant change from the cramped jetliner quarters in which he had just spent five hours.

The soft, almost inaudible sound of Beethoven's Fifth Symphony filtered through the air while James nursed the glass of champagne Tor handed him. The circumstances surrounding Donald Peck's death had fascinated James and he came right to the point. "Are you sure about the film wrappers?" he asked.

Tor shrugged. "It's only a guess at this time, but it seems strange that when the police checked the camera in the trunk there was no exposed film. The film didn't come from Peck's camera. It had to have come from somewhere else."

"And the Muniz killing had the same type of wrappers?"

Tor nodded. "The same, Fuji 35 millimeter, 24 explosures, 400 ASA. Even Kodak film would be too coincidental to be taken lightly, but there's not that many people around using Fuji film. Thta's what makes me believe the two murders were handled by the same person. After I asked the police in Geneva about the film, they double-checked the murder site again. The footprints they found all around the car suddenly made sense to them. It looked like someone took pictures from all angles before leaving the scene, the same as with the Muniz killing. Do you think Peck's death was ordered by Cordaro?''

James shrugged his shoulders. "It's hard to say. Peck had his share of enemies, same as Cordaro, but the film thing does seem strange. Muniz threatened to kill my brother, but I don't see why Cordaro would have stopped him. Getting rid of my brother is more in line with what Cordaro wanted and there were no film wrappers there. I don't know what to think of it. There's a connection somewhere but exactly what it is is anybody's guess."

James paused, sipped more champagne, then continued. "What about the jurors, what's happening there?" he asked.

Tor recounted the problems he had experienced since the death of Amos Westland. "And now," he continued, "the police are considering calling Westland's death a suicide since the two kids who said they saw someone throw him off the balcony are beginning to get a little scared. All of a sudden they say they can't be sure. Someone probably got to them too!''

James disagreed, shaking his head. "If Cordaro had Westland killed, the last thing he would want is for the police to call it suicide. His point would be negated. He wants to scare the other jurors. What we better hope for is that they *do* list it as a suicide. Then some of our juror friends might gain some confidence and loosen their tongues."

"What do you think our chances are of getting the grand jury to return a jury-tampering indictment if the jury doesn't cooperate?"

James pulled a small pencil-thin cigar from his pocket and lit it. "There's enough evidence on record to get him to court again," James answered, exhaling a puff of smoke. "If the jurors don't talk then, well . . ." he hesitated, thought a moment, then went on. "I have to hope the jurors will cooperate. Meanwhile, stay on it. Keep pushing them. Get our investigators to reassure them of their safety. Push their patriotism buttons—it may be our only chance. Without them, we're sure to lose Cordaro again."

James stood, walked to the window and stared out. Then his eyes fell to the champagne glass in his hand. "I don't have to tell you how busy I am and how helpless I feel about handing you something I originally started. But I want you to know it's still just as important to me now. I need you to understand that."

"I never thought any differently," Tor answered.

Looking at the mass of traffic below, James turned to look at Tor who had joined him at the window. "Looks like the boys proved their point today," he said, pointing at the bridge.

"Yeah, they sure did. They called it off a while ago but it won't clear up for hours."

James nodded. "I heard about it when we landed. I couldn't believe the streets when we flew over. It looked like a parking lot as far as you could see. It's a damn shame."

"The walkout, you mean?"

James continued to look at the traffic, then turned to Tor shaking his head. "No," he said. "Walkouts are part of the bargaining process and I don't believe that should ever change. This one just underlines what the union can do to the economy if they've a mind to do it. It's awesome! It's wrong, but that's the way it is. That's why it's important for the unions to be run by people who demonstrate an understanding for their power and don't abuse it. We can't let Cordaro go on calling the shots."

"What don't you agree with, then?" Tor asked.

"I object to any police officer belonging to any national union! Police should be particularly responsive to local control. With the Cordaro union representing them, local citizens will have no control over their own police force and that's exactly what I object to. Shit, everybody's got a right to organize, but this is a different situation. It's not a factory where what the union does affects us economically. It's a situation where what they do could affect our rights, even our lives. That's the difference!''

''Well, anyway,'' Tor offered, ''with the union convention starting Monday, Cordaro will be in town. We probably won't see any more problems like this for a while. The city and the union will need all the help they can get to get the convention off to a smooth start.''

The telephone rang but neither Tor nor James paid attention. A moment later, a Secret Service agent who was waiting in the next room rapped lightly on the den door.

''There's a call for you, Mr. Slagle,'' he said, opening the door.

''Ask him to leave a message,'' Tor answered.

''I already tried that,'' the agent said, ''whoever it is says he has to talk to you now. He says it's important but he wouldn't give me his name.''

Tor poured himself a glass of champagne as he picked up the phone. He recognized the voice instantly. It was the same muffled voice he had heard before. He quickly motioned for James to pick up the extension phone in the other room.

''I know Hawk's with you,'' the voice began. ''I want you to listen carefully. Don't ask questions. You need to get to Sidney Bonnam. He's got something to tell you about Cordaro you ought to know. But be careful. Don't let anybody see you talking to him or you'll lose him just like you lost Peck.'' There was a pause, followed by a loud click.

Tor was still holding the phone when James reentered the den a few second later. ''Your mystery man?'' he asked.

Tor nodded.

''The same as before?''

''The same.''

''Judging from what he said about Peck, he knows what he's talking about.''

"Yeah, but . . ."

"But?"

Tor's champagne suddenly tasted bitter in his mouth. "Well, thanks to Mikki we already know about Bonnam," he began. "That's no secret. We could hang him out to dry any time we want. I don't see what use it would be to talk to Bonnam. We'd only end up exposing Mikki."

James drew near and placed both palms flat on Tor's desk. He leaned closer, staring directly at Tor. "But can we take the chance of *not* confronting Bonnam?" he challenged. "If we don't, Bonnam could meet the same fate as Peck. He could be our key witness."

Tor was still wary. "And if we do confront him and he isn't cooperative, he'll run straight to Cordaro. Then they'll know they've got an informer in their ranks and it won't take long for them to figure out who that is. Nobody knew anything about what Bonnam was up to but Mikki, Borg Trenier, and Cordaro."

Both men became silent, realizing at the exact time the significance of what Tor had said. The identity of the mystery caller suddenly was no longer a mystery. Mikki Parker wasn't making the anonymous phone calls and it certainly wasn't Cordaro. By steering Tor to Bonnam, the caller had left only one possibility.

"That's it," yelled Tor. "Trenier's been submarining Cordaro! I'll be damned!"

James was skeptical, his brow furrowed. "Unless Bonnam's been making the calls himself," he added seriously.

"Why should he do that?" Tor asked incredulously.

"Who knows? He was a Secret Service agent before he went into law practice. His record is clean. He may have had his own private reasons for taking up with Cordaro. He may be doing a little investigative work. It just doesn't make sense that Trenier made the calls. He wouldn't be assured of taking over if Cordaro went to jail. The union constitution calls for an open election if the president steps down and there's a number of union vice-presidents that could easily step into the presidency. Trenier could be our caller or it could be Bonnam. We'll never know for sure

313

unless we talk with Bonnam." James ran his fingers through his hair and turned to face the window again. "Well, I guess we know what you'll be doing for the next few days, don't we?"

Tor said nothing as he stared at the ring on his desk left by the champagne bottle which he had just emptied. In many ways, he thought, he and James were much alike. They both had very few illusions left. Neither man would ever admit it to the other, but both felt a sense of defeat as they silently reflected on the degenerate attitudes of so many that were going unchecked without scorn or censure by the people of their country.

James looked to the den door and saw the Secret Service agent pointing to his watch. He glanced back at Tor, who needed no further instructions. He knew what James wanted.

"I'll try and locate Bonnam in the morning," he said.

Chapter 39

ON THE AFTERNOON of August ninth, a soft-spoken, mild-mannered man walked into the Senate Office Building and asked the receptionist for an envelope that he was told would be waiting for him. Even though Sidney Bonnam had worked for the committee as a special investigator, this was the first time he had ever been in the Senate Office Building. Bonnam followed the directions in the envelope to the second floor, walked to the end of the east corridor and entered the unmarked door designated only by an arrow on the crudely drawn map he clutched in his hand.

Tor Slagle sat at his desk, his feet propped up and a half-eaten sandwich in his hand, thumbing through a staff investigator's report. When he looked up, Bonnam was already standing in his office.

"You wanted to see me?" Bonnam asked.

"I guess if you call leaving over ten unanswered messages with your wife means I want to talk to you, you're right," Tor answered, a slight grin crossing his face as he extended his hand to Bonnam who reluctantly reciprocated with a tentative extension of his own.

They wasted no time as Tor listened for over an hour while Bonnam fidgeted his way through his story, still quite unaware that Tor already knew of his covert activities. Tor's mind constantly toyed with suggestions as to why Bonnam had suddenly decided to cooperate with the committee. He would have liked to believe that Bonnam was a man to whom principle meant more than his own safety, but he had warned himself against any such pre-judgment. On the surface, his story made sense but something told Tor there was a different reason for Bonnam spilling his guts. When it came time to bring into the open the fact that Louie Cordaro had hired him to spy on the committee as well as carry the bribe to the jurors from the Sky City trial, Bonnam would suffer regardless of how noble his motives had been. What Tor couldn't understand was why he had accepted the assignment from Cordaro to spy on the committee in the first place.

"Why didn't you come to us when Cordaro first made the offer?" Tor asked.

Bonnam was prepared for the question. "I've been in the business long enough to know that the fewer people who know about something like this the better. I wanted to work alone until I was sure I could be of some use to the committee. Now, I think I can."

Tor was blunt. "I assume you're aware of the complications you'll face after you've testified. People who cross Louie Cordaro usually find their health in very precarious shape."

Bonnam's eyebrows soared and a cryptic smile crossed his lips. "Who said I was going to testify?" he asked.

Tor's face remained expressionless. He felt he knew what Bonnam wanted. "What's your price?" he asked.

Bonnam thought a moment about his half-million dollar agreement with Borg Trenier. The money was what was giving him the strength to continue his charade. "I want protection—a new identity," he began. "My wife and I have talked about it. We have no real ties, so we could easily disappear. All I want is assurance that I'll be given a choice as to where I'll be living and that a new background will be set up so that it's impossible to trace my true identity. Without that, I'd be a dead man."

Tor was standing now, his hands deep in his pockets. "That's all you want?"

"That's all. I just want out when it's over. Nothing else."

Tor's faith in common civic pride was beginning to rebuild. "You just said you wanted to wait until you could be of use to the committee before reporting Cordaro. Can you now prove what you just told me?"

"Do I get what I asked for?"

Tor nodded. "That can be arranged."

"Then I can prove it."

"You may be lying to me," Tor tested.

"Why should I? I have nothing to gain and you're certainly not going to tell me anything I can take back to Cordaro. All you have to do is go to each person on the jury and ask them to verify what I've told you. Ask them exactly what I said when I spoke with them."

"Okay." Tor answered, quickly making up his mind. "Let's go to work."

For the remainder of the day and most of the evening, Bonnam worked with Tor and the F.B.I. Director J. Robert Wallace, detailing with exacting precision the incidents he had outlined earlier to Tor. Later, Wallace stated that there was no question in his mind that Bonnam had indeed chronicled a documented history that would hold up under the most penetrating of courtroom challenges. It was after midnight when Bonnam finally left Wallace's office. He was exhausted from his long testimony and Wallace's interrogation. The city was still asleep when he got home, confident that Wallace and Tor would honor their agreement. For the first time in weeks, he fell asleep quickly.

The next morning, exactly fifty-eight days after Billy Hawk's death and only twenty-one days after Don Peck's assassination, it seemed the public had all but forgotten about the two men. The questions concerning their deaths had long since disappeared from the newspapers as well as most radio and television broadcasts. Even the presidential campaign stories on this day were shifted from the front pages of the *Washington Post* in favor of the coverage of a District of Columbia liquor store robbery in the ghetto in which two men were killed.

James Hawk sat with Tor behind the closed doors in his Senate office quietly discussing the subject of Sidney Bonnam. While cautious, both men were elated in their sudden change of luck. Bonnam's cooperation had been totally unexpected.

James spread his hands. "This is all we need to convince the grand jury to indict," he said, an excited and optimistic tone in his voice. "They can't come to any other conclusion. The evidence is overwhelming."

Tor was less enthusiastic. "What if the jurors don't cooperate and stay close-mouthed about the whole thing?" he asked.

James brushed his hands briskly in the air. "Don't worry. The indictment will convince them. They still don't know that none of their fellow jurors are talking to us. When we confront them individually, one of them is bound to crack and corroborate Bonnam's story. Once one starts talking, the others will follow. I'd bet on it."

Tor looked at James with a thin smile. "Do you think Bonnam's telling us everything he knows?"

"What do you think?"

"They grilled him pretty hard last night. His story checks out from all angles. I don't see how he could be hiding anything but, then again, nothing would surprise me anymore. I keep telling myself that there would be nothing for him to gain by holding anything back now. I only hope I'm right."

"Did you ask him if he was the one making the anonymous phone calls to you?"

"I asked, but he became awfully uneasy when I pressed him. He seemed surprised at first, as if he didn't know what I was talking about. It's funny, because after a while he started questioning *me* about it. I still don't know what to think about his reaction, but I got a definite feeling he hasn't been the one making the calls."

James shifted uncomfortably in his chair. Something about Bonnam made him feel uneasy. He looked up at

Tor, his eyes flashing. "Then if Bonnam didn't make the calls, that leaves only one other person."

Tor nodded. Borg Trenier was the only other choice.

Chapter 40

THEY MET FOR a late afternoon lunch at a small outdoor café only a few blocks away from union headquarters. Several empty beer bottles remained scattered on the table. They drank mostly in silence, Louie Cordaro having finally run out of complaints about the government. Cordaro had needed a release from the tensions that had been knotting his insides and Bartie Bonano just happened to be around with nothing better to do after collecting his final monetary installment for completing his latest assignment.

Cordaro sat hunched over his beer. "Bastards," he muttered, more to himself than to Bonano.

Bonano grunted in the same monotone in which he had been intermittently responding all afternoon, "What?"

"Don't want to talk about it anymore," Cordaro replied thickly. "I'm fucking tired of talking. Let's have another drink."

Cordaro waved at the waiter, simultaneously downing the last warm swallow from the beer in front of him. The waiter reappeared with two more bottles. Still hunched, Cordaro stared at his friend through a tired set of narrowing eyes as he lifted the fresh beer to his lips.

Bonano was already guzzling, taking the final swallow before slamming the bottle to the table. He worked himself out of the chair and stood up unsteadily. "Gotta go, boss," he replied, anchoring his massive frame to a nearby chair.

Cordaro cleared his throat. "Sit down," he said, pointing to Bonano's empty chair. "I've got another little job I want you to do."

Bonano sat down heavily, his mountainous frame again filling the small chair. He always listened when Cordaro had a job for him. That was how he made his living. Even after nine beers, he was sober enough to take on a new assignment.

Chapter 41

SIDNEY BONNAM'S HANDS were shaking.

Borg Trenier listened, his ear pressed hard against the telephone as Bonnam spoke. Bonnam was nervous, concerned about his personal safety.

"I'm not sure I can stay with this thing," Bonnam announced. "There's too many people over there who know about this. What if one of those committee guys slips and talks to someone? It could get back to Cordaro. I mean, I don't feel safe."

Trenier was impatient with Bonnam's sudden lack of courage. "Why didn't you ask them for protection? They could do that without anyone finding out."

Bonnam's voice cracked. "They asked me about that. They wanted to know if I'd accept protective custody but I wasn't sure I really wanted to do that. Hell, they could put me away for a long time if I agreed to that. Once they got me, I might not be able to get back out if I changed my mind about testifying."

Even over the phone, Trenier could recognize the quiver in Bonnam's high-pitched voice. Bonnam was frightened, unsure of himself and that frightened him. Such people weren't stable enough to be predictable. Somehow he needed to calm Bonnam down, control him. He thought of the money. "Sid, if it'll ease your mind, I can come up with part of the first installment now. You can salt it away and use some of it to hide out until you feel better about this whole thing. What do you think of that?"

There was a long pause. Bonnam remained silent, thinking as fast as he could considering the circumstances. "How much are you talking about?" Bonnam asked at last, clearing his throat.

"A hundred grand. I can have it for you by tomorrow."

No response.

Trenier became impatient. "Come on, Sid, that's the smart thing to do. You must know that. You can take off while you're waiting for the trial. You don't even have to tell me where you are. Just keep in touch from time to time and be sure and show up when they need you for the trial. That's all I ask."

Several seconds passed. Then, Bonnam's response was quick, unexpected. "Get the money by tomorrow. But . . ."

Trenier cut him short. "Great."

"*Listen* to me, dammit," Bonnam demanded, his voice abruptly becoming more authoritative. "I don't want a hundred grand, I want the whole first installment—a quarter-million."

"Wait a minute," Trenier objected. "I can't do that. The others won't go along with it. You could just take off without testifying, you know."

"By tomorrow, Trenier, or you'll never know whether or not I would have testified. Take it or leave it. That's my deal!"

A click hammered in Trenier's ear. He sat with the phone still in his hand, trying to anaylze what Bonnam had just told him. He replaced the receiver in the cradle. But he had already made up his mind. He had to take the chance. He would get the money.

Chapter 42

IT WAS NICE lying next to him. The anxieties of the past month seemed to have drained away as he lay peacefully asleep, snoring lightly. It had been weeks since Gloria Bonnam had seen her husband sleep so soundly. Perhaps their love-making a few hours earlier had exhausted him. If that was the panacea to assure his relaxation, she intended to continue the therapy.

She lay quietly, just looking at him, her skin sensitive to his every movement, from the tempo of his breathing to the fine hair on his bony legs that brushed against her. It was so simple. She loved him very much. Their twelve-year age difference had become more of an asset than the hindrance everybody had warned her about before their marriage. Despite his recent propensity to tire easily during their love-making, his gentleness and kindness warmed her heart. Even his taciturn manner was far removed from the brashness of the men she had dated through college and he could be very funny when he wasn't too preoccupied. That was what had attracted her to him most when they had first met four years earlier.

He moved, rolled toward her, his arm reaching across her stomach. In the soft early morning light, she could see their reflections in the door mirror beside their bed. She enjoyed the images. His milk-white skin contrasted with the golden tan highlighting the gracefully smooth but athletic lines of her own body. She tugged at his arm, trying to get him to move closer.

"What?" He was startled, still barely awake.

"Just trying to get close to you," she said, snuggling closer.

His arm tightened across her middle, the fingers curling slowly around the naked soft flesh of her narrow waist. "I love you," he murmured, burying his face against her back.

"I love you too."

He rested a moment, then came up on his knees embracing her from behind, his hands moving upward to cover her breasts. He cupped her nipples in his palms and massaged them gently. When they became erect, he turned her around and laid her on her back, his mouth searching. First, around her breasts, and then gradually lower.

She spread her legs to accommodate the gentle flicking of his tongue. She loved it when he did that. No other man who had ever done it to her before could come close to giving her the same pleasure. Most men would put their tongue too far inside but he always moistened her clitoris area first, making circles with his tongue all around it.

He was purposely avoiding going too fast, kissing only the insides of her thighs. She raised her legs higher, locking her arms behind her legs and holding her knees tight and close to her chest. His mouth teased, then moved leisurely but deliberately over her vaginal opening, sucking it lightly while increasing the pressure gradually. He often did this in the morning, after they had made love the night before. He knew her sexual appetite far exceeded his capacity and it gave him great pleasure to satisfy her needs in this manner.

She moaned as he increased the tempo. The pressure of his tongue made her move faster and her body slammed hard against his face as she neared the finish. Even when she screamed uncontrollably he did not stop, choosing to imbibe every drop of her wetness. She squirmed violently as he cupped her buttocks hard to force her still against his mouth.

Her body wracked with orgasms. "I'm coming," she

screamed. "I'm coming. God, I'm coming. Fuck me, fuck me!"

Afterwards, they lay together quietly, saying nothing, both thinking the same thoughts. She knew they would not make love again for a long time and that saddened her. They had already decided it would be best if he disappeared until the trial.

Later, he showered, packed a single bag, called a cab, kissed her good-bye, and left. She nestled close to her pillow and cried herself to sleep.

Chapter 43

IT WAS A FEW minutes before nine P.M. when Mikki Parker walked anxiously down the hall toward her room on the forty-fifth floor of New York City's Plaza Hotel. She hadn't talked to her sister since early that morning and was looking forward to hearing her voice after another boring day of following Louie Cordaro around the streets of New York, watching him visit several different union locals on yet another backslapping goodwill tour that had for her become all too frequent during the last few weeks.

Louie Cordaro was determined to show his critics how much his people supported and loved him. The strength he demonstrated was impressive in terms of numbers but the audience lacked much of the old enthusiasm accorded him during similar visits in the past. Even he had noticed that something was different but blocked it out of his mind as he urged the members to wage war at the polls by not supporting those who hadn't clearly demonstrated their support of organized labor. Lists were handed out with the names of people to vote against. It was no surprise that James Hawk occupied the list's top position.

Mikki was nearly at her door when she heard a crashing sound. For security reasons, she and Cordaro had been frequently exchanging rooms when they traveled and tonight room 4512 was occupied by Cordaro, though it was registered in her name.

The door was ajar and she cautiously entered. The room was dark and she had difficulty adjusting her eyes. She

stood still, listening. Then, without warning, a sharp pain
shot through the back of her neck as she was thrown
forward, her body viciously slamming against the thickly
carpeted floor. Something cold was thrust against her
cheek and the ominous clicking noise of a cocked gun,
only a life-taking millimeter away from firing, seemed to
echo throughout her brain. She didn't move a muscle as
she lay her face flat against the floor, held in place by what
she thought to be the sole of someone's powerful foot.

Her words were muffled, barely discernible. "I'm Mikki
Parker."

The pain behind her head began to disappear as the foot
holding her down slowly lifted. "You fuckin' idiot, don't
ever come into my room that way!"

She recognized the voice and was never more relieved. It
was Cordaro. A profuse sweat broke out all over her body.
She rose to one elbow and stumbled to her feet, grasping
for her balance in the still darkened room. A fumbling
noise preceded the lights. Cordaro stood only a few feet
away, the gun still in his hand.

Mikki tried to explain. "I heard a noise. I only wanted
to check if you were all right," she said apologetically.

Cordaro was fierce, still storming. "I could a killed ya!
What in the fuck did you pull a trick like that for? You
oughta know better!"

"Like I said, I heard a noise," she said, picking up her
purse from the floor. "What was it, anyway?"

"Oh, I bumped into a table. I just knocked that lamp
over," Cordaro explained, pointing to the lamp on the
floor. He looked at the pistol he was still clutching in his
hand and self-consciously looked for a place to set it down,
finally settling for the pillow on his bed. "Sorry. Well you
know, I can't be too careful."

There was an awkward silence. Then Cordaro turned
away and looked at the whiskey bottle on the table. "How
about a drink?" he asked.

She could tell that he had had a liquid dinner. It was the
same pattern he had been following for the past two weeks
on the road. Up early, working through the day without

lunch, then excusing himself early after dinner for the balance of the evening. While she hadn't actually seen him drinking away the night in his room, his bloodshot eyes and liquored breath each morning gave him away. She looked at an empty bottle of Jim Beam on the nightstand. Another freshly opened fifth sat beside it. Cordaro's eyes, contracted because of the sudden light, didn't give him away but his slurred speech, something that he couldn't control whenever he had over three drinks, did. His room was scattered with the remains of the *New York Times,* several empty glasses, and two plastic buckets half filled with water where the ice had long since melted.

He pointed to the sofa and she sat down, not wishing to antagonize him.

Cordaro turned away, visibly embarrassed at the disorderly appearance of his room. After a few feeble attempts to fold the newspapers that lay scattered on the floor, he gave up and sat down on the sofa next to her. He stared at her, his eyes now open wide and blinking. "I guess I owe you an apology."

She only nodded.

He looked pleased, assuming he was excused even though he had offered no formal apology, letting only his suggestion suffice.

She stared at him. A gulf of silence separated them. She became even more uneasy as his eyes dropped from hers and began to scan her body. She knew what he was thinking and thought about the time he had raped her. She knew he would never try to do such a thing again. It was strange. He respected her. He had told her that when she offered to come back to work after the attack. It wasn't her threat to turn him in if he ever touched her again that kept him at bay, she felt sure of that. He could have had her eliminated the same as he had others that threatened to get in his way. There was something else, something she had felt ever since she was a little girl. The flowers, the gifts, the money he had showered on her and her sister over the years now seemed as if he had been trying to make up for something.

He was close to her, their thighs barely touching as they sat side by side. She took the glass he was offering, even though she didn't care for whiskey.

Cordaro continued to ramble. "Lousy bastards," he muttered. "They think they can scare me, but I'll show 'em who's boss. The fuckin' joke is going to be on them."

A damp and stale stink from some spilled whiskey made her stomach uneasy. She turned her head away but he paid no attention, continuing to talk, still expecting no response. "Ya know, I can control this country," he said.

She looked back at him. His face had become more serious. The blank stare of only moments earlier was beginning to disappear. He was more lucid now, even though his speech was still slurred.

"Those bastards!" he screamed. "They need us, we don't need them. They can't even get elected without our support. You know something? We could take whichever party that loses the next election and build it into a labor party with our own people that could rule the whole fuckin' country. We'd have the strongest labor political party in history! We could elect anybody we wanted. Shit, we're doing it now and we're not even a political party. I could be president in four years. What do you think of that? Me! President of the United States! Sounds kinda good, don't it? President Louie Cordaro. I like it."

She toyed with her glass of whiskey, swirled it about and watched it continue to revolve in the glass before setting it down. "Don't you think you better get some sleep?" she asked. "We've got to go to Cleveland in the morning."

"Aw, fuck those yo-yo's in Cleveland. They don't know shit anyway. I don't even know why I let 'em talk me into going there. They're just a bunch of dumb bastards that'll do anything I say anyway. I could send them a letter telling them what to do and how to vote and they'd do it, no questions asked. Not like these tough New York guys. They gotta see me in person before they'll listen. Why do you suppose that is?"

"Maybe they're smarter in New York," she offered, with a faint smile.

He scratched his head. "Well, no matter anyway," he said, shaking his head. "The point is I'm smarter than all those dummies put together and they know it. They don't dare cross me 'cause I got lots of friends and I can buy any son-of-a-bitch who *isn't* my friend. Every man's got his price, even the fuckin' president."

She looked away again, surprised at his last comment. She looked back at him. "The president?" she asked.

"Yeah."

Her interest was more than piqued. "What president?"

"Jordan! Who else? He's the only one we got, ain't he?" he said, his face only inches away from hers. She offered no response other than visibly arched brows as he draped his arm around her shoulders. "Look, honey," he boasted, "I told you when you came to work for me that you'd see me do things you didn't think was possible. I even surprise myself sometimes. Hell, the president's no different than the rest of us. He's working for a living, collects a salary just like all the other suckers in the world. If the price is right, he'll take money. He's done it before more than once, and he'll do it again."

"You mean you've actually bribed the president?" she asked, trying to be as casual as she could under the circumstances.

His arm became tighter around her shoulder, his face even closer than before. "Not bribed, not bribed! That's the wrong word. It always sounds so illegal. *Bought!* Bought, that's the word. Let's just say for services rendered. That sounds clearer."

"Call it what you want, it's still the same thing," she said with a smile, trying not to be too serious for fear of arousing his volatile temper. She wanted more specifics; she had to push ahead. "Whatever did you need that you had to bribe the president?" she asked innocently.

A frown drew his thick brows together. She feared that she had pressed too far.

He looked her in the eyes, then leaned forward and kissed her forehead. After a brief silence, he returned to the subject. "You don't wanna know. But believe me, he can be bought. Just like anybody else. Ain't no saints in this world, particularly Jordan."

She became nervous but didn't show it. His face was still only inches away. "How much did you have to pay him?" she asked.

Cordaro only shook his head.

She tried to collect her thoughts, to convince him to be more specific, but her mind failed to respond. She decided to wait for a more propitious moment. She thought about her friend Frank Billings and what he had told her about Cordaro. Maybe now was the time to bring up the subject. She hesitated a moment, then, "Have you ever killed anybody?" she asked.

The color rose in Cordaro's cheeks. She watched him closely, trying to detect from his reaction how close she was to finding out if what Billings had told her was true. She had never seen a face so stunned—not frightened, just stunned. His mouth opened a moment before the first word came out. "What did you say?"

She repeated her question exactly as before, although purposely more casually, but she didn't really need an answer. His reaction gave him away. He had killed. She was sure of that.

"Who wants to know?" he asked, removing his arm from around her shoulder.

"Just curious. I mean, I read the papers. It seems somebody is always getting killed in this business, just like that fellow from Puerto Rico."

"I didn't have nothin' to do with that!" he shouted, standing up quickly.

She held his hand, trying to calm him. "Louie, I just used that as an example. I was just curious, that's all."

Cordaro weighed what she was saying. Either she was being perfectly honest or she represented something other than what he thought her to be. He had to find out.

He reached down and cupped her face with his hands.

She made no effort to move as he lowered his face to hers, kissing her on the lips this time. "I'm tired," he said. "Let's get some rest. We can discuss this another time, maybe in the morning."

She wasn't sure what he meant but it only took a moment before she knew. He took her by the hand and led her to the bedroom. "Get undressed," he said.

This time there would be no rape, she had already decided that. She wanted to know more about who he had killed. If she had to use her body to get the information, she would. She sat on the edge of the bed. He could feel the heat beginning to build in his loins as she began to roll her sweater over her head. She wasn't wearing a bra, and he followed her hands with his eyes as she began to move them seductively down over her body.

"Now what?" she asked quietly, a challenging tone to her voice.

He stepped closer, running his fingers through her hair before reaching down, searching. Her eyes closed. She let him fondle her breasts, remaining still all the while. Her mind was blank now, in a near trance.

He began to roll her onto her back but she stopped him, sliding her hands between her legs.

"Lie down," she commanded, reaching for his belt.

He rolled heavily onto the bed, landing on his back. She tugged at his belt, then at his zipper which opened easily. He reached under her skirt, trying to slide his hand as high as possible but she pushed him back gently. "Lie back," she said, parting her lips. Expertly, her fingers found their way between his legs and the elastic on the leg of his underwear. She reached inside freeing him and placed her head between his legs. Her mouth felt hot and he lay back, letting the juices flow. Tonight, at least for now, he had no trouble.

Chapter 44

TOR DROPPED HIS briefcase on James Hawk's cluttered desk and opened it. "It's a dead-end street," he announced. "We'll just have to wait and see."

James looked down at the battered old case, then back at Tor. "Do you believe her?" he asked.

"What else can I do? She says he's on vacation and can't be contacted. She's not even sure herself where Bonnam is. After all, she is his wife and she didn't seem concerned, so maybe . . ."

Tor didn't complete the sentence. He knew what James was thinking. If Mikki Parker's assessment of Louie Cordaro's remarks the day before about finding Sidney Bonnam was correct, a contract had been let on Bonnam's life. Now they couldn't even be sure whether he was dead or alive. While the F.B.I. had Bonnam's signed confession, it would be of little use as evidence if the defense didn't have the right to cross-examine. There also was no assurance that the jurors would testify even if confronted with Bonnam's statement. Even the threat of contempt of court charges if they refused to cooperate was no guarantee. Cordaro's history of eluding convictions also could not be ignored. Cordaro was capable of anything.

Pushing against his desk, James slid himself backward in his chair. "All right," he began. "We'll proceed as if that's exactly where Bonnam is, on vacation. The trial preparation will assume Bonnam will be here to testify. In the meantime, I want to be sure the jurors know that we have him as our witness. That just might shake them loose.''

James shifted in his chair and continued. "Keep a close watch on Bonnam's wife but don't alarm her. Just tell her that it's very important that we talk with her husband. Without him, we're dead. Even if the jurors admit that Bonnam tried to bribe them, we can't tie Cordaro directly into it without Bonnam's testimony. He's our proof, our hammer to nail Cordaro. I don't want to go through this whole damn exercise and end up with nothing more than a handful of jurors admitting that someone they'd never seen before tried to bribe them. Particularly someone we can't even produce.''

"Or even prove exists," Tor added.

"There is a way, you know.''

Tor did know. "Mikki," he said.

James nodded. "Her testimony could make the difference in whether or not we have a chance at getting to Cordaro. If Bonnam doesn't show, that's an option we'll have to face.''

"Let's wait until the time comes.''

James slowly nodded his head.

Tor shifted his attention to his briefcase and pulled out a miniature tape recorder. "There's something I want you to hear," he said.

He set the recorder on top of his briefcase and engaged it. "The voice is Mikki's. I asked her to tape some things she told me last night.''

Tor leaned forward, turned up the volume slightly and sat back in his chair, his arms crossed loosely on his chest. James listened as Mikki described what Cordaro had told her about bribing President Jordan. James had to struggle to fully comprehend what he was hearing. It was so antithetical to him he found it difficult to believe. Even if he discovered Mikki Parker's accusations to be true, he would never be able to bring himself to reveal them to the public, let alone exploit them. That the president of the United States had apparently succumbed to the same temptations as many private citizens was a tragedy, but unless his indiscretions jeopardized the national security, James felt it would be best to let it be. If he were successful in defeating the president in the November elections, the problem would be eliminated. There would be no sense in tearing down the public trust to get at one man who could do no more harm.

The tape ran out. Tor stopped the machine, returned it to his briefcase and waited for a response.

James broke from his reflections. "I would be careful with that tape," he said. "We can't let this get out. We can't be sure what Cordaro was talking about. Mikki did say he was drunk."

"Don't you want to pursue it?"

James thought a moment and then spoke slowly. "Any other time we could handle this differently. But this is an election year. Any charges I make against the president, even if we had all the facts, would be received by the public as mudslinging on my part. There's less than three months before the election. Jordan simply has to be defeated. If what he's done turns out to be something that merits prosecution, we can handle it later. It's better to prosecute an ex-president than one still in office. That way, the nation wouldn't be weakened by a scandal that could only result in an interim government that would have a caretaker function at best. I don't believe our country can afford that right now."

James rubbed his forehead with the back of his hand and continued. "You know, we've had bad policemen, district attorneys, judges, even bad presidents. There's no guarantee that a person will do the right thing once he has been given a badge or is elected to office. There's always the danger that people will succumb to the power of politics that can corrupt any office, high or low. The problem is, every time something like this happens it erodes a little of the people's confidence. It begins to fade until one day, it's vanished. Then you have revolution. Unless we begin to correct some of these things and rebuild the public's confidence, get them involved in what's going on around them, we'll be ripe for something just like that. I can actually see the deterioration process setting in. Cordaro's union is infested with members of organized crime—you might even say they're controlled by the mob—the union can control the economy of the United States on a moment's notice if they want to, and the politicians know it. We're going to need legislation to defend ourselves against union control and that will have to come quickly because more Cordaro-sponsored congressmen are coming in every year. They know to whom their loyalties belong. If organized crime controls Cordaro, and Cordaro's union in turn controls many of the police forces that enforce the laws in our cities that are made by politicians backed in the elections by Cordaro, who in the hell controls the country? Cordaro and his union, that's who! They're gradually going to strangle us if we don't wake up.''

The two men sat silently, each lost in his own thoughts. They knew what had to be done. How and when were the questions they could not answer.

Tor rose to his feet. "Come on," he said. "Enough of this bullshit about solving the world's problems in one night. We're getting out of here.''

"Where are we going.''

"Well, since I can't safely see Mikki, I have an old friend in town. I asked her to join us for dinner.''

James looked puzzled. "What's that got to do with me? You two will be better off alone. Call me in the morning after you've had your horns trimmed.''

"That's precisely what I'm getting at! I asked her to invite a friend. I told you a few weeks ago I'd get you laid discreetly. They're already at the hotel and neither one of them are coming out of their rooms until after we leave tomorrow morning. You can slip in, fuck your socks off all night, and get out in the morning without so much as a whisper. Even the future president needs a little ass once in a while.''

James was hesitant, concerned about his image.

Tor persisted. "Look, turkey, to be good is noble but

you should just concentrate on teaching others how to be good—that's even nobler and a whole lot less trouble. Now let's go have some fun."

James smiled. "Let's go," he said.

Chapter 45

TOR SAT IN HIS office at the Senate Office Building writing a letter. It was nearly three o'clock in the afternoon and his mind still reflected on what James had said two days earlier about the possibility of Louie Cordaro and his union controlling the country. He finished the letter, affixed a stemp and threw it in the out box. He had never been able to tell Mikki of any of his frustrations about their relationship but he had tried to do just that in his letter. He thought a lot of her and wanted her to understand that fact. Somehow writing made it seem clearer. He stared moodily out the open window and rubbed the day's fatigue from his eyes.

Outside, a young man knocked lightly on Tor's office door, entering without waiting for a response. ''Mr. Slagle?'' he asked in a muted tone. ''My name is Mark Tripp. I believe I have an appointment with you.''

Tor was embarrassed. His mind's wanderings had caused him to forget the boy's phone call earlier that morning. He didn't know what the boy wanted to discuss but he had been insistent, saying only that it was confidential.

The boy looked about seventeen with long red hair that nearly hid his fading freckles. He spoke with his head down. ''I heard that you're with the Hawk Committee,'' he said.

Tor nodded and the boy continued. ''Then there's a man I think you should know about.''

The boy was nervous, fidgeting, not sure where to start

his story, but he soon settled in and his facts became clearer as his confidence began to grow. "I became suspicious several months ago," he said. "My girlfriend began buying a lot of expensive clothes with money she said her grandmother gave her. When she kept buying more clothes I asked her mother about it. She told me that both of my girlfriend's grandmothers had died several years ago."

The boy went silent and looked to Tor for some reaction. Tor only smiled, still not sure of what the boy was leading up to. "Go on," he said.

"So, I asked her mother about the new clothes and she told me that Sheila, that's my girlfriend, was getting her money from her part-time job. She was a typist for a lawyer in Columbus, but I knew the money she made there couldn't have come close to what she was spending."

The boy pressed on. "It wasn't until she returned from a ski trip with broken ribs and a black eye that I knew something was wrong. I knew she hadn't been skiing. I could just tell. I finally threatened to go to her mother, so she broke down and told me about the beating she got from the senator."

Tor nearly bolted from his chair. "What senator?" he asked quickly.

The boy eyed Tor, as if he distrusted him. His words came with venom and not without difficulty. "Gregory—Senator Benjamin Gregory," he said tersely.

"Who knows about this?" Tor asked, his mind already sorting out the potential implications.

The boy's head bowed slightly. "We haven't told anybody," he answered.

Tor's voice was reassuring. "Why have you come to me?" he asked.

"Because I've read about your position with the committee."

"What's that got to do with it?"

"Don't you see? It's because of the union that Sheila got beat up."

Tor was stupefied. "I think you're going to have to

explain that. I really don't understand the connection.''

The boy tried to regain his composure. He had spent three days trying to convince himself that what he was about to do was right. Haltingly, he continued.

He told about the party arranged by Everett Richardson where Sheila had been beaten. ''She didn't recognize the name she saw on the driver's license until a few weeks ago when she saw him on television,'' he said. ''When she told me who it was, I decided to come here.''

''And Sheila worked for Everett Richardson?''

''If you can call it that!''

''Please, go on,'' Tor asked.

''Richardson paid her a hundred dollars each time she went to one of the parties as a hostess, but she didn't have to have sex. It was okay up until the last party.''

''The last party?''

''Yeah. Richardson asked her to go to another party and said he's pay her five hundred dollars if she slept with someone. That's when she got beat up. She called me the next morning, real early. I could tell she'd been crying but she just said she was lonely without me and wanted to hear my voice. She hung up before I could say anything. That's when Richardson came into her room.''

James asked, ''What then?''

The boy became silent, looking at he floor.

''You have my word,'' Tor said. ''This is between us.''

The boy continued to look down for a minute, studying the laces on his tennis shoes, then continued in a weakened and broken tone, ''Well, he told her he was sorry about what had happened and said he'd take her to a doctor. He offered her another five hundred dollars to keep quiet. All she wanted to do was get out of there so she agreed. That was when he said he had to be sure.''

''To be sure?''

''Yeah, you know what I mean. Be sure that she wouldn't talk.''

''And?''

The boy's voice was breaking, but he continued. ''He made her take off her clothes and lie on the bed while he took pictures of her. Then another lady came in and they took more pictures. Sheila was scared so she went along with it.''

''What kind of pictures?''

He hesitated, then his speech became more deliberate. ''Pornographic pictures . . . they made her do all kinds of things, first to some guy she'd never seen before and then to the other lady while they took more pictures. They said that if she ever said anything to anybody about the beating they'd sell the pictures to some porno magazine and send a copy to her mother.''

The boy started crying. Tor reached over, touched his arm, and sat patiently for a moment until the tears began to subside.

''I want you to know that I want to help you and I will,'' Tor said. ''I promise you that. But I still need to know why you think this has anything to do with the union or the committee.''

The boy's face stiffened; his fists clenched, driving his fingernails into sweaty palms. ''I did some checking,'' he said. ''Richardson's been the defending attorney for a lot of union officials in the past. I figure he must be involved with them in some way or another. That's why I came to you. I just didn't know where else to go. So, here I am.''

Later, as Tor watched the boy leave the room, he came to grips with the problem of how to deal with Senator Gregory. It was a real can of worms, but it had to be addressed without delay. Because of the senator's position on the committee, any public investigation would jeopardize the credibility of the committee itself, but coverup could be potentially even more damaging. Gregory was a pawn for Cordaro, easily sacrificed. If the investigation of Gregory was discovered by Cordaro, he would exploit it to the fullest by blasting at Gregory's credibility as a member of the committee that sought to destroy him. It was ironic that Senator Gregory possibly stood to help Louie Cordaro more as a lawmaker under investigation for his sexual deviations than he ever had as a Hawk Committee member.

It took only a few days for Tor to discover that Everett Richardson was involved in much more than arranging parties for influential people. His discussions with the boy's girl friend confirmed that there were at least six other girls under eighteen employed by Richardson for their sexual favors. Since the girls were under age, Richardson was subject to prosecution under the White Slave Act, but Tor's interest was of a much broader scope. The relationship between the union and Richardson had to be detailed.

Tor wondered how many judges had been paid off through favors from people such as Richardson. How, he thought, do you know when you prosecute a union official that the judge doesn't owe his election to the backing of Louie Cordaro? What about the prosecuting attorney? How can you convict someone the prosecuting attorney doesn't want to convict? All he needs to do is prepare a weak case, not present enough facts to eliminate any reasonable doubt in the minds of the juror.

Tor worked closely with the Columbus, Ohio district attorney, convincing him that the committee's interest in Richardson's activities with several other state politicians as an unregisterred union lobbyist would require a closed grand jury inquiry. He sent for one of the committee's top investigators to assist the district attorney after assuring him that Senator Gregory's involvement would be kept quiet temporarily as it would be included as part of the grand jury's closed hearings.

In an immediate action to stop the continued practice of using under-age girls for prostitution, Everett Richardson was arrested and charged with violation of the White Slave Act as well as pandering.

Within hours of Richardson's arrest, he flexed his muscles and showed his uncommonly strong influence within the state's judicial system by having himself released on his own recognizance. Even though Tor was confident that the grand jury's probe would implicate Richardson for things far more serious than being a pimp, the harsh reality of Richardson's power settled in for Tor only after the grand jury returned their indictment against Richardson. For no apparent reason, Richardson's trial was shifted from Columbus to Cincinnati.

Tor's preliminary inquiries into the shifting of trial sites showed that Richardson's political influence was stronger in Cincinnati than Columbus. The fact that one man could openly manipulate his own judicial destiny was infuriating. Once again Tor began to resent being trapped by the responsibility thrust upon him first by Billy Hawk and now by his brother James. Unscrupulous politicians and judicial officials threatened the serenity of the life that he had once enjoyed what now seemed to be an eternity away. He yearned to return to his old life but knew that regardless of the outcome of his commitment to James Hawk and the committee, he could never view his country through the same rose-colored glasses as he had in the past. He was watching firsthand as his government was being stripped to the buff, bearing scars that seemed would never heal.

Just after Labor Day, the sensations that had been churning in Tor's insides temporarily disappeared when he read the morning paper. The United States District Attorney in Virginia announced the formal indictment of Louie Cordaro for jury tampering.

Chapter 46

"WITHOUT DOUBT," JAMES Hawk declared to nobody in particular, "that is one bullshit collection of lies!"

In what had become a pattern, Marshall Tucker's front page editorial had been mailed to every major newspaper in the country. Captioned "Road to Dictatorship," it was republished by many of the papers receiving copies, and, like so many of the other Tucker Globe editorials, it was a scathing attack on James Hawk:

> The latest announcement that Louie Cordaro has once again been indicted makes you think of the kid who lost the ballgame and then accused the victors of cheating. Last June, in Virginia, James Hawk lost another of his many attempts to hang something on Louie Cordaro. In the Sky City fiasco, the jury couldn't agree to convict Cordaro of anything and now the government, under constant prodding by Hawk, has announced that they've indicted Cordaro on the grounds that he and some of his associates conspired to fix the jury.
>
> Cordaro has experienced indictments numerous times before and each time has either been acquitted, or, as in the last case, the jury was divided and a mistrial declared under our judicial system proving his innocence. Under any just system of government it would seem that this persecution of one individual should cease since the only thing Cordaro is guilty of is not kneeling to James Hawk in humble obedience as do other smaller union leaders

around the country. Louie Cordaro and his union are as independent and proud as James Hawk and they have a right to be. Since when has that been a crime in this country? The battle of Cordaro versus Hawk has become the battle of all working Americans who want to stay free. Is this the man we want as our president? I think not.

James was dispirited. He sat in his chartered jet with his legs resting on the seat across the aisle. He dropped the newspaper across his lap and looked over his shoulder at the company of media reporters in the aft cabin. They had been paying no attention to his muffled comments while he was reading the editorial.

A fever of impatience crept into his soul as he looked at the entourage accompanying him on the first day of a grueling two-week campaign tour that was to begin within two hours in Atlanta. He wanted to vent his frustrations, but booze and backgammon games were taking precedence over even a presidential candidate.

He began to thumb through his itinerary for the next two weeks. It resembled an hourly chronology for an efficiency study. Each day's schedule required two single-spaced typewritten pages. It was incomprehensible even to him how anybody could keep up such a pace. Not only did a sequence of such days exhaust his own vitality and perceptions, is exhausted his staff. Moreover, it exhausted the press, which was even more important. It was important to inform the public. His thinking and proposals had to be made clear. If not, he risked the reporters giving only a mechanical summary, which was exactly what he wanted to avoid. Marshall Tucker's editorials gave only one side of the story and to meet the Cordaro problem head-on could cause even more problems.

Then, a young reporter from the *Los Angeles Times* brushed James's arm accidentally as he was returning to his seat from the forward restroom.

"Sorry, Mr. Hawk," he said sheepishly over his shoulder. James smiled an understanding acknowledgement and returned his attention to the papers in his lap.

For the first time, he was going to address the union situation publicly and his advisors had worked intently on the speech he was to give that evening. He had to ignore the real issues and differences between the president and himself, something he felt needed to be aired, and concentrate instead on his survival. The union issue would kill him politically and he knew it. Tonight's speech was critical.

The speech was purposely scheduled at the beginning of the hectic two-week schedule to guard against the reporter fatigue he feared so much. Most of the wire service reporters were scheduled to be at his side for the entire two weeks and he knew too well the schedule's energy-sapping drain that would be evident at the end. The speech had to come now. His views had to be reported and interpreted accurately.

While James studied his speech, the young reporter from the *Times* sat several rows behind, fidgeting in his seat in a fever of impatience, waiting for his chance. He intently down the aisle into the first class section. James's eyes never left the pages he was studying. Then, several minutes later, James dropped the papers into the empty seat alongside his own and stood to stretch his legs. The young reporter leaped from his seat.

"Mr. Hawk," he called.

James turned and recognized him with a lukewarm but polite smile. "Yes, Mr. Hobbs, what can I do for you?"

The reporter hesitated momentarily. "I'm s-sorry, sir," he apologized, with a slight stutter. "I guess I'm surprised that you know my name."

"Goddammit, boy," James said loudly, "if I have to travel with you guys for two weeks than I damn well better know who my companions are!" He put his arm around the young reporter's shoulder. "Now, as I said before, what can I do for you?"

Hobbs was grinning now, gaining confidence. This was his first assignment as a national political reporter after having spent three years in Sacramento covering state politics. He didn't want to blow his chance. "I—I'd like to

351

ask you your opinion of the union's national convention that was just held."

"Why do you ask?" James asked.

"Why shouldn't I?" Hobbs blurted without thinking, then quickly retrenching. "I mean, isn't it important?"

"Damn right it is! It's just interesting that you're the first reporter to ask me about it. I'd like to know what makes you so different from the others."

"Aren't you addressing the subject in your speech tonight?"

"Yes, but it's not about the union's convention."

"It's not?"

"No."

"Why not?"

"Because that's not what the public wants to hear," James answered tersely.

An inquisitive look crossed Hobbs's face. He wanted to speak but couldn't. The answer to his question had caught him off-guard.

James smiled. "Do you want to know why I'm not going to discuss the convention?"

Hobbs nodded.

"Then sit down and listen," James answered, pointing to the seat next to his own.

James aired his frustrations in dealing with the union issue . . . the difficulty of a political candidate's attacking the leader of the strongest political force in the United States outside of the Democratic and Republican parties and still expect to get elected. The labor vote was important and Louie Cordaro was at the helm of the largest labor union in the world. James explained that in most elections, the union could sway the opinion of most of their members. Newsletters would be mailed to members of every local praising the endorsed candidate and denouncing the other as antilabor, whether or not their past voting record supported or rejected such claims. This was going to be a close election and there wasn't any question that those voters currently undecided would carry the fate of both candidates into voting booths.

"So you can see why I haven't wanted to make this union thing an issue during the campaign," James proclaimed. "Hell, I've supported the workingman all through my legislative life—my voting record will support that. But Louie Cordaro runs the union and I know whom he's supporting. I'm not naive enough to think that the majority of the voting public will dig out my voting record to see if I've supported labor. Shit, most people don't even know who their congressmen are, so how can I expect them to examine my record? They'll believe the bullshit Cordaro's slinging about my being antilabor and I'll have to spend half the campaign defending fake allegations which will cloud the real issues of the campaign. The fact is, Jordan's done a lousy job of running this country for the last four years and he can't defend that no matter how hard he tries. His record simply won't stand up to it."

Hobb's nervousness had disappeared. "But you wouldn't have had the labor vote anyway as long as Cordaro is president of the union. Why do you think the union issue is so critical to your getting elected? You knew when you started your campaign that you wouldn't have their vote."

"Yes, but I didn't plan on such an all-out campaign against me," James answered, pointing to the typewritten pages he had been studying earlier. "Look at that. What you see is an outline of a half-hour speech that two very intelligent members of my staff took over three days to research and write. *Three days* spent to try and defend myself against allegations from Jordan and Cordaro. They've got me on the run. I'll have to spend valuable time on defense instead of offense where I can be most effective. I thought if I could keep the union issue at bay during the election the public could concentrate on the real issues and make their choices accordingly. My record speaks for itself. I'm ready for the presidency. Jordan's already proved he can't handle the job! This country needs a change. Hell, ten years ago when the inflation rate was three and one-half percent, I can remember the people screaming about runaway inflation. Now, it's over ten percent, down from an annual rate of over eighteen percent only a few months ago, and Jordan's running around the country claiming he's whipped inflation. Bullshit! At ten percent? Who in the hell's he trying to kid? Even if it levels out at six percent, we've still gone through twelve months at eighteen percent. Prices will never come down to where they were before Jordan took office. We're stuck with paying exhorbitant prices for basic essentials because of his damned ineptness.''

"Now you're sounding like a politician," Hobbs offered.

"Well, Goddammit it, it's the truth," James shot back.

"So why did you get involved with the investigation in the first place if you knew there was a possibility it could hurt your chances of getting elected?"

James quickly held up two fingers. "Two reasons. First of all, I didn't expect this thing to come to a head as fast as it has. I thought after being elected I would be in a much stronger position to insure Cordaro's conviction. He's guilty as hell and all we need is a little more time to prove it. I just miscalculated the timing, that's all."

"You mean he's guilty of jury tampering?"

"Keep this off the record and I'll answer that."

"Okay. Off the record," Hobbs said, placing his pen in his shirt pocket.

James shook his head. "I can't say about the tampering charge for sure, but I know for a fact we can nail him on misuse of union funds. That's what we set out to do and we'll do it. The jury tampering issue is what's blowing up in my face. He got to someone on the jury and created a hung jury when we should have had him cold. His conviction would have proved my point. Now the jury tampering indictment looks to the public like sour grapes on my part because he didn't get the conviction. It's become such an issue that I have to address it, which keeps me from getting on with my original campaign strategy."

"Which it to attack Jordan's record."

"Exactly! Every day I spend defending myself against Cordaro takes precious time from the offense I need to win the election. I'll lose votes; I know it, but it has to be done."

"Catch-22?"

James sighed and responded emphatically, "Catch-22!"

"You said there were two reasons you got involved in the investigation. What's number two?"

James turned his head to look out the window. He wondered now if he should answer the question. After all, he reasoned, only a few people really knew and understood his intense emotion about Louie Cordaro. How could he convey in a brief moment what had been building in his gut for ten years? He wasn't afraid of his explanation, only how it would be interpreted.

A stewardess broke his concentration. "Excuse me, sir, would you care for some more coffee?"

James lifted his cup silently as she poured. Her tongue pressed hard between her lips as she concentrated.

"Spilling coffee on our next president would never do," she said, breaking the formality.

James laughed heartily. "I certainly hope you're right!"

Hobbs waited patiently for his answer.

"Let me ask you a question before I explain the second reason," James said.

Hobbs nodded, saying nothing.

"Why did you ask me about the convention? I'd bet a thousand dollars that I could spend the next two weeks on this plane with all those reporters back there and not be asked that question again."

Hobbs settled himself in his seat before answering the question. He sipped his coffee. "I've had an interest in labor unions for a long time," he began, "ever since I had a job in a manufacturing plant for the summer and they told me I had to join the union within one month of my hire date or be fired. That didn't sit too well with me."

"That almost sounds as if you don't like unions, Mr. Hobbs," James challenged with a dead-calm smile.

Hobbs shook his head. "Not exactly. I've just made it a point to study their organizations and what they stand for and try to let the public know whenever I can what I think, good or bad.''

"And just what *do* you think?''

"I'll answer that after you've told me reason number two for getting involved with the committee. It's still off the record.''

James looked into Hobbs's eyes. They were steady, honest eyes. His instincts told him to trust him. "Perhaps I can explain my second reason best by answering your original question.''

"You mean about the convention?''

"Exactly. What we saw during the convention was an accurately recorded demonstration of Cordaro's democracy, or should I say the absence thereof. The audience was filled with over eighteen-hundred voting union delegates, most of whom came from the pro-Cordaro locals he's so carefully staffed over the last two years. Cordaro even made sure that the media passes for the newspaper, radio, and television reporters only went to those who in the past demonstrated a friendly position toward the union. With preselected delegates who wouldn't dare vote against any proposal that Cordaro endorsed, the whole damn convention thumbed its nose at democracy. It was a Goddamn sham! No honest working-man would have voted for some of the shit Cordaro dumped on that convention.''

"Like raising the dues by a dollar a month?''

"Not so much that, although with membership of over two million people, it adds twenty-four million more dollars a year to an International treasury that's already overflowing with more than two hundred million dollars in reserve. Hell, the whole pension and health and welfare funds are now totally financed by employers who have to contribute one hundred dollars a month for every employee. Why it was necessary to stick the workingman with an extra dollar a month for dues is something I'm still trying to comprehend.''

"What did you think of Cordaro's rewriting the union's constitution?''

"You mean about creating a new office of general vice-president?"

Hobbs nodded.

James sighed and pushed his coffee aside. "It's another sham! Cordaro's covering his ass just in case he gets thrown in prison. By appointing Borg Trenier general vice-president, it automatically provides for Trenier to succeed to the presidency without a vote by the delegates until the next election if anything should happen to Cordaro. He won't have to worry about any political surprises within his own organization."

"But Cordaro denied that Trenier would just be a caretaker president. I was there. I heard him say it."

"Bullshit! Trenier wouldn't dare make any changes or rock the boat while Cordaro's in prison because he'd have to recken with him when he got out and that wouldn't be healthy. If Cordaro goes to prison, he'll still run his union. Behind the scenes, but he'll be running it. That's why he created the new position. He can trust Trenier to carry out his plan. If any of the others were to succeed him he couldn't be so sure."

Hobbs nodded. "It sounds as if you don't think much of Cordaro's democracy."

"There's no such word in the man's vocabulary. How many politicians do you suppose could pass legislation that would provide public funds from the taxpayers for legal fees to defend themselves in criminal cases?"

"I don't understand."

"That's exactly what Cordaro did during the convention! He presented a resolution, which the delegates approved, that provides funds for the defense for any union official in a criminal case. I find it very strange that union members would use their own funds to defend somebody accused of defrauding them of their own money."

"Meaning if Cordaro hadn't stacked the deck with his own hand-picked delegates he would never have gotten it through."

"Now you're beginning to understand. The working-man may have voted for the bit about the general vice-president, but not the funds for the defense of a common criminal. In Cordaro's case alone, it amounts to over a million dollars and he's bound to run up a bill twice that size now that he doesn't have to foot the bill personally."

Hobbs asked the obvious question, stepping right into James's favorite topic. "What can be done about it?"

"We need legislation against such a process, whether it's a union organization or a public company. Somebody has to look out for the little guy whose voice is never heard in such matters, usually because he never hears about it. Most of the union members never even find out what goes on at their own annual convention. Oh, there's a lot of news about general things, but little things such as allocations of funds for the legal defense of the union's officials are tacked on to the bottom of less controversial resolutions to keep from drawing too much attention."

"But that's the American way! Politicians do it all the time. It's usually the way they vote themselves a raise—by tacking it on to another bit of legislation they know the public wants and wouldn't dare vote against. One vote carries everything in the bill, including their raise in the small print at the bottom."

James admitted the truth in Hobbs's comment. "I can't dispute what you say, but I rather doubt our public servants would tag along with their raise a provision to have their full salaries continued in the event they spent their term of office in prison."

"Cordaro did that?"

"You didn't read the small print, Mr. Hobbs. He even *raised* his salary. Most of the delegates thought all they were voting for was for the creation of a new office called general vice-president."

James was just beginning to get warmed up. He went on. "And that's only the beginning. What boondoggles Cordaro's pulling on a national basis are being repeated daily on a smaller scale by hundreds of others at the local level. Our whole society is threatened by this mess. The workingman isn't properly represented even though he pays his dues. Corporations and small businesses suffer under excessive contract demands that divert funds away that should go to the worker in wage benefits but instead goes to the International Pension and Health and Welfare Fund, which has a slush fund used to support the whims of a very select few at the top of the union's hierarchy. If all the dollars funneled into those two funds were actually used to benefit the worker, I'd have no complaints, but our estimates are that less than half of it ever comes out at the other end as health and retirement benefits.''

''Where's the rest go?''

''That's what the committee is all about. It wasn't structured to punish Louie Cordaro. It's just that as president of the union, he was an obvious focal point and it became very clear that his laundry wasn't very clean.''

''And the committee intends to wash it in the street for him?'' Hobbs asked casually.

''He's up to his ears in corruption. He exercises absolute control in the union with virtually no system within the organization for checks and balances. When he runs into difficulty of any kind he resorts to threats and bribery to get what he wants. This jury-tampering thing is just one example of how far that man will go. For the good of the workingman, he must be stopped.''

''But would that rid the union of corruption?''

''It would be one helluva start!''

''If the corruption has been so obvious, why haven't the rank and file members organized and thrown Cordaro out?''

James smiled and leaned his head back on the seat, adjusting the air flow valve above. A cool stream of air blew on his face. ''A few brave souls have tried to go against Cordaro in the past but they've always failed. Some have been beaten, some even killed. There'll be no rank and file revolution, not in the near future anyway. The silent majority within that organization needs help. I intend to give it to them.''

"Through the committee?"

James nodded.

"You sound as though you're committed to see this thing through."

"Even if it costs me the presidency."

"It means that much to you?"

"I don't think there's any other choice."

"Meaning?"

"Our country can't survive as it exists today if we permit this corruption to continue. Our whole judicial and political systems as we know them will erode. We'd have politicians elected and judges then appointed by those same politicians who owe their election to the union's support and votes. It's no secret that Cordaro's union is heavily supported by organized crime. Cordaro and those folks go back a long way and they're so intertwined now it's hard to tell them apart. Most of Cordaro's union muscle comes from organized crime. In exchange, the mob gets their hands on the wealth of the union's pension and health and welfare funds to finance some of their supposedly 'legitimate' businesses. Cordaro gets the muscle to run his union; the mob gets the money. What the politicians and appointed judges get is to keep their jobs by staying on the good side of Cordaro. They won't get to keep that support if they start introducing or supporting legislation detrimental to the cause of the union or organized crime. You can sure as hell bet judges would look with a lenient eye on any accused individual they were told to go easy on. So that's what you'd have. Three entities: Organized crime, Cordaro's union, which I might add already represents many of our police forces, and the United States government composed of union-supported judges and politicians. All struggling for a common goal."

"What's that?"

"Power and survival. Power and survival."

There was a long silence as Hobbs looked away. He was beginning to understand why James was willing to jeopardize his chance of winning the election. He knew that it would take him time to understand all the ramifications of Hawk's ideas and thoughts.

"What do you think your chances are?" Hobbs asked.

"You mean in the election?"

"No, not that. I've read the polls. I mean about straightening this union mess out."

"That depends."

"On?"

"If I'm elected, I think we can lick it. It'll take a lot of time and effort, but we can begin."

"And if you're not elected?"

James shook his head and did not answer. He didn't want to consider the possibility.

Chapter 47

LOUIE CORDARO LOOKED down from his office window and saw the reporters and photographers had gathered near the entrance to the parking lot. He had ordered them removed from the premises when they began to flood his outer office insisting on a statement about his indictment for jury-tampering.

He turned to Borg Trenier who stood by his side, watching with equal interest. "Fuck 'em! I'm not going to dignify the bastards with a statement," Cordaro said defiantly.

Trenier disagreed. "You'll have to do something," he countered. "They're not just going to disappear. They'll hang around until they get a statement no matter how long they have to wait. If you don't give 'em one, they'll make a fool of you. You know that."

Cordaro glared at him, his face crimson. He knew Trenier was right. "Okay, okay, I'll give," he said reluctantly. "But I don't want those jerk reporters down there askin' their own questions. Get McCallum to arrange a press conference for this afternoon. He knows the reporters that are on our side. I don't want anybody there askin' any questions that would be embarrassing."

"You want an approved list of questions to be handed out beforehand?"

"Yeah, yeah. That's it. Give 'em a list of questions. McCallum and me will work out some sort of statement and the answers to the questions we give 'em."

Trenier puffed on his short cigar, rolled it from side to side in his mouth and smiled wryly. "I guess now we'll see how good a public relations man McCallum really is," he said.

"What do you mean?"

"I don't know how some of those reporters down there are going to take to being excluded from any press conference of yours."

Cordaro's features were livid. "It's my fuckin' conference! I'll invite whoever I damn well please! Now get McCallum. Tell him I want him here right away."

Within moments, Trenier returned. "He'll schedule the conference for two o'clock so there will be enough time to get it on this evening's news on the west coast. He'll work out the details on the questions and answers with you over lunch."

Cordaro nodded his approval, his face expressionless. Trenier twisted his cigar in his fingers uneasily, unsure if he should stay or leave. The telephone interrupted his awkward moment. It was Senator Gregory. Cordaro took the call and motioned for Trenier to sit down, raising a finger to indicate that he would only be a moment.

Before Cordaro could express his views about the indictment, the senator stopped him in his tracks.

"When?" Cordaro asked.

"This morning," the senator answered. "I just got the message. I thought you should know. I mean, something has to be done."

Cordaro began to pace as far back and forth as the phone line would permit. "What do they know?" he asked.

The senator continued. "He's been indicted for pandering. There's a lot of people that could go down in flames if he talks. My phone's been ringing off the hook. At least four judges have called and they all want to know what you're going to do about it. This whole damn thing can be traced back to the union, you know."

"I don't know what you're talking about!" Cordaro shouted, hanging up the phone violently. "That stupid fucking son-of-a-bitch!'' he yelled.

Trenier's eyes followed Cordaro who was now nervously pacing. Cordaro's cheeks were flushed with anger, his breathing short. Creases around his eyes became more profound as he began to frown menacingly.

"Can you imagine that stupid bastard calling me on that phone and making that kind of statement?'' Cordaro asked. "Hell, anybody could've been listening in!''

Having heard only one side of the conversation, Trenier had no idea what his boss was raving about.

Trenier shook his head. "What are you talking about?'' he asked.

Cordaro allowed himself a frustrated smile. "Everett Richardson got indicted for pandering. Gregory's been getting a lot of flak from some of the state officials. They want to know what we can do to stop it. But that witless ass has to broadcast over *my* phone that they can trace Richardson's little sex parties back to us!''

"Can they?''

"It won't be easy, but they could if they're smart enough.''

"How?''

"Richardson worked through McCallum's Public Relations Agency. McCallum paid all Richardson's bills and billed us back his normal retainer plus any extra costs. If they get into McCallum's operation and start asking questions about some of those billings, things could get sticky.''

"What's that got to do with the state officials?''

"If those whores open up and start talking about who their clients are, half the fuckin' judges and district attorneys in the state will be dragged into it. It wouldn't take any genius to put the pieces together. Some of those judges ain't too swift about covering their tracks.''

Giving away sex in exchange for favorable court rulings regarding the union was nothing new to Trenier. There was an Everett Richardson in almost every state performing similar duties. It wasn't until now that he understood how those people had financed their operations. "What are you going to do?'' he asked.

"When McCallum gets here, we can have . . .'' Cordaro stopped and thought for a moment. "No, no that won't work.'' His voice trailed off. He was about to suggest that McCallum hire a lawyer to defend Richardson but the absurdity of that idea quickly surfaced in his mind. His wits returning, Cordaro had another idea. "Get to Tom Wilson and tell him what's happening up in Ohio. Tell him to get us a good mouthpiece that can't be traced back to us and send him up there to see what he can do to get Richardson off the hook. I got enough fuckin' problems without that thing blowing up in my face.''

Cordaro's mood suddenly changed again. He began to laugh almost uncontrollably, as he thought about Senator Gregory. "What sweet justice it would be to have Gregory linked with a sex scandal! If it wasn't for the shit that'd hit the fan, I'd just as soon help the damned investigation along. But hell, I can't do that. Go ahead and get Wilson on it, but keep me posted. This thing may work to our advantage yet.''

Trenier snuffed his cigar and decided to leave before Cordaro's mood deteriorated again. He really wasn't sure what Cordaro was thinking but that wasn't unusual.

One hour later, an uncomfortable heat pierced through Cordaro's sports jacket as the sun of September's eighth day blazed through the window from behind his desk. He sat alone and rubbed the fatigue from his eyes. When he stood to pull the blinds, he saw Bob McCallum walking up the steps from the parking lot without his usual entourage of well-dressed assistants. He never did like McCallum's little helpers. Their appearance was always too refined. Ivy League suits, blow-dried hair, button-down shirt collars, and wing-tipped shoes were, for him, the sign of sissies. His own taste in clothes, while expensive, usually defied the tailor's original intent. His choice of accessories more often than not included brown shoes with a black belt and a flourescent tie that looked like it came off a rack at the corner drug store. No matter how well the suit fit his stumplike body, he somehow always managed to destroy the effect with a garish collection of accessories.

Cordaro listened for over an hour as McCallum previewed his proposal for what would be the opening statement for the press conference. As he had been instructed, all questions would be submitted to the press in advance.

Cordaro developed a headache that pounded in his forehead like a slowly swinging pendulum, each beat hurting more than the last. He toyed with and occasionally clenched his hand around a silver-plated Cross pen as McCallum repeated over and over what his prepared responses to the questions should be.

Just outside, Mikki Parker glanced at her watch as she leaned against the wall in the corridor that led to Cordaro's office. She had been there all morning and, apart from Trenier, she wasn't to let anybody enter. Her day had been boring and her mind wandered frequently, skipping at random from thoughts of Shana to how much she hated being where she was. Her face remained expressionless, giving no indication of the emotions she was feeling.

The door to Cordaro's office opened in a flurry and an electricity filled the air when Cordaro suddenly exploded past her into the corridor with Bob McCallum in close pursuit.

"Let's get this over with!" Cordaro commanded. Mikki quickly fell into line and they all walked briskly toward Borg Trenier's office.

When they arrived, Trenier was already outside, waiting to escort his boss to the press conference. They took only a few steps into the main corridor before a voice rang out from behind.

"Louie!" a man yelled.

The voice came from behind them, from an elderly unkempt man, his left arm missing, who anxiously approached. He wore brown shoes with dried mud on the heels and sides that met his lime green stretch socks. He wore gray pants which were much too short for his long legs and his frayed plaid sportcoat made his appearance even more disreputable.

"You remember me," he said to Cordaro anxiously. "We worked together in Chicago a long time ago."

Unimpressed, Cordaro turned away without acknowledging the man and started walking again.

The man persisted, stepping up his pace. "Please, Louie. You gotta talk to me!"

Cordaro kept walking.

Frustrated by Cordaro's stone-faced silence, the old man suddenly reached out, seizing Cordaro's arm, trying to stop him. The old man's frustrations were met with an equally untamed rage as Cordaro slammed his fist into the man's face, threw him to the floor and began to kick him with unrestrained fury.

"You want to talk to me, get an appointment!" Cordaro yelled.

A sense of shock filled both Trenier and McCallum as they stood by, doing nothing. Mikki Parker was closest to the altercation and finally intervened, pulling Cordaro away from his helpless victim while several people in the lobby who witnessed the attack chose to keep distant.

The veins on Cordaro's neck throbbed as he was restrained by both Trenier and McCallum. "Get that asshole outta here!" he screamed.

"You go ahead," Mikki offered. "I'll take care of this."

After helping to clean the blood from his face, she took the old man to the employees cafeteria where she bought him an egg sandwich and a bowl of tomato soup. She offered him some cigarettes and he accepted, letting her light one for him. While his shaky hands tried to guide the cigarette to his mouth, the man sucked in his breath, exhaled, and started to talk. "My name is Ivan Pilcher," he began . . .

Chapter 48

JAMES HAWK LAY awake in bed, a victim of a smild case of insomnia. He found it difficult to sleep, especially over the past few days. The effect of Louie Cordaro's carefully controlled press conference had gone exactly as planned. There were no surprises or potentially embarrassing questions while Cordaro skillfully used the national media coverage to portray James Hawk as an ogre and himself as an unfairly persecuted soul about to be obliterated unless the people of the country recognized his tormentor for what he was.

The power of the media, particularly television, to shape the American mind was never more evident, and James knew his already precarious lead over President Jordan in the polls was now in danger of slipping even further. Had it been a political adversary rather than Louie Cordaro who had made the damaging accusations about him, he could have demanded equal air time from the network to express and clarify his views. But the media hadn't asked for his rebuttal to Cordaro's statements. Even if they had, Cordaro had struck the first blow and any defense couldn't have erased the entire effect.

The constant chipping away by Cordaro and the media was definitely beginning to hurt. Cordaro, not President Jordan, was presenting the most formidable competition during this presidential campaign. Cordaro had become the opposition; it was he who was taking two steps forward for every one backward. It wouldn't take long now for him to reach his goal. The president was closing in on the lead.

The same night, Tor Slagle sat alone, occupying himself with a report that had been dropped on his desk only minutes before he was to leave to meet Mikki Parker.

As he sat in a parked car on a dead-end street, he used a penlight and leafed quickly through a committee investigative interviewer's comments concerning the assault only two days earlier on Ivan Pilcher by Louie Cordaro.

Pilcher's story was not unusual within the union organization. While he refused to press charges against Cordaro for assault, he did agree to tell his story when he was assured by the committee's investigator that the government would try to help him.

Tor soon found himself deeply involved in the interview between Pilcher and the investigator, which began with generalities but quickly spread to a broader terrain.

Questioner:	How old are you, Mr. Pilcher?
Pilcher:	Sixty-three.
Questioner:	Are you a member of the union?
Pilcher:	Yes. I have been for over thirty-six years.
Questioner:	Are you working now?
Pilcher:	No. That's the whole problem. That's why I went to ask Louie for help.
Questioner:	Louie Cordaro?
Pilcher:	Yeah.
Questioner:	What was it you wanted to talk to Mr. Cordaro about?
Pilcher:	My retirement benefits. The bastards never gave me my retirement benefits.
Questioner:	You mean the union?
Pilcher:	Yeah.
Questioner:	Are you retired now?
Pilcher:	Uh huh.
Questioner:	When did you retire?
Pilcher:	Last year. I was a warehouse maintenance man. Before that I drove a trunk for twenty-eight years. I lost my arm in a trucking accicent eight years ago so I had to look for another job. There aren't

	many one-armed men that can handle a sixteen-wheeler, ya know.
Questioner:	Why weren't your retirement benefits honored?
Pilcher:	They said I didn't qualify.
Questioner:	Who said you didn't qualify?
Pilcher:	The trustees of the pension fund, I guess. All I got was a letter. I don't remember exactly who from.
Questioner:	What did the letter say?
Pilcher:	It said because I had broken service between my time as a truck driver and a warehouseman, that they couldn't combine my years between the two jobs to make me eligible for retirement benefits.
Questioner:	But you had twenty-eight years as a truck driver. Didn't that qualify you?
Pilcher:	Not accordin' to them. When I had my accident I was only fifty-five and I didn't qualify for early retirement; the rules said you had to be sixty-two. That's why I worked another eight years. I figured then I'd have thirty-six years which would qualify me for a nice pension. That's why I quit my job and applied for my retirement. But when I applied, I never got an answer so I wrote again. In fact I wrote several letters and even made phone calls but it didn't do no good. It was over six months before they finally answered my letters. They said in the letter that I didn't qualify because I hadn't been working ten consecutive years when I retired. Hell, I thought I'd been working *thirty-six* years!
Questioner:	Hadn't you?
Pilcher:	I guess not. They said that because when I was between jobs I was off for over a

	year. They told me that anytime you're not a dues-paying member for more than one year you lose all benefits. Nobody never told me that before. I tried hard to find a job but there aren't many jobs around for one-armed men. It took me that long just to land the job in the warehouse.
Questioner:	Was your accident job-related?
Pilcher:	No. If it had been, I would have been covered, but I guess I can't even be sure of that now. They tell you about all the great benefits the union has to offer but I never read no small print. You just figure they'll take care of you when you need them. That's the only thing that kept me going after the accident. I figured with my pension and Social Security I could retire with almost as much income as I had when I worked. I was wrong.
Questioner:	Why did you try to approach Mr. Cordaro with your problem?
Pilcher:	Because I didn't know what else to do. Nobody else would even listen to me.
Questioner:	And you thought Cordaro would?
Pilcher:	Yeah. We worked together on the docks in Chicago when he first started out. That was a long time ago but he still remembered me, I know.
Questioner:	You were friends?
Pilcher:	Not exactly. He's always sent me a Christmas card, every year ya know. He signed it himself even though I haven't seen him personally in over twenty years. That's the kind of guy he was. He never forgot a friend. That's why I can't understand why he did what he did. Do you suppose he didn't recognize me?

Questioner:	You did say it had been a long time. I understand that you don't want to press charges. Is that correct?
Pilcher:	That's right.
Questioner:	Would you mind telling me why not?
Pilcher:	Because I know what happens to people who cross Louie. When he's your friend you want to keep it that way. I saw him turn on a friend once. It wasn't real pretty.
Questioner:	Who was that?
Pilcher:	It don't matter now.
Questioner:	Why?
Pilcher:	Because he's dead!
Questioner:	Did he kill him?
Pilcher:	No, at least I don't think so. He has others that can do that sort of thing for him, that much I do know.
Questioner:	How do you know that?
Pilcher:	Never mind. I just know.
Questioner:	Has he ever hurt or tried to hurt you before this?
Pilcher:	No.
Questioner:	Why do you suppose he hit you?
Pilcher:	Christ! How in the hell should I know? He just started beating the shit out of me. I can't explain it! Look, all I want is for you guys to help me. You said you'd help me if I answered some questions. Are you going to help me or not? I need your help, dammit! Please!
Questioner:	We'll try, that's all I can say. What you've told us here today will go a long way in helping to stop some of these things. Is there anything we can do for you in the meantime?
Pilcher:	I don't think so, not now. But . . .
Questioner:	But?
Pilcher:	You know, people like me . . . the little

guy . . . we can't do nothing unless you folks help. Where can we go? If we go to the union, we get bogged down in red tape and still don't get no answers. If we raise our voice to the public we stand a chance to get hurt. It's a no-win situation. I can't understand how somebody like Louie could have changed so much. He used to be such a nice guy. I really liked him. There was a time I would have given the man the shirt off my back. But no more. Even if I wanted to, I'm not so sure I'd have one to give anymore.

Tor flipped off his penlight momentarily. He sat in the darkness and wondered how many more Ivan Pilchers there were in the world.

He looked up the narrow street. There still was no sign of Mikki. He remembered that the agent who interviewed Pilcher had included with the interrogatory an additional commentary outlining his personal investigations over the past several months. He pulled the report from a manila folder, sat back, and began to read the agent's comments.

"The administration of the union's pension fund is so bureaucratic that many potential pensioners such as Pilcher aren't being given the benefit of a clear refusal, thereby making it virtually impossible to make an effective challenge to the trustees' rulings.

"It appears that pension claims frequently sit unanswered until the claimant dies or ultimately gives up writing letters. Many claimants interviewed in the last twelve months purport that their former employers have secretly cooperated with the union by altering records and fitting them into an employment category that could be considered by the trustees as questionable for pension eligibility, thus absolving the pension fund of responsibility for payments.

"A large number of individuals of questionable character are living well on the proceeds of investments made possible by the pension fund's loans while many deserving and qualified retired union employees can't get their earned benefits. Our investigators have shown that hundreds of millions of pension fund dollars have been squandered on bad loans, many of which have gone to businesses run by racketeers and ex-convicts. Many legitimate businesses are actually owned by members of organized crime that were initially financed by loans from the union's pension fund. They use these businesses to launder or funnel illegal profits from their other activities such as prostitution and narcotics. In many cases, these businesses never repay the loan and no explanation is given when the pension fund writes it off as an uncollectable debt. The Pension Fund remains a source for unlimited funds for organized crime in exchange for providing a protection service for a few select union officials that insures their power for a period sufficient in duration to assure an independently wealthy retirement. All of this is at the expense of people such as Ivan Pilcher.''

Tor turned off the penlight again and sat back. He had been working on the committee for nearly five months. He thought there was nothing that the union could do that would surprise him, but he was incredulous at what was happening to so many of the union's retirees. The very concept of unionism and brotherhood apparently meant nothing to the union leaders. Originally, he had believed that if the union could rid itself of Louie Cordaro, much of the corruption that infested the union would automatically be eliminated. He thought that no longer. His empathy for Ivan Pilcher made him feel a twinge of guilt about his own personal wealth. He knew now why Billy Hawk had fought so hard. It wasn't just one man, it was an institution.

He looked around for Mikki once more, and saw a figure standing alone near a darkened lamp post. He felt a sudden pulsation pound at his insides when the figure began to move toward the car. For the first time in his life, he wished he had a handgun. He was unarmed, exposed. He turned the ignition key, simultaneously turning the headlights toward the moving shadow ahead. His heart began to beat even faster. Then he saw who it was—Mikki.

She got quickly inside.

"Damn," Tor growled, turning the lights off. "You scared the hell out of me!"

Mikki responded with only a hint of emotion. "I guess I'm being a little over cautious these days," she said, kissing him on the cheek.

They wasted no time in systematically reviewing the notes each had made since their last meeting.

"What's behind the Everett Richardson indictment?" she questioned.

"Why do you ask?"

"The phone's been ringing constantly in Louie's office. A lot of people are concerned about what Richardson knows. It's even got Louie on edge. What's it all about?"

"We know that Senator Gregory is definitely involved but we're not sure how to handle it just yet. The district attorney in Ohio is handling most of the investigation. What's Cordaro said about it?"

Mikki shook her head. "Nothing. But he's been getting calls from some judges and a few others in Ohio. When I'm in the office, he always tells the caller he'll return the call, but I haven't been around when he calls back so I don't know what he's been telling them. I don't even know if he does call them back, but he looks plenty worried."

"He should be, but that's not my concern just now. We still can't find Bonnam and we're only a week away from the start of the trial. Do you know anything?"

"Not a word. I asked Louie yesterday if he'd ever found him, and he only muttered something I couldn't understand. I offered to help him but when I mentioned it, Louie changed the subject."

Tor's frustration was beginning to show. "Damn!" he said loudly.

Mikki ignored Tor's outburst. "How are you doing with the jurors? Are they talking?"

"They're all still scared. I thought they'd crack by now. It's got me worried. We need at least one of them to corroborate Bonnam's story and that's assuming we come up with Bonnam and his testimony."

"How about Bonnam's wife?"

"Nothing there either. She won't even answer her phone and she's been sending out for her groceries. When we go to her house, she won't open the door. She just talks through it."

"Do you think she knows where Bonnam is?"

"No, no . . ." he said, his voice trailing off as he turned away and looked out the window.

Tor turned back to Mikki, a careful and observant look on his face. "I told Jack Hawk about what Cordaro said concerning the possibility the president took a bribe. He wants you to keep on it. Have you gotten any more information?"

Mikki shook her head again, this time more slowly. "No. In fact, when I pressed him on it a couple of days ago he said he never said anything of the sort. He denied even remembering our conversation."

"Cordaro's smart." Tor sighed. "I was surprised he even mentioned it in the first place. Even for him, that's pretty heavy stuff to be mouthing off about."

Mikki just nodded. Tor knew she wanted out of her commitment to help the committee, but he wasn't about to bring up the subject, at least not for now. He knew there was something more than simple patriotism that was holding her where she was. He wished he could penetrate her thoughts, find out what was driving her, what made her so persistent.

She was still lost in thought when Tor interrupted her. "What do you know about Borg Trenier?"

Shrugging, she answered, "What's to know? He goes around running errands for Louie, same as I do. Why do you ask?"

"Nothing much, except there's a possibility he's the one that's been making those anonymous calls to me about Peck and Bonnam."

Mikki's interest was piqued, but she disagreed quickly. "He wouldn't dare cross Louie. Even if Louie went to prison, he would get back at him if he thought Borg was trying to undermine his authority. Trenier's too smart to pull a stunt like that."

"Just the same, I'd like you to nose around a bit. He's played it pretty low-key through the years but I'm not sure I buy his verbiage about not wanting the union presidency. I think he might be just waiting to strike."

"What makes you think he's behind the calls?" she asked.

"It boils down to only two people, Bonnam and Trenier. One of the calls specifically said to get to Bonnam. Except for Cordaro and Trenier, the only other people we think knew about Bonnam's spying activities were you, Jim Hawk, and me. I hardly think Bonnam would call me and point the finger at himself. That only leaves Trenier, but we can't be one hundred percent certain. I asked Bonnam but he denied it. He even seemed scared when I told him about the calls. I'm counting on you to see what you can find out."

Mikki continued to dwell on her own thoughts. Her life was filled with fear and hatred and suspicion. She couldn't even allow herself time to develop a relationship with the person sitting next to her, though she knew he possessed all the qualities she had ever hoped for in a man. In the beginning, when they had first met, she felt he was a ray of sunlight in a world suddenly cloudy and dark in the aftermath of her father's death. But now, thanks to Louie Cordaro, her emotions were spent. He had hardened her heart. She trusted nobody, not even Tor, but there was nothing she could do to change the way she felt.

Tor could guess some of what was going on in Mikki's mind. He was experiencing much of the same frustrations, but there was no way for him to know what was going on between her and Louie Cordaro. As for Mikki, she had to call on all her reserves of inner strength just to carry on, her thoughts centered around Shana. Shana was the only reason she could keep going. For now, working for Louie

Cordaro was serving a purpose. There was unfinished business that had to be completed.

They looked at each other without speaking for what seemed to them hours, although it was actually less than two minutes.

"Anything else?" Mikki said at last.

Tor smiled slightly. "No," he answered. "Just stay alert and remember that it's better to keep your mouth shut and appear stupid than to open it and remove all doubt."

The seriousness on Mikki's face suddenly disappeared. She began to laugh. Tor's feeble joke had made her relax and she appreciated his recognizing that she needed something to smile about right now. "Okay," she said, reaching for the door. "I'll go home and tape my mouth shut."

"Not yet. There's something I have to do first," Tor said.

"What's that?"

"This," he said, reaching for her. He kissed her lightly then reached his arm around her to draw her nearer.

She moved away, letting herself out. "Not tonight, Tor, I have to go," she said quietly. Then she was gone.

The next morning Tor sat in his office chair and reflected on the night before. He felt more depressed than at any time he could remember. He had no idea how much longer it would take the committee to satisfactorily complete its business and he was puzzled by Mikki's sudden departure the night before. He had wanted to make love to her and worried that his intent had been too obvious. He was mad at himself for being so insensitive to her feelings and wanted desperately to talk to her, to apologize. He sat chewing on the end of the plastic pen and leaned back in his chair, propping his feet on his desk. Only the sound of the squeaking springs beneath his oak chair broke the silence. It was then that he noticed the envelope propped against the calendar on his desk. He'd seen it earlier but it hadn't registered. It was a telegram sent from New York City.

The message was simple, made its point, and Tor's day: "Will show when trial starts. S.B."

Tor's depression quickly vanished. Sidney Bonnam had come back into the picture.

Chapter 49

ELAINE HAWK'S VOICE came through the telephone with unexpected news. "I think I've found what you've been looking for," she said.

Tor leaned forward in his chair, pressing the phone tightly to his ear. "You mean the diary?"

"I think so. I was cleaning Billy's den and decided to listen to some music. That's when I found it. It was in the recorder."

"A cassette?"

"Yes, can you believe it? It's been there all this time! I never use that machine but since I was going to be in there for a while I . . ."

Before she could finish, Tor cut her off. "Where is it now?" he asked.

"Here. Right here in my hand. But there's something else."

"What?"

"I know this may sound silly, but I think somebody has been in Billy's den."

"What makes you think that?"

"I specifically remember locking Billy's file cabinet after you were here. I have the only two keys, but when I came in this morning it was unlocked. I know I didn't leave it that way. I haven't been in here in weeks."

Tor was alarmed. He remembered seeing the safe unlocked when he was searching for Billy's diary. He also remembered locking it. "Elaine, I want you to take the tape and put it in your safety deposit box until I get there. Do it now. I'll fly in by early evening. We'll go get it out in the morning," he said, already leafing through his pocket airline schedule.

It was only nine A.M. but with a flight time of over five hours and a three hour time change, he wouldn't be in Newport until long after the bank closed for the day.

"I'll call you from the airport when I get in," he said. "Meanwhile, I want you out that door on the way to the bank as soon as we hang up. Understand?"

"I understand," she answered.

"And, Elaine?"

'Yes?'

He was silent for a moment, almost hesitant to say what was on his mind. "Get someone to come over and stay with you today," he said. "Don't let them leave until I get there."

Elaine ignored Tor's warning and spent the day alone. She hadn't taken the cassette to her safety deposit box as he had asked. She considered his concern to be an over-reaction. The cassette was hidden where only she could find it and she felt comfortable alone.

Still, throughout the day, she was aware of her nervousness. She hadn't seen Tor for nearly two months, although she had talked with him over the phone several times. She wasn't sure why she was tense but the sharp pain in the right side of her neck that extended down to her shoulder blade was a dead giveaway. It always did that when she felt uneasy.

Somewhere deep inside her strange feelings on the day Billy had been killed became confused with Tor's return to her home. Perhaps his presence would remind her too much of Billy's death, but she discounted the idea almost as quickly as it came. Tor had been like a brother to her husband and his presence had always been comforting for her. She was looking forward to his visit despite her nervous reactions.

It was midday, while drinking her cup of herb tea, that the actuality of her concern hit her with the subtlety of a freight train. It wasn't Tor's visit that was making her uneasy, it was Billy's tape.

Listening to Billy's voice on the tape had been so unexpected it caused her to relive the full force of that dreadful day in May all over again, and she knew when Tor arrived she would hear the tape again. For a moment she thought she could just turn the recording over to Tor and let him listen to it alone, but for some reason she knew she had to be there.

That evening she was resting on the sofa when the sound of the doorbell filtered into the library and she jumped to open the door. Tor stood there with a wide smile and a small bouquet of flowers he had bought from a flower shop a few blocks away.

He knew something was wrong as soon as she opened the door. Her face was pale with a slight trace of tears in the corners of her eyes. She put her arms around him without saying a word, the tears creeping down her face. He put his hands on her shoulders and they stood together for over a minute, holding on tightly.

She was no longer America's widow as she had been immediately after Billy's assassination. In an age of instant mourning, where even dead heroes are rushed to the grave, she was left behind—expected first to suffer, then to mend, then finally to forget. She hadn't forgotten; she never would. It was comforting to her to be in the arms of someone who shared her devotion to Billy's memory.

As they sat together in the den and listened to Billy's recorded diary, Elaine shifted uneasily on the edge of her chair. She was watching Tor closely, looking to see if his reactions would be similar to those she had experienced, but he was offering no clue to his feelings as he sat impassively.

In a lengthy narrative, Billy outlined Cordaro's earlier union history and compared his past exploits with strategies that he was beginning to launch on a national scale. He told of how Cordaro had gained control of his first local in Chicago and how he had quickly broadened that strength by gaining support from the surrounding unions and local city government officials by using various forms of bribery and coercion.

"Within a short time," Billy's narrative continued, "Cordaro controlled Chicago and for the most part the state of Illinois but not until he had managed to convince a grossly underpaid Chicago police department that the only way to maintain their dignity and to regain economic stature was to allow his union to represent them in negotiations. In exchange for that service, Cordaro told the police force that he would not ask them to actually join the union if they would support him in a demonstration of statewide union strength in upcoming negotiations with the railroads and the trucking industry. At the time, the contracts for the two largest intrastate trucking companies were about to expire and both trucking companies indicated that they would never accede to the proposed forty-five percent wage increase Cordaro was demanding throughout the state. Thinking that their cargo could be shipped by rail if a strike were to occur, the trucking companies stood firm in their refusal to negotiate until the initial wage demands were reduced."

The tape shut off, breaking Tor's concentration. He looked at Elaine.

"There's more," she said calmly. "Turn it over."

Tor reversed the tape and sat down again, reaching for a small pad from Billy's desk to scribble some notes. The tape continued.

"Without publicly acknowledging the contract expiration date at the time, nearly three years earlier Cordaro had negotiated a settlement with the railroads that called for the termination of the rail contract only two days after the trucking company's contract expiration date. Because of the simultaneous expiration dates, Cordaro had insured both the trucking and rail workers a stranglehold on the economy of Illinois by freezing intrastate shipping if their wage demands weren't met. The state could only withstand a few days of such a debacle without declaring a state of emergency and eventually acceding to the union's demands. To insure the success of such a strike, Cordaro had a sympathetic Chicago police force neatly tucked into his pocket ready to avert their eyes in the event of any illegal or rough strike activities that would have been necessary to bring about an early settlement.''

Tor remained silent, writing an occasional note as he listened.

''Because the strike was averted by a quick settlement, it never became necessary for Cordaro to flex his muscles and the potential crisis received very little publicity. Louie Cordaro had established himself unofficially as the most powerful man in the state. Even the governor didn't possess his political strength and that is precisely my point.''

Billy's voice was slower now, more deliberate. ''If Cordaro could establish such a mastery of the economy of one of the most industrialized sections of the country, then why wouldn't the same type of plan be successful on a national scale? His union's strength is now so vast that any major contracts in competing industries such as trucking and railroads with similar contract expiration dates would be disastrous to the American economy. The union could demand wages that would fuel inflation to the extent that the nation would find itself in an untenable situation that would take decades to correct. Cities such as Chicago are already experiencing the phenomenon. I plan to assign an investigator to a special project that will screen all major union contracts under Cordaro's control for every state as well as all national contracts for all industries to establish whether or not a trend toward common contract expiration dates appears. If Cordaro has such a plan for a 'Master Contract' we need to know about it now. Even then we may be too late.''

Billy had prefaced the tape with the date, which was only two days before his death. Tor doubted that he had ever had time to assign such an investigator.

Tor scratched at his chin. Elaine got up, walked over to the bookcase and popped the cassette from the recorder.

''There's another tape,'' she said matter-of-factly, replacing a second tape in the player.

This time BIlly's subject was President Jordan. His information had come from an unidentified telephone caller only days before his death.

The tape went on to detail a period of time six years earlier when Jordan, then a United States senator, served on the Senate Labor Committee that was drafting highly controversial legislation designed to remove high ranking labor officials with felony criminal records from office. Tor vaguely remembered that the law was designed to preclude a person from holding union office for five years after conviction of certain crimes. Before the bill could get out of committee to be presented on the Senate Floor for passage, it had to survive what was projected to be a close committee vote. According to Billy's anonymous caller, Louie Cordaro wanted insurance that the bill would die in committee. The caller said that Cordaro had personally ordered Peter Denning, armed with a hundred thousand dollars of the union's money, to visit Senator Jordan to specifically ask for his support in voting against the proposed legislation. The caller had told of how the money was passed to the senator at a Washington party as Jordan and Denning strolled alone by the swimming pool while the other guests were preoccupied with a charity auction inside. The money had come from a huge unaccountable slush fund maintained by Denning from his insurance firm's proceeds from the union's pension fund.

"According to the caller," Billy proceeded to explain, "Cordaro always wanted ready cash available for such purposes and he saw to it that the fund was always full by approving occasional special unaudited charges submitted to the union by Denning. My source didn't confirm whether or not any of the other senators on the committee accepted bribes but a review of a little history shows that Jordan's negative vote was the deciding factor in killing the bill."

Billy's voice was clear, determined. "I suspect that only three people, other than the caller whom I can't identify, know if this story is true—Jordan, Cordaro, and Denning. If it is true, I am sure none of them would be kind enough to corroborate any of it for us. However, I believe we could check the slush fund with a complete audit of Denning's records and payments received from the union at the time in question. It's a complex issue that will take a lot of time to investigate. If we knew who the caller was, then our attack would be more clearly defined. That being absent, I'm afraid the road will be long and rough before we can verify the truth. However, I feel we must pursue the story. Every lead should be checked out.''

The tape clicked off. Tor and Elaine looked at each other.

Elaine spoke first. ''You must admit,'' she said, ''it's a rather monstrous situation. I find it hard to believe that our own president is no better than a common criminal.''

Billy's statement about the possibility of Cordaro planning to control the United States was a theory that deserved to be researched alongside the caller's charge that the president had accepted a bribe while serving on the Senate Labor Committee. Both issues were important but Tor temporarily pushed them to the back of his mind. What interested him more now was the identity of the caller. It was entirely possible that Billy's caller had the same motive as that of the person that had called Tor about Don Peck. Both obviously wanted Cordaro put away, out of control of the union. The person who made the calls to Tor had to be one of two people: Borg Trenier or Sidney Bonnam. If Billy's caller was the same person, then the selection was narrowed to one—Trenier. Sid Bonnam couldn't possibly have known about the slush fund with the Denning Insurance Company or about Jordan's bribe. He had only recently been hired and prior to that his work had nothing to do with the union. Suddenly things were beginning to make sense. Despite Trenier's outward nonchalance about the union hierarchy, there was now no denying that he wanted Cordaro's job.

Tor reached out and picked up the cassettes, toying with them. ''Has anybody else heard these?'' he asked.

Elaine shook her head.

''Can you put them in a safe place tomorrow?''

"Sure."

"Where?"

"My safety deposit box."

"Which is where they were supposed to be today," he reminded her.

Elaine didn't share Tor's concern. "Who could possibly know about them?" she asked.

"Just do it," he said. "I'll explain later."

The next day James Hawk sat in bed at home and replaced the phone in its cradle, then rested his head on his pillow. It was still early morning and he had just finished talking with Tor, who had described the content of Billy's recorded diary in detail. He had already missed seven-thirty mass because of Tor's call so he decided to sleep in a little longer, skip breakfast, then drive directly to Boston where he was scheduled to record an interview for CBS's "Meet the Press," which was to air that evening.

While dressing, his mind skipped about furiously, rehashing what Tor had just told him. If the president had taken a bribe, it was going to be difficult to prove. With proper research and a few key witnesses, it was conceivable that enough evidence could be gathered to force Jordan to an admission.

He tried to fight his inclination to consider the president guilty without benefit of trial but he couldn't help believing it. He had never respected President Jordan, either as a man or a politician.

The threat of the president's winning the election coupled with the possibility of Louie Cordaro being acquitted and set free to continue spreading his influence throughout the nation gave him a sudden sick feeling.

There really was no way for him to be sure what Trenier's possible promotion to the union presidency would mean if Cordaro were convicted. Trenier had been a forgotten figure in the committee's investigations, his name rarely mentioned. But that didn't mean his hands were clean. Trenier would have to be looked at more closely but that would have to wait. Cordaro remained top priority.

It was another twenty minutes before James got out of bed. Five hours later he was on his way back home from Boston. His thoughts never strayed from Tor's phone call, even during the taping of ''Meet the Press.''

Chapter 50

THOMAS BARRETT WILSON sat in his office and listened to the amplified voice over the speaker phone on his desk while picking at two small pieces of lint that clung stubbornly to the lapel of his suit, all the while continuing to be a polite audience as Judge George Marconi aired his frustrations.

"You know," the judge continued, "there's a lot of us here in Chicago that stand to lose our asses if Richardson talks. You know what I mean?"

Wilson repeated what he had been telling the judge for the last ten minutes. "I hear you George. Like I said before, we've got it under control. Richardson won't embarrass anybody."

Marconi wasn't satisfied. "How can you be so damn sure?" he asked.

"Trust me."

"That would be a hell of a lot easier if you'd tell me what makes you so certain Richardson won't talk."

Wilson sat silently, picking at yet another bit of lint he discovered on his pant leg as he crossed his legs. He chuckled to himself as he envisioned Marconi sitting at his desk, sweating, handkerchief in hand, mopping at his brow. Marconi was over sixty years old and had served for twenty-one years on the bench in Chicago. His presence at the same party where Sheila Lancaster had been badly beaten by Senator Gregory made him extremely vulnerable even though the investigation into

Richardson's activities was at least temporarily centered in Ohio. The district attorney in Columbus had such a tight grip on the pre-trial investigation that Wilson's normal reliable informational fountains had gone dry and that worried him. Whether the Senator or Judge Marconi would be implicated were questions he knew he simply could not answer but chose not to share those concerns with Marconi. The only sure thing was Richardson's use of minors for prostitution. Richardson was a good bet for a prison sentence, but whose reputations would be destroyed along the way was still pure conjecture.

Wilson's only assignment from Louie Cordaro was to see to it that the source of the funds that sponsored the parties was not traced back to the union. He didn't give a damn about Judge Marconi but he didn't allow his personal distaste for the man to show over the phone. "George, all I can say is Everett Richardson won't be the source of any embarrassing information for you. What is said by others I have no control over. Do you understand what I am saying?"

"No, no I don't," the judge countered.

"Look, Everett's one of our boys. He knows the rules. He assured our attorney that he'll take the Fifth. Now whatever the D.A. in Columbus drags out beyond that is anybody's guess. If I hear anything more than what I know already, I'll pass it on to you. Meanwhile, you can help us along."

Marconi was skeptical. "What do you mean?"

"I can't get involved in this thing anymore. I've been discreetly counseling Richardson's attorney behind the scenes but if I do more than that, the D.A. just might start looking at the union's involvement in this problem a little closer than we'd like. You could help us by passing along the word to some of the judges in Illinois and Ohio that we need character witnesses on Richardson's behalf. If we can build Richardson's character with some testimony from a few well selected influential citizens, it will make any complaints by the Columbus D.A. look like a witch-hunt."

It was an old trick and Marconi didn't have to have it explained any further. He knew he had to do whatever Wilson asked. "How many do you want?" he asked resignedly.

"At least six judges. I'll give you their names but you'll have to make the contact. It's too risky for any of us to do it."

"What about me? Do you want me to testify?"

Wilson was incredulous that Marconi could ask such a stupid question. "Are you kidding? All we need is for you to testify to Richardson's good character and then have the D.A. pull out a witness placing you at one of those parties! The whole thing would turn to shit if that happened. Stay the hell out of it!"

An even more worried tone filtered through Marconi's voice. "Do you think there's a chance they might have witnesses placing me at the party?" he asked.

"How in the hell would I know? Just do your job and let us handle the rest. Understand?"

"How do you know we can get some of the other judges to testify?"

"They'll cooperate when you tell them Cordaro wants a favor. They have no other choice." Wilson hesitated, then added, "You do understand?"

Marconi nodded to himself unconsciously, as if Wilson could see him. The other judges would cooperate, just as he would. Louie Cordaro always got what he wanted.

Wilson called off the names and Marconi dutifully wrote them down on the bottom portion of a frayed legal pad he had been scribbling on, notes for a trial or a hearing, he couldn't remember which. All the confusion since Richardson's indictment had put him in a state of near mental and physical exhaustion. He hadn't slept for more than two hours in the last two days. Wilson's casual optimism about the trial gave him his first encouraging news in over ten days, but he still sat nervously tapping his left leg up and down for several minutes after he hung up the phone. After several false starts, he finally picked up the phone and dialed the first name on his list.

Chapter 51

FOR EVERETT RICHARDSON, not knowing what his future held was a torture far more severe than any he had seen meted out by union thugs during his college days when he had worked part-time as a finger man on the picket line. In those days, his job was to point out to union organizers employees who weren't sympathetic to the union's organizing drive. He couldn't remember how many times he had watched a person he had identified as a company commiserator have his or her arm broken for their disloyalty to the union. Usually they would have their arm placed flat on a curb, held stationary on one side by one person while another jumped with full force on the part hanging over the curb. The limb would break with a sickening sound that he had never gotten used to or forgotten.

With a trembling hand, he took a long swallow of Scotch as he sat in the vast sitting room of his suite at the Hotel Excelsior in Cincinnati.

He wanted to believe it was all a bad dream, that he would awaken in the morning to find himself at home with his family. He sat deep in the brown velvet armchair, staring dejectedly at his Scotch while swirling it about in the glass.

For the second night, he had retired alone to his suite to brood. The prior evening he had placed one call to his wife, and he had managed to evade her questions about what was going on and why he had left home to stay in a hotel. He had promised to see her the following night, which, too soon, had become tonight. The encounter would be a miserable event, one he knew he couldn't handle.

His impending trial had a guilty verdict even if he were to be absolved of the charges. Win or lose, he knew he could no longer effectively practice law and Tom Wilson's promise that the union would find a place for him somewhere regardless of the outcome of the trial gave him no solace. Wilson's words still rang in his ears, "If you cooperate." They hammered constantly, like the throbbing pulsations of a nagging toothache.

Earlier in the day Wilson had made it very clear that when Richardson went to trial, he was to answer only the simplest of questions, and to plead the Fifth Amendment whenever signaled to do so by his attorney. Wilson's smooth and confident approach to the matter made prison life sound like a restive sabbatical with pay, but full pay while in prison wasn't what he wanted to hear. Money wasn't one of his problems. What he wanted, but couldn't have, was his dignity.

He had spent well over twenty years honing his law practice into what he considered to be an artistically creative labor lobby unmatched in the history of Ohio politics. Constructing the adhesion that existed between the state's government officials and the union was an accomplishment that had resulted in his being the state's most influential nonelected official, a position he cherished. Now it was gone.

He didn't feel that what he had done through the years to build his friendships with judges and politicians had ever been illegal, although he knew the law, if taken literally, would lead to a different conclusion. The suddenness of his indictment brought him back to reality.

He remembered the first time he had arranged for a prostitute to provide an evening's entertainment for a young district attorney in exchange for a favorable recommendation to the court that was about to sentence a client he was representing. He worried about his role in that exchange, fearing that the district attorney may have been

396

baiting him and in turn would charge him with bribery. His fears were alleviated when the quid pro quo was met, bringing down the curtain on his first lesson in judicial politics. His first lesson was followed by a second, then a third. With each new venture his butterflies over getting caught gradually abated until after only a few years he grew callous about what he considered a political fact of life. He had proved Louie Cordaro's personal theory that everybody had his price and he was proud of the friendships and successes that it brought him over the years. He'd come a long way from his struggling youth when he had lived in eight different foster homes in six years. Now he was on the threshold of losing what was to him his entire life.

The thought of prison was abhorrent to him. He had been around long enough to know what happens when men are incarcerated. Prison was a jungle where a man was stripped of his human rights the day he entered.

His influence with the union and his money would buy him some considerations, but not enough. He could have certain comforts, but escaping the initial humiliation would be impossible and he couldn't cope with that.

He pulled himself up from the chair and filled his glass again from a nearly empty fifth of Chivas Regal, which he had purchased only two hours earlier. He walked awkwardly to the desk, then sat down again. He drank some more and began to write, not remembering exactly when it was that suicide had first seemed a logical panacea to his troubles. An ending, he thought, a release. It was the only way, there was no other.

When he finished writing, the hollow shell of his aloneness seemed to float about the room like the river of Scotch he had just spilled on the desk.

He pushed himself away from the desk and stumbled toward the closet where he removed a long slim felt bag. The shotgun slipped out easily.

His hands suddenly became steady; his perception of what he was about to do was clear. He slipped in two shells, then lowered the gun butt carefully to the floor.

Sitting on the bed, he leaned forward, pressed the twin barrels against his forehead just above his eyebrows and tripped both triggers.

Chapter 52

SUFFOLK, VIRGINIA. IT was the first trial day of Louie Cordaro. Tor looked anxiously around the courtroom. He rapped his pencil sharply on the chair in front of him when it became apparent to him that Sidney Bonnam wasn't part of the crowded gallery.

Tor's best estimate pegged the trial's duration at two weeks and he had already crossed off his calendar any other commitments for fourteen consecutive days. Bonnam's continued absence was about to free up about twelve of those days. Without him, the trial wouldn't get past the afternoon of the second day.

The United States Attorney assigned as chief prosecutor was a seasoned veteran named Mark West with delicate facial features that belied his inner intensity. His light eyes and cropped blond hair suggested an innocence and naivete that had in reality disappeared long ago. There would be no repeat performance of ineptitude on the part of the prosecution as there had been at Cordaro's last trial. For the defense, Thomas Barrett Wilson stood his normal ground, alongside Louie Cordaro.

West had been reluctant even to make opening remarks without the assurance of Bonnam's testimony, but a last minute phone call from James Hawk convinced him to start the trial against his better judgment.

No one was more aware of the importance of Bonnam's testimony than West. He looked over his shoulder at Tor who was shaking his head from side to side. He knew what the signal meant.

Unlike the first trial where the prosecution was second rate and ill prepared, West began with a carefully detailed outline of the charges and how he would prove them. His reputation as a hard-nosed prosecutor for over thirty years was exactly why Tor had pushed to get him assigned to the case. He was doing a masterful job of convincing the jury that he meant to convict Louie Cordaro and that he had the ammunition to do it.

The first day, except for Bonnam's absence, went exactly as planned. Wilson was cool, confident in his delivery, but as expected offered no hint of any surprises.

By jockeying the agenda slightly, West was able to schedule the morning of the second day for the questioning of minor witnesses whose testimony would not rely on any corroboration from other witnesses such as Bonnam or the still silent Sky City jurors.

If the afternoon session came and Bonnam still hadn't shown, both Tor and West had already decided that the charges against Cordaro would have to be dropped.

The start of the second day found Mark West shuffling his notes. Tor occupied the same chair he had the day before, directly behind the railing in the first gallery row, surveying each member of the gallery as they filed in. There was still no sign of Sidney Bonnam.

It was nearly ten A.M. when Louie Cordaro abruptly burst into the courtroom with his customary flamboyant brashness only a few seconds before the judge's entrance.

Tor watched as Cordaro took his seat with an obnoxious air of superiority. He wondered if he knew of Everett Richardson's suicide. If he did, there was no sign of it. His demeanor was the same as always. The Columbus district attorney had told Tor that he had information that linked Richardson's expensive parties with a union local in Columbus that had been paying Richardson's entertainment bills but the records indicating the reimbursement to Richardson had suddenly disappeared. With Richardson's suicide, the trail back to the local would now be long and difficult.

The matter concerning Senator Gregory was being given

top priority, but there were indications that the girl's parents, in an effort to avoid publicity, were contemplating dropping charges.

Mark West began by questioning patrolman Ed Patterson and Tor couldn't help acknowledging a slow ache that began to tie a knot in his stomach. He knew Cordaro was on the verge of slipping away again.

It was nearly noon when Wilson finished with his cross-examination of Ed Patterson. Both Tor and West were desperately hoping that the judge would call a lunch recess. Patterson was their last witness before they had to call Bonnam.

They both held their breath as the judge shuffled some legal briefs and then stared out from the bench directly at West. "I believe it's your prerogative to call another witness, Mr. West," the judge said, making it clear that, at least for the moment, there would be no recess.

Tor took another quick glance around the courtroom. Nothing. Nobody that even looked like Bonnam was present.

Mark West sucked in a deep breath. "Your honor, I call to the stand Mr. Sidney Robert Bonnam," he stated.

Tor's eyes first went to Cordaro, then Wilson. Wilson was calm, unruffled, but Cordaro's face paled and his eyes narrowed. He quickly turned and delivered a searching glare around the gallery. After a few seconds, the color began to filter back into Cordaro's face and a relieved smile crept to the corners of his lips.

Fury built up inside Tor as he stared at Cordaro. It was all he could to to restrain himself from acting on an intense desire to tear Cordaro apart. It frightened him to realize himself capable of such an emotion.

Suddenly a movement from the rear of the room magnetized the still searching eyes of the gallery. A small bearded man with black hair, wearing faded jeans and sandals, was struggling to get through myriad legs that blocked his passage to the main aisle from his seat at the end of the spectators' row. His open-neck shirt revealed a brightly colored string of turquoise beads mounted in a silver necklace. He adjusted rimless glasses as he strode silently down the aisle toward the front of the courtroom, followed by a low ripple of whispers that grew progressively louder with each step.

Tor watched him closely. Who was this man?

The man spoke briefly into the ear of the court bailiff who had quickly moved to block his path. Slowly, almost reluctantly, the man pulled a wallet from his rear pocket. He opened it, showed it to the bailiff, then stood motionless, looking straight ahead at the judge as the bailiff approached the bench.

The judge reviewed the identification. Then, "You are Sidney Robert Bonnam?" he asked.

"I am," the man replied, his voice cracking. "I am Sidney Bonnam."

"Bullshit!" Cordaro yelled, standing and pointing an accusing finger. "That's a goddamn lie!"

Wilson grabbed Cordaro's arm pullling him down.

The judge pounded his gavel loudly and looked squarely at Cordaro. "Mr. Cordaro, another outburst like that and you'll be found in contempt of court."

A recess was called to verify Bonnam's identity, but Cordaro knew it wasn't necessary. Even with the beard and the dyed black hair, he knew it was Bonnam. He sensed it immediately. He remembered a small v-shaped scar over Bonnam's left eye, which was unmistakable. He could see it now.

Mikki Parker was in the gallery. She trailed behind the others as Cordaro was escorted by a bailiff into a nearby conference room where he quickly unleashed his fury by picking up a chair and throwing it across the room. "That motherfucker can't do shit to me!" he yelled.

Mikki thought it a strange comment from Cordaro to make if Bonnam's sudden appearance really *did* mean nothing. She knew the damage Bonnam could do to Cordaro and she also understood his anger. Inside she rejoiced; outwardly there was no emotion.

Within minutes, Thomas Barrett Wilson joined them in the room, confirming the authenticity of Bonnam's credentials. "It's Bonnam," he explained angrily. "Now do you want to tell me what the hell this is all about?"

Cordaro was sullen, having cooled down from his earlier tirade. "Yeah, yeah," he said. "But I want to talk alone. Not in here. Let's go outside."

Outside, Wilson walked slowly at Cordaro's side, listening to his story. The summer's midday sun made the eighty degree temperature seem much warmer and Cordaro slung his coat over his shoulder as he continued to relate his story. Wilson remained unruffled, every hair in place, his suit without wrinkles. Mikki sauntered behind watching closely, a few paces back but still within hearing distance.

Remaining tightlipped, Wilson was offering no opinions. He took no notes. Mikki had seen enough of him to know that controlling his emotions was one of his many talents, but his glances at Cordaro as he listened to the narrative unfold made it very clear that he was more than casually upset. Cordaro frequently withheld information from union attorneys and Wilson was no exception. Wilson considered himself one of the premier attorneys in the United States. Cordaro's tampering with a jury in a case where he was the principal defense attorney was an incredible insult. It was surprising to many insiders that he had not resigned as he had threatened to do after the Sky City trial. The resultant embarrassment had been excruciating to him but for some unknown reason he had come back to defend Cordaro agin. That puzzled Mikki as she continued to listen to Cordaro confess his involvement with Bonnam. Cordaro knew there was no reason to hide the facts now, for Wilson was sure to hear them for himself inside the courtroom.

"I've got to go inside and think this through," Wilson finally said. "Meet me in an hour, I'll have something by then." He turned away and hurried up the floral-lined walkway that led to the courthouse.

Cordaro glanced back at Mikki, then turned away. "I'm going to take a walk," he said.

"Where are you going?" she asked.

Cordaro just shook his pockets and rattled his coins. "To buy some insurance."

Mikki watched him disappear around a corner.

"Keep your eyes open and your mind open. Suspect and question everything." That's what Tor had said when she had first accepted the assignment, and Mikki knew Cordaro's last statement about buying some insurance could mean just about anything. Cordaro was up to something. She had to talk to Tor.

Chapter 53

GLORIA BONNAM PREPARED herself to meet her husband. It would be the first time she had seen him since he had left over a month ago. It scared her to think about the future, it was so full of the unknown. As the day wore on, she began to feel more serene for the first time in weeks. Suddenly she didn't care what the future held. She was going to meet her husband. That was the most important thing in her life. She wasn't sure if the two of them would be able to be alone, his phone call the night before was too brief for details, but she wanted to be prepared. She dropped her robe, draped it across the bed and began to pack her clothes. She picked up a beige crepe dress, her husband's favorite, placed it in front of her and looked at her reflection in the mirror. She was nude, her tanned body the darkest it had been all season. The traces of white where her bikini had been were the only marks on an otherwise unblemished skin. She was proud of her youthful figure and had always kept a watchful eye for any signs of physical deterioration, even though she was only twenty-seven.

The hot bath water steamed as she slowly descended, inching in a little at a time. It was almost an hour later when she flipped the lever to let the water drain. It was then she heard the noise. It sounded like glass breaking and came from the front of the house.

She quickly wrapped a towel around her body but couldn't make herself open the bathroom door. She sat on the john, staring at the door. Then she heard more noises, more muffled this time, as if someone were moving about the living room. She remembered the bedroom door. She always locked it when she was alone. A sudden hammering echoed off the bathroom walls, followed by an even more terrorizing silence. Someone was in the bedroom.

She sat motionless. A minute passed, then another. No sound came from the other side of the door. She licked her dry lips, praying that whoever it was had gone. She kept her eyes glued to the door.

Another five minutes passed. Still no movement, no sound. She was frightened but it was more frightening to think of staying cooped up in the small windowless bathroom. She couldn't stand it much longer. She had to make a move, and the only way out was through the bedroom.

Cautiously, she placed her hand on the doorknob and opened the door. She took a step. She was not alone.

A clicking sound cracked through the air. Instinct, nothing else, told her to stand still. Then she recognized the sound. It was that of a gun cocking.

"Smart girl," a man's voice advised.

She slowly turned her head. A hulking man stood with his back to the wall, the gun pointed to her head. She watched him survey her body with his eyes.

"Over there," he commanded, pointing to the bed. The long barrel of his 357 magnum flailed about, aiming first at the bed, then at her.

Bartie Bonano knew what he was there for, but he couldn't help feeling the hardness that began to swell in his loins as he watched her walking slowly backward, feeling her way toward the bed.

She knew she had no chance against the man. Even if he didn't have a gun she would be no match for him physically. She had often thought about rape and how she would react but her mind went blank. She could think of nothing.

Then the unexpected came.

"Get dressed," he ordered.

She couldn't believe what she'd heard. "What?"

"I said get dressed. We're getting outta here," he bellowed.

She began to panic. Being in her own home, even if he raped her, gave her a sense of comfort she couldn't explain. Going somewhere else with him exposed her to the unknown.

"I—I don't understand. What do you want? I . . ."

"Hurry up. We don't have much time," he rasped. "Now do as I say!"

He watched as she reached for her panties, wetting his mouth as she balanced precariously on one leg trying to step into them.

"Wait," he said, beginning to walk toward her. He walked slowly but with a deliberateness that terrified her.

She froze when he stopped in front of her.

"Sit down," he commanded, pushing her down to the bed.

With the gun still pointed at her abdomen, he touched her shoulder with a finger, traced the curve of her collarbone, then dropped his huge hand and cupped her breast.

"Lie back," he commanded.

She hesitated.

"*Now* bitch!"

She dutifully lay back, her feet raising slightly off the floor. He placed his hand over her panties, pulling them apart from her leg at the crotch. She could feel his finger first pushing then probing. A sharp pain made her jerk her legs upward as he forced the calloused appendage inside, scraping the walls of her vagina with his long fingernail.

A low guttural groan came from deep inside his throat. She tried to see where he had placed the gun but his huge body was blocking her vision. She closed her eyes and remained still, resigning herself to his fondling without a struggle.

He was leaning over her now, one arm fully extended on the bed holding his body only inches above hers as he continued to force his finger in and out, occasionally pulling it out long enough to smell it and lick it lightly before replacing it. Still, she dared not move. He stood, took her hand and placed it on the bulge in his pants. She didn't open her eyes or move.

"You know what to do," he whispered.

Slowly, she opened her eyes. He pulled her from the bed and stood her upright directly in front of him.

"Do it now, cunt," he commanded, pressing her hand harder on his crotch, pushing her to her knees.

She knew what he wanted and didn't hesitate. She feared any resistance would cost her life. Her fingers quickly opened his trousers and she thrust her hand inside, freeing him. She began to stroke him.

"No, no," he demanded. "Use your mouth. I want to come in your mouth."

"I—I can't! I—"

"Suck it, you fuckin' cunt, or I'll shove it all the way up your ass!"

It was nearly two P.M. when the judge finally called Tor and Mark West to his chambers where Thomas Barrett Wilson was already waiting.

The judge looked tired, somber. "Mr. West," he began, "the defense has requested a recess until Monday since the introduction of your witness into the case comes as a complete surprise to him. It's up to you, but I must warn you that if you disagree it could become grounds for appeal if the testimony of your witness leads to a conviction."

It wasn't necessary for West to agree and Tor knew it. They had prepared their case together as if Bonnam would be there to testify and they were prepared to proceed. It was an unnecessary delay, but Tor couldn't erase from his mind the question Sidney Bonnam had asked him only minutes earlier, a question he couldn't answer.

Everyone had been so concerned with Bonnam's disappearance during the past weeks that it was only when he asked about protection for his wife that Tor realized his own insensitivity to Gloria Bonnam's precarious position.

If Cordaro couldn't stop Bonnam, then his wife was the obvious second choice. Until Bonnam appeared in court, there had been no reason for Cordaro to be concerned with Gloria Bonnam. Now that Bonnam had appeared, the danger was patently clear and Bonnam was now refusing to testify until he was assured of his wife's safety.

Without explaining why, Tor asked West to agree to the recess. West complied.

Several hours later the prosecution once again couldn't be sure of Sidney Bonnam's testimony. Gloria Bonnam was missing.

Chapter 54

ON FRIDAY MORNING, Sidney Bonnam uttered a heavy sigh, exited and walked alone down the hall to the lunchroom. Tor sat and gazed about the sheriff's office. The two telephones were silent now, although they had been ringing nearly nonstop since the night before. Notepaper listing potential locations to look for Gloria Bonnam now lay crumpled on the floor.

It was quiet. The room earlier filled with ten people, now had Tor as its only tenant. The ticking of the old school clock on the wall seemed to get louder and louder until the telephone's ringing drowned out its hypnotic effect. It was James Hawk.

"What's going on down there?" he asked.

"Well, I guess you've heard about our problem," Tor answered.

"All I've heard is that Bonnam showed. Why did you agree to a recess?"

"Bonnam's wife is missing," he explained. "He says he won't testify until he can be sure she's safe. We're not having any luck finding her."

"Shit!" James growled. He paused for a few seconds, then said, "Where in the hell was the surveillance security we ordered to watch her?" he asked.

"I don't know, Jim. The city police chief mentioned something about changing the schedule to nights only a couple of weeks ago. I don't know why, but he did. He didn't consult with us."

"Have you talked to Mikki?"

"Not yet. She called late last night to say where to meet her and then hung up. I'll know more after I talk to her later tonight."

"Who else knows about this?"

"Nobody except the police. But it won't take long for the press to pick it up. The police are looking all over the state for her. I've alerted the F.B.I. and they're checking everything they can, including the airlines."

"How about the trains and buses?"

"Those too. The judge has ordered the jury sequestered."

Tor swiveled around in his chair and reached for the cup of coffee he had started earlier. It was cold and he spit it back into the cup. "I was thinking—" he began, then hesitated.

"What?"

"What if we can't find her by Monday? Why not spring Mikki on them? Have her testify instead of Bonnam."

James wasn't convinced. "That could create a problem. The defense would scream that she was a government plant inside Cordaro's headquarters. Besides, I doubt that her testimony would carry much weight with the jury after Cordaro's attorney got through with her. Wilson would discredit her testimony by claiming she was being paid to testify. He wouldn't convince all the jurors but all he needs is one for a hung jury. We'd end up right back where we started. I think we have to go with Bonnam. We didn't plant him like we did Mikki. It's our only way out of this mess."

Tor agreed. "I'll talk to Mikki then get back to you," he said.

That night, Sidney Bonnam was safely secluded in protective custody at the Suffolk County jail. As he slept, Tor was keeping his appointment with Mikki Parker.

It was after midnight. Tor arrived at an old hotel on the west side of town and asked the hotel keeper for Mikki's room, which she had rented earlier under an assumed name.

He walked up the stairs to the fourth floor where Mikki was waiting.

"We've got to stop meeting like this," Tor kidded, kissing her gently.

"You name the time," she answered. "I've never been much of a night person."

As a precaution against eavesdroppers, she had the television on at a volume loud enough to drown their subdued conversation but not loud enough to evoke any complaints from the management.

"Bonnam's wife?"

"She's missing."

"So that's it!"

"What do you mean," Tor asked.

"Louie has been nervous as hell since yesterday afternoon. He won't talk to anybody, not even Wilson, and just barely to say hello to me. He's been after me to find Bartie Bonano. He says he needs to talk with him."

"Who's Bartie Bonano?"

"He's an old buddy of Louie's. If you ever saw him, you'd never forget him. That's why I called you. Bonano is Louie's private muscle. He's never been caught at it, but it's no big secret that he's a hit man. I figured if Louie wanted to talk with him so badly, something must be up. Maybe they're going to try to hit Bonnam before Monday."

"Do you think Bonano could have anything to do with Gloria Bonnam's disappearance?"

"Cordaro hadn't said anything."

"Nothing other than he wants to talk to Bonano. He won't say why."

"Do you know where Bonano is?"

"All I have is a contact number Louie gave me. He said to keep trying until Bartie answers. I've called a half a dozen times but there's no answer."

"It makes sense."

"What?"

"Cordaro knows he can't get to Sid Bonnam. He's locked up tighter than the gold at Fort Knox. If he can't

413

get to Bonnam, then his wife is the most obvious target. I can't believe we were so damned stupid!''

Mikki's eyebrows raised. ''Do you think he had her killed?''

Tor shook his head. ''No, there's no need for that right now. They'll have to prove to Bonnam that she's alive to keep him from talking.''

''And without Bonnam's testimony, you lose the case.''

''Exactly. We can't get by Monday without it. We could always appeal if we lost. We could bring Cordaro to trial again if we could be sure Bonnam would testify but that could take another year, and I doubt if Bonnam will stay in protective custody beyond Monday if we can't find his wife. He says he's sure Cordaro is behind her disappearance and he knows he'll have to be accessible to a phone if it's an extortion attempt. He's going to want out of custody fast if we don't find her.''

''Meaning Louie will bribe him with the release of his wife if he agrees not to testify?'' Mikki suggested.

''That's what Bonnam thinks. I don't, but I didn't tell him that.''

''I don't understand.''

Tor inhaled deeply, exhaling with a profound sigh. ''Bonnam thinks if he can bargain with his wife's release he'll be able to disappear afterward with the new identity that we agreed to provide. We'd lose the case, but at least he would have upheld his end of the bargain. The only problem is I don't think his wife will ever be released. There would be no point in it.''

''Why?''

''Because Cordaro's not dumb enough to risk getting caught in extortion and kidnapping. Any bargain with Bonnam would involve him personally and he can't afford that either. I don't think he plans to keep her alive.''

Mikki looked away, then down at the floor, her mind reeling.

''Do you agree with my theory?'' Tor asked.

Mikki avoided his question. ''Now what?'' she asked.

''I was afraid you'd ask that,'' Tor confessed. ''I don't

really know. We just have to sit and wait."

"Unless we do something to flush them out."

"What?"

"I think I have a way to find out where she is," Mikki offered. Tor noticed an intensity in Mikki's voice he had never heard before, as if an inner hatred were surfacing. She began haltingly, but gradually her mind began to clear as she revealed her plan. Soon, her words flowed effortlessly. Tor listened in silence, never interrupting, adding only a few nods of cautious encouragement along the way.

Tor accepted her plan because it was logical. He had no choice. They decided to operate under the assumption that the reason Cordaro wanted to talk to Bonano was because Bonano in fact had Gloria Bonnam. Somehow, Mikki was to convince Bonano to take her to Gloria by telling him that Cordaro wanted Mrs. Bonnam moved to a more secure location and that he wanted her to go along to help. If Bonano bought the story, it would be a fairly simple maneuver for plainclothes agents to follow along behind undetected.

They both agreed that getting over the first hurdle would represent Mikki's largest risk. If Bonano knew nothing of Mrs. Bonnam's whereabouts, she would be no physical match for Bonano's strength, and it was a virtual certainty that Bonano would hold her and call Cordaro to check out what was going on. It wouldn't take long for Cordaro to backtrack and unwind the story. His questions about how the authorities knew about Bob Kane and his association with patrolman Patterson would be answered. Cordaro never had bought Bonnam's theory that either Kane or Patterson had turned themselves in, telling Mikki several times in the past few weeks that he was still puzzled over their apparent confessions. In fact he had brought it up so often that it was making her very uneasy. It wouldn't take him more than a few seconds to add two plus two and come up with her name as the snitch who had turned in Kane. There was also no guarantee that Cordaro wouldn't order her killed immediately. It was a risk she was willing to take. This would be her last assignment for the committee. She had already decided that.

"Look at it this way," she jested. "Either way I get out of this assignment."

Tor didn't share her uncharacteristic levity. "You'll have to give me time to get a tail on you before you talk to Bonano," he said seriously.

"Do you actually think it'll work?"

"If Bonano becomes suspicious, you're dead," Tor reminded her. "I wouldn't trust either of those bastards one damn inch."

Mikki became impatient. "We don't have any choice! If I don't get to Bonano before Louie does we'll blow our chance to pull this off. Either way, I'm getting out of this mess. Now I can help before I go or I can take a walk and you go back to court Monday empty-handed and watch him walk away free again."

Mikki looked at Tor, suddenly feeling guilty about her short temper. "I want to apologize for shooting off my mouth about quitting the way I did," she said.

"I understand. It's not an easy time for any of us."

"That's just it," she said, tears suddenly welling in her eyes. "I don't think you *do* understand. There's something I need to tell you."

Tor listened for nearly an hour. He was so shocked at what she was relating to him that he found it difficult to offer any meaningful response. How does a man react when his lover tells him her boss raped her and that she has been sleeping with him ever since to pry even more information from him? Especially when he knew the only reason she was still working for the man was because he had repeatedly convinced her to stay on. She told of her last meeting with Frank Billings after he had testified against Louie Cordaro. As one of her father's best friends, Billings had felt it his duty to explain to her about her father and what motivated him. Frank Billings had told her about Louie Cordaro and Bartie Bonano, about what her father suspected . . . that they were responsible for the murders of her father's mother and sister when he was a boy. It wasn't until Cordaro told her only a few days earlier that he had killed before that she knew her father had been correct and that his death on the streets of San Francisco had been no accident.

Tor's insides were tied in a vicious knot by the time Mikki finished, the sickening reality of it all finally settling in. Only time would allow him to respond adequately and that was something neither of them had at the moment.

They held each other close, neither saying anything. Then they made love.

Chapter 55

MIKKI PARKER FELT better about her relationship with Tor than she had since she met him. Their lovemaking the night before had transformed the ties between them into a bond cemented with trust, love, and above all, new hope for their future.

As agreed, she remained in her hotel room waiting until her phone rang two times as a signal that F.B.I. agents had her under surveillance. She would than be free to leave. Once she made contact with Bonano, she was to try to bring both him and Gloria Bonnam to an abandoned sporting goods warehouse Tor knew of on Suffolk's south side. Agents would be waiting inside. The outside area was to be surrounded immediately after they entered through the rear door.

The surveillance teams were in place at her hotel less than two hours after she arrived. If Bonano called, she was to leave a note in her room telling of the location of their meeting. That would be her last communication. The balance depended on the success of the surveillance teams.

If they lost her before she arrived at the warehouse, the results would be all too predictable. Everyone knew that, particularly Mikki, though she had displayed a stoic confidence when outlining her plan. Every minute that passed increased the chances that Louie Cordaro might talk to Bonano before she did. Even then, there was no way of knowing if Bonano would call Cordaro to confirm her story about his wanting Gloria Bonnam moved.

It was nearly noon when she finally made contact. Bonano was apparently intoxicated but nevertheless coherent, readily agreeing to meet with her later that day.

She managed to sleep a bit then, after first lying awake for over an hour sorting out her life. She felt a strange sense of completeness, as if her path were suddenly clear. For a reason she could not explain, it was no longer important for her to avenge her father. Cordaro would get his due, she was sure of that. Her mission was almost finished. She would soon be starting afresh with a new outlook and purpose for her own existence and that of her sister.

She awoke with the same confidence and promptly called Shana.

"Mikki, where are you?" Shana demanded excitedly. "Miss Oliver said you were all right but I was worried when you didn't call last night."

"Sorry, honey. I got called out of town but I'll be home tonight. You can count on it. I told Miss Oliver but you were sleeping when I called last night."

"I miss you," Shana announced. "Be sure and come home tonight. I took three more steps yesterday and I want to show you how good I'm doing."

"I'll be there, honey. Nothing can stop me. I promise."

"You know what I heard on the radio last night?"

"No, why don't you tell me, darling?"

"I heard the record of *Camelot*. There weren't any commercials or anything. Oh, Mikki, it was wonderful! Can we get the record? Please?"

"Tell you what, sweetheart. I'll bring it home with me tonight. How's that?"

"I'll wait up for you."

"See you tonight."

"Mikki?"

"Yes?"

"I love you."

"I love you too, darlin'."

Mikki tucked a note under the telephone of her hotel room telling of her destination, a coffee shop off Expressway 395, about thirty miles southwest of Washington, D.C. She took a deep breath and walked out the door and down the stairs, avoiding the slow elevator.

She had experienced a lot of frightening moments during the last few months, but none so frightening as the feeling she experienced as she waited in the coffee shop for Bonana to arrive. Even with her newfound inner peace, reality was still with her. The importance of how she conducted her meeting with Bonano was sinking in. A fear of Bonano himself was beginning to set in. Was there to be no Camelot? What would become of Shana if she failed?

She looked out the window then back inside the coffee shop where she and two truck drivers two booths away, were the only customers. The waitress and cook were in deep conversation. The minutes passed slowly. Then, just as she was about to abandon hope, a car pulled into the parking lot outside and stopped. The door opened and a man moved slowly out, closed the door and walked toward the coffee shop entrance. Bartie Bonano was keeping his appointment.

To think that Bonano was once considered a ladies' man was beyond her comprehension. Age and added weight made him totally gross. His cropped haircut sat atop a face that had been reshaped by a large fist many years earlier. His eyes sat back in their sockets above a bent nose and discolored teeth. He gave the illusion of having no neck at all, making him look like a squat Suma wrestler in a cheap business suit. Suddenly he was standing beside the table.

He sat down across from her, simultaneously uttering an unintelligible greeting before turning his attention to the buttocks of the young waitress who was still talking to the cook. He stared at her for what seemed to Mikki like ages before returning his eyes back to her. "What's this shit about Louie wanting us to work together?" he asked.

Mikki sucked in her breath silently. "He didn't cover it with you?"

"Nah, I was out most of the night."

She held her breath and hoped her next question went as planned. "Louie said he wants the lady moved to a new location. He said I should go along in case she gave you any trouble," she said calmly.

That was it. It was done. She bit her nail, awaiting Bonano's response. There was no turning back.

Bonano cocked his head and raised a brow. He turned, looked over at the waitress who was still ignoring them, then back over his shoulder at the two truck drivers. They were laughing at a joke one had told the other and were in a world of their own. He looked back at Mikki with an ominous glare. "What trouble?" he asked. "She's not gonna give me any shit. I got her just where I want her."

Mikki tried her best to look unruffled but she was afraid she was failing miserably. She had been right. Bonano had Gloria Bonnam. "Louie wants her moved right away," she insisted.

"When?" Bonano asked.

"Tonight."

"Where to?"

"A vacant sporting goods warehouse in Suffolk. I have the directions. Louie said you'd know how to handle it."

Bonano finally displayed some emotion. "Fuck, now I gotta go all the way back to D.C.!" he said irritably. "Why didn't you tell me this over the phone? You coulda saved me a drive!" The undercurrent of menace in Bonano's tone was frightening.

Mikki hid her fear well. "I couldn't risk it over the phone," she answered. "Where do you have her now?"

Mikki glued her eyes to Bonano, and he returned the stare. *Christ! What's he thinking? Say something! Don't panic!*

Bonano was lost in thought and Mikki became even more frightened, not knowing what was going on in his mind. "That's not important," he finally answered. "You can just follow me. We'll wait awhile. I gotta eat first. Then we'll go and get her."

He believed her! Following in a separate car was more than she could possibly have hoped. The agents would now have two targets to follow, making it even easier, and reducing her own risk even more. She could simply drive off if she thought he was becoming suspicious.

Later, as they drove toward Washington, she could see an older model pickup truck, a Chevrolet, she thought, in her rear view mirror about a quarter of a mile behind. She could only hope it was part of the surveillance team. A helicopter flying overhead about a mile west was only occasionally in view and she hoped Bonano wasn't as aware of it as she was.

She was filled with a deep sense of relief as she drove behind Bonano's car, being careful to keep her distance yet not get too far away. Not only was her plan working, she wasn't even in the same car with the man and that in itself was comforting.

They drove for over an hour, taking an indirect route toward the capital. She surmised that it was a crude attempt for Bonano to confuse anybody that might possibly try to follow. When they turned off onto a service road from the Beltway, the Chevrolet pickup went straight ahead but a sedan that had been following several car lengths behind the pickup for the last few minutes did make the turn-off. A moment later, she followed Bonano into a multistoried public garage near Watergate where their tires squealed and echoed as they climbed three levels before coming to a stop on the fourth floor. The trailing sedan had apparently stopped outside or at a lower level, she couldn't be sure which. She felt a sense of panic as she pulled the car to a stop in the stall next to Bonano's.

"Quick," Bonano ordered. "Over there." He was already out of his car, motioning for her to get inside yet another car. She reluctantly complied, not wanting to show any hint of hesitancy. Bonano ordered her to put on a large brimmed man's cowboy hat and a pair of mirrored sunglasses that nearly covered her entire face, then got in the back.

"You drive," he ordered.

She started the car and drove slowly toward the exit ramp. Bonano's hulking body lay spread across the rear seat safely camouflaged under a blanket.

Her hands started shaking as she desperately looked for

the sedan as they exited. *Too many cars! Damn!*

She knew Bonano had to suspect something was wrong. There could be no other answer. If he had fully believed her there wouldn't be any reason for this carefully planned diversion. A cold sweat permeated her blouse as they pulled away from the parking lot. She watched her rear view mirror. They were not being followed, she was certain of that. What now?

She drove out Wisconsin Avenue until they hit the Beltway again where Bonano, still hidden in the backseat, instructed her to head toward Baltimore. She drove without further instructions for over an hour.

They had nearly circled the Beltway and were almost back where they had started. She looked in the rearview mirror and saw the reflection of Bonano's massive head. "Take the next turn-off," he ordered.

They went a few blocks through a commercial district, then took two more turns and were suddenly in the midst of a rundown neighborhood filled with old Victorian houses. They stopped in front of one in the middle of the block, which appeared to be in a worse state of repair than the others.

"In there," Bonana grunted, pointing to the scalloped and bracketed house.

She got out and walked to the front door, Bonano close behind. Without being obvious she tried to look about the street for any sign of the surveillance team. Nothing, not a trace of movement. No cars, no people.

Bonano fumbled with the keys and had difficulty with the front door's sticky and rusted latch. A loud click followed after several unsuccessful attempts and the door swung open. Bonano motioned and she stepped in.

The door slammed behind him and the sound of a gun cocking to the ready position confirmed her worst fears.

Bonano laughed heartily. "Louie was right—you're a fuckin' spy for the Feds! Aren't you?" he demanded.

Her stomach sank even further, but somehow she managed to remain calm. "I don't know what you're talking about," she responded authoritatively.

"Cut the bullshit! I already know."

"I still don't know what you're talking about."

Bonano's patience wore thin. "In there," he commanded gruffly, pointing to a door at the end of a dimly lit hallway.

They walked into the room. It was sparsely furnished. An old, faded green, overstuffed sofa crowded the north wall while a matching chair sat facing the sofa on the opposite wall. A tarnished brass-plated lamp with a long crack up the base sat atop a painted cylindrical table, illuminating a faded print of a winter scene that hung crookedly on the wall behind it.

Mikki listened for some sound from the adjoining room but heard nothing. If Gloria Bonnam was on the other side of the door, she couldn't tell.

A whiskey bottle, three quarters empty, sat under the lamp and Bonano wasted no time picking it up before settling in on the sofa. He pointed toward the chair with the barrel of his gun. Mikki gave no resistance, quickly sitting down. She waited in silence, watching Bonano empty the contents of the whiskey bottle with one big swallow. Her mind frantically searched for something to say. Bonano's eyes were riveted on her, but strangely she no longer felt afraid. Somehow she was sure her intelligence would win over Bonano's brawn. All she had to do was stay calm.

Bonano dropped the bottle on the floor and leaned forward, still waving the pistol precariously. "Ya know," he began, "Louie figured something was funny when Bob Kane got fingered for talking to that cop. He figured Bonnam done it, but Louie don't like no loose ends. He wanted to check you out, too. Says you two were the only ones who coulda possibly talked to the Feds. Kinda looks to me like he found two squealers instead of one."

Mikki's stomach constricted and she swallowed hard. She could hardly have been more wrong. The plan she thought she had so carefully devised had fallen to Cordaro's more cleverly designed conspiracy. Her mind raced back, back to the time in the car when Bonnam had described Kane's arrest to Cordaro. How stupid she had been to think that Cordaro would let such a question go unanswered! She had let Cordaro's apparent lack of concern about Kane slip by unnoticed because of her own urge for self-preservation. She had thought at the time that Bonnam's suggestion that Patterson and Kane may have turned themselves in was a plausible solution that Cordaro could have accepted, but now she knew it made no sense.

Bonano wiped his mouth on his sleeve and lifted his bulky frame from the sofa. "In there," he said, pointing to the next room with his free hand.

Prodded from behind with the barrel of Bonano's gun, she pushed the door open and walked in.

It was then that she saw Gloria Bonnam. She lay spread-eagled on the bed, naked, and on her back. Both legs and arms were fastened to the four corners of the bed with surgical tape, her mouth stuffed with a wash cloth and taped over, the sheets wet with urine.

Bonano pointed to her genitals. "Look there!" he ordered.

It was difficult for Mikki not to notice what was between her legs. A small pool of dried blood on the sheet framed the butt of a handgun, its barrel fully penetrating her vagina. Cocked and loaded, it was Bonano's sick way of keeping her still. The slightest movement of her body would have tripped the firing mechanism.

"Take the gun out," Bonana commanded. "But only use your thumb and one finger."

Mikki's eyes were cold and unyielding as she stared at Bonano, then back again at Gloria Bonnam. Reluctantly, nervously, she began to disengage the trigger. She gradually tugged the long barrel out carefully, trying not to hurt the woman. Gloria flinched in pain as the pointed gunsite at the barrel's tip tore at her already wounded vaginal walls. Mikki stood with the handle between her thumb and index finger, the barrel pointing straight down. Her mind toyed desperately with the idea of turning the gun on Bonano, but she was unsure of herself.

426

If she failed to do it fast enough, she and Gloria would be dead.

"Drop it," Bonano commanded.

She dropped the gun to the floor.

"Kick it over here!"

She kicked at the gun and Bonano picked it up, never moving his eyes from her.

"Now take off her gag. We're going to have some fun." Bonano laughed loudly, leaning against the wall.

Mikki carefully peeled the tape from Gloria's face. Bonano was watching closely, all the while removing a thirty-five millimeter camera from a camera bag that lay in the corner of the room. He began focusing it on Gloria Bonnam's body. Satisfied, he looked away and back at Mikki.

"Take off your skirt," he demanded.

"Come on. Is this really necessary?" she protested.

Bonano's words were chilling. "Do it or I'll break your fuckin' neck!"

She had no choice. She removed her skirt, then her panties. Gloria Bonnam lay motionless, her eyes closed, her tongue lightly circling her chafed lips.

Mikki watched Bonano closely. He was sitting now, his gun in one hand while the other balanced the camera on the back of an old painted chair he was sitting on sideways.

Mikki protested again. "Look," she pleaded, "I can't do this. You must understand. It's just that . . ."

"Get over there and sit on her face or I'll stick this gun up your ass," Bonano yelled, his voice going hoarse. "Stick your cunt in her mouth."

Slowly, Mikki inched closer to Gloria. She was on her knees, her naked pelvis only inches from Gloria's face.

Her eyes half open, Gloria was watching now. Bonano fidgeted and became increasingly impatient as Mikki continued to hesitate.

"Let me help," she whispered. "Here," she said, opening her mouth.

Mikki hesitated again.

"For Christ's sakes," Gloria whispered hysterically, "do

427

it or he'll kill us both!''

Mikki braced herself with her arms above the headboard as she lowered her body. Bonano's oversized head dwarfed the small camera as he intermittently peered through and over the viewfinder while watching every move they made.

Bonano could feel a tightness in his testicles as he became hard. "Stop," he commanded.

Mikki paused momentarily. Her pelvis remained poised directly above Gloria's twisting face only inches away. Mikki's eyes closed, knowing what to expect next.

"Eat her," he commanded. "Eat her pussy."

Mikki caught her breath, slowly lifted her leg off, and turned her body around facing Gloria. She slid lower, positioning herself between Gloria's legs and then mechanically lowered her face downward pressing her mouth against Gloria who screamed slightly as Mikki's tongue entered her already inflamed and tender vagina.

Gloria thrust her hips upward hoping the change of position would lessen her pain.

"Eat her *hard*, dammit!" Bonano screamed, watching intently while rubbing his crotch. He just sat, watching every move as the two women performed. From time to time, he would move closer, snapping still more pictures.

He wasn't satisfied. He wanted more action. "Untie her and roll her over," he demanded. "Shove this in her ass," he said, producing from the bureau drawer a large rubber dildo.

"Can't we . . ."

"I said in her ass! Spit on it if you have to."

A few hours later, Mikki drove alone in the front seat as Bonano sat directly behind her with Gloria beside him in the rear. To think that she could hate one man so much defied her imagination. The indignity of what he had just had them do was enough to make any person want to kill but that alone wasn't what was fueling the rage that poured through her veins. She had to keep calm. She had to survive this night.

The day was dying now, the darkness deep, but not so

deep as the depression Mikki felt in her heart. How naive she had been! She still harbored a faint trace of hope, that grew weaker each minute.

It was past two in the morning when he finally directed her to stop at a marina near Annapolis. For the past hour it had been a quiet ride, but now Bonano was restless, uneasy. Mikki watched him closely. He was getting ready for something, psyching himself up.

He escorted them down a freshly painted gangway, following closely behind carrying over his hunched shoulders two large plastic bags. "Here," he said. "Stop here."

Mikki clutched Gloria's arm tightly. She felt totally helpless, unable to offer any encouragement for escape. To make a move now would mean instant death. She looked back over her shoulder at Bonano. He had a look of satisfaction on his grotesque face as if he were thriving on their adversity. It was the most horrible sight she had ever seen.

The plastic bags Bonano carried aboard the small pleasure craft in which they set out into Chesapeake Bay were filled with assorted meat and ground fish, designed to attract sharks once they were out to sea. The remains of their bodies would never be found, he was sure of that. The only trace of how they met their death would be in his camera. For him, it was always that way.

Chapter 56

TOR KNEW, WITH terrible clarity, that he would not see Mikki again. He tried to clear his head, to convince himself that there was no need to worry as his mind frantically reviewed all the plans he and Mikki had discussed. Many times during the previous day he had sat near the phone in his Washington office waiting to hear from her, but she never called; now he was sure she never would. In a few short months she had captured his imagination, his respect, his love. She was beautiful, fine, and gentle but now it was necessary that he face reality. The world was still revolving. Louie Cordaro still existed. The tears in his heart welled to his eyes before he finally found sleep. Tomorrow would begin without hope, but it would begin. Tonight all he had was prayer. It alone provided the strength he needed to face the inevitable.

Shortly after six A.M. the next morning Sidney Bonnam walked out of his comparatively plush unlocked jail cell and strolled down the hall toward the outer office, where he telephoned Tor to tell him of his decision. He had decided to testify against Louie Cordaro.

Tor had been giving him daily detailed chronologies of the F.B.I.'s and the local and state authorities' frustrating efforts to locate his wife and Mikki Parker. It was all too obvious to him that Mikki had failed in her attempt to lead the authorities to his wife, and now the F.B.I. didn't have a clue where they might find Bartie Bonano. Tor had been candid with him, telling him that even if Bonano were located it was doubtful that he would be held for charges of any kind. The surveillance teams had been too far away to make a positive identification that would have placed him with Mikki on the day of the disappearance, nor could the waitress and the cook at the restaurant identify Bonano's picture. The two truck drivers who had sat a few booths away were transients. As far as the employees knew, they had never been in the restaurant before. Locating them was deemed to be next to impossible. While some still expressed optimism that his wife and Mikki would still be found, Bonnam no longer shared the same feelings. He couldn't explain it but he knew in his heart that they were both dead.

Court was scheduled to start that morning after the weekend recess. Now he would be there. He had nothing more to lose.

When the court reconvened at the scheduled hour, Bonnam repositioned himself in the witness chair he had occupied only momentarily before the recess.

Reminded he was still under oath, he focused his eyes on Louie Cordaro who sat slumped in his chair, his arms folded defiantly across his chest. Their eyes met and Cordaro conveyed his contempt first by scowling, then with a raised fist.

Hatred seethed through Bonnam's body. He sat motionless, staring at his adversary with laserlike penetration. Several seconds passed before Cordaro looked up and laughed lightly, turning his attention away from Bonnam to Thomas Barrett Wilson, who was sitting at his side waiting for the prosecution to begin questioning.

Mark West sat at the table to Wilson's right, barely ten feet away. He looked at Wilson and admired his calm. If their positions were reversed, he knew his demeanor would be far less reserved than Wilson's. Earlier that morning the judge had virtually assured Cordaro's conviction. Wilson had shown no emotion during a meeting in chambers when the judge ruled against Wilson's request that the

432

prosecution not be allowed to introduce to the jury Sidney Bonnam's dual role both as a committee investigator and as a paid Cordaro spy against the committee. By introducing Bonnam as a spy against the committee it was going to be much easier for the prosecution to convince the jury of Bonnam's story that he had been involved in the juror bribery attempts at Cordaro's request.

It was a solid victory for the prosecution. West knew that but couldn't help being apprehensive. West went over and over in his mind the judge's ruling that morning. Maybe he had missed something, a loophole somewhere that Wilson recognized but was not revealing. The judge's words were still clear in his mind: "I admit that Mr. Bonnam's participation as a union spy against the committee is a separate crime to be dealt with in yet another courtroom. However, Mr. Wilson," the judge had said, "the fact that he was employed by Mr. Cordaro specifically to gather information in an illegal manner for Mr. Cordaro's defense at the time the alleged bribes being reviewed by this court took place makes it germane to the prosecution in this particular case. The jury will be instructed that the crime of spying on the Hawk Committee is not pertinent to this case at this time and that Mr. Bonnam's testimony is to be considered only when pertaining to the specific issues concerning this particular trial."

Soon, West's daydreaming was over and he found himself questioning Sidney Bonnam. The trial had started. There was no turning back.

When Bonnam described his initial introduction to Louie Cordaro, Tor sat in his front aisle seat watching, his mind temporarily removed from thoughts about Mikki. He silently wondered about Borg Trenier's involvement in the bribe attempts. Mikki had said Trenier was present at the time Cordaro ordered Bonnam to bribe the jurors, albeit a passive role. Trenier's possible crime as that of an accessory was a seperate issue, but, with Bonnam's cooperation, West could possibly call on Trenier to testify. The only problem was that Bonnam, for an unknown reason, was stubbornly refusing to corroborate Mikki's story that Trenier was present when the bribes were being discussed with Cordaro. He didn't deny it, he just refused to comment on it. What bothered Tor was why Bonnam was protecting him. Some day he would find out. Right now, the target was Louie Cordaro.

Bonnam's years as a Secret Service agent enabled him to give his testimony with penetrating detail, something not normally displayed by an inexperienced witness. By introducing him as a former Secret Service agent, West gained an added edge with the jury by lending even more credibility to Bonnam's story. The jury wouldn't perceive him as just another thug hired to do a job.

The day dragged on. Wilson's objections, more frequent earlier, gradually grew further apart. Even Cordaro's outbursts were dulled as the court day drew to a close. Bonnam's testimony was irreversible. Wilson's challenges were amost totally ineffective as Bonnam uniformly dissected each day he worked for Cordaro up until the time he was ordered to bribe the jurors.

It was then that Mark West unexpectedly excused Bonnam from the witness chair.

"Your honor, I'd like to request an adjournment," West announced. "I also want to ask that any Sky City juror who wishes to testify be prepared to do so as my first witness tomorrow morning."

The judge agreed, adjourning the trial for the day without further comment. West had insured the presence in the courtroom that day of all Sky City jurors. Having been subpoenaed, they all had been present. Now they had the entire evening to think about West's closing comment.

West had insured against any attempts being made to influence them by having the Suffolk police provide twenty-four hour protection at the home of each subpoenaed juror. He was taking no chances.

That night Tor spent a long and restless evening with

West detailing a contingency plan if the jurors still remained silent. They had to have at least one of the jurors corroborate Bonnam's story to insure a conviction. If not, they had to try something else.

The next morning, Amos Alonzo Rutherford was the first Sky City juror called to the stand. He was a tall and proud black man with a bony frame and bald head. He had always been quiet but was extremely articulate when pressed to speak.

West had chosen Rutherford as his first witness because of what Bonnam had told him the day before. Bonnam had approached Rutherford at his home and asked if he would accept five thousand dollars in exchange for a vote for Cordaro's acquittal. Of the five jurors Bonnam said he personally approached, Rutherford was the only one to physically threaten him when the offer was made. Two of the five accepted the funds while the remaining two initially indicated they would consider the offer but later refused.

West was gambling that Rutherford would be the most likely member of the group to cooperate. Rutherford described the incident with Bonnam and publicly apologized for his previous silence, saying that he had feared for the safety of his family, but could no longer consider himself a citizen if he didn't come forth with the truth.

When Rutherford left the stand, West looked across the room, located Tor, and winked.

The balance of the day as well as the next two were carbon copies of Rutherford's testimony. Previously mute jurors suddenly turned loquacious about their experiences.

On the fourth day of the trial, Sidney Bonnam was recalled to the witness stand to corroborate the jurors' testimonies. The moment of truth had arrived. Bonnam's testimony was so devastating to Cordaro's defense that Wilson didn't bother to call Cordaro to the stand to dispute the charges. It was unlike Wilson to go down without a fight and that concerned West. Even Cordaro was sitting quietly with uncharacteristic nonchalance.

There was more to their demeanor than they showed outwardly, West was sure of that. It bothered him even though he was confident that the jury would now support the prosecution's case.

It took only six hours of deliberation before an intense jury returned to announce their verdict.

The jury foreman read the verdict: "We find the defendant Louie Cordaro guilty as charged."

The courtroom was strikingly quiet, even somber; the verdict was obviously no surprise. A few reporters squirmed in their seats, anxious to get to the telephones in the corridor, but reluctant to leave before the judge's closing remarks. Tor and Mark West sat equally quiet, each feeling only a slight sense of victory. Until Louie Cordaro was behind bars, nothing could be certain. The guilty verdict was only a start.

A few minor rumblings in the gallery subsided when the judge began to speak. "Mr. Cordaro," he began, "it is the opinion of this court that the verdict of the jury in this case is clearly supported by the evidence that you did knowingly attempt to arrange to bribe jurors involved in a criminal trial.

"It is difficult for the court to imagine a more willful violation of the law. Most defendants that stand before this court have either been accused of violating the property rights of other individuals or violating the personal rights of individuals."

The judge's voice became stern, slightly strained, but noticeably louder. "You stand here convicted of seeking to corrupt the administration of justice itself, having tampered with the very foundation of this great nation. Without fair, proper, and lawfully administered court procedures, nothing would be possible in this country— the administration of labor unions, of business, everything that we call civilization, depends ultimately upon the proper administration of justice itself.

"If such a crime were to go unpunished it would destroy our country more quickly than any combination of foreign enemies that we could possibly ever imagine.

"I personally find your acts deplorable! Sentencing is set for October fourth in this courtroom at ten A.M."

Chapter 57

LOUIE CORDARO HAD been fully prepared for the verdict. That fact was clearly evident to Tor within two days after Cordaro's conviction. Bumper stickers appeared throughout the country proclaiming his innocence, asking sympathizers to write to their congressman to save Louie Cordaro.

An appeal to overturn the conviction was filed and scheduled to be heard within three weeks. Full page newspaper ads appeared in every major U.S. city offering a $10,000 reward for information that could prove that Sidney Bonnam was a government agent whose sole assignment was to entrap Cordaro.

Editorials from Marshall Tucker's newspaper appeared nationally in sister newspapers calling the conviction a "foul and filthy frameup" and accused James Hawk of being "the architect of the diabolical plot."

Myriad political cartoons depicting James as a tyrant became commonplace and scurrilous pamphlets attacking his civil rights record were distributed throughout the most impoverished ghetto areas in all the major cities of the nation. Attached to the pamphlets were bumper stickers that stated simply, "Save Louie" with requests that the recipients promptly place the stickers on their own or their neighbor's car.

Louie Cordaro was a long way from prison and not about to go without a fight. Sympathy for his plight, as carefully planned, flourished as each hour passed.

A week later, the ocean sparkled in the sun while James and Tor sat on the patio of the clapboard and shingle Hawk mansion. The house had been in the Hawk family for over forty years and although Tor had been there several times before, he was still impressed.

A slight offshore breeze blew off the water, and the dune grass bent gently with the wind. James brushed his hair out of his eyes as he studied a single gull that flew overhead. What Tor had just told him was beyond his immediate comprehension and he wanted to think a moment before responding.

Mikki Parker had frequently told Tor about President Jordan accepting bribes. Until now, Tor had never mentioned to him what else Mikki had suspected. Now he felt he had to reveal her theory and the reasons behind it.

"It's incredible," James said, still staring at the sea. "When someone tells you that the president of the United States may have had your brother murdered, it takes your breath away."

Tor nodded his head in silent agreement.

"What gave Mikki the idea that Jordan may have been behind my brother's death?"

"Some time ago she was with Cordaro at dinner. This time he got really plastered. She said he could hardly talk he was so drunk. He kept bragging that he was going to get you, said that he got your brother and he could get you, too. Mikki finally came out and asked him how he got Billy. He didn't hesitate. He said he did it through the president. He said a million dollars will buy anybody. That's all she got out of him before he passed out. I didn't want to say anything to you until we had a chance to check out the story about the million dollars. A million dollars is pretty hard to camouflage, even for a president."

"Particularly if Jordan didn't think anybody would be scrutinizing his finances. He wouldn't cover it up too well," James added.

"Exactly."

"Have you looked into it yet?" James asked.

"We're doing it now but to be honest I've been out of

touch for the past few days. I've been spending as much time as possible with Shana, Mikki's little sister."

"How is she?" James asked. He was only being polite, making small talk, Tor knew. Normally intensely sensitive, James's mind was completely absorbed in the ramifications of what he had just heard.

"She's coming along fine, physically. But I hate to think of what's going to happen if we have to tell her that her Mikki's never coming home."

Tor turned away then, looked out across the sea. "There's another thing," he said, turning back again.

"More?" James asked.

Tor spoke softly without looking up. "The last night, when Mikki was at dinner with Cordaro, he told her why he always hired people to do his dirty work. He said when he was young and first starting out with the union his first job on the payroll was as an enforcer. He and another thug broke the arms and legs of anybody who was uncooperative with the union movement. One afternoon he and this other fellow were instructed to go out to the home of an uncooperative company president and scare the hell out of his family. It ended up with the other fellow raping one of the executive's daughters. Then he asked Cordaro to prove his loyalty to the union by killing the witnesses. Cordaro told Mikki he was young and didn't know what to do. He was scared."

James stared at Tor for a moment. "Go on," he said.

"Cordaro killed the witnesses. He said he was sick for months afterwards. That's when he decided he would always get someone else to do his killing for him. He's never had the stomach for it since."

Tor looked past James, his jaw tightened. "That's what makes all of this so damn sick," he said.

James hesitated. "I'm afraid I don't understand," he said.

Tor took a deep breath. "The people Cordaro killed were part of Mikki's family—her father's mother and sister. Ed Parker and his other sister were hidden in the coal bin. They witnessed the whole thing. They couldn't

441

do a damn thing to help, or they would have been killed too. Mikki's father devoted his life looking for the bastard that killed them. If Cordaro hadn't passed out dead drunk after he told her, Mikki said she probably would have killed him. She'd only known about her father's obsession since his death. Frank Billings told her about it a couple of months ago. He also told her he didn't believe her father's death had been an accident. He was convinced that Parker had found out that Cordaro killed his mother and sister.''

"And Mikki believed it too?"

Tor nodded. "You got it," he answered, looking out toward the sea again, trying to fight back the tears that persisted in surfacing. The thought of being without her was excruciatingly painful, but he knew his suffering was nothing compared to what she must have been experiencing during the last few weeks.

He looked back at James who was standing quietly at his side. "You know," Tor began, "it took a lot of guts for her to stick with this thing. She never mentioned any of it until the last time I saw her."

"Did Mikki know who the other thug was?" James asked, referring to the Parker family murders.

Tor nodded. "Bartie Bonano. At least that's what Billings told her. Bonano looked different then, not nearly as bloated and much more presentable. But after her father had thought about it awhile, he was sure it was Bonano."

James looked at Tor, his face solemn. "No wonder she was so willing to help us nail Cordaro," he said, with obvious respect for Mikki's actions.

James stepped off the deck and began to stroll toward the beach. Tor stayed behind. He could tell James wanted to be alone with his thoughts, just as he did.

James stood alone at the water's edge, kicked off his sneakers and waded in a few steps. He looked over his shoulder back at the compound and then back out to the sea. What he saw normally soothed him, but not today. He would remember this day for it was the first time he could recall ever taking a pessimistic point of view about his future. Even Billy's death hadn't had the same effect on him as the news about Mikki Parker. He didn't feel responsible for his brother's death, but if Mikki were dead, that was another story. She had voluntarily risked her life, and James knew that as committee chairman he was the only one who could have put a stop to using her as a plant; and he hadn't stopped it.

The water slapped against his legs and his energy seemed to drain with the receding waves. He had gone against his instincts. He had let his obsession with Louie Cordaro get in the way of good judgment. He began to question his own worthiness to ask the American public to elect him as their president.

That evening, after dinner, Tor and James sat in the parlor and continued their conversation. James placed his feet on the ottoman and shifted in his chair.

He stared into the fireplace, not looking at Tor. "Without Mikki," he began, "even if you trace the million dollars Jordan was supposed to have received, I'm not sure it would prove anything."

"If we find evidence though, we can force Jordan to offer some sort of explanation. If he lies about it, we can nail him."

James nodded, deciding to change the subject again. "What about Bonnam?" he asked. "Where have you got him?"

"He's been placed under Army guard at the Presidio in San Francisco until we set him up with new identification. I figured that since the trial is over he might as well be somewhere convenient to me. I plan to go home for a while."

"You know he'll have to stay there until we're sure the appeals are denied. We can't take a chance and expose him if he ends up having to testify again. He'll end up a dead man."

Tor nodded, his face serious. "He knows that. With Gloria missing, he doesn't seem to care anymore. He's convinced she's dead."

"What do you think?" James tested.

Tor responded, "That he's probably right."

James's face flushed, pale crimson etching his cheekbones. "That bastard won't stop at anything," he said angrily.

Tor sat on the floor and shielded his eyes from the light above his head with his forearm. He looked up at James. "There's more," he said. "We checked out the union's national contracts. The expiration dates are going to be a problem."

"Then Billy was right?"

Tor nodded. "The contracts are all set to expire within two weeks of each other. Everything—the railroads, most of the airline contracts, and all the trucking contracts. Cordaro's even had some of the smaller intrastate trucking lines alter their expiration dates. The only thing he left out was the shipping lines but he doesn't need them to make his plan effective. He can cripple the economy very effectively as it is."

"When are they set to expire?"

"Just short of two years from now, between August first and the fifteenth."

"Who else knows about this?"

"Only a handful of committee investigators," Tor answered. "It's funny—those dates are common knowledge, but nobody has ever thought to look at the expiration dates outside their own industry. If all those unions go for a big pay boost at the same time, there won't be much anybody can do except give in."

James turned in his chair, looking away from Tor. "And Cordaro's calling the shots, in or out of prison. How in the hell did we ever let ourselves get into this position?" he asked, not really expecting a response.

"What do you think he's going to do with it?" Tor asked.

James turned to look at Tor and spoke assertively. "I doubt if he'll do anything with it just now. It's his ace in the hole to get himself out of prison. If he announces the common expiration dates now, it would be taken as a threat to Jordan. And if his association with the president is as tight as it appears, then he's got to keep it quiet. If he plays the martyr role long enough, there's a chance Jordan could pardon him after a couple of months without causing a big public furor. If Cordaro brought up the master contract now and Jordan pardoned him, everyone would say the president was giving in to pressure."

Tor shielded his eyes again. "What if Jordan won't pardon him?" he asked.

"Then we'll see a gun put to the nation's head. Not only would the unions seek exorbitant increases, Cordaro's freedom would be a contingency for their agreements. You can bet on that!"

The evening was still early, the parlor a comforting temporary refuge from crowds. They sat for another two hours discussing Louie Cordaro. Occasionally, they dropped the subject altogether and talked of the campaign.

James was concerned about the president. He didn't know how he would handle Mikki's accusations for the present because he lacked sufficient evidence to pursue the story, but he knew there would come a time when the issue would have to be faced.

He asked Tor to be sure that Billy's tape be kept in Elaine's safety deposit box until he instructed otherwise and for him to research the million dollar bribe issue personally in order to keep it top secret. James trusted nobody other than Tor.

The next morning, they went sailing together. It was nearly noon when they finally returned, their minds refreshed and purified by the salt water and crystal air. They moored the boat and walked slowly back toward the compound.

As they walked, a phone was ringing in Washington, D.C. Louie Cordaro was calling the president.

Chapter 58

IT WAS PAST two A.M. Sunday morning when the President
called and asked his most trustworthy personal bodyguard,
Terence Clavell, to remain on duty past his normal quitting time, saying that he wanted to get some fresh air and
asking Clavell to park his car a few blocks away from the
White House so they could slip away undetected. Clavell
was ordered to bring the black box with him, an unusual
request. It was the first time the president had ever asked
him to do such a thing. The black box was a device from
which it was mandated that the president could never be
more than one minute away. About the size of a briefcase,
the box contained the electronic equipment that allowed
the president to maintain communications between
himself and the entire network of the nation's defense
forces in case of surprise military attack.

Clavell had dutifully arranged to carry the box, but he
was concerned. Secret Service rules strictly prohibited such
a thing and only his loyalty kept Clavell from reporting the
president's request to his superiors.

The president instructed him to drive toward Georgetown on some of the lesser traveled roads, which to Clavell
meant avoiding busy Wisconsin Avenue. They drove along
the cobblestoned side streets until the president instructed
him to turn into the driveway of a plain brick Georgetown
house. He pulled the car to a halt, stopped the engine and
jumped out, surveying the area. Satisfied, he opened the
door. The president, wearing a gray trench coat and his

hunting cap, slipped out, closing the door quietly behind himself.

The house was dark and the president cast a quick look up and down the road befor darting through a squeaky iron gate that led to the rear of the house, with Clavell trailing closely behind pointing a pencil-sized flashlight at the president's feet.

Before they could knock, the door opened, swinging partially open. Clavell already had his revolver in his hand when a short stocky man wearing a wrinkled business suit without a tie peered suspiciously over their shoulders. It was dark but Clavell's eyes had adjusted well enough to the filtered light to recognize Louie Cordaro.

"Are you alone?" the president asked.

"As we agreed," Cordaro answered.

"Check it," the president said, motioning Clavell toward the other rooms. Cordaro closed the door quietly as Clavell hastened to search, using only his small flashlight. He was uneasy about leaving the president alone with Cordaro and hurried back toward the rear door from the front of the house.

"All clear," he announced.

Cordaro grinned and shuffled carefully in the dark toward the living room where he turned on a small table lamp. The president followed, excusing Clavell who went outside to wait.

Clavell squatted on the front porch, affording himself a view of everything but the rear of the house, which he worried about, but working alone left him no choice. He decided to stay on the porch with his gun drawn, trained on the room where he could see the president sitting on the sofa.

Inside the house, the president sat contently. He knew why Cordaro had requested their meeting but it was his idea to keep it totally secret from everyone but Clavell.

Jordan spoke slowly, raising his eyes from a note pad he had been studying. "I agree with you, Louie, that it would be a great injustice if you were to go to prison. Now I know there are those who would disagree with me, say that I'm all wrong and that you're guilty. But I was taught that if there's a reasonable doubt, then the accused is, by law, innocent. I'm here tonight to tell you that I believe there's a reasonable doubt in your case. That's why I'd like to help you, but you must understand it isn't going to be easy. There are complications which have to be considered.''

Cordaro was unusually calm even though he sensed that the president wasn't going to accede to his request that he be pardoned in the event he was sentenced to prison. He studied Jordan. He had spoken with him many times before but never alone. He was impressed with himself. Here he was, sitting alone with the president of the United States. He had come a long way from his humble beginnings.

''What complications?'' Cordaro asked.

The president gave him a stern look. ''Well now, Louie, you know I want to help and that I personally covet the support of your union in this election. Let's both understand that. No doubt about it.''

The president was hedging and Cordaro knew it. He sipped his coffee. ''Like I said, what complications?'' he asked again.

The president slumped deeper into his chair, adjusting his feet on the hassock. A pleased smile crossed his face. ''I could offer you the pardon but there are some conditions that would have to be met.'' The president raised the note pad and gestured with it. ''I've made some notes,'' he said.

Cordaro sat staring, not knowing what to expect. ''Go on,'' he said.

Combing his fingers nervously through his hair, the president continued. ''I have some information that disturbs me and maybe you can help me alleviate some of those concerns.''

''I'm listening.''

President Jordan shifted his attention from his note pad and looked directly at Cordaro. ''There's been some talk that Peter Denning's files may be audited. It seems that there's some concern over whether a certain payment to an individual a few years ago may have been made illegally. I would hope that Mr. Denning has taken enough precautions to preclude such an investigation turning up anything potentially embarrassing to the individual."

"Meaning yourself?"

"I didn't say that!" the president countered quickly.

Cordaro couldn't resist the chance to rub the president's nose in a past indiscretion. "Consider it done," he offered.

The president fidgeted with the note pad again, looking back across the room at Cordaro. "There's more," he said bluntly. "Billy Hawk made a tape recording that is of interest to both of us. I want it."

Cordaro leaned forward in his chair. "How do you know that?"

"Come now, Louie. I'm the president. There's not much that can be kept from me, especially when I want to know something."

"What's on it?" Cordaro tested, still unclear what it all meant.

"Let's just say that Billy Hawk suspected more than he led us to believe when he was alive. Neither of us needs the kind of publicity we'd get if that tape were ever made public."

Cordaro sat up irritably, unsatisfied. "I gotta know what's in it," he demanded. "Hell, if I get it for you, I'll damn well listen to it first. You can bet on that!"

The president bristled, his voice became louder. "Your master contract is mentioned. Need I say more?"

This was the first time Cordaro had ever heard anybody use the term "master contract" outside of his own organization. It didn't really matter now anyway, he thought. The plan was already in effect. Any attempt to stop it with legislation by retroactively making the master contract illegal would be met with a nationwide shutdown. He had the country at his mercy and he knew it, but he needed to be a free man to enjoy it. That had to come first. The president's interest in the tape extended beyond the master contract. It had to. He was convinced of that.

He studied the president's face for a moment. "If I get the tape, what would that solve? There must be others who know about it."

Jordan hesitated before answering. "I'll take care of those people when the time comes. Just get the tape," he said coolly.

Even for Cordaro it was hard to comprehend what the president was saying. He was sure James Hawk had to know about Billy Hawk's tape and its contents. The way he was reading the president, James Hawk's life meant nothing to Jordan either. Cordaro was used to such facts of life but never on such a high level. It was one thing to act as enforcer, even to order the killing of an annoying and uncooperative labor opponent, but for a leader of the free world to apply those same principles in such a casual matter-of-fact manner produced a tension in his gut. To think that the president would order the assassination of a political opponent was almost unbelievable.

Cordaro sighed heavily, trying to calm himself. "I can handle the tape. Just tell me where it is."

"Good," the president said. "I . . ."

Cordaro stopped him before he could continue. "There's still the small matter of *why* I should do it," he interrupted. "You're asking me to get you the tape plus you want continued support from my union in the election. You know, there's something missing here. You haven't offered anything in return for those favors. Let's talk price. You know what I mean."

The president had expected Cordaro's response. "That's why we need to talk," he said. "An unconditional pardon, under the current circumstances, wouldn't sit well with the public despite the fact that you have a lot of support there."

"What do you mean by unconditional?" Cordaro asked, suddenly leaning forward in his chair again.

"If your appeal results in a sustained conviction, you'll have to go to prison. It could take a year before you've exhausted the appeal process and you could still be sitting where you are today—free on bail but still convicted, with a long prison sentence ahead of you."

"I know that! But I still don't know what you're driving at."

"It's simple. If I'm not reelected, there would be nothing I could do to help you when you'd need me most. You'll just go to prison and serve your time. I can't very well pardon you if I'm just a private citizen. I *could* lose the election, you know."

"So pardon me now! Let's not worry about whether or not you win the election!"

"It's not that easy, Louie. The public would say I acted too quickly, that I should have waited for the appeal process to run out and that the courts should have decided your fate. It could cost me a lot of votes, not to mention the election."

"So if you lose the election, I got to prison. Is that it?"

"Not exactly. If you do as I ask, we can work it out."

Cordaro sat back. "I'm listening."

"Your support out there among the public is beginning to build. But it'll take a long time to convince the majority of the public that you're innocent. The way for you to get their sympathy is to continue your persecution campaign. Convince them, whether you're guilty or not, that no man should be subjected to what you've been through."

"But that's what we're doing now. I've got the whole fuckin' public relations firm doing nothing but that!"

"I know, I know. But it's not enough. It'll take too long, way past January the way I figure it. And that will be too late."

Cordaro's eyes narrowed. "Okay, so what's your plan?" he asked.

"Surrender now."

Cordaro was incredulous. He nearly leaped from his chair. "What? Are you nuts?"

The president persisted. "Hear me out. It makes sense."

Cordaro squirmed uncomfortably back into his chair as the president continued.

"The worst thing that could happen to you is to spend time going through the appeal process and still wind up with a guilty verdict. You must know you stand a good chance of that or you wouldn't have shown up here tonight. You can voluntarily submit to imprisonment without an appeal. Don't you see, it would dramatize your persecution. The public would accept a presidential pardon on that basis. I can claim that you went to prison without due process. With a continued campaign on your part to stress your sacrifice to the judicial system, we can pull it off. Oh, there'll be a little flak but nothing like I'd get if I pardoned you now. Hell, they might try to impeach me!"

Cordaro raced through a series of thoughts in his mind. "What's the timing?" he asked, not sure if he wanted to hear the answer.

"As soon as possible. You need to spend at least a few months in prison. I can't very well pardon you a couple of days after you go in. It wouldn't look good. I'll let the word out that I'm reviewing the case. That way it won't come as a complete surprise when I pardon you."

"When will the pardon come?"

"Before Christmas, whether I win or lose the election. I can guarantee that."

"And you'll do this for me just for getting you that tape?"

"Don't forget the continued union support," the president added quickly. "A real stepped-up effort is needed."

"That's all?"

"For now."

Cordaro's eyes narrowed. "For now?"

"If I win the election, consider the debt even. If I lose, it will be another story."

"I'm listening."

The president went on. "I want to remain in office, that's rather obvious. It's more important to me than anything else in the world. But if I lose the election, I must consider the future. I come from humble beginnings, just like you. I am not a rich man, at least not yet. If I lose the election, I'll need money to help me invest in my future."

"How much?"

"Two million dollars has a nice ring to it."

"That's twice as much as before!"

The president took offense. "If you don't like the terms, you can stay in prison. I'll get by, with or without you. I have other resources at my disposal."

"I'm not so sure," Cordaro challenged through clenched teeth.

There was a long silence. Neither man was in a position to bargain and both knew it, despite their bluffs. The stakes were too high; neither could afford to alienate the other.

"I don't know," Cordaro said slowly, biting his nail. "I get a little anxious thinkin' about sitting in the can waiting for someone else to press the button that springs me. I'd have no control over it and I don't like that one damn bit. I want to talk it over with some people first."

"Absolutely not!" the president yelled, suddenly on his feet. "This has to be kept strictly between the two of us. No outsiders. I've never reneged on a deal between us yet. I believe you know what I mean."

Cordaro stared malevolently at the man who he knew controlled his fate. There was no use kidding himself. He knew Jordan needed him and what his union could do for him politically, if not financially. One other thing kept sticking in his mind—Billy Hawk. The fact that Jordan had handled his end of that transaction spoke for itself. He could have taken the million dollars and done nothing, with no reprisals. There had been no guarantees then, either. Each man had acted on faith that the other would hold his end of the deal. Billy Hawk was dead. That was what had been bargained for; that was what had been achieved.

There was no choice. Both men knew that. Neither could reach his goals without help from the other.

The president's eyes narrowed as he sat back down. "Do you agree?" he asked.

Cordaro nodded.

Chapter 59

"WHEN'S MY SISTER coming home?"

Tor rationalized that while there was still a sliver of hope for finding Mikki, he couldn't very well tell Shana that he feared her sister was dead. For a precious eight-year-old girl who had spent much of her brief life reading poetry and fairy tales, it would be too brutal. Shana couldn't take another devastating loss right now.

Tor changed the subject. "You try and get some sleep," he said. "It's been a long day."

She looked up at him as he sat on the edge of the bed in the room Tor had set aside for her in his apartment. "Is this going to be my room?" she asked.

Tor nodded. "For a while," he answered.

Shana turned up her nose, making a face.

"What's wrong with it?" he asked.

"There's no dolls or animals or any of those kind of things. Everything is so *plain*. I want my dolls. And Merlin too."

"Merlin?"

"He's my stuffed frog. He's almost as big as I am. Actually, Merlin is my friend the magician. He can make himself into anything he wants. With me, he's always been a frog. My daddy gave him to me."

"Where is Merlin now?"

She turned from him, shrugging her shoulders. "I don't know anymore. When Mommy died, Daddy had all the furniture and things picked up by the moving people. I haven't seen him since. That's when we came to San Francisco. Do you think Merlin's here somewhere? He's always been able to go wherever he wants. I think maybe he's around. You know, disguised as something else.''

"I don't know about that, but I'll sure try and find out. Now, you get some sleep and I'll see you in the morning."

Shana reached up and kissed his cheek.

He returned her kiss, tucked her in, and started out the bedroom door.

"Mr. Slagle," she called.

He turned and looked back. She was sitting up in bed.

"Yes?" he answered.

"Thanks for taking care of me," she said. "I like you almost as much as Merlyn."

Tor spent most of the night thinking about the little girl who was now sharing his home. She had spent so much time away from her sister during the past few months that Mikki's absence now was not all that unusual for her, and she had asked no questions when he had told her that she was going to stay with him in California until Mikki returned.

The next morning, the gentle hug and kiss she gave him as he left for the office brought a trace of tears to his eyes. "Goodby, Lancelot," she whispered. "Please help bring my sister home."

She was still in his mind as he sat at his office desk hours later, trying to sort through an array of papers that were spread out before him. He kept wondering how he would ever be able to tell her Mikki might never be coming home.

An hour later, Percy Tinsley left Tor's office with another long list of items to check out. It was the sixth time in two days he had been given similar assignments. Tor was relying heavily on him for a grass-roots assessment of the union movement within the city and in his store in particular, and he didn't like what Tinsley was telling him.

The city had already succumbed to the demands of the police force, allowing them to be represented by Cordaro's union and a threatened strike was on the horizon if their wage demands weren't met.

Police Commissioner Hardy, who had threatened to resign if the union was recognized, had already fulfilled that pledge. His termination date was set for the first of the year and had prematurely solved the mayor's secret dilemma of how to comply with Louie Cordaro's earlier request that Hardy by dumped.

There were rumors that the next police force targeted for a union organization drive was Phoenix, Arizona, and nobody had to tell Tor why. The heavy drug traffic funneled in from Mexico made it an ideal location for strengthening the union's relationship with organized crime. Like San Francisco, union organizers were promising big salary increases to the rank and file peace officers and their words were already falling on attentive ears.

Winston Sheffield, whom Tor hadn't talked with since their meeting in May, apparently was losing his battle in San Francisco to keep Hemp, Lathrop and Company and the other smaller retailers free from unionism. While the initial election to determine if the employees wanted union representation had not been held, the fact that the union had for the first time gathered enough signatures to require an election spoke for the strength of the union's organizing efforts and the weakness in Sheffield's efforts to thwart the drive.

Tinsley warned that Slagle's was now the last store to survive the drive, but the situation was precarious. Employees who used to call Tinsley by his first name had suddenly begun calling him "Mr. Tinsley" and were aloof and unresponsive when he tried to talk to them. It was Tinsley's view that they were ambivalent about Tor's commitment to Slagle's and consequently, they were concerned about their own job security. The union continued to circulate the rumor that Tor was considering selling the company in order to devote full time to politics and that the only way the employees could be certain of retaining their jobs when a new owner took over was to be unionized.

Tor was so enraged at the erroneous report that he scheduled a full store meeting for the next morning to dispel the rumor. When unions couldn't offer prospective organizing employees more money, the next step was frequently to promote job security by promising employees that they couldn't be fired without the union's approval. Tor wanted to be sure everybody knew that the only security his employees would ever need was to do a good job and that the union could never keep him or any other employer from terminating an employee for cause.

At mid-afternoon, Tor sat staring out his office window after dispatching the final piece of paperwork that required his review and signature. The silence was peaceful as he sipped a diet soda and watched the people below battle the stiff San Francisco winds. Then Willie Ray poked his uninvited head through the office door and ushered himself in.

Ray was jovially caustic. "I thought I'd stop by and see if you really do exist," he said. "I've been talking to a recording for the past two months."

"It's nice to be back but I'm afraid it probably won't be for long." Tor responded.

After pouring himself a Perrier from the office bar, Ray came right to the point of his visit. "I suppose Percy has filled you in on the local happenings," he said.

Tor nodded. "I'm afraid so."

"Sick, isn't it?" he said, not expecting an answer to his question.

Tor sighed. "The toughest part is trying to sort through all the rumors that have built up since I've been gone. I don't know what to believe."

"Tain't just rumors," Ray interjected, shaking his head in disgust. "This fuckin' city is going under. Anybody with more than a handful of employees will have Cordaro and the union to deal with by the end of the year, you included. I'm afraid I haven't been much help to you on this one."

Tor flicked his hands in a gesture of resignation. "Don't worry about it. I still think we've got a chance, but that doesn't bother me as much as what's going on in City Hall. Percy tells me even the mayor is running scared."

"Hell, that prick's been in the union's back pocket ever since he was elected. The only thing different is that now they're not *asking* him, they're *telling* him what to do."

"Like naming a new police commissioner?"

"Sure! Cordaro wants to keep the boys in the mob happy by making sure the mayor names someone that'll be a little softer on vice than Hardy has been. Hardy's been a thorn in the side of the rackets for a long time. His resignation is playing right into their hands."

"But Hardy must know that."

"Yeah, but that won't change his mind. He's always known where the mayor is coming from, but Hardy's biggest problem has been the D.A. The cops keep arresting the prostitutes and the dope peddlers and they keep gettin' turned loose by Jackson who always seems to find a reason not to prosecute. Hardy's just had it. Nobody can talk him out of it. We've lost him."

"Cordaro representing his police force didn't help him much either, did it?"

"That was the last straw. When that happened, Hardy decided there wasn't any hope. The boys in the streets are laughing their asses off. They figure once we get a new commissioner, this place could become as sophisticated as Las Vegas, only underground, with privileged members."

Tor only stared at Ray. After a moment, he responded. "And you can bet the new commissioner will take his orders from the mayor. Otherwise, he won't get the job," he added.

"It's a beautiful world we have. The name of the game is 'cooperate and graduate'."

The telephone interrupted. It was Percy Tinsley. "Turn the T.V. to Channel Four," he began. "There's something you'll want to see."

Tor searched for the remote unit that was hidden somewhere under the papers on his desk. A moment later the

461

screen was filled with a close-up shot of Louie Cordaro standing on the steps of union headquarters. His voice was loud and clear as he read from a prepared script. "Something is happening in this country by the name of James Hawk," he shouted. "That man assigned an elite squad of deputy attorneys to work his dictates on me and as a result of his obsessive actions I have been hounded and harassed to a degree that has affected my health. I am here today to say I cannot take this punishment any longer either physically or emotionally. James Hawk has beaten me into the ground unmercifully for things I had no control over. He's even paid people to spy on me. This man will stop at nothing until he sees Louie Cordaro behind bars."

Cordaro paused, turned the pages, and continued. "He's a spoiled millionaire that never had to go out and make a living by his own efforts. He's used me as a pawn to get publicity for his political campaign. I am here today to say that I am about to submit myself for incarceration in Federal prison. Not because I am guilty, which I am not, but to demonstrate to the American citizens what a travesty it is when an individual like Hawk is allowed to point a gun in the name of authority at an innocent citizen's head and pull the trigger. I don't feel there is a need for me to wait out the appeals' process. James Hawk would only buy more witnesses to lie about me and I would stand no more chance of acquitting myself than I did during the last trial. Contrary to our great Constitution, I have been considered guilty first and forced to prove my innocence. I will surrender and go to prison with the hope that my sacrifice to the government and James Hawk will prevent similar injustices to any of my fellow citizens in the future. Putting me in jail is a crime, perpetrated by a crazed individual who must be eradicated. I will return to public life someday, but only when that person is no longer in the powerful position he now occupies. I cannot live a normal life until then. That's all I have to say at this time."

Newsmen scurried to ask questions but Cordaro quickly disappeared behind guarded doors.

Stunned, Tor snapped off the television. Cordaro's unexpected decision simply made no sense. It was totally out of character. There had to be a hidden motive. Tor couldn't imagine what it was.

"What do you think?" Ray asked.

"I don't know. I just don't know," Tor responded. "But I do know that little speech about Jim couldn't have been better timed. It'll be all over the national networks tonight and Jim's debate with the president tomorrow night is bound to suffer."

"What do you mean?" Ray asked, not following Tor's thoughts.

"The public will spend the rest of tonight and all of tomorrow waiting for Jim to defend himself against Cordaro's charges, the media will see to that. They won't even listen to what Jim has to say about the other issues. Jim's spent months trying to get the president in front of the cameras to talk about the economy and now that he's done it, nobody will hear a word he says. Hell, they won't want to hear about the economy now. They'll want to hear about Louie Cordaro!"

Ray cleaned his glasses on his shirt sleeve. "Will Hawk address the issue tomorrow night?"

"I doubt it," Tor said, shaking his head. "Too much has gone into the debate format to change it now. Besides, Jordan wants no part of the Cordaro issue. Neither does Jim for that matter."

"I don't understand," he said slowly. "I can see why *Hawk* would want to avoid the issue, but why wouldn't Jordan jump at the chance to bring it up? It can only make Jim Hawk look like a fool."

"Jordan doesn't *need* to bring the issue up. That's the point," Tor explained, his voice rising. "Technically, because he's the president, the Hawk Committee is part of his administration and he doesn't want to remind the public of that. Besides, if Jordan remains neutral, he can't get hurt. By avoiding it, he stays clean, offending nobody. Meanwhile, Jim's on the defensive for the rest of the campaign. He won't win any votes diverting his attention to Cordaro and away from the basic issues. That's where Jordan has to be attacked. The fact is, he's been a lousy president. Our economy proves that. He's been a fuckin' disaster but that's going to get glossed over now.''

Tor's eyes came back to Ray's and for a moment the two men simultaneously felt diminished. They were small, virtually helpless.

At that very moment, the doorbell was ringing at the Slagle residence. A dozen roses were being delivered to Shana Parker. There was no name on the card. It simply read: ''To Shana, all my love.''

Chapter 60

PALACE OF FINE ARTS, San Francisco. It was October fourteenth, a long way from the old wintry days of the first campaign in the New Hampshire primary. Election day was less than one month away and at 6:00 P.M., Pacific Daylight Time, the evening news faded away, to be followed immediately by a commercial for Chevrolet. The debate between the two presidential candidates was only seconds away.

For ninety minutes, the technology of television was about to bring the campaign to over one hundred forty million people gathered in front of television sets across the land in order that they might ponder their choice between the two men in what was called by the morning wire services "the biggest political forum in history."

What James Hawk and his brain trust had worked so hard for was about to come true. They finally had the president where they wanted him, in front of the cameras for direct comparison.

The events concerning Louie Cordaro during the past two weeks made the debate unnecessary as far as the president was concerned but it was too late to pull out. The debate had been scheduled when the president and his advisors had felt they had no other choice but to agree. They were trailing in the polls by only two to five percentage points and gaining, but at a pace they calculated too slow to overtake James Hawk by election day. At the time, the debate appeared to be the only answer despite the president's campaign committee's reservations about James Hawk's stronger oratorical abilities.

But things were different now. The unexpected anti-Hawk backlash as a result of the union campaign to discredit him, had narrowed the gap. The latest polls rated the two candidates even. James Hawk had lost his once seemingly insurmountable lead.

The issues to be discussed this evening by the candidates had been decided upon at earlier meetings but the exact questions were not to be revealed to either candidate in advance. Questions were to be asked of each alternately.

James's preparation was imprinted with his patented attention to organization and his casual surface approach to the task at hand. He behaved, as he did in any period of stress, as if the crisis would only be complicated if his emotions were permitted to interfere. He had spent the last two days secluded with aides at his home, studying as if he were cramming for a college final. When he finished, he had nineteen typewritten pages covering the broadest range of subject matter that could possibly be presented by the commentator or panel members. Answers on such things as unemployment, steel production, cost of living, and gross national product were synopsized into concise paragraphs that simplified his point of view on complicated subjects far too deep to be reviewed effectively in the two-and-a-half minute response allowed for each question.

In contrast, President Jordan had spent his time preparing in solitude. He was tired and had noticeably lost weight over the past six weeks because of his rigorous schedule. His campaign had been a hell of a lot easier four years earlier when all he had to worry about was the campaign itself. Now, he was running both his campaign and the country. His physical appearance wasn't good and he worried about it as he sat quietly waiting. He was concerned over his television image and the makeup artists were working on him feverishly. His deep eye shadows and beard stubble were being corrected by using spotlights to eliminate the shadows, and theater makeup was used to hide the coarseness of his features.

The two candidates entered the studio, spoke briefly, and exchanged terse pleasantries. In their careers, they had met on a casual basis many times before and the president's cordial manner had always impressed James. But tonight he seemed nervous, aloof. He was short-tempered, easily agitated, and found it hard to look at James directly. His mind was preoccupied, and it was obvious to James that he only spoke because decorum dictated that he do so.

The president's representatives sat tensely as the background lights lowered for the beginning of the debate while the Hawk camp appeared as cocky and bold as their leader.

As soon as the cameras brought the image of the two candidates to the viewers, James bagged his first victory of the evening. Up until now, he had been the young challenger under constant verbal attack from the president as too inexperienced and immature to seek the presidency. Now, as they sat side by side, James was projected into the public's imagination as an equal to the president of the United States. That alone was Jordan's major objection against the idea of the debate.

The two candidates sat quietly off screen as the N.B.C. moderator opened the program. "Good evening," he began with a plastic smile. "The television and radio stations of the United States are proud to present a discussion of domestic issues in the current political campaign by the two major candidates for the presidency."

Then they were on the air. For the next sixteen and one half minutes each candidate would use his allotted time to give an opening statement from which many of the points of the debate would emanate.

James spoke first, spending his eight minutes appealing to the emotions of the people across the nation for support in the election while, at the same time, promising to improve unemployment and to bring inflation down. "The posture of America in the world rests primarily on how our country functions at home," James emphasized. He cited the poor health of the economy during the Jordan administration and vowed to get America moving again. He was appealing to no particular ethnic or political groups, but to the masses.

During President Jordan's opening remarks, he stated similar goals for the next four years, but differed in the method to attain them.

Perhaps it was because James had spoken first that the president made his fatal mistake and became defensive. As the debate wore on, he repeatedly rebutted and refuted James's statements and generally failed to address himself, as James did continually, to the people. He offered no idealistic vision of the future as James had done so skillfully in his opening remarks.

James repeatedly ignored the president's inferences about his immature solutions to the country's internal problems, choosing instead to use each question as an opening for another appeal to the minds and imaginations of his audience. As the minutes ticked away, the president slowly and methodically continued defeating himself.

James was unruffled by the president's constant barrage of insults, remaining characteristically calm, which contrasted sharply with the president's obvious tenseness.

Sensing his performance was weak, Jordan seemed to sink deeper into the pit he was digging for himself. He looked frightened and was occasionally caught by the cameras scowling at James.

When the debate came to a close, the president was haggard as he slouched over his podium fidgeting with his notes. His makeup began to streak as the tremendous heat from the lights made his brow bead with sweat. It was obvious to the seasoned observers present that he lacked the energy to match that of James Hawk's youth. In ninety minutes, James had snatched away what had been predicted as an easy Jordan victory over an inexperienced challenger.

When it was over, the consensus of reporters across the country was that the debate had been a disaster for the president. He had wanted to expose James as a young, excitable, and inexperienced kid down the block that wanted to ride his big brother's bicycle, and had failed miserably.

James was ecstatic over the sudden turn of events. He wasn't sure how much good the debate had done him but it had repaired some of the image problem he faced in the shadow of Louie Cordaro. The impact of the debate would have to come later after the pollsters had assessed the public pulse once again.

Chapter 61

IT WAS 9:15 A.M., Tuesday, October 18, when Louie Cordaro officially began serving time. He was facing an eight-year prison term, the commencement of which was recorded for history by no less than fifty newspaper, radio, and television reporters who chronicled every move he made as he surrendered at the United States Marshall's office in Washington, D.C.

At 4:05 that afternoon, less than three weeks after his conviction, he arrived unceremoniously by automobile at the federal penitentiary of Lewisburg, Pennsylvania. It seemed that Louie Cordaro had finally been brought to his knees.

Two days later, a group of thirty-two well-dressed and well-manicured men gathered on a palatial fifteen-acre estate in upper New York. They came from all over the country—Colorado, Texas, New York, Florida. Collectively, the group represented every area in the United States.

Twenty-nine of the thirty-two men had arrest records with over forty convictions. Sixteen had been arrested or questioned in connection with narcotics, twelve for murder, and twenty-two for illegal use of firearms. The leader of the meeting was Joe Coppola, a man who had been a prime suspect in several different murders within the last four years, each time being released for lack of evidence.

All the men present at the meeting were active in legitimate businesses as well as their other activities. Garment manufacturing, vending machines, and electronic games were by far the most popular vocations, with a scattering of representations from the trucking industry. In one way or another, each man was involved with labor or labor-management relations. Simply, it was a select gathering from the world of organized crime.

The security that surrounded the riverstone wall around the mansion outmatched any ever provided for the heads of many of the world's largest countries. Electronic equipment jammed the airwaves for miles around to prevent eavesdropping, and a helicopter hovering overhead kept in close contact with ground surveillance crews surrounding the sanctuary.

This was to be a strategy meeting, carefully designed to develop and approve the marketing plans for the coming year in narcotics and gambling, with a special emphasis on continuing efforts to seize more control of legitimate businesses and labor racketeering.

Today was the annual meeting, the meeting of the stockholders, so to speak. Discussion would be brief. The carefully prepared agenda had been in each delegate's possession for over two weeks. The only decisions, beyond the actual vote to decide for or against a proposition, would be to decide how to divide the territories for management responsibility if an approved proposal encompassed more than one leader's geographical locations as they stretched their tentacles of authority.

The agenda called for two days of decision making with the end of the second day reserved for general open discussion. Everyone knew what the main topic would be.

In the past, the group had always found a friendly ear when they needed it in Louie Cordaro. Cordaro knew he couldn't attain all his personal and union goals without reciprocal favors from organized crime. But Cordaro's brashness and flair for publicity never set well with this group of allies. They preferred to remain anonymous. It was difficult for the group to operate their legitimate businesses while being investigated by federal and local governmental agencies interested in their operations simply because of something Louie Cordaro had said or done. Cordaro was stubborn and that trait frequently led to trouble, not only for him but his associates as well.

Cordaro had never dealt directly with any of the men attending the meeting today and it seemed ironic to Peter Denning that today they would be discussing Cordaro's fate. Denning had always been Cordaro's liaison with the group, his personal go-between with organized crime. He had always thought it best that their communications were handled through Denning but the truth was that he had no choice. The group would have it no other way. Denning was one of their own. His appointment by Cordaro a few years earlier as underwriter to the National Union Health and Welfare and Pension Funds helped cement a relationship between himself and the group's secluded community that had been fequently strained over the years due to his own stubbornness.

Today, an air of relief filled the smoke-filled room as the men casually discussed the imprisonement of Louie Cordaro. Their future relationship with the union was suddenly uncertain because of Cordaro's absence and as the day drew to a close the discussion was going nowhere. No solutions, no proposals, only uncertainty. Their conversations continued in an unbroken hum for over an hour until Coppola finally interrupted, tapping his pipe against the table in front of him. "Gentlemen, I'd like you to meet someone who might solve our dilemma," he announced.

There was a long silence. Except for the faint ticking of an antique wall clock that hung over the fireplace and the hiss of a match lighting Coppola's twelve-inch cigar, the quiet remained unbroken. All eyes were riveted on Coppola, who delighted in his surprise. The meeting had run its course. The only "unfinished business" stood outside, awaiting an invitation to join the conference.

"Gentlemen, I'd like you to meet Borg Trenier,"

Coppola announced, opening a door that led to the hallway where Trenier had been waiting for over an hour.

Trenier tightly gripped his own hands, trying desperately to appear calm as he entered the room. He looked into Coppola's face and smiled weakly, never once allowing his eyes to stray from his host. He felt as though he were on a pedestal, afraid to move for fear of falling from a dangerous height.

Coppola cast an anxious glance toward his colleagues as Trenier made his way toward an empty chair beside him. Never before had an outsider been permitted to attend such a meeting. Trenier knew why he was there. He wasn't anybody's fool. He had not been invited to the meeting simply as a temporary replacement for Louie Cordaro. The group considered him union president, fully empowered to operate accordingly with no restrictions. As far as they were concerned, it was as if Louie Cordaro never existed. It was as easy as erasing Stalin's name from the Soviet Union's history books. He could breathe easier now and he settled into his chair a bit more comfortably. For the first time in his life, he was out of Louie Cordaro's reach.

The next day, Borg Trenier named Peter Denning as a consultant to the union's pension fund and took over Cordaro's role as the ultimate decision-maker on the board of trustees for dispensing the funds. Trenier was sure conflict of interest charges from some of the other trustees would be brought, but he decided to disregard the potential consequences and go ahead with Denning's appointment. If it appeared that Denning's unique dual position as both consultant and underwriter to the fund would bring legal action, he would simply have Denning transfer his ownership of the Denning Insurance Company to another individual, enabling him to silently maintain his majority interest in his insurance company. Trenier's only concern was to get Denning the job for which he was so strongly recommended. James Coppola wanted Denning in that position, a point he had made very clear the day before. Trenier had to move swiftly. He had a

474

carefully devised game plan that allowed for no mistakes or compromises either in execution or timing. James Coppola had seen to that.

Chapter 62

THERE WAS NO explanation, no press release. Only a brief handshake after a very one-sided conversation.

Thomas Barrett Wilson felt relieved as he walked away from Borg Trenier's office. He was surprised, but welcomed the decision. He had wanted to quit his position as chief counsel for the union for over a year. Now the choice had been taken out of his hands. While his professional reputation was still high, it had nevertheless been tarnished because of his close association with Louie Cordaro. Lawyers couldn't always defend an innocent client and too frequently he had found himself working with only threads of hope while defending Cordaro. Louie's ideas concerning justice had never coincided with his own and it had become increasingly difficult over the past year for him to maintain his professional ethics. A great weight had been lifted from his shoulders with his termination. He was now free to do as he wished without fear of reprisal. He wasn't sure why Trenier had relieved him of his responsibilities but he didn't really care. They had always gotten along in the past, and as far as he was concerned, Trenier remained a friend. It was Cordaro's problem now. He could worry about what motivated Trenier.

Wilson walked briskly through the union parking lot, thinking about what Cordaro's reactions would be to Trenier's rearrangement of the union's brain trust. He was sure that the naming of Denning as pension fund consultant and now his own dismissal as legal counsel would be enough to cause a Cordaro tirade loud enough to be heard throughout the Lewisburg Penitentiary.

It was 8:15 A.M., when Louie Cordaro finished breakfast. He strolled with an anxious gait in the exercise yard, awaiting permission to go to the visitors area in Section B. For the last two weeks, he had repeatedly left messages for Borg Trenier to come to Lewisburg for a conference, but the requests were always ignored. Out of frustration, he finally turned to Thomas Barrett Wilson. He knew Wilson wouldn't refuse to come.

Cordaro tapped his foot nervously on the cracking cement as he stood and waited. He was worried. What he thought was impossible was actually happening to him. Trenier was challenging his authority while he was in prison and there was nothing he could do about it. Not only had Trenier ignored him but Peter Denning, along with other union officials, was not equally inaccessible. Cordaro wondered what he would do if he had to spend more than a few weeks in prison. The indignity he had already suffered was barely palatable only because he knew it would soon be over, that he would be free to resume his private and public life in any manner he chose. But now things were different. He was no longer confident. Fear of the unknown unsettled him to a point of near frenzy. He hadn't slept for two nights and his swollen eyes were bleary, but not so much as to be unable to recognize the guard that was approaching. He was a tall, big-boned Swede with a broad face, large nose, and legs like fireplugs.

"You got a visitor," the guard grunted.

Cordaro's pace quickened as he plodded across the exercise area toward the visiting room where Wilson patiently sat waiting behind a bullet-proof glass window.

Cordaro felt nervous sweat running from his armpits as he picked up the headphones and inched toward the microphone to speak. He offered Wilson no greeting, instead squaring up to the window with an ominous stare. "What the fuck's goin' on out there?" he asked abruptly, his teeth clenched.

478

"I guess you've heard about Denning," Wilson said calmly.

"Yeah, yeah. And you too. I had to read about it in the papers. Why didn't you come over here and tell me yourself?"

Wilson responded without a trace of compassion or recrimination. "Pennsylvania is a long way from Washington. I had business to conduct."

Cordaro snarled derisively. "Goddamit, Tom, we've been together too long for you to pull this shit too! All I want to know is what Trenier's trying to pull. Now give me some fuckin' answers! I'm tired of sitting here and stewing in my own shit and not knowin' what's happening."

Wilson hesitated, then shook his head. "Sorry, Louie, but I really don't know what the deal is. From what I can see, Trenier is just doing his own thing. I'm on the outside now. I don't know any more than the next guy."

"Bullshit! You must have heard something."

Wilson shrugged noncommittally. "I can only tell you what I've picked up here and there. Nobody's told me anything. To be truthful, I haven't asked because it wouldn't do any good. Nobody's talking."

Cordaro's lips tightened. He reached up and snatched a cigarette from his breast pocket and lit it. "Then tell me what you *do* know," he said, exhaling a puff of smoke.

Wilson thought a moment. He had to be careful with what he was about to say. Even in prison, Louie Cordaro's power was not to be underestimated. "Word has it that Trenier's told everyone to cool the campaign to get you out of prison. He's handling the negotiations for your freedom through the attorney general and doesn't want anybody rocking the boat. He's put a stop to everything, even the bumper stickers."

Cordaro took a deep drag on his cigarette and stared at Wilson, shaking his head. "That fucker doesn't even *know* the attorney general!" he growled. "What about Tucker? Why hasn't he answered my messages?"

"I hear he's in Europe on vacation and won't be back for a month. I doubt that he even knows you're trying to contact him."

"Son-of-a-bitch!" Cordaro shouted, his face reddening. "I'm in here less than two fuckin' weeks and the whole world turns to shit! Wait till I get my hands on that bastard, I'll kill him!"

Wilson's voice remained cool.

"The worst part of it is, your boys seem to be following him. As far as I can see, nobody's taken offense at any of Trenier's orders. There's no resistance."

"I don't understand it!" Cordaro yelled again, his hand slamming on the table. "That asshole couldn't lead a horse to water!"

"If you ask me, you've been had. I think he planned it all along. From the looks of it, he's been waiting for a chance like this. He couldn't wait for you to go to prison."

"That doesn't make sense," Cordaro snapped. "The union presidency doesn't mean shit. You gotta have friends to back it up. Trenier doesn't have the influence I do. I got *people* to back up the power."

Wilson was unable to resist the opportunity to repay his former employer just once for the myraid indignities and insults he had been subjected to during the past several years. "Where are they now, Louie?" he asked cynically.

Cordaro was wordless. Nothing in his previous experience had prepared him for this sudden isolation from those he considered his friends. He had never considered Wilson a friend, only an employee. For that reason, he let Wilson's caustic statement pass. He wondered about President Jordan, what he was thinking. If the president backed down from their agreement, he would be forced to serve at least three years of the eight-year sentence. The thought of remaining in prison more than a few weeks was one he dared not consider. For the first time since he could remember, he was frightened.

Cordaro blew out another puff of smoke. "What makes you think Trenier's planned this whole thing?" he asked.

He chose his words carefully, answering matter-of-factly. "He's moved too fast, with too much authority. I think he's tested his strength somewhere else before jumping into these decisions. I don't believe he's so stupid

480

that he'd try these things without knowing he has some support."

"The board?" Cordaro asked.

Wilson nodded.

"Those fuckin' bastards! That's it! Trenier told me they'd try and dump me if I went to prison. Now that I'm in, they think they can sweep me under the carpet."

Cordaro became silent for a moment, chewing on a fingernail, still trying to sort things out. "That still doesn't make sense," he said, more to himself than Wilson. "The board knows when I get outta here they'll have to answer to me. I don't get it. Either Trenier's crazy or he knows something I don't."

Wilson smiled coldly. "I hate to say this, but I warned you about surrendering. Without the union's campaign to free you, I don't see how in hell you can expect to get out of here before your parole date. Trenier's apparently got you where he wants you. He's pulled your plug."

Cordaro was instantly livid and began yelling again. "Bullshit! He knows I'll get out one way or another and when I do, that son-of-a-bitch will regret it. Meanwhile, I want you to get hold of Marshall Tucker and tell him I gotta see him. Fast!"

Somehow Louie's request for favors always sounded like irrevocable orders and Wilson resented more than ever being told to find Tucker. He was about to tell Cordaro to go to hell but at the last moment he changed his mind. One last indignity could be endured. After all, Cordaro was right. Sooner or later, he would be out of prison and people would have to answer to him for their actions. He didn't want to be one of them.

"Anything else?" Wilson asked with s sigh, not really expecting an answer.

"Yeah, get hold of Bartie Bonano. Tell him I want to see him."

Chapter 63

BORG TRENIER WAS moving swiftly. He had managed to arrest or retard most officially sanctioned union campaigns to free Louie but he hadn't been able to stop everything. A few dissident Cordaro loyalists refused to relent and continued their efforts independent of union sanctions. They would be a bother but Trenier decided there was nothing he could do to stop them.

A nationwide letter-written campaign by rank and file union members and their wives was still in full swing. Local 492 in Michigan had a "Win A Car, Help Louie" contest. The union member who produced the largest number of letters to the president demanding Louie Cordaro's release would win a new Chevrolet. Sample form letters and prepaid envelopes were stuffed in each member's pay envelope to insure the success of the contest. Despite Trenier's objections, it was proving to be a huge success. Thousands of letters were already being sent to the White House on a daily basis.

Before leaving for Europe, Marshall Tucker drafted a scathing editorial that was circulating throughout the nation's leading newspapers: "One of the greatest labor leaders in the history of this great country of ours is presently confined at Lewisburg Prison. He's there because of a personal vendetta by a very small minority who could not stand the likes of Louie Cordaro unselfishly representing the millions of American working men and women. We all know that Louie Cordaro is one of America's most understanding and compassionate men and that he has never turned his back on the working man's needs. I ask all of you to write your congressman. Demand the release of this persecuted man. If the tables were turned, he would certainly do it for you.''

Despite these efforts on Cordaro's behalf, Trenier still felt comfortable that his new position as union president would remain secure. Even so, he took precautions against any unforeseen reprisals by having a personal bodyguard on duty around the clock.

He was enjoying his new position as head of the world's largest labor union. In only two weeks, Trenier had managed to firmly establish himself as the undisputed king of labor and his insatiable appetite for even more power was growing daily. He was working nearly twenty-four hours a day at his new job and the long days were beginning to take their toll on his rotund fifty-six-year-old body. His mind remained alert, but physically, he was no match for such a grueling schedule. He decided to accept an inviation from James Coppola to take a golfing vacation. They were to stay at Coppola's summer home that bordered the fifteen fairway at Rancho La Costa outside of San Diego. Trenier was familiar with the area because the union's pension fund had provided the financing for the project's developme. Many years earlier, a group of investors headed by Coppola had conceived the idea for a year-round golfing paradise. San Diego's climate was perfect and it proved to be a wise investment for all concerned. It was financed with over sixty million dollars of union money and many high-ranking union officials had free use of several homes that bordered the fairways. The golf course was officially rated as one of the best in the world and the climate drew a wealthy clientele from around the world to enjoy themselves in its posh restaurants and hotels. Trenier was now part of the choicest part of society. His once powerful body had over the years become far softer than his mind. It was time to take a rest.

It was an unusual day at La Costa, sunny and oppressively warm for the first day of November. The five and one half hours spent on the course, along with the three prior days in which his routine was exactly the same, finally began to decimate Trenier's strength and his body was aching. He decided to avoid the sauna, deciding instead to shower early and keep his four o'clock massage appointment.

He walked slowly across the grounds with his bodyguard, a stout twenty-nine-year-old dock worker recruited for the week from a union local in Los Angeles. The sky was clear, and the towering palm trees mixed with a scattering of pines presented a rich variety of greens that he thoroughly enjoyed. He didn't look forward to leaving.

After showering, Trenier laid himself comfortably on his stomach across the sheeted massage table. It was only 3:30. His solitude would not be broken for at least another half hour and a short nap before his massage was too tempting to refuse. He began to doze off.

In what seemed like only a minute, he heard the door behind him open and close. He cast his eyes blearily at his watch; it was 3:40. He clumsily tried to cover his nakedness with a sheet as he struggled to roll over. Then, suddenly, he was brutally slammed face down to the table.

"Louie wants some questions answered," whispered a gruff voice that was all too familiar to him.

Dressed in an all-white cotton uniform, Bartie Bonano had his forearm jammed tightly under Trenier's throat, pressing hard against his head with the palm of his opposite hand making it nearly impossible for him to utter even the smallest sound.

Trenier's face quickly suffused a deep red, his blood flow almost completely choked off. He coughed violently, offering no resistance as he grasped for the slightest breath of air.

Suddenly the stranglehold was released and Trenier lay motionless, catching his breath as the seconds ticked by. Then he felt another painful grip, this time in his lower body. The excruciating pain increased and before he could cry out, a rolled-up pair of tennis socks was stuffed into his mouth, quickly secured by a towel wrapped around and tied behind his head.

Trenier's eyes widened, rolling from side to side as he tried to see what his tormentor was doing. The unbelievable pain in his groin was still there even though Bonano had long before released his grip on his testicles. Trenier heard noises—drawers opening and closing, then footsteps from behind. Still, he did not move. He was sure Bonano had a gun. *Stay calm,* he told himself. It would be his only chance.

Bonano's voice struck terror in him. "Like I said," Bonano said, "Louie wants some questions answered and I don't want to take back any fuckin' lies so we're gonna be sure you feel like tellin' ol' Bartie the truth."

Bonano reached for a jar of vaseline he had found in the supply cupboard and forced a thumbful into Trenier's exposed anus quickly followed by a cold and full penetration of the six-inch barrel from his handgun. The sound of the hammer clicking to the ready position made Trenier forget about the pain. Sweat began to stream profusely from his body as he lay totally immobile.

Bonano muttered a few obscenities, walked around to the front of the table and pulled up a chair. He reversed it, then sat down heavily in front of Trenier. "Move a muscle and your asshole will be twelve inches bigger," he boasted, laughing heartily.

Trenier lifted his head slowly, his head still swirling from the pain.

"Give me your hand," Bonano ordered.

Slowly, Trenier obeyed, not knowing what else to do. Bonano took hold of his little finger and bent it backwards until it broke with a sickening crack that caused Trenier to vomit into the socks. He began to choke.

Bonano snarled contemptuously through his teeth, keeping his voice low. "I'm gonna take the gag off, motherfucker, and if you so much as utter a noise above a whisper, I'm gonna reach down and jerk one of your balls off. You understand, fatso?"

Trenier tried nodding his head.

Slowly, Bonano eased off the towel and pulled the vomit strained socks from his mouth.

Trenier's mouth dropped open. "You bastard," he whispered. "I'll get you for this! You can tell your friend to go fuck himself! I—"

Trenier's words were cut short. The socks were suddenly crammed back into his mouth, followed by the towel being tied around his head even tighter than before.

Bonano slammed Trenier's head down on the table. "Like I said, I don't want no trouble outta you, asshole."

Trenier closed his eyes, sweat rolling off his body even more heavily. He could still feel the pain in his backside. Bonano grabbed another of his fingers and bent it back so far the nail touched the back of his hand. For some reason, the break didn't seem to hurt as much as the earlier one, but it was still painful. Tears began to roll down his cheeks.

Bonano was breathing heavily now, his patience worn thin. "You fat prick, I'll pull every finger off your hands and stuff 'em down your throat. Now, cut the bullshit," he commanded as he reached down between Trenier's legs. He jammed the pistol even further inside, twisting it from side to side, increasing the pain.

"Now, you're going to get up and tell your little body-guard outside that you're going to take a steam bath. Have him disappear so we can talk."

Bonano stood in front of him. His huge hands picked up Trenier's head by the ears. "And you can forget about your massage appointment. I cancelled it." Bonano ripped the barrel from Trenier's rectum, replacing it squarely in the middle of his back. He allowed Trenier a moment to calm himself before disappearing behind the half open door while Trenier got rid of the bodyguard. When the man was gone, Bonano motioned for him to get back on the table, again face down. The pistol was promptly replaced in its original position and cocked.

Trenier talked.

Chapter 64

DURING THE LAST three days of his presidential campaign, James Hawk had traveled over thirteen thousand miles and given twenty-one speeches. Now it was election eve day. He sat alone in his late brother's den editing what would be his final campaign speech. He didn't discount the importance of the half hour that would bring his final plea to television viewers nationwide, but he found it difficult to concentrate on the draft in front of him. While it was the best of the four alternative speeches submitted for his review, somehow it didn't seem to convey what he really wanted to say.

His pen dropped on the paper-scattered desk as he sat quietly and reflected on the campaign that was about to close. It had been much different than what he had originally thought it would be. There would be no roaring climax as there had been in other presidential years, no violent arguments or unmanageable crowds. An enormous indifference had overtaken the American citizens. Politics had been dulled by television, replacing the personal touch, the handshakes, baby kissing, and all the other familiar political games that, over the years, had traditionally brought the candidates face-to-face with their constituency. A few minutes in front of a television camera exposed each candidate to more people than a year of barnstorming the country could ever have accomplished.

He wondered what he would do if he lost the election, a possibility that he had refused to consider until now. He wasn't the same man as he had been before he decided to run for the presidency. Billy's death, the long campaign, the president's dishonesty, and Louie Cordaro's grip on the nation collectively had served to harden his heart. He felt no compassion, no sense of fair play, not even love for his own family and friends. A few months earlier he had set out like a knight in armor, but that seemed an eternity away. He slumped morosely behind Billy's desk, hating yet understanding what the last few months had done to him. He was still tormented by his proposed speech. It simply wasn't what he wanted to say at all. Even with an apathetic public, he couldn't lower himself to that same threshold by offering a spiritless, middle-of-the-road recitation as a parting shot.

"To hell with it," he said to himself, finally tearing up the pages in front of him. It would be a gamble, but he would scrap the prepared speech. He would write his own.

The news Tor had brought him the night before weighed heavily on his mind as he searched for a new pad of writing paper. It had been confirmed that six years earlier the president had indeed taken a bribe from the union through Peter Denning. It couldn't be proved, James knew that, but that didn't change the fact that it was true. Denning's records for that year were destroyed by a fire but now there was a more incriminating question to be answered. A five-hundred-thousand-dollar deposit had been credited to a personal savings account in the president's name three days after Billy's assassination. That money had not been so neatly disguised. An identical sum was also credited on the same day as the bank deposit to the Jordan Campaign Fund in the names of over a hundred separate donors, all of whom, according to Tor, turned out to be either fictitious names or names of individuals who had not actually contributed.

The president had violated campaign laws that required the reporting of all donations from companies or individuals in amounts over one hundred dollars. The half-million dollars in his personal account would also be difficult to explain. Tor hadn't traced the origin of the half-million dollars but James was sure it would lead back to the source of the other half-million dollars in the president's campaign fund. The pieces of the puzzle were beginning to fall into place.

James tried again to outline a new speech. His mind kept wandering to the fate of Mikki Parker and Gloria Bonnam. The roles they played had cost them their lives, he knew that in his gut. Then there was Sidney Bonnam who was still in protective custody in San Francisco. He wondered what it must be like to be completely shut off from those you love. In a way, he was feeling the same loneliness Bonnam must be experiencing. The world Bonnam had divorced himself from by testifying against Louie Cordaro was hostile to him now, not entirely unlike the world James felt closing in on himself.

It was past three P.M., when James completed the final draft of his new speech. Despite the objections of his campaign manager as well as several of his key aides, he was going to do it his way. He had something to say and he was going to say it to several million people simultaneously. He knew it could cost him the election but then, there was no guarantee he would win anyway.

"On the other hand," he explained to his aides, "it just may be enough to swing the deciding votes in our favor." It was going to be done the Hawk way, the only way he knew how. Both barrels would be blasting.

Two hours earlier, Elaine had told him the tape recording in which Billy had described the president's bribe as a senator and the union's master contract was missing. The bank manager was insistant that there was no way that something could be removed from a safety deposit box without the depositor's key because the bank didn't keep duplicates. If a depositor lost the key, a certified locksmith was always called in to release the customer's lock while the bank provided its own safety key for the second lock. Nevertheless, the tape was missing with no explanations as to how it could have happened.

The tape was of little importance as far as James was concerned because nothing Billy had said was concrete fact, although many of his brother's suspicions were proving to be true.

In the television studio, he closed his eyes. A young woman applied a light dusting of powder to his face to absorb the perspiration once the heat from the studio lights started to take their toll. He opened his eyes and watched the studio personnel moving their gear and equipment around. Members of the major media sat in the gallery in front of him talking among themselves.

At five minutes before air time, the missing tape still stuck in his mind. It wasn't the contents of the tape itself that was weighing on his mind, but the fact that it was missing and what that meant. Someone else not only knew of the tape's existence but the same person responsible for its theft had to be reasonably sure that there wasn't a duplicate. It had to be President Jordan. Besides Louie Cordaro, the president was the only other person that would benefit from the destruction of the tape. How he or Cordaro knew of the tape was a question James had to address but not this evening—there wasn't time.

Three successive beeping tones. Ten seconds to air time.

As always, James declined the use of a teleprompter, preferring to work instead with the crude outline he had prepared earlier. The red light on the center camera came on. Without introduction, he sat alone before nationwide television, addressing over one hundred million of his fellow citizens:

"Good evening," James began. "As this campaign comes to a close, I'd like to speak about some things that I have in the past touched upon only briefly in this campaign because I have been advised that the issues were too sensitive and could possibly cost me some of your votes. However, I cannot sit here tonight in good conscience and not reveal my feelings concerning these matters. It's no secret that my drive to rid our country of corruption has already been detrimental to my campaign."

There was total silence in the studio as James continued.

His voice was electrifying.

"The president and I see differently on many issues. But on nothing so much as the corruptive element in the labor movement about which he has chosen to remain mute while I have, along with several others, spent many long, hard years attempting to put respect and credibility back into the philosophy and practice of unionism.

"For our nation to survive in this perilous period, we must reaffirm the cherished values bestowed upon us by our forefathers.

"There is no room in our country for the oppressor, the bully, or the corruptor. Labor leaders, who have become thieves, cheating those whose trust has been placed in them, dishonor our country as much as any traitor by imposing an irrevocable cloud of distrust over what is basically an honest labor movement, one which has in the past meant so much to the growth of this nation. I speak of Louie Cordaro and his union. They, along with equally dishonest businessmen who, in their greed to obtain an unfair advantage over their competitors by making illegal concessions to labor leaders at the expense of their employees, have perversely affected the morality of our American economic system.

"We, as a nation, are incapable of withstanding the potentially paralyzing corruption of this particular labor movement. In the last few weeks, I have been advised of a heinous plot against our nation by a high-ranking labor official. Though he currently is in prison, his strength still lingers in the form of what he calls a master contract. If the master contract were implemented, it could cripple our economy for years, leaving a lasting scar."

James went on for over twenty minutes to explain in detail the master contract that Louie Cordaro developed, equating it to a surprise missile attack by the Soviet Union. To say that it came as a shock to most Americans that one man, or even one union, could have more power than even the president of the United States would have been an understatement, judging by the reactions viewed by James's campaign manager as he watched the faces of the more than two hundred reporters present in the studio.

James went on, "People have often asked me why I have concentrated so much of my life on the labor movement and, just as often, I have been severely criticized for pursuing the truth. To that, I must say that I have done, and will continue to do, what I feel is necessary to save our country. You don't *ask* someone to bail water when the boat you are in is sinking. You expect it. If they don't bail, you work even harder and you don't take time to discuss the matter. That discussion will have to come later. Tonight, I say to you, it's time to discuss Louie Cordaro.

"These are uncertain times for us. We must all begin to bail water by taking a greater interest in our country and the affairs within it by letting our legislators know where we stand on the issues and, in particular, the labor movement and the problems it poses.

"I shall, whether I win or lose this election, introduce regulative legislation that will help combat the problems that have been exposed within the labor movement and subsequently prevent any such events occurring again. Those of you who have followed my efforts in this area know of the injustices of which I speak; for those of you who are unaware of the problems, I can only ask your support and that you believe me and study the issues and ask questions.

"It is imperative that the lesson of our nation's past be heeded now more than ever. The idealism and toughness that have guided us in the past must dominate our thoughts. We must trade our concern for self, for wealth and security, for an equally intense desire to fight whatever is evil and to serve in whatever capacity necessary to achieve victory over this cancer that has spread through the country we love.

"President Jordan has chosen throughout his political career to remain indifferent to the problems within the labor movement. I have not. Foreign leaders have said that we are a dying nation, a decadent society, that dishonesty and corruption have combined with a physical and moral flabbiness throughout our country. Of that, I say there can

494

be no doubt. I believe it's true.

"Our forefathers faced quite different battles, yet their willingness to risk their personal security and future for what they believed in is the reason we became a powerful and prosperous nation.

"But, now we have a new problem, one of apathy— apathy on the part of the current administration, apathy on the part of ourselves.

"Franklin D. Roosevelt, accepting his second presidential nomination, said, 'Governments can err, Presidents make mistakes, but the immortal Dante tells us that Divine Justice weighs the sins of the cold-blooded and the sins of the warm-hearted on a different scale. Better the occasional faults of a government living in the spirit of charity, than the consistent omissions of a government frozen in the ice of its own indifference.'

"That is where the president and I differ. The greatest sin of all is indifference and he is guilty of that. I ask for your help, not just your votes. Good night."

With that, James Hawk closed his presidential campaign. He spoke briefly with the group of reporters who had followed his every footstep for the past twelve months and then left the studio amid cheers from his supporters. Like the exhausted reporters who began to slip away to their home cities for a night of rest before the election, James was on his way to Boston and then home. The speech he had just delivered gave him, in the opinions of most who saw or heard it, a last minute advantage. He would go to bed that night a slight favorite to become the next President of the United States.

Chapter 65

HE TRIED TO look ahead, beyond the election, but President Jordan knew that regardless of the results James Hawk represented a far more lethal personal than political enemy. Hawk was a problem that would have to be solved and the president was uncomfortably aware that there was no time to waste.

Since the Hawk Committee's inception, information about their investigations were routinely passed on to the Oval Office and for the last six months Jordan had been receiving special top-secret reports from CIA Director Addleton. It was those reports that disturbed him to a point where there was not a moment within the last two weeks when they weren't on his mind. Jordan couldn't be sure now how James Hawk would handle his past indiscretions and that made him uneasy, even though he felt confident that any bribery charges against him couldn't be substantiated. But even so, the matter wouldn't rest. He was sure of that.

It was two A.M. on election morning. The president shut off the lamp beside his bed and turned over on his side. He lay awake with the covers turned down halfway, exposing the upper portion of his naked body. The election occupied his mind only briefly during the two hours it took him to fall asleep. James Hawk continued to haunt him as he tossed from side to side. The pattern had been the same for the past month and sleep continued to remain at a premium for him. The omnipresent impression of James Hawk stalking him from behind would remain in his future no matter which candidate won the election. He could stand it no longer. Something had to be done.

When James Hawk awoke, millions of people across the country had already cast their votes and, as always in America, the early vote would be decidedly Republican. It wouldn't be until later in the day when the working men and women had a chance to vote that the country's Democrats would begin to make their presence felt.

He was very tired when he walked out of his house. He was on his way to vote, preferring to walk the short distance to the neighborhood polling station. It was about a half mile away, the final leg of a full year of journeys that had begun humbly in the streets of New Hampshire when Hawk was a relatively unknown candidate and had slowly built to a thundering cavalcade of supporters across the nation as the months wore on.

The walk was peaceful compared to what he had been through during the past twelve months. There were no crowds, no outstretched hands, no ripples of sound that would grow to a deafening roar as he came nearer.

A handful of Secret Service agents stationed strategically along the autumnally colorful maplelined street were the only people he saw and he chatted with one of the agents who walked alongside. He felt serene, almost melancholy, in stark contrast to the hustling busy mornings to which he had grown accustomed over the last few weeks.

If past crowds were any indication of voter support, he felt he should be a landslide winner. Wherever he went, he had consistently generated more enthusiasm from more people than those who had turned out to meet the president. Nevertheless, he was still concerned about the outcome. While he had captured the imaginations of America's youth, the quiet people, those who didn't stand for hours alongside a city street just to catch a glimpse of him pass by in a motorcade, also had a vote. He would have to wait to see what effect he had had on them. The silent majority would have their say.

James dined early that afternoon with his parents at their home, then went across the lawn back to his own house. He was restless and wanted to be alone and decided he would wait in the privacy of his own home for the voters' mandate.

For a while, he sat huddled alone against the wind on his porch. He was exhausted, but felt an anticipatory energy that slowly began to rebuild his strength as the minutes passed and the temperature dropped. He felt the cold creep into his bones, a trancelike feeling that was even stronger, a sensation that nothing mattered now. Win or lose, he would have to deal with President Jordan and that took the edge off an event for which he had been waiting for what seemed to him an eternity. Within hours, he could be President of the United States, and the thought of such an awesome responsibility didn't faze him in the least; he was prepared for that. What he feared was he had built no foundation to support himself or the world's citizens for what was sure to be the biggest scandal in the history of politics. To live with the responsibility of tearing down a nation's political leader and the country's morale was becoming an unavoidable reality, and only he could weigh the initial negative effect against the benefits of such a disclosure. The country had a right to know the truth.

The smell of the sea was a temporary comfort as he savored the last few moments of peace he would have before settling inside to await the returns. Darkness began to crawl across the sky, gradually at first, then with a lightninglike pace. He sat for over an hour before going back inside.

At precisely eight P.M., an assemblange of family and close friends gathered in his living room which had now become a temporary communications center. Three television sets, tuned to the three major networks, were turned on. The long night's vigil was beginning.

The polls on the East Coast were closed. Now, the voters' choices could legally be broadcast for the first time. At nine P.M., the first piece of news came in. Campbell

County, Kentucky, which had never voted for the loser in a presidential election, had turned out heavily in favor of James Hawk.

Shortly afterwards, a second item followed that showed the first full precinct count in New Hampshire. Also favorable.

Half an hour later the first national summary total of voting figures was released: 291,061 for Jordan, 242,626 for Hawk. While that deficit could be discounted because of the usual Republican pattern of early voters, the count nevertheless had a dampening effect on everyone in the room.

James knew that the industrial states were the real key to his winning the election. The heavy concentration of union propaganda against him there had hurt him and the more recent polls showed him losing those states. Without them, he could not win. The polls had also shown that the majority of states were in the Hawk camp, but that wouldn't help in the electoral college. He needed 270 votes to win there, and the key states with the most electoral votes were mostly industrial and heavily unionized. Illinois, California, Pennsylvania, New York and New Jersey would be tough.

Midnight. The national margin finally shifted and, for the first time, James held a majority of the popular vote across the nation. By twelve-thirty, he had increased from a 902,000 vote lead to over one million votes and the number was rising by the minute.

He grew even more restless as the night inched its way into the early morning hours. While his guests watched the popular vote total, James's entire concentration was focused on the critical industrial states where the vote was still too close to call, except for the eastern states. He had already lost New York, New Jersey, and Maine by a slim margin, and they shared a combined total of fifty-six electoral votes. His lead in Pennsylvania with twenty-six electoral votes was shrinking to a dangerously precarious ten thousand votes and North Carolina's thirteen electoral votes were also showing signs of slipping away. For the moment, Georgia was rated dead even.

Tension began to show on his face as he abandoned his usual loquaciousness and sat with an emotionless stare watching the TV screen as the reports from the Midwest and West began to take final form. With the exception of California, the early returns showed him to have a substantial lead in every state west of the Mississippi, and his popular vote margin had spread another 200,000 to over 1,200,000. He was clearly leading in thirty-two states, too close to call in seven others. The rest were going, for the moment at least, to the president.

Occasionally the telephone would ring and James would answer it to help ease the tension. His running mate, Senator Griffith from Virginia, called shortly after one A.M., and humorously announced that as a team they were doing fine in Virginia, while disclaiming any responsibility for James's poor showing in New York. All eyes in the room were now on the electoral college vote tally that was slowly finalizing at what seemed to be an agonizingly sluggish pace.

Two A.M. The eastern states had over eight percent of the vote tallied, enough to safely project the final results. James had suffered heavy electoral vote losses in New York, New Jersey, Maine, North Carolina, Georgia, Pennsylvania, and Ohio. Those six states, despite the fact that he had lost the popular vote by less than one percent in each of them, had cost him 129 precious electoral votes, giving President Jordan nearly half the electoral votes needed to be reelected. The trend in Michigan and Illinois was toward the president as well. James mentally scribbled their combined forty-four votes on the opponent's ledger that he was keeping privately in his head.

That gave President Jordan one hundred seventy-three. Texas, with twenty-nine, had likewise slipped away from James. That made ten states and two hundred two electoral votes for the incumbent president.

Everyone present felt a gripping frustration as they watched the television commentators systematically place magnetic white and black states on a map of the United States, indicating each state's preference. The map was heavily unbalanced in favor of white, designating Democratic, but the few black states on the map were imposing. Because of their electoral significance, the Republican states became more worrisome as the minutes ticked by.

An hour later, another state fell into the Jordan column when Minnesota's ten votes were officially awarded by the computer to the president. Jordan now had two hundred twelve electoral votes but he was stalled.

For the first time in over three hours James felt a sense of relief as he continued to chalk up wins in state after state. He had already clearly won thirty-three states and his national popular vote tally was up by over two million over the president. Now, only six states were in doubt.

Jordan had won only eleven states. Three of the six remaining states showed James ahead by margins that the television commentators said appeared as if they would hold. That left only three in doubt—Indiana, which was still too close to call, then Washington, where James had a slight edge, and California, where the president was leading by nearly twenty thousand votes.

Even if California's forty-seven electoral votes fell into the president's column, James knew that he could still win. Without Washington and Indiana, the president would fall eleven votes short. Even Washington's ten votes, could go to the president and James would still win if Indiana went Democratic. Even with just three states in doubt, the possibilities multiplied confusingly.

Ninety minutes later, California swung to President Jordan, bringing the president's count to twelve states and two hundred fifty-nine electoral votes. Washington's ten votes were projected for James.

The count was insane. James had won thirty-seven states and was winning the popular vote by over two million, yet his electoral vote count stood three votes short at two hundred sixty-seven to the president's two hundred fifty-nine. The future was clear. Indiana, with their twelve electoral votes, would decide who would lead the country for the next four years.

Forty minutes later, the same nucleus of people that only thirteen months earlier had set in motion the machinery that was to offer to the American public the youngest presidential candidate in over one hundred years watched and listened in stunned silence to the final results. James Hawk, truly the majority favorite of the country's citizens, had lost the election. Indiana fell to the president. By winning only thirteen states, the president nevertheless had two hundred seventy-one electoral votes, one over the required majority for election.

James had lost; he was prepared for that, but not for the manner in which he had lost.

While he didn't say so that night, he knew that the unions, not Jordan, had won the election. The lost states were all heavily industrialized; their union-supported strength had been underestimated. The American political system changed that night. No longer did the majority rule.

Chapter 66

PRESIDENT JORDAN'S VICTORY was barely an hour old when the *New York Times*, in an unprecedented move that made their deliveries over two hours later than normal, hit the streets. The *Times* had supported James Hawk's presidential bid even though it had previously reprinted some of Marshall Tucker's editorials.

An editorial appeared that morning that had obviously been prepared in advance. It was headed ''What Price Union Support?'' and carried the *Times* editorial staff's message without a trace of undefined intent. It said in part:

> The budding love affair between the Jordan Administration and the union has some ugly overtones never more evident than in the results of yesterday's elections. The ardor with which the president courted Louie Cordaro's two-million-member union would be questionable enough if it were regarded solely as a bid for political support. But, in the cynical environment that enshrouds this rich union, no amount of official denials can erase the suspicion of a deal to free Louie Cordaro. The fact that a man can win a presidential election with a plurality of thirteen of the fifty states speaks for the strength of that union, strength that, until recently, has never been so visible. While it is understandable that the union would be against James Hawk, it's membership had never before demonstrated an affinity for President Jordan. To suddenly and without any public

explanation turn their awesome political strength in support for the president makes one wonder. It is a sorry aggregation that the president is clutching to his bosom . . . Before entering the penitentiary, Cordaro often boasted that every man—especially every politician— could be bought. The truth of those words was never more evident than yesterday. We wonder what will follow, now that Mr. Cordaro has kept his part of the bargain. What price will the nation pay for the favor?

There was much still to be done but James felt no compulsion to accomplish it quickly. He was physically and, even more, emotionally drained and decided to take a few weeks off to be alone, to sort out his life and plans. At first, it seemed that something within him had died, that he could never awaken the same spirit and energy he once felt, but the sensation soon evaporated. He needed time to rekindle the fire. There was always a low point or a period of uncertainty whenever he had to undertake an unpleasant task. He was faced with that now; the president had to be exposed for what he was. Action had to be taken. It was only because he wasn't exactly precise in his own mind on how to attack an institution as formidable as the executive branch of the United States government that he didn't act immediately. But he would act and soon. He was a life-giver, not a taker. It was going to be difficult for him to take away what was to the president his life, the presidency itself, but he had no other choice.

Four weeks later, on December twenty-third, Tor Slagle had already been home for three weeks, dead locked in his bitter battle to stall the union organizational drive within Slagle's. He had accomplished what James Hawk had originally asked him to do—put Louie Cordaro in prison, but when his mission was accomplished, he and James both knew there was more to come. Their lives would never be the same. Both were resigned to that. For now, Tor was trying to get back into the flow of Slagle's daily activities. What happened after the new year would be anybody's guess.

On that same day, as the sun was setting in Washington, D. C., the president quietly signed an executive grant of clemency for twenty-one persons incarcerated in federal penitentiaries across the land. Included in that list was the name of Louie Cordaro. His sentence had been commuted by the president to time served. Less than two months after he began his eight-year sentence, Louie Cordaro was to be set free.

Chapter 67

CHRISTMAS EVE. MUCH paler and thinner than on the day he entered prison, Louie Cordaro looked through the iron gates and saw the reporters and photographers that were waiting for him as he prepared to leave Lewisburg Penitentiary. He turned to the guard escorting him and asked, "Is there another way out of here?"

"No, sir," the guard chuckled. "One way in and one way out. We don't like a lot of doors around here."

Cordaro shrugged his shoulders, then continued to the gate. A few more steps and he was outside, the door closed behind him. The reporters were suddenly ubiquitous, relentless.

"Can you comment on why the president commuted your sentence?"

"What about the claim that you made a deal with the president?"

"Where will you spend Christmas?"

"Louie, who do you plan to see first?"

"No comment, no comment," Cordaro answered briskly as he tried his best to bully his way toward a limousine that awaited behind the mob of reporters.

Just as the limo door opened, another question stopped him cold. He turned to find the reporter who asked it. "What, what did you say?" Cordaro asked heatedly.

A white-haired veteran reporter from Associated Press stepped forward. "I asked if you were aware of the restriction attached to your commutation of sentence.''

"What restriction?'' Cordaro retorted. "What restriction?''

"It says that as a condition of your continued release, you're not to engage in direct or indirect management of your union or any other labor organization for five years.''

"Bullshit! I don't believe it! Who said that?''

"It was attached to the executive clemency order. I read it this morning,'' the reporter replied.

"I signed that yesterday. It was just a formality to get out of prison,'' Cordaro responded. "There was no restriction. I don't know what you're talking about.''

Cordaro glared at the reporter and then turned to the car. The crowd, suddenly silent, parted a little and Cordaro stepped into the limo without another word.

"There is now, Mr. Cordaro. There is now,'' the reporter replied calmly to no one in particular as the limo sped off.

The next afternoon, Louie Cordaro sat in the Oval Office of the White House with President Jordan. It was Christmas Day, but his business with the president couldn't wait.

They sat alone. The president knew how badly Cordaro wanted to regain his position within the union and he waited patiently to allow Cordaro time to think over the offer he had just made. It was a trade, a rescinding of the commutation restriction for another favor to the president. Another quid pro quo.

Cordaro wasn't sure. He distrusted Jordan. He had been tricked before. He was out of prison, but not the way they had discussed originally. He hadn't agreed to any restriction upon his release and he couldn't be sure that the president wouldn't do something similar again.

Being careful to guard against any recorded reprisal, Cordaro finally responded by incriminating both the president and himself at the same time. "You dumped his brother, so why do you need my help to bump him off?'' he said arrogantly.

The president smiled cautiously, as if he had expected the question. "There are no recording devices here, Louie, I can assure you of that. I don't need the publicity any more than you do so it's not necessary for you to worry about covering your own ass. My skirts aren't clean in this matter, I admit that. Now, do we understand each other?''

Cordaro nodded. The two men sat silently staring into each other's eyes.

The president broke the silence. "It's one thing to eliminate a problem that the CIA considers a threat to national security," he began. "Billy Hawk was definitely a threat. It's quite another to eliminate a man that has just missed becoming president of the United States. I have power, but I'm afraid the CIA would draw the line at assassinating James Hawk. I could never convince Mr. Addleton that it would be for the good of the country.''

Another silence fell between them. It was Cordaro who broke it abuptly. "How do I know you'll carry out your end of the deal? You just finished shitting on me when you attached that fuckin' condition to my commutation.''

Slowly, the president let some smoke from his cigarette drift from his mouth. He held it in front of him and rolled it in his fingers, watching it critically before he resumed. "Neither of us is in a position to bargain, Mr. Cordaro. I trust you understand that. If Hawk has his way, we'll both be embarrassed about that million dollars. We were stupid. I didn't cover my tracks properly and the money can be traced back to Denning or to the false names on the campaign donation list. I believe you understand that it's no big secret where Denning gets his cash. I think you know what I mean. Now, do we understand each other?''

"Why don't we just destroy the records like we did before?'' Cordaro asked matter-of-factly.

"It's too late. Hawk already knows. I'm sure he has copies of whatever he needs. So you see why we need to act fast.''

"Are you sure he has copies?"

"I know it for a fact. That Slagle fellow has the information about our little transaction. He'll have to be taken care of as well."

Cordaro was suddenly incredulous. "Shit, this is wholesale murder! Cheaper by the dozen!"

The president's voice was cold, terse. "Do we have a choice?"

Cordaro's eyes seemed dulled, almost lost as they narrowed. "Maybe I'm getting old, but all this sounds a little risky to me."

The president looked surprised. "You've arranged such things before. This time the target is a little more prominent, that's all," he said coolly.

Cordaro thought a moment, let out a deep sigh and leaned back in his seat resignedly. "What about Slagle? How do you want that handled?"

The president thought for a moment. "Let it ride for now. I need Slagle around to find out if anyone else worked with him on the investigation. When I find out, we'll work something out. If others are involved, it's going to get a little messier. For now, James Hawk is the target. Can you handle it?"

Cordaro nodded.

"Quickly?"

Another nod.

Louie Cordaro was under no illusions about what had to be done and he had another reason to expedite the president's suggestions. With the restriction on his commutation, he couldn't even walk into union headquarters without violating the conditions of his release and Borg Trenier knew it. There was no way of knowing how Trenier was reacting to his release from prison and Cordaro wasn't naive enough to think Trenier would welcome him with open arms. He had to stay away until he was released from his conditional commutation. Until then he himself wouldn't be safe. He didn't know who his real friends were anymore or whom he could trust. But there was one person who he was confident would always stand by his side, the same person who would be commissioned to carry out the president's unofficial execution order, Bartie Bonano.

Chapter 68

JAMES HAWK HAD lost an election for the first time in his life, but not the hearts of an enraged public who felt betrayed by their own election process.

He was still their champion, but as snow dusted the pavement of New York's Fifth Avenue on December twenty-seventh, he was struck down at 1:16 P.M. by three perfectly aimed shots from an unknown assassin's rifle as he walked from the Plaza Hotel after giving a fund-raising speech for the state's Democratic Party.

Gone forever was the familiar New England twang, the jabbing finger, the authoritative staccato voice that had captured the imaginations of the majority of his country's citizens. A piece of the nation's heart had been cut out and people in offices, stores, bars, and parks gathered, stunned, around radios and televisions throughout the country to hear about the death of the man who had in the past twelve months come to exemplify the finest qualities of the nation he loved and served.

The country reeled, stunned and incredulous at the second assassination within the same family that year. Two leaders of promise had been snatched away from those they chose to serve.

On the afternoon of the assassination, President Jordan issued a Presidential Proclamation ordering the nation's flags to be flown at half-mast for the next thirty days in tribute to James Hawk.

It was a chilly afternoon but the president wore no overcoat as he spoke into a bank of microphones set up just outside the Oval Office next to the Rose Garden. "I earnestly recommend," the president said, "that people assemble on the day of Mr. Hawk's funeral in their respective places of worship, there to bow down in submission to the will of Almighty God, and to pay homage to the memory of a great and good man. Our nation has suffered a great loss."

James Hawk was dead. Like his brother's death seven months earlier, there was no public explanation. Lawmakers were suddenly engulfed in debate over guncontrol and street philosophers discussed the nature of violence as the grieving nation awaited the funeral. The body was to lie in state in the Capitol Rotunda for two days while dignitaries from around the country and the world offered, as one body without political considerations, their condolences and respect.

The day of James Hawk's funeral found the sun bright and the sky clear as the entire country readied themselves in front of their television sets to vicariously help lay to rest this man of distinction in Arlington National Cemetery. For over three hours, from the beginning in the Capitol Rotunda when his body was removed by an honor guard and escorted ceremoniously to St. Matthew's Cathedral and then to Arlington, the public watched. Muffled drums could be heard in the distance; then stopped, followed by three cannons firing in turn, sounding the final twenty-one gun salute. The flag that draped the coffin was folded with care, then passed from hand to hand to James's mother. Taps rippled over the Virginia hills as the sun began to sink. The Lord's Prayer was intoned and, at 3:52 P.M., on December thirty-first, James Hawk slipped out of sight forever.

High above, on a hill within Arlington looking down on the gravesite some six hundred yards away, a man stood watching as the official funeral party departed and a long line of mourners began to file past.

It was New Year's Eve, and Bartie Bonano watched, wondering how long it would be before the seemingly endless line of people would dissipate. He smoked the last of several cigarettes just before the sun finally set at 4:40. He stood there leaning against a tree for another hour, bundled in a heavy wool coat and muffler against the evening chill. It was the first time he had ever attended, albeit indirectly, the funeral of a man whom he had murdered. James Hawk was either his twenty-first or twenty-second victim—he couldn't remember which. He chuckled as he thought of the fifty thousand dollars he was about to receive and how unexpectedly easy it had been for him to earn it. He had balked at first when Louie Cordaro asked him to do it. He had always killed punks, unknowns, whose demise aroused little concern beyond the usual newspaper articles and routine police investigations. When the ante was raised to fifty thousand dollars for the assassination of James Hawk, he decided he liked the odds and accepted the job.

James proved to be an easy mark. In the confusion that had followed, Bonano even found he had time to walk within ten feet of the man he had just felled as a hysterical crowd surrounded his victim. He even paused momentarily to photograph the confusion before disappearing into the crowd, pleased with the thought that he had captured in his camera the most significant moment in his long career of paid violence. The pictures would make a fine addition to his private scrapbook that he had kept secretly all his adult life. The habit of photographing his victims as a precaution against nonpayment from clients had started long ago when Bonano was unable to provide proof to a client that he had in fact been responsible for the killing of a young lawyer as they had agreed. His client wanted proof that the man was dead and it took over six months before the client finally consented to pay the second half of his fee. Since then, he had always provided proof of his efforts. It was neater that way and payments were speedier.

Aside from photographing his victims, he had no interest in cameras. For him, a camera was strictly a tool of the trade, to be brought out only when on a mission.

An uneasiness began to build, making him anxious to leave Arlington. The line of mourners had grown even longer, stretching far beyond his line of vision and he could no longer see the end as the night crept closer to the year's end.

He left without turning to look back at the gravesite he had watched so intently since ten o'clock that morning. For the first time in his life, he experienced an emotion he had never felt before. He had actually admired James Hawk; he had even voted for him. James Hawk was a good man. But business was business . . .

Louie Cordaro sat in his living room in a mood of intense irritation. The limousine service was having difficulty in confirming his last-minute request to be picked up at seven-thirty. The fact that it was New Year's Eve and every limousine service had long since reserved all their cars cut little ice for him as he profanely demanded an immediate response to his request.

It was unusual for Bartie Bonano to ask him to handle the payment of his fee personally, but it was equally unusual for his fee to be fifty thousand dollars, so Cordaro thought little of Bonano's request. Besides, he reasoned, it would also give him an opportunity to talk to Bonano about Borg Trenier and Peter Denning. Cordaro had been out of prison for over a week and he had still heard nothing from either despite leaving several messages for them to call. He knew Trenier had double-crossed him but he couldn't believe that Peter Denning would do the same. Denning had to have a reason for not responding to his calls. Perhaps he was trying to avoid making waves, following Trenier's orders until Cordaro could legally regain control of the union. Nevertheless, the unanswered phone calls still disturbed him. He couldn't understand why his best friend would be evading him.

He picked up the phone to call the limousine service again but remembered something and hung up. He reached for his wallet, found a business card with a toll-free number on it, picked up the phone and dialed that number instead.

A voice answered. "Federal Flowers," the lady announced.

"I'd like to send some flowers," he informed her. "I want them delivered tomorrow."

"Yes, sir, that can be arranged. Where did you want them sent?"

"To San Francisco. No, wait—Sausalito, California. It's right next to San Francisco. I've sent them there before."

"All right, sir. What's the recipient's name?"

"Parker, Shana Parker."

A half hour later, the limousine problem resolved itself when a last-minute cancellation provided an extra car. As the door of the limousine shut behind him, Cordaro directed the driver to a small restaurant in the heart of Washington, D.C. He thought about Shana Parker and hoped the flowers he had been sending helped to cheer her up. He wished he could see her again, but since she was living with Tor Slagle it presented a problem. He didn't want to think about the consequences to Shana if Tor had to be eliminated as well. Even for Cordaro, it went against the grain to thrust such problems on one so young. Somehow, someday, he thought, he was going to make it all up to her.

The noise of the city was shut out by the closed windows of the limousine, and Cordaro leaned his head back and closed his eyes. He reflected on being cut off from the outside world. Until his business with the president was finalized, he would continue to be an outcast.

He could feel the bulge of the package in his breast pocket press lightly against his chest. Absently, he tapped at it with his right hand. Fifty thousand dollars was a lot of money, but what it was buying was worth every penny. It was comforting to know that within the next few days the president would lift the restriction to his commutation.

Twenty minutes later, the limousine came to a stop. He exited quickly, ordering the driver to return in an hour. He did not go inside the restaurant, choosing instead to wait on the corner across the street. He stood alone, out in the open. He felt uncomfortable, vulnerable, more susceptible to danger than he had ever been in the last fifteen years.

A fat woman came out of a restaurant across the street and walked toward him. She looked frightened and he watched her closely. She put her hand into a big leather bag that hung from her shoulder. Louie tightened, then relaxed when she pulled out a handkerchief and stopped to wipe her nose before continuing to cross the street.

They exchanged cautious glances as she came nearer. When she continued down the walkway, he broke into a cold sweat.

A familiar car finally pulled alongside the curb and he got in, relieved to be enclosed once more. His hand was quickly swallowed in the viselike grip of Bartie Bonano's that reached out to greet him. Bonano pulled the car away, driving carefully, fighting the light feeling in his head from the whiskey he had been drinking most of the afternoon. He never drank when on the job, but tonight was different. It was New Year's Eve and he had just spent the day watching a public burial of the biggest hit of his life.

Cordaro held out the envelope he was carrying and passed it over for Bonano's inspection.

"That's for the job," he said. "You really got me out of a tight spot with that one."

Bonano grunted something unintelligible, looked at the envelope and then back at Cordaro. He nodded, continuing to drive cautiously.

A moment later, a car pulled unexpectedly from a curbside parking space and Bonano swerved sharply to avoid a collision, causing something to fall to the floor from the back seat. Cordaro turned to look to see what had fallen but couldn't make out the outline of the object.

"What's that?" he asked, leaning over the back seat.

"Just my camera," Bonano responded.

Louie Cordaro was a dead man less than thirty minutes later. He died at the hands of his longtime friend, never knowing why he had been betrayed. He never knew his old friend had been employed by Borg Trenier ever since his November visit to La Costa. Trenier was a politician not to be underestimated. Louie Cordaro died because every man, as he had often stated, had his price. Especially Bartie Bonano.

Chapter 69

As SEVEN days after Louie Cordaro's disappearance went by, President Jordan's depression deepened. Despite what he said publicly in the past, he had never liked the man. Never for an instant had he trusted Cordaro's integrity and he was livid with himself for having allowed himself to get into such a vulnerable position.

From the moment he learned that Cordaro hadn't returned home on New Year's Eve, Jordan had panicked. The secret of James Hawk's assassination rested with two people besides himself: Cordaro and the assassin. Now, one of them was missing. Without Cordaro, the president knew he couldn't be sure what to expect from the assassin. Did the assassin, whoever he was, know about the arrangement between him and Cordaro? Had the assassin been paid? Was Cordaro dead? How could he be sure Cordaro hadn't told others of their arrangement before he disappeared? And what about Borg Trenier? How much did he know? Did somebody have Cordaro alive and captive? Were they asking him questions, torturing him until he was forced to talk? What if Cordaro's disappearance was voluntary and he was planning a conspiracy against Jordan? Any man who could arrange to have somebody killed at the drop of a hat was capable of anything.

F.B.I. Director J. Robert Wallace had been sending progress reports to the president daily. Presidential orders had been issued to use every available method to find Cordaro, but there was no escaping the fact that after one week there still were no realistic leads for the F.B.I. to follow. The president's temper became so short that his aides began to communicate with him exclusively by written memos, which were delivered twice daily through his personal secretary.

Jordan had vacillated through a long and neurotic weekend before making up his mind to call a meeting with Borg Trenier. He could no longer withstand the mounting pressures of the unknown. He had to find out if Trenier knew anything potentially dangerous. If Louie Cordaro was permanently out of the picture, there were matters that he would have to get Trenier to handle. He was enough of a politician to steer the conversation of the meeting with Trenier in the proper direction without appearing overanxious. Casual concern, that would be the tone of their meeting.

Borg Trenier stepped proudly from his limousine to the steps of the White House. He had waited all his life for such a moment and had wasted no time in honoring the president's personal invitation for a meeting in the Oval Office. He was very pleased with himself. Today he had achieved the ultimate, a private meeting with the most powerful man in the world. A smug feeling encompassed him as he sat waiting in the outer office. He didn't mind waiting. He was savoring every moment. For every minute he spent in the White House, he was paying back a year of frustration at the beck and call of Louie Cordaro. There would be no more subservience, no obsequious errands. He was president of the world's largest labor union now and with his title came new privileges and honors. His meeting with the president was just the beginning.

Within a few minutes, he was inside the Oval Office and found himself exchanging mundane pleasantries with the president. Despite their cordiality, both men knew that the subject of Louie Cordaro could not be avoided for long.

The mood soon became more somber as President Jordan pressed on with the matters at hand. "Borg, there are some things I need to know, private matters that you can be assured will never go further than this office. I hope you understand what I'm saying.''

Trenier sat tensely, somewhat uncomfortable with his impressive surroundings. Not being sure what to say, he simply nodded and took a deep drag on his cigar.

The president stared intently at him, arranging his thoughts carefully. ''Louie and I were never close friends,'' he said slowly. ''But, of course, you must know that. We respected each other and for that reason I am deeply concerned about him. I think you know I've asked the F.B.I. to pull out all stops in a full-scale effort to locate him. I want you to know I've done that because I feel it's important to both of us to find out what has happened to him. I am sure you are aware that there are some grave matters that are complicated by Cordaro's absence.''

Trenier knew what the president was driving at, but still opted to say nothing. Underneath his calm appearance, he had figured out that the president was worried. He began to relax.

The president studied Trenier's expressionless face, wondering why the man was not responding. Trenier was portly and looked vulgar to the president, with his patent leather shoes and thin, nylon hose that clung around his ankles, exposing the skin between the end of his trousers and the tops of his socks as he crossed his legs. There was a food stain on his tie and his hair, while curly, was naturally greasy. Untidy, the president thought, the man was simply untidy. There were men who could never look sophisticated in a business suit, no matter what the price, and Trenier was one of them. Louie Cordaro certainly was another.

They stared at each other for several seconds. The president fidgeted with his tie while Trenier began puffing more and more confidently on his cigar.

Trenier glanced at his ankles and tugged up one sock before breaking the silence. ''Mr. President,'' he began, ''I frankly don't think that you called me here just to discuss Louie Cordaro's disappearance. I'm sure you'll agree there are other matters of far more importance that need to be dealt with.''

The president was unprepared for Trenier's directness. He became uneasy, unsure of what Trenier meant. He had to respond but he couldn't reveal too much. He still wasn't sure how much Trenier knew. He decided to play it safe, to avoid momentarily any mention of James Hawk's assassination.

"I assume you're talking of the master contract," Jordan finally offered.

Trenier allowed a little of his complacence to show. "That's a good starting point."

"I assume you know that before James Hawk's death, he was authorizing legislation that would preclude the union from ever implementing such a strike."

The president's statement had an explosive effect on Trenier. "You can take that legislation and shove it up your ass!" Trenier intoned loudly. "If they ever try and pass it, I'll call a national walkout that'll bring this country to its knees. You can tell the Senate that they can bet on that."

"There's no need for threats," the president retorted quickly.

"That's no threat, Mr. President, it's reality. We've worked hard to get our people into a bargaining position that will get them the kind of contracts they deserve and we won't sit still while the rich folks try and pass laws to take that right away."

Trenier snuffed out his cigar in a large silver ashtray on the president's desk and continued, "I thought that after the support we gave you during the election there would be a new spirit of cooperation between your administration and my union. After all, we are responsible for getting you elected. I certainly wouldn't expect that you'd sign a bill that would take away any of our rights."

Weighing Trenier's comments carefully, the president sat silently, still thoughtful. Trenier's outburst amazed him. He hadn't expected from him the same brashness that had so long been Cordaro's trademark. While the master contract was important, it wasn't what he wanted to talk to Trenier about. He was confused as to how he could steer the conversation back to Cordaro, back to what he had to know. He had to keep Trenier talking, keep him off guard until he could bring up the subject naturally.

"Borg, I wouldn't be too concerned about the master contract just now. I'm sure that with mutual cooperation we'll never have to cross that bridge."

Trenier waved his hands palms up in a halting gesture. "I wouldn't go so far as to say that," he said. "We would prefer not to ever have to call such a strike. The master contract is a bargaining tool, like anything else. We'll use it only if I deem it necessary, I can assure you of that, but we *would* use it."

"It's a pretty lethal tool."

"Damn right it is, thanks to Louie."

There it was! The opening he wanted. Trenier had voluntarily brought Cordaro back into the conversation. The president seized the opportunity. "You know, Cordaro's disappearance causes me some personal concern."

Trenier answered without hesitation. "I know that."

A surprised look came across the president's face. "You do?"

"I said I did."

"Would you mind explaining?"

"You called the meeting, Mr. President. Why don't you tell me?"

Without mentioning a specific sum, the president reluctantly began to tell Trenier of the union's donation to his campaign fund and of his concern that it be kept quiet. "Without Cordaro around," he cautioned, "there is no way I can be sure that the donation will go unremarked. All I want is your assurance that union records would be properly handled if any inquiries are ever made."

Trenier was candid. "I'm aware of the donation," he pointed out. "But there is a problem."

The president's brow furrowed. He looked worried. "What problem?"

"Rumor has it that there's going to be more pressure to start investigating our pension fund again. If that happens, then the Denning Insurance Agency will be a part of that investigation. That's where the million dollars came from."

Now President Jordan knew that others besides Cordaro knew of the money. The fact that Trenier knew the exact amount confirmed it. "Then you know *why* the money was paid to my campaign fund?" he asked cautiously.

"A million isn't much to pay for a man's freedom. It's too bad Louie didn't get a chance to enjoy it."

"Then Cordaro told you why he needed the money?"

Trenier shook his head slowly. "No, but I have ways of finding out what I want to know."

"Who told you?"

"Peter Denning."

"Cordaro told Denning?"

"No, not exactly. Denning just figured out that Louie was buying some insurance, in case he had to go to prison."

Trenier's answer was so quick and without any trace of doubt that it prompted the president to exhale an audible sigh of relief. Now he was sure that nobody knew the real reason for the passing of the funds was for the elimination of Billy Hawk. Nobody except Cordaro, and that still bothered him. "What do you know about Cordaro's disappearance?" he asked.

Trenier considered the question carefully. "I hear rumors that we'll never see him again," he answered matter-of-factly.

Trenier's voice had such an ominous tone that it was all the president could do to keep from smiling. He leaned back in his chair. The tension he felt earlier began to drain from his body. With Cordaro out of the way, his only concern now was the million dollars. Because of the CIA's electronic surveillance of Billy Hawk's den, he had infornation that suggested that Tor Slagle perhaps had already gotten to Peter Denning's files. He told Trenier of his concerns.

"What do we do now?" Trenier asked, his relaxed posture stiffening slightly.

The president's eyes focused directly on Trenier. His voice was stern. "Cover it up any way you can. Slagle can't possibly have the original records and without them he could never prove a damn thing. Just destroy the records and do it fast!"

"What about Slagle?"

"He's harmless for now. But I'm sure he was working with someone else when he discovered the money transfer. I still don't know who that is, but we're working on it."

"Destroying the records helps you, not me. It doesn't solve *my* problem."

"You mean with the pension fund investigation?"

"Exactly."

"What are the problems?"

"Let's just say I don't need people nosing around the fund or the Denning Insurance Agency. I'd like to keep things quiet for a while until I can correct some factors that I'd rather never be made public."

"How bad is it?"

"Let's just say it's going to take a long time to straighten out. I need time."

The president's mind was working like a machine now. He needed to make a trade. There had to be an incentive to get Trenier to cooperate and agree to cover up Denning's records. "I think I know a way to take the heat off the investigation before it gets rolling," he said.

"Go on, I'm listening."

The president's words became calculating, slow and deliberate. "The big complaint about the fund is that half the trustees are union officials and that most of them have their greedy little fingers into the investments. If you voluntarily turn the fund over to an independent bank trust to administer it, then I could stop the investigation from getting started."

"Wait a minute," Trenier protested. "I didn't say I wanted to give up control over the pension fund. I just don't want anybody nosing around right now. I can't agree to that.''

"Why not?" the president snapped.

"Because this thing is too damned one-sided, that's why! I've got nothing to gain by saving your ass. I had nothing to do with passing you that million dollars.''

The president didn't need an explanation for Trenier's resistance. Trenier's interests in the pension fund were purely mercenary. He was stalling for more time to implement his own plans to extort investment money for his personal gain.

Jordan's face was serious, his voice low. "Without a voluntary resignation of the union trustees, I don't think even I could prevent an inquiry. There have been so many complaints of bankrupt and mismanaged programs by various retirement funds, it's only a matter of time before all pension programs throughout the country will be under direct government control. There's legislation addressing that very subject being prepared right now in several different committees.''

Trenier stirred restlessly. Despite what he wanted to believe, the president's assessment was painfully true. He exchanged an uneasy glance with Jordan but remained silent, choosing only to puff on his cigar and listen.

"I think I know a way we can solve this dilemma," the president continued, easing forward in his seat.

"Which is?" Trenier responded, his lips tightening around his cigar.

"The union's health and welfare fund isn't an object of concern to the legislature and never has been. It's only the pension fund that, so far, had gotten all the attention. Since there is no legal provision as to how the union divides employer donations between the pension or health and welfare funds, it would be a simple matter to divert any additional funds required by the union into the health and welfare fund instead of the pension fund. Then, those revenues could be dispersed in any manner you choose without fear of governmental interference. The Hawk Committee's after the pension fund, not the health and welfare fund. It's so simple, it stinks.''

Trenier liked what he heard. A smile began to relax the previously pursed lips. "You mean if I clean up the pension fund, they'll stop there? They won't pursue the health and welfare fund?"

"Exactly."

"What makes you so sure?"

"What would be the reason? I initiated formation of the Hawk Committee in the first place. Once their objective has been accomplished, it'll be disbanded. They're not authorized to go any further and there won't be any reason to if they're satisfied you're correcting the problems in the pension fund. By turning it over to a bank trust, you'll get everyone off the hook. The public, the legislators, the union, the whole damn bunch will forget about it. Justice will have been served. You can have your cake and eat it too."

The coolness between them that had prevailed only moments before had quickly disappeared. Trenier knew that he and the president were about to commence a long and mutually profitable relationship. While each man could live comfortably for the rest of their lives if they were to retire, neither considered themselves extremely wealthy. During the next two hours, they discreetly outlined a plan to correct that oversight.

Several days later, the president walked at Trenier's side as he gave him a personal guided tour of union head-quarters. It was the first time a president had ever publicly shown support of the union. Trenier tried but failed miserably to conceal his smile as they walked the halls of the marble palace, followed by an entourage of reporters and aides. The day ended with Trenier continuing to bask in the president's friendship. He knew that Peter Denning would be pleased with the relationship they had developed. He had become president of the union because of the support he had gained from Denning and his contacts with organized crime. Now he had added another weapon to his powerful arsenal—the president of the United States.

It was a troika, he thought. Three powerful organizations working together cooperatively toward a mutually beneficial goal. Unholy as it was, it was reality. To him, it was beautiful. An American troika had been born. The union, organized crime, and the U.S. government. Now they were one, working together for a common cause.

Chapter 70

TOR LOOKED DOWN at the photographs on his desk. They confirmed what he suspected.

When James was assassinated, newspaper photographers covering his speech at the Plaza Hotel had graphically recorded the tragedy and it was one of those photographs that had captured his attention and curiosity.

James had been dead two days before Tor could find the inner strength to look at a newspaper and it was then that he noticed someone familiar in the crowd that surrounded his slain friend's bloodstained body.

Initially, he wasn't sure. It wasn't the face that attracted his attention, but the size of the man who towered like a giant over the others on the New York City sidewalk.

He remembered the night in Geneva after dinner with Don Peck when he had nearly collided outside the restaurant with a person who appeared to be the man in the photograph. If it weren't for his recollections of seeing the same man a second time after clearing customs in San Francisco, he probably would never have given a second look at the newspaper photo.

But he was certain now.

It was one thing to recognize a face in a crowd but quite another to attach a name to that face and he knew it would be difficult. He considered going to the F.B.I. with his discovery but decided against it, at least temporarily, until he had a chance to think things through. All he had was a hunch, nothing more, and he wanted to research it completely until he was certain it merited mentioning to anyone.

That night, after tucking Shana into bed, he lay on his sofa listening to Beethoven's Fifth Symphony. He sipped on a glass of wine mixed with Perrier water, letting his morning speculation shift to a more realistic form. As the evening wore on, unconfirmed parts of the puzzle began to evolve from the embryonic stage to a more advanced theorum, but just as each piece seemingly began to fit, another more complex question would surface.

Tor hypothesized that the man in the photograph was connected in some way with Donald Peck's assassination and, perhaps, to that of James as well. His mind wandered past midnight until he finally discarded the last of the evening's many theories. Yet there was one thought that continued to surface. If the man in the photograph had killed both Peck and James, then he was sure that his orders must have come from the same source. If Peck had been killed on the orders of Louie Cordaro, Tor could not understand why James would have been assassinated by the same person. Cordaro was already out of prison at the time of James's assassination and James represented no immediate threat to him. Shortly thereafter, Cordaro himself had disappeared. It was ironic that the two men would both exit from the world under such unusual circumstances on the exact same day, but Tor was under no illusions as to Cordaro's disappearance. Mikki Parker's sudden disappearance had killed whatever ideals he had left about fair play in the world of politics and crime. He didn't believe Cordaro could have been vindictive enough to order James assassination simply out of spite. There had to be more to it than that. If Cordaro was behind it, Tor was sure there was an intricate path somewhere that had led to that decision.

The next morning, Tor took Shana to her physical therapy session at the hospital, then sat over a cup of black coffee in the commisssary as he waited, still thinking about the single assassin. By now, he had changed his tactics. He had eliminated Cordaro's name as the source of the order to kill James and Don Peck and substituted for it that of the union.

He then put Cordaro's disappearance out of the picture and the muddied waters became clearer. It was obvious to him that the commutation of Cordaro's prison sentence so soon after his incarceration was an underhanded "thank you" from the president to the union for their election support. Of that, he was certain. But he was still perplexed. If Cordaro or the union wanted James dead, the order had to have been issued because of something far more serious than anything that had transpired publicly. If it were their intent to kill James because of his interest in the union's activities, James would have been disposed of long before the investigations that had led to Cordaro's conviction. Perhaps Billy's tragic death was meant to be a warning that had gone unheeded by James.

If the man in the photograph could be identified as the killer of Donald Peck, the ramifications would be staggering. If the union and the president had plotted James's assassination, Tor was sure that it was the president who stood to gain. James represented a potential danger to the president in exposing the million dollars that had found its way into the president's campaign fund and personal savings account. But Tor's theory stopped there. He could come up with no reasonable explanation of how Jordan could possibly have known anything about James's intentions to expose him. No one besides Tor himself knew the overall scope or intent of the investigation of President Jordan's activities. Each investigator had worked separately. Each individual part of the investigation meant nothing to the others involved. Only Tor saw the final incriminating pieces assembled. As a further safeguard, he had even used Elaine Hawk and Percy Tinsley to do some of the research, but like the others, they too only possessed isolated pieces of the puzzle.

Tor remained in the hospital commissary for over an hour, his mind reeling with unanswered theories and questions that only led to even more elusive speculations. He decided to place first things first and attempt to identify the man in the photograph. If he could not confirm his suspicions that the same man might have killed both James and Donald Peck, all his other theories would be void.

He remembered a conversation he had once had with one of the Hawk Committee investigators about the union's methods of eliminating troublesome individuals, and the investigator's graphic description of Bartie Bonano. Tor had never seen Bonano but his description dovetailed with the photograph of the man standing in the crowd. There was an outside chance someone else could identify that face. All Tor knew for sure was that the man in the photograph was the same man he had seen in Europe. He decided that after taking Shana home he would drive to the Presidio and visit Sidney Bonnam.

"Are you sure?"

Sidney Bonnam fingered the cropped photograph as he and Tor sat in Bonnam's heavily guarded quarters on the grounds of San Francisco's Presidio Army Base.

"Of course. I saw him twice when I worked for Cordaro. It's Bonano, no question about it."

"I think he may have been involved in the assassination," Tor said.

Bonnam didn't speak, staring down at the floor. The memory of his wife and the F.B.I.'s unproved suspicion that Bonano might have been responsible for her disappearance temporarily dulled his responses. Then, a moment later, he asked, "What makes you think that?"

Instinctively, Tor decided to let Bonnam know no more. He wasn't sure why, but he suddenly felt uncomfortable talking about his theory. He no longer knew whom he could trust. He had cropped the newspaper photograph enough to show only Bonano's face. It was impossible for anybody to know the original source.

Tor shook his head.

"You're ignoring my question," Bonnam protested.

"No, it's not that. I just don't really know what to think right now. It's only a guess, nothing more."

A frightened look crossed Bonnam's face. "Bonano's not a person you want to mess with."

Tor ignored Bonnam's warning. "Any idea where I could find him?" he asked.

"I can guess," Bonnam responded. "Try looking in D.C. That's where the F.B.I. finally found him when they questioned him about my wife's disappearance. He's never very far away from union headquarters but I don't think anybody knows where he lives."

Tor changed the subject and talked with Bonnam about more mundane matters for another hour, trying to cheer him up. It depressed him to see Bonnam locked away from the outside world, cast aside with only books and television to pass the hours until he could resume a normal life. It was unfair that Bonnam should be forced to live in such a manner simply because he had tried to help rid his country of a sickness. Even when he gained a new identity, Bonnam would still live in constant fear of reprisal.

That night, Bonnam lay awake in his security cell for most of the evening as he had night after night before. He let his mind drift. He knew that if Borg Trenier kept his promise at least his financial future was secure. But even that was of little comfort. Life without his wife would be empty, meaningless, and possibly unbearable. He vacillated between telling and not telling Tor of his arrangement with Trenier and blowing the lid off the union hierarchy again. He changed his mind over and over again when he thought of the penalty he would eventually have to pay if he testified again. His was a strange fate for a man who only eight months earlier had dreamed only of strengthening his law practice. He had had a beautiful loving wife and hoped to raise a family. Now, as far as he knew, he had nothing. Somehow death didn't scare him as much as it once did. In fact, it seemed an escape. Self-preservation was no longer his strongest motivation.

The next day, four hundred miles south in Newport Beach, Tor and Elaine Hawk sat in Billy's den. Tor looked about the den and thought of the many conversations he had shared there with both Billy and James. The two brothers had always seemed to prefer that particular room over the rest of the house. Together, they would often sit there intensely discussing their various philosophies on just about any subject.

That morning, Elaine had dedicated a new elementary school in the name of her husband and Tor had taken the opportunity to join her in the ceremony. There was still a piece missing from his puzzle, but he had no idea what it was he was searching for. His mind kept toying with the same questions that had been perplexing him for days.

He glanced about Billy's den. "You know," he said, "this whole thing would begin to make some sort of sense if somehow Jordan knew about the information we had."

"What?" Elaine asked, confused by Tor's train of thought.

Tor hesitated before answering. He realized his rambling made no sense as Elaine had been purposely kept uninformed about the bribe money. "I'm sorry—just thinking out loud."

"Well, you've managed to lose me," she said.

Then it struck. The idea was so simple Tor berated himself for not thinking of it sooner.

He began to crawl on the floor.

"What in the hell are you doing?" Elaine asked incredulously.

"Looking for something," he answered, without further explanation. He was already under Billy's desk.

A moment later, he found it. Taped to the back of the right-hand top drawer was a miniature microphone about the size of a dime with a two-inch wire attached.

"What's that?" Elaine asked.

"You've been bugged," Tor answered, after smashing the device on the desk.

A chill shot through Elaine's body. "Why would anyone want to do that?" she asked.

"I don't know, but I intend to find out," he said. Tor knew that he could trust no one, not even Elaine. He remembered the unlocked safe when he had first searched

536

Billy's den for the missing diary and Elaine's comments a few weeks after Billy's death when she had found Billy's file cabinet unlocked. The safe, the file cabinet, and now the microphone all pointed in the same direction—straight to the Oval Office. Many of the conversations he had had with James had been in that room. Billy's taped diary had been played there for the first time as well. Nothing had ever been said in that room that would have induced anybody other than the president to search for Billy's diary. It didn't take a genius to conclude that the electronic surveillance had been ordered by President Jordan. Cordaro would have had nothing to gain by searching or monitoring Billy's den and the president's authority to order the surveillance of Billy through the CIA would have easily gone unquestioned. Even his own home in Sausalito had probably been bugged, perhaps his office as well. A desolate sensation gripped him when he realized that he couldn't possibly go to the F.B.I. with his theory.

It was apparent that he too was probably ticketed for assassination. If the president had ordered the assassination of James to prevent personal embarrassment, then his own life was in danger as well. The president had to know that Tor knew as much about the bribes as James had.

Why he was still alive was a question he didn't care to think about. He would have to act fast to preserve that luxury. Once the president found out that Tor had discovered the surveillance device, Tor was sure he would act quickly. He realized now it had been a mistake to destroy the bug. How stupid! If he had only left it in place, Jordan would have no way of knowing that he had discovered it. Now it was too late.

Without telling Elaine that he feared for her safety as well as his own, Tor insisted that she accompany him back to San Francisco that night. He couldn't be sure that the surveillance had been ordered by the president but there was a way to find out. If his own home were wired, then it was obvious that the surveillance had been ordered by the same person and the trail would most likely lead directly to the president. He remembered the previous day and how sorry he had felt for Sidney Bonnam. Now he was no better off than Bonnam.

It wasn't until the plane landed and was taxiing to the boarding ramp that a final thought pierced Tor's confusion. If the president had ordered the surveillance of Billy's den as part of a monitoring system to determine what the Hawk Committee was investigating, then Sidney Bonnam would have been bugged as well. If that were true, it meant that Jordan knew of Tor's interest in Bartie Bonano and his association with the union. An empty sensation settled in Tor's stomach as he realized that the chances of his own early demise were increasing every minute.

Elaine struggled to keep up as Tor raced to a phone after deplaning. It was past midnight. He called the Presidio where Sidney Bonnam was sleeping. Using a prearranged code number to identify himself, it was only a matter of seconds before Tor was connected with a sleepy voice that he recognized as Bonnam's.

Tor's stomach was twisting. "Don't ask questions," he said. "Just look around your quarters for any signs of electronic surveillance. Check the phone, lamps, anything. I'll wait. Take your time."

A tormenting silence, interrupted by occasional noises, filtered through the phone as Tor waited apprehensively. Then the words came. "Yes, it is affirmative," Bonnam answered methodically.

"Don't do anything," Tor ordered. "Just remember that it's there. I'll be back to you."

A sickening panic shot through Tor and his face drained of color. The problem now was to stay alive. He wasn't sure that he wasn't already dead.

Chapter 71

IT WAS ON the evening of January eighteenth that Borg Trenier finally realized the scope of his station in the troika composed of the union, his new friends from the world of organized crime and the president of the United States.

Jordan's phone call was without compromise and left no room for irresolute questions regarding his message. Trenier's years in the union had left him with a callousness he had thought impenetrable. He thought he had seen and heard it all, but for the president to call him personally and unemotionally demand the assassination of another human being was, even for him, unnerving.

Trenier sat for over an hour reflecting on what the president had said. He remembered every word.

"Borg, we've got a problem with your Mr. Bonano," the president opened coldly.

"Bartie Bonano?"

"Yes, he's the one."

"I don't understand."

"Let's just say that it's in both of our interests that the man isn't around to answer any questions."

"I'm afraid I still don't understand."

Jordan lost patience. "Dammit, I don't give a goddamn if you understand or not! Just do as I say. Now, I want this Bonano matter taken care of and I don't mean temporarily. He's one of your boys, so you handle it. I don't care how, just do it. Do I make myself clear?"

"Yes, I think so."

"Fuck the indecision, Trenier! Either you do or you don't. Now, give me an answer."

"Yes, sir, I'll handle it," Trenier answered firmly.

"Do you know where to find him?"

"Yes, I think so," he answered, fully aware that at that very moment he was the only person in the world who knew exactly how to get in touch with Bonano. He felt some sense of security in that. Not even the president had that information.

"Trenier?"

"Yes."

"I don't mean some time soon. I want it done *now*."

"When?"

"By tomorrow."

"I'll handle it," Trenier repeated. He was still shaken, but managed to camouflage his feelings.

"And another thing," the president added, almost as an afterthought. "I want this Slagle fellow taken care of as well. Neitehr of us needs the potential problems that man could create."

"Is he onto something?"

The president hung up the phone without responding. Trenier would do as he asked. By having Trenier arrange the elimination of both Bonano and Tor Slagle, he wouldn't have to involve the CIA again. Their surveillance of Billy's den, Tor's home and Bonnam's private cell had resulted in tapes of all conversations from each and Addleton had personally relayed the information to the president. He and Addleton were the only two people in the world who had ever heard those recordings.

Addleton had a large ego, the president had known that for a long time. Any exposure of the tapes would threaten his position as CIA director. The fact that he had ordered Billy Hawk's assassination at the president's request underlined Addleton's continued loyalty, but Jordan didn't want to test him again. They understood each other and he wanted to leave it that way. Asking Addleton to eliminate Bonano and Tor would only propagate a relationship that would require him to return future favors.

The president had had enough. He wasn't proud of what he had done but it couldn't be avoided. He wanted to spend the remaining years of his life free of any more indebtedness to Addleton.

Trenier sat alone at his desk, his eyes cast downward. He was thinking about his conversation with President Jordan. The authoritative firmness of the president's voice still rang in his ears as he weighed the implications of what had transpired. For the first time, he felt he knew the identity of James Hawk's assassin. He had always suspected that Cordaro and the president had made some sort of arrangement to guarantee Cordaro's release from prison in exchange for the union's election support, but he had not been able to confirm it.

With the president's sudden insistence that both Bartie Bonano and Tor Slagle be eliminated simultaneously, the reasons behind the president's concerns had become clear. If Slagle had to be eliminated for something he knew, it only made sense to Trenier that James Hawk had known the same things and had been destroyed because of it. He was sure that Cordaro had once received similiar presidential orders as he had tonight. For Cordaro, the target had been James Hawk. For himself, it would be Bartie Bonano and Tor Slagle. It seemed a small price to pay to keep his relationship with the president intact. If he handled it well, he was sure that their bond would be strengthened even more. There was no need to rationalize the matter any further. He would do as the president asked. His only problem was that one of the two who were to be killed was the only man he personally knew to call upon to assassinate the other. Slagle would have to be first. It would be Bonano's last paycheck. He would deal with Bonano afterwards, but that would take more planning. He would need more time. First, he needed to call Bonano.

It was just before eleven in the morning when Tor decided to go outside his home for the first time in two days. A need to mail a letter forced the issue. The postman had already passed. It was Saturday, the post office closed at noon, and he wanted to be sure the letter got off that day. After the letter was mailed, it would be too late for anyone to stop him and he felt better about that.

He had holed himself up, a prisoner in his own home. Elaine Hawk, his house guest, was unaware of his concerns. She had thought nothing of Tor's occasional requests over the past two days for her to run any errands that would have taken him outside the house. He spent his days poring over every shred of evidence that could possibly support the scenario he had decided to present to the F.B.I. on the following Monday. He had outlined in detail the events that had led to his conclusion that the president, in collusion with Louie Cordaro, had ordered James Hawk's assassination.

While he hadn't yet pieced together all the facts, he felt confident that he had compiled evidence sufficient for a grand jury investigation. He had photo copies of both the president's campaign checking account and his personal savings account during the month of May when one million dollars was divided and credited to the two accounts. That coupled with the records showing that Peter Denning's insurance company had dispersed those funds was enough in itself to initiate even more questions of the president, which was what he wanted.

He planned to ask the F.B.I. about the electronic surveillance of the quarters of Sidney Bonnam and the homes of Billy and James Hawk, as well as his own—who had ordered the surveillance and why? He wanted to ask why the president had received a million dollars from the union right after Billy Hawk's assassination. He wanted to ask about Bartie Bonano—who he was, who he worked for, and why he had been in Geneva at the time of Donald Peck's assassination. He wanted to know why Bonano was in New York City on December twenty-seventh, looking over the body of James Hawk only minutes after he was shot down. He wanted to ask the real reason why Louie

Cordaro's sentence had been commuted after he had served only slightly more than two months of an eight-year sentence. He would ask all these questions, but only for show. He already knew the answers. He wanted the public to demand the same answers. It was only then that his efforts would be rewarded with justice.

His days of seclusion had made his initial fears for his own safety subside sufficiently to go outside today for the first time. Elaine had some shopping to do and he had already decided he would bring her up to date on what he had been working on the past few days when she returned. After all she had been through and the support she had been offering him, he owed her that much. The details would be kept for the F.B.I. He had decided against going to the F.B.I. authorities in San Francisco with his evidence. To be safe, he would fly unannounced on Monday morning to the regional office in Phoenix instead. It was there that he would tell his story and ask his questions.

When Elaine returned home that night from her shopping trip, Tor's stiff and bloodstained body lay cold, draped over the steps to the entryway of his home. Minutes later, the county coroner's ambulance was negotiating the steep grade up the hill past a squadron of Sausalito police cars that were already lining the narrow pathway. Tor had been shot six times, through the heart and head, with a powerful handgun. There was no sign of a struggle. An empty 35mm film wrapper lay at his side.

Chapter 72

AS HE HAD been instructed, Bartie Bonano sat waiting, albeit impatiently, in a small Mission District motel room on San Francisco's south side. He had done his job and was anxious to leave, but Borg Trenier had ordered him to wait in the motel for a phone call. He had felt no emotion about killing Tor Slagle that night and it amused him momentarily to remember how nervous he had been when he had first killed for money. A friend in the business had once told him that having a conscience was like having a wheel of knives spinning in your gut that dulled a little more each time they spun. The first spin was nearly unbearable but, with constant use, the blades would dull to a point where they were virtually unnoticeable. If the blades had been spinning this afternoon, he hadn't felt them.

He had waited outside Tor's home for nearly two days after Trenier had given him the assignment. He was tired, so much so that he had fallen asleep in his car and nearly missed his chance when Tor finally left the house. He had followed him down the hill to the post office and then back again. The killing was quick, uneventful. Now he sat waiting again, for what, he did not know.

He could hear noises outside, people walking past and cars coming in and out of the parking lot but he didn't bother to look out. He sat toying with his camera. He didn't like motels. They never had room service and, like tonight, they were often without radios or televisions to help pass the time. He didn't know why Trenier had sent him to such a rundown motel but he did know he wouldn't be spending the night there. The room had an odor that he couldn't identify and the stains on the worn chenille bedspread were all too familiar. He would wait until midnight for Trenier's call before leaving, no longer.

Two miles away, San Francisco district attorney Richard Jackson was on the telephone with the city's new police commissioner, acting out his assigned role. They both reveled in thinking about the favorable publicity they would receive for assisting in the capture of Tor Slagle's assassin as well as the points they were sure to receive for doing a favor for Borg Trenier. The spoils of that goodwill gesture would be far-reaching for both men and they asked no questions of each other or anyone else before setting their plan in motion.

Trenier had made it clear to both men that Tor's killer was not to be taken alive. He gave no explanations, just told them where Bonano was hiding and that the police were to be told that the suspect would be armed and uncooperative.

It took only thirty minutes for the police SWAT team to completely evacuate and surround the dingy motel. That was when the phone rang in Bonano's room.

Bonano was napping. The phone's incessant ringing jarred him to a slightly more lucid state. He could hear voices outside. The room was dark. A faint hint of light came through the window. The phone continued ringing.

Slowly, he leaned forward, reaching for the phone. It had to be the call he had been told to expect.

"Bonano?"

It was a strange voice, not Trenier's, as he had expected.
"Yes," he responded tentatively.

"This is Richard Jackson, district attorney for the City of San Francisco. I've got a message for you."

A silence followed.

"Bonano?"

"What do you want?"

"We've got your room surrounded. Come out peacefully or we'll shoot to kill."

Bonano dropped the phone, ran to the window and peered through a hole in the draperies. Several empty police cars were lined up in a half circle around the door to his room. Quickly, he ran to the bathroom window in the rear of the room and saw more of the same. More cars, more red lights flashing. He began to laugh hysterically. "Go fuck yourself!" he said aloud, reaching for his handgun. His maniacal laughter was cut short by a voice over a bullhorn from outside demanding his surrender.

A stillness followed. Twelve marksmen sighted their rifles on the motel door and the rear window of his room. There would be no escape. They knew that. Bonano knew it as well.

A minute passed, then another, but nobody was counting. Then the motel door opened. Slowly at first, then with a sudden inward thrust that pulled it off its hinges. A stream of fire blasted through the darkness from the six-inch barrel of Bonano's gun as he bolted out the door into the glaring floodlights.

A blinding series of explosions returned Bonano's random fire and within seconds, Bonano lay immobile across the hood of a police sedan he had charged in his frenzy, his arms and legs spasmodically jerking, his gun lying nearly ten feet away on the asphalt parking lot.

In all, twenty-seven bullets permeated Bartie Bonano's body. Nevertheless, it took over an hour before he expired without regaining consciousness. He had done what a few people knew he would if he were ever trapped. He had not been taken alive. Louie Cordaro had always known that. More recently, Borg Trenier and Richard Jackson had been made aware of Bonano's lifetime boast. Tor Slagle was not Bartie Bonano's last victim. The last was himself.

The news of Tor Slagle's death was barely a few hours old when it was announced over the wire services that his suspected slayer had been killed. At that precise moment, Borg Trenier became aware of an easing of the breathlessness and fluttering in his stomach he had been feeling for the last few days. A cold sweat broke out over his body. It was nearly morning when he finally went to bed. The job was done. Trenier fell asleep easily.

As he slept, President Jordan was up early, editing the final draft of his inauguration speech which, until he heard the news of Tor Slagle's death, he had found impossible to concentrate on. It was nearly noon when he completed the draft. Before leaving for lunch, he scrawled a note to his secretary, ordering a personal V.I.P. car and an invitation to his inauguration to be sent to Borg Trenier.

Chapter 73

Tor Slagle died without knowing the results of the Slagle employees' union election.

Only hours before the discovery of his body, the National Labor Relations Board's representative announced that Slagle had voted in favor of union organization by the slimmest possible majority—one vote.

Tuesday, January twenty-second, Inauguration Day, and also the day of Tor's funeral. Elaine Hawk and Winston Sheffield helped with the arrangements, initially planning a simple and quiet early morning ceremony; but it soon became apparent that it would be impossible to do so. Tor's friends numbered in the hundreds.

Over five hundred mourners, including an official presidential representative, quietly and respectfully jammed the inside of Grace Episcopal Cathedral for the ceremony. An overflow of friends and employees waited outside the church, lining both sides of California Street. They would have to be content to attend the graveside services in the Presidio.

Percy Tinsley, dressed somberly in black, sat in the second row behind Elaine and Winston Sheffield. Having no close relatives, Tor had named Tinsley executor of his estate and for that Tinsley felt proud and honored. Tinsley's wife, Samantha, sat at his side. A stunningly beautiful woman, she held the hand of their twelve-year-old daughter, Jennifer. On his other side sat another small girl and Tinsley's mind moved away for a moment from the funeral to Shana Parker who sat quietly holding his hand. Since Tor's death, she had been staying with his family while he assisted with the funeral arrangements. Having been spared the gruesomeness of Tor's death only because of an all-day physical therapy session, Shana was displaying courage in the face of yet another tragedy in her young life.

Shana hadn't spoken much since she was told of Tor's death, preferring to keep to herself. Her best friends always seemed to be adults and those she had been closest to had been violently taken away from her. First her mother and father, then her sister, and now Tor. On this day, she had awakened early, dressed herself in her favorite pink dress, made her own breakfast, read an article in the morning paper about Tor, and then sat quietly in the living room waiting for the others to rise, thinking of the man who had become her closest real-life friend. Tor had tried to answer every question she had about her sister and why she was gone. He had even explained about James and Billy Hawk and how her sister's work related to their own goals. Tor had treated her as an adult, and for that she felt a fondness for him which she had formerly reserved only for her own family. It had taken her three days to assimilate all that had happened but she had finally done it. She even felt she knew *why* it had happened. It was over, but her life had to go on. She still had her memories, and she knew they could never be taken away. Shana thought of what Tor had told her the night before his death. She was so impressed with the message she had made him write it down for her. As she sat there, waiting for the funeral to begin, she read what Tor had written. That piece of paper was now her most prized possession. She read it over and over:

Tomorrow is the most important thing in life. It comes to us at midnight very clean. It's perfect when it arrives and puts itself in our hands. It hopes we've learned something from yesterday.

She had learned from the days and months before. There was nothing she could do to change the past. She would live for tomorrow; she owed it to herself, to Mikki; to Tor.

Tinsley found it hard to concentrate on the funeral. A phone call he had received the day before kept coming back to his mind. He had been told by Tor's secretary that an envelope marked "Confidential" had come to his office by registered mail. She was sure that it was in Tor's handwriting and asked him if he wanted her to deliver it to his home. He declined, instructing her to lock it up, but now he wished he had had her deliver it. If Tor had sent it, it had to be important. He was worried. He tried to shrug off his concerns but they oppressed him as the funeral began. There was nothing he could do for the next two hours.

Despite his usual detachment from emotion, Tinsley's eyes filled with tears as the priest performed the simple ceremony. The man who had come into his life as a college roommate was leaving it as a beloved friend. Death had created a gap that would never be closed.

Outside, the California Street cable cars filled with morning commuters clinging to the sides rang loudly as they passed Grace Cathedral where the sidewalks were jammed with men and women who waited patiently to pay their last respects. One spectator, one of many Slagle's employees present, studied the stream of commuters. This day was like any other, he thought. Nothing, not even Tor's funeral or the inauguration, could change it. Life and death went hand in hand.

As the mourners began to file out, Tinsley looked at Elaine who stood with her head bowed in front of him. He reached gently for her hand and she clutched it tightly. The day before she had requested that she be allowed to say the graveside eulogy. He asked if she were still up to it, offering to fill in if she was not. She thanked him, but declined the offer.

The solemnity of the church was quickly transformed outside by the noisy police motorcycle escort at the head of the procession. The long black hearse pulled from the curb carrying Tor's body from the cathedral. It turned left, then glided smoothly down California Street toward its destination five miles away. The day was bright and sunny with only a hint of an early morning chill. San Francisco's weather was in stark contrast to the gray and cold windy late morning being experienced three thousand miles away in the nation's capital, where President John Jordan was about to take the inaugural oath of office for his second term.

Traffic outside the church had been diverted, and the cortege began to move slowly. Tinsley looked through the window at the television cameramen who were photographing the mourners who had come to pay homage to his friend.

People attending the funeral didn't know why Tor Slagle had been murdered, or why he had traded his carefree life-style for that of chief counsel to the Hawk Committee.

Some, who knew Tor only indirectly, had attended from a sense of loyalty and duty to his late father and mother. Others came because of curiosity about the unexplained death of the third member of the Hawk Committee in eight months. But the majority came because they knew and loved the man, either through personal relationships or as an employer or benefactor.

At the Presidio, the cars at the head of the cortege were already inching to a stop near the gravesite as those at the end of the line were just beginning to enter the army base nearly a mile away.

Shana Parker moved ahead of Elaine as they led the mourners in a quiet procession following the plain copper coffin being wheeled by the pallbearers toward the gravesite.

They walked slowly, waiting several minutes at the burial site for the rest of the cars to arrive. The immediate area around the grave soon became too crowded and the late arrivals chose to simply stand near their parked cars. The movement around the gravesite slowed, then stopped. Elaine began to deliver the eulogy.

In the background, a car radio turned to the president's inaugural address could be heard, but Elaine ignored the intrusion. An older couple standing beside their car were listening intently to the president's speech and failed to notice or recognize the significance of the glares from the crowd at the gravesite.

Elaine was strong and determined in her delivery, despite her grief. "I stand here today not to honor Tor, because his life has already done that for him. For whatever reason, beyond my comprehension, he has been taken away from us after having given so much and asking for so little in return."

Lost in his grief, Tinsley could nevertheless still hear the radio and found himself involuntarily picking up intermittent parts of the president's speech.

"The greatest honor history can bestow," the president was saying, "is the title of peacemaker. We find ourselves in a time of low spirit, when crime and corruption seem to have overtaken our lives by threatening the very foundations of this great nation . . ."

"To Tor," Elaine continued, "indifference was the greatest sin of all and he shared that feeling with many of his friends and colleagues. The sins of the cold-hearted will be weighed by our Lord on a different scale than the one in which Tor will be measured . . ."

"America has suffered greatly in the past few months, and, as your president, I can not promise you an overnight solution to the problems of discontent and hatred. We are torn by divisions, seeking unity . . ."

With her voice beginning to show signs of strain, Elaine delivered her final words. "The work started by others and later magnificiently continued by the man we bury today must not be forgotten. Let his death mark not the conclusion of his task, but the inception of a new effort on behalf of all of us to carry on the fight which cost their strongest advocates."

Elaine's voice began to crack and tears filled her eyes. She paused a moment and looked at Shana who stood at attention, absorbing every word. There was hope, she decided. The job could still be done. Shana's concentration and concern gave her the strength to continue. She reached out and pulled the child to her side, her arm around Shana's shoulders. "Let the world know there's a story to be told! Each day as we live our lives we must ask ourselves if everyone has heard the message—heard what James and Billy Hawk wanted for their country and what Tor Slagle sought to help them achieve. Think back on how it all began and why. Think about why we must tell that story loud and clear. Yes, once there was a fleeting glimpse of glory. With our diligence, it will not all have been in vain. We need your help. God bless you, Tor; God bless you, Billy; God bless you, James; God bless us all."

Elaine stepped back, her arm still around Shana. She bent down, kissed Shana's head and they gently embraced, their tears mingling.

The crowd started to disperse. Elaine and Shana stayed behind, alone with their thoughts while Tinsley waited patiently with the limousine. Doors of other cars were slamming as figured disappeared inside.

Tinsley watched silently as the coffin was lowered. Elaine and Shana continued to stand at the graveside. Elaine held a red rose given to her by the priest who had plucked it from atop Tor's coffin.

The older couple with the car radio had not yet left. The inaugural address was coming to an end.

"The peace we seek within our country will come only when we are able to win the hearts and minds of those who do not understand our ways. Law and order will prevail. As your president, I shall stand for nothing less. This is a great nation, unparalleled by any in history, and I am proud to have been your leader for the past four years, proud that you have allowed me to continue the work I have begun. My fellow Americans, I can only thank you for your support. You may rest assured, I shall never let you down."

Tinsley watched as the couple got into their car and nosed into the stream of cars that was pouring out the narrow and winding cemetery drive. As their car slowed, stopped, and started forward again, he overheard the old woman speaking.

"At least," she said, "we can sleep a little easier knowing we have such a fine man as our president!"

the commandos

elliot arnold

SABOTAGE IN THE ENEMY'S CAMP!

They were expert dealers in death, men who would stop at nothing to destroy the enemy. When American Alan Lowell led an expedition to capture a Nazi garrison on the Norwegian coast, he encountered an unexpected complication in the beautiful Nicole, mistress of a Nazi captain!

If their liaison were discovered, it would mean death for Nicole—and untold disaster for the commandos' mission!

Price: $2.75
0-8439-2009-2
pp. 304

Category: War

FAST EDDIE

Neil Bayne and Wes Sarginson

THE MODERN JESSE JAMES

He's held up 61 banks and stolen over $6 million—but he's never harmed a soul!

While the FBI put him on the Ten Most Wanted list, Dun & Bradstreet hailed him as an up-and-coming business executive.

Prisons can't hold him—once he escaped while recovering from a heart attack, and another time he just jogged away through the prison gates.

He's Fast Eddie, the last of America's classic bank robbers—we hope!

LEISURE BOOKS

1070-4/$3.50

THE SCORPIO CIPHER

RALPH HAYES

Rosenfeld was the man who invented America's greatest weapon—the deadly laser cannon.

Now Rosenfeld was the captive of Iranian zealots who were determined to learn the secret of his design.

Gage was the man the President sent into Iran to get Rosenfeld out.

It wasn't routine—even for Gage, whose assignments were never routine. Rosenfeld was held under heavy guard. Rosenfeld was being tortured by a twisted master of pain.

And Gage was supposed to take Rosenfeld's place!

LEISURE BOOKS

1060-7/$3.25